"What you need to do is arrive tonight with a fiancé."

"What?" Camilla frowned, confused. Had the fellow not understood what she had been telling him? "How could I—? Who—?"

Sedgewick smiled and nodded toward the other man in the room. "Benedict will be your fiancé."

Camilla gaped at Sedgewick.

Benedict expressed her fears more forcibly. "For God's sake, Jermyn, have you run mad?"

"Not at all. If you will all think about it, you will see that it is the perfect solution."

"I see that it is perfect insanity," Benedict retorted. "If you think that I am going to become engaged to that…that…"

Camilla looked at him, her eyes sparkling dangerously. "To that *what?*"

"Candace Camp is renowned as a storyteller who touches the heart of her readers time and again."

—Romantic Times

CANDACE CAMP

Indiscreet

MIRA BOOKS

MIRA

ISBN 1-55166-297-3

INDISCREET

Copyright © 1997 by Candace Camp.

Printed in U.S.A.

Indiscreet

1

1812

She was lost.

Camilla had suspected it for some time, and now, as she pushed aside the curtain and peered out into the night, she was sure. Her post chaise was enshrouded by fog. She might as well have been sitting inside a cloud. She had no idea where they were. The carriage could be sitting ten yards from her grandfather's house—or on the edge of a cliff.

"Wot should I do, miss?" the coachman called down from atop the conveyance.

"Just sit here for a moment." It would be foolhardy to press on through this pea soup of a fog. There was no telling where they would wind up. "Let me think."

With a sigh, she let the curtain fall and leaned back against the cushioned seat. This was all her fault, she knew. If only she hadn't been so sunk in her thoughts, so immersed in her problems, she might have noticed the fog creeping in or seen that the hired coachman, unfamiliar with the local terrain, had taken a wrong turn. Indeed, she should have stopped in the village and hired a local postboy to show the driver the way. Instead, she had been cudgeling her brain for a way to get herself out of her predicament, so intent on the trap she had sprung on herself with her lie—*why had Grandpapa told Aunt Beryl?*—that she had not paid any attention to the coach's progress. Well, now she would have to pay for that inattention.

Camilla opened the door of the chaise and leaned out. She could not even see the heads of the lead horses clearly. She looked down at the road. She could see that—clearly enough to realize that it was little more than a track through the heath, certainly not the road leading to Chevington Park. *God knew where the London-bred driver had taken them.*

Wrapping her cloak around her and tying it at the neck, she jumped lightly down to the ground. The driver swiveled around and looked down at her. "But, miss—wot are you doing?" He moved as though he were about to climb down. "I ain't even put the steps down."

Camilla waved him back. "That's all right. No need to bother. I'm already down, you see. I am going to take a look around."

The coachman looked worried. "Now, don't go wanderin' off, miss. You can't see your hand in front of your face in this weather." Bitterly he added, "Heathen place, Dorset."

Camilla smiled to herself, but refrained from asking him whether London did not have fog, too. Instead, she inquired, "Have you a lantern? That would be of use."

"Yes, miss." He leaned over, handing down the

lantern to her, still looking doubtful. Obviously, in his experience, young ladies of Quality did not go tramping about in the fog, lantern or no lantern.

Camilla ignored him and went to the horses' heads, holding up the lantern to cast more light about her. The light did little to penetrate the fog, but it did illuminate the ground beneath her feet, enabling her to see the narrow cart track. The lead horse on the right rolled his eyes apprehensively at her approach, but she spoke in soothing tones to him and stroked his neck, and he quickly quieted down.

She turned back to the coachman. "The thing to do, I think, is for me to walk beside the horses and guide them," she told him. "That way we can be sure of not going off the road or tumbling into a hole. I can see the ground in front of me quite well for several feet."

The driver looked as horrified as if she had suggested stripping off her clothes and running screaming through the night. "Miss! 'Ere, you can't do that."

"Why not? It is the sensible thing to do."

"It wouldn't be proper. I'll guide 'em." He started to lay his reins aside, but Camilla's voice stopped him.

"Nonsense! Who would stop the horses, then, if they should take it into their heads to bolt? I assure you, I am not skilled in handling the reins. However, I am quite capable of walking and watching the ground in front of me. Besides, I lived here nearly all my life. It isn't logical for you to lead the horses."

"But, miss...it just wouldn't be prop—"

"Oh, hang propriety. Propriety won't help us to get out of this mess, now, will it?"

She turned her back on him, ending the conversation, and walked back to the horses' heads. She slid a hand beneath the strap of one of the horses' bridles and started forward, holding the lantern aloft with the other hand. The horses plodded along docilely beside her.

The track was a trifle muddy—it had rained earlier in the evening—and Camilla kept to the grass beside the rutted trail to avoid getting her shoes caked with mud. However, the moisture of the bedewed grass soon crept through her shoes. The fog began to lift a little, revealing a patch of gorse or a briar bush here and there, but at the same time, it began to drizzle. Sighing, Camilla pulled up the hood of her cloak to protect her face from the chilly, persistent drops.

The drizzle, she soon noticed, was turning into a definite rain. Her feet slipped on the wet grass, but when she stepped into the track, the slick mud was just as bad. Moreover, the rain was beginning to penetrate her light cloak. She thought of getting her umbrella out of the post chaise, but she could think of no way that she could carry it and the lantern, and still hold the horse's head. Her only other choice was to wait for the rain to stop, but she did not relish the thought of being stuck out here any longer than she had to be. So she trudged on, grateful that at least the fog was disappearing, reduced to wisps and patches.

Then, off to her right, she saw a movement, and she jumped, startled, letting out a squeak of surprise. She held her lantern higher and peered into the night. It was a man standing beside a small tree, almost hidden by its branches.

"Sir!" she exclaimed, letting go of the horse's head

and starting toward him eagerly. "Sir, can you help me? I fear we are lost, and—"

The man whirled toward her, frowning fiercely, his face pale in the dark. There was a long-barreled pistol in his hand. "Hush!" he hissed. "Do you want to get us all killed?"

At that moment, her lantern exploded in her hand, the explosion accompanied by a loud pop. The horses whinnied and danced nervously. The lantern, torn from her grasp, hit the ground and went out, plunging her into complete darkness. Camilla screamed and turned to run back to the carriage.

But before she could take a step, the man launched himself across the space separating them and rammed into her with all his weight, sending them both tumbling to the ground. Camilla hit the earth hard, the breath knocked from her. The stranger lay sprawled atop her, his weight pressing her into the ground. Camilla struggled to get out from under him, gasping for air.

"Stop squirming, dammit!" he growled, pinning her to the ground. "They're firing at us. Silly chit, do you want to be killed?"

It was then that she realized what that pop had been and why the lantern had shattered. Someone had shot at her! She realized, too, that she had heard more pops as the man drove her to the ground. Camilla went limp with shock.

There were shouts in the distance, but no more bangs. Nearer to them, the horses, upset by the shots, were whinnying and dancing about, tossing their heads. The coachman, cursing, was struggling to control them.

The stranger lifted his head and looked behind them. Camilla stared up at him. His face was fierce and dark, all sharp angles and jutting cheekbones and black, slanting eyebrows. He looked, she thought, quite dangerous, and instinctively she was certain that it was *he* the others had been shooting at.

"Bloody hell!" He rasped the words out. "I think they're coming after us."

"What?" Her voice rose sharply. "What is going on?"

He shook his head and rose to a crouch. Before she realized what he was going to do, he had grasped her upper arms with hands of steel and jerked her to her feet, rising with her.

"Run!" he ordered, and with the word, he ran to the coach, dragging her along with him.

"Let go of me!" Camilla tried to wrest her arm away from him, but he was too strong.

There were two more gunshots behind them, and Camilla heard something splat into the side of the chaise. Her companion jerked open the door of the coach and tossed her up into it. Camilla screamed again as she hit the floor, and the carriage jerked and took off, the coachman apparently unable to hold the frightened horses any longer.

The stranger was clinging to the door. She thought he meant to crawl inside, too, but then, to her amazement, he grasped something on the roof of the carriage and used the door as a stepping-stone to climb onto the top of it.

"Watch out!" she shouted to the driver, and she heard the coachman's shout of surprise and the sound of a struggle, then the thud of a body—undoubtedly the poor coachman's—falling to the seat.

The coach gathered speed quickly, the horses panicked and with the bits between their teeth. The vehicle rocked and bounced along the rough path. Camilla grabbed hold of the seat, afraid that she would go sliding out the open door when the carriage tilted that way.

There were more shots, and she realized that they were hurtling straight toward the men who were firing upon them. She had a glimpse of dark shapes that resolved themselves into men and ponies. Suddenly a large man jumped out of the darkness, grabbing the door and swinging his feet up into the carriage. Camilla shrieked and scrambled away from him. As she did so, her flailing hand landed on her umbrella, lying there on the floor.

She picked it up and swung it hard at the man, cracking him on the shins. He let out a howl, and she gave him a hard poke in the stomach with the tip of the umbrella. He let out another cry of pain, and his fingers slipped on the door. He fell backward out of the carriage.

Camilla sat down on the seat, grasping the strap on the wall for purchase. With the other hand, she held her umbrella at the ready, keeping a sharp lookout for any other intruders. They tore along at a reckless speed, the door of the carriage swinging back and forth, the carriage jouncing wildly over the rutted track. Camilla was certain that they were going to overturn at any moment. It was raining in earnest now, too, and rain was slanting in through the open door.

She realized after a while that they were slowing

down to a more sedate pace, and after a moment, she slid across the seat and grabbed the door as it swung back toward the carriage and pulled it firmly shut. She looked with distaste at the puddle of water that had formed on the floor, but there was little she could do about that. She could, however, remove her soaked mantle, the back of which, she discovered, was thoroughly smeared with mud from when the stranger had thrown her to the ground.

The stranger. Her eyes narrowed as her thoughts turned toward that man. *Who was he, and what had he been up to out here in the wilds of the Dorset coast?* He was up to no good, she was sure. Those men had been shooting at him, and, now that she thought about it, it was obvious that he had been hiding behind that tree—no doubt lying in wait for someone. It was no wonder he had looked at her with such fury when she called to him; she had broadcast his presence to the other men, giving them a chance to protect themselves. She wondered if he was a highwayman, or merely some ruffian looking to attack one of his enemies.

Of course, she mused, given where they were, it just might have something to do with "the gentlemen"— the name, uttered only in lowered voices, given to the men engaged in the age-old occupation of smuggling. Everyone knew about it, and, if truth be known, many an upstanding local citizen, even among the magistrates and judges, was known to turn a blind eye to the illegal trade. Indeed, many of them had a regular delivery of French brandy waiting on their back doorsteps in the early-morning light after a moonless night. There were those who, hating the duty laws, considered "the gentlemen" within their rights in evading the laws. The people of the outlying coastal areas were often known to resent the intrusion of the central government in what they considered their business. In the previous century, the smugglers had been so strong that there were even pitched battles between the Hawkridge gang and the soldiers. Though those lawless times had passed, the business of smuggling went on, especially now, with coveted French goods cut off from England by the war.

Camilla thought back to the man, remembering his face as he had loomed above her in the dark—the fierce upward slash of cheekbones and the hard mouth, the dark eyes beneath peaked black eyebrows, the dark, rough clothes. Yes, she decided, he had definitely looked as if he might be a smuggler, at odds with his fellows, or a highwayman looking to rob a traveler, or simply a ruffian seeking revenge upon someone. Whatever he was, she was certain that she was not in a safe position. She had seen him where he had not wanted to be seen, and she had been the unwitting cause of the other men shooting at him and chasing him. He had been furious with her earlier, and she had little doubt that he still was. This rough ride in the post chaise might be nothing compared to what happened when the vehicle stopped.

Which it was doing right now. Camilla could feel the chaise slowing down. In a moment, she knew, it would rock to a halt, and then he would jump down and come back here and open the door. He would pull her out and— Well, she was not sure what he would do, but she had no trouble imagining him doing anything from hitting her to strangling her, including the

despoiling that old women always warned of in lowered voices to girls who were rash enough to go out
unaccompanied.

Camilla took a firm grip on her umbrella. It had
served well enough as a weapon before. *Perhaps if
she took him by surprise, she might disable him
enough to get away.*

As the carriage rolled to a halt, she crouched down
beside the door and waited, the blood pounding in her
ears, every nerve stretched, listening for his approach.
She heard the thud as he jumped down, and the crunch
of his boots upon pebbles as he strode to the door. The
latch turned and the door swung outward. "Are
you—"

Camilla erupted from her crouched position with a
shriek, launching herself out of the chaise. She swung
her umbrella with all her might at the man's face, and
the handle cracked satisfyingly against his cheek. The
umbrella broke in two, and the man staggered back
with a roared oath, his hand going to his cheek.

Camilla hit the ground running, screaming with all
her might. She knew that they were probably too far
away for anyone to hear her, but she had to try, just
as she had to run. She lifted her skirts and flew across
the ground, heading down the muddy road in front of
the carriage. She didn't even notice the rain falling on
her, or the mud that pulled at her shoes.

He was after her in an instant. She could hear him
behind her, but even though she ran so fast she thought
her heart would burst, he caught up with her. His hand
wrapped around one of her arms like an iron band and
pulled her to a stop.

"Stop that caterwauling!" he snarled. "Dammit,

woman, what is wrong with you? You'll bring the whole countryside down upon us.''

Camilla did stop screaming, but only because she was out of breath. She sucked in a lungful of air as she whipped around and struck out at him with her doubled-up fist.

She hit only his chest, and it sent a dart of pain shooting up her arm. He let out a string of curses and grabbed for her wrist, but Camilla twisted and struggled, hitting out and kicking at him.

''Bloody hell, woman, would you stop it? Are you mad?''

They were both thoroughly soaked by the rain now, but neither of them noticed as they grappled in the dark. The man was far larger and taller than Camilla, and the conclusion was never in doubt, but she was fighting for her life, and she struggled wildly, connecting with several kicks and blows as he struggled to subdue her. He managed to wrap one arm around her and pull her off her feet, but Camilla twisted and reached for his face with her nails. He jerked back as her fingers scraped down his cheek, barely missing his eye, and he lost his balance and staggered backward.

They crashed to the ground, but their fall was softened by the mud into which they fell. The man received the brunt of the blow, and he loosened his grasp involuntarily. Camilla seized the opportunity to pull away from him, but before she could crawl to her feet, he had grabbed her arm, jerking her to a stop, and she fell face first into the mud. She came up spluttering and enraged, lashing out at him. He grabbed for her arms, trying to pin them to her sides, but she was slippery with rain and mud, and he could not get a good hold on her. They rolled across the muddy ground, grappling.

Camilla squirmed and twisted, trying to get away, and he tried to wrap his arms around her to pin her arms to her sides. Once, as they struggled, she felt his hand slide across her breast, and she sucked in her breath sharply at the intimate touch. It startled and alarmed her, almost as much for the strange, sudden heat that shot through her body as for the effrontery of the contact.

He, too, seemed surprised at the touch, and he froze for an instant. She seized the opportunity to try to rise, but he grabbed at her arm to stop her, and the sodden material of her dress ripped, leaving the sleeve in his hand. She tore away, and he lunged after her. They went sprawling in the mud again, his weight bearing her down into the soft muck. He grabbed her wrists, hauling them up over her head, and sat up, leaning on her arms to hold her to the ground. His legs clamped tightly around hers, holding her immobile beneath him.

The man gazed down at her, his chest rising and falling in rapid pants. He was soaked and smeared with mud, his rough dark shirt hanging open down the front, where buttons had been torn off in their struggle. His bare skin showed through the gap, sleek and tanned and wet. His hair clung to his head. There was a cut high on his cheekbone where she had hit him with her umbrella, and his eyes glittered fiercely.

Camilla's throat went dry. The man looked elemental and furious, quite male and quite angry. Camilla was very aware of the suggestive nature of their position, of his weight upon her legs. She was conscious, too, of an odd feeling in the center of her being, a strange mixture of fury and excitement and some other elusive emotion she could not have named. His eyes skimmed down her, taking in the wet bodice that clung to her breasts, and she could feel the response of his body.

"Let go of me!"

"Not until I get some answers!" he growled back. "Who the devil are you, and what are you doing here?"

"What am I doing here?" she gasped, outraged. "I have every right to be driving through here. It is you who are obviously up to no good, skulking about the countryside in the dark, people firing at you. Release me at once, or you'll be in even more trouble than you already are."

"You are hardly in a position to be issuing commands," he reminded her, and a faint smile touched his lips.

His mouth was wide, with a generous lower lip, and he should have had an appealing smile, but his face was set in cold, sardonic lines that ruined any hint of charm. His amusement at her expense infuriated Camilla, and she lunged upward with all her might, trying to throw him off. He was far too heavy and strong for her, of course, and her efforts did little to dislodge him, but the glitter in his eyes turned dangerously brighter, reminding Camilla chillingly of the helplessness and intimacy of her position.

To hide her fear, she curled her lip in contempt. "It is obvious that you are a villain," she said coldly. "I suggest that you refrain from turning yourself into a felon, as well."

His eyebrows quirked up in inverted vees, giving his dark visage an even more demonic look. "Well said, madam. But I scarcely need remind you that without witnesses, it is hard to charge a man with a felony." He paused, letting the threat of his words sink in, then smiled coldly and said, "Besides, I know of no felony that has been committed this night. 'Tis scarcely a crime to take charge of a carriage in order to save a lady from a gang of men who are attacking her."

"You know as well as I that those men were not concerned with me," Camilla shot back. "It was *you* they were firing at."

His mouth twisted grimly. "Perhaps, but they would certainly not have been if you had not blundered into the scene, shouting and waving a lantern about."

"How was I supposed to know that you were engaged in clandestine doings? I was seeking your help—a futile quest, obviously, but I was not as aware of your character then as I am now. I did not know that I was dealing with a thief."

"I am not a thief." He ground out the words.

"Ha!" Camilla shot him a scornful look. "What were you doing hiding out there on a foggy night, then?"

"That is none of your business, and if you weren't such a blasted busybody, we wouldn't be in this mess."

"I should have known that you were the sort to try to shift the blame. As if I were responsible for your cohorts or your enemies or whoever those people were."

"Lord, you've got a wasp's tongue on you." Suddenly, swiftly, he stood up, hauling her up with him. "But I've no desire to hang about here bandying quips with you. Those men might very well be upon us at any minute."

He clamped one hand tightly around her arm and began to walk her toward the post chaise. Camilla dug in her heels. "Wait! I am not going anywhere with you."

"I think you would be far better off back in Edgecombe than you would be standing around in the dark in the middle of the countryside with a large group of men with guns wandering about."

"I didn't say that I was staying here! What I meant was that *you* are not going anywhere in my carriage."

He looked at her for a long moment, then dropped her arm and stepped back. "Of course. You are right. It is your carriage, and I have no claim to it. I shall leave you, then. Good day, madam."

He turned and started striding away. Stunned, Camilla stared after him. Then she remembered that her coachman was unconscious—*oh, Lord, might he even have killed the poor man?*—and while she could handle a gig, it was quite beyond her powers to drive a coach-and-four. Not only that, there was a band of men with guns who were perhaps still pursuing her carriage.

"Wait!" she called, and when the stranger did not stop, she took a few running steps after him. "Stop! Please?"

He turned and looked back at her, his eyebrows raised inquisitively. "Yes?"

"Don't go. I—I cannot drive the post chaise back to Edgecombe."

"Mmm. Then it would seem that you have a certain problem with *your* carriage. Good night."

"Oh, stop being so exasperating! I am telling you that you can go with me to Edgecombe."

"You mean that you are allowing me the honor of working for you?" he asked sardonically. "How kind of you. But I am afraid I must decline the honor. You see, I think it would be better for me to walk. One man in the fog is far less noticeable than a great carriage."

"Horses are faster."

He shrugged and turned to walk off again.

"Stop! You cannot leave me here! No gentleman would leave a lady stranded like this."

"Well, as you have no doubt realized, I am not much of a gentleman, and, frankly, I have yet to see any ladylike qualities in you."

Camilla glared at him. "All right. Have you satisfied your need to insult me? Let us go, then. We both know that it would be absurd for you to walk when there is a coach right here. We do not like each other, but surely we can trade—your skill at driving the horses for the use of my post chaise."

He said nothing, just walked back and swung up to the top of the coach. Camilla quickly climbed back in, and they set out again, this time at a speed more suited to the rutted track. It was fast enough to rattle and jounce Camilla around in her seat, and she suspected darkly that the awful man was doing it simply to annoy her.

Adding to her discomfort was the state of her hair and clothes. This morning she had been dressed quite charmingly in a sprigged muslin gown and green kid half boots, and her hair had been pulled up to the crown of her head, from which point it hung in a cluster of fetching curls. Now her shoes were a sodden mess, soaked through and caked with mud, inside and out, and her dress and hair were in almost as bad a state. She was wet clear through to her underthings. Her curls, too, were thick with mud, and she could feel it drying on her skin, as well.

How was she going to explain her state when she arrived at the Park? Tears welled up in her eyes. *As if she did not have problems enough already, what with Grandpapa and the terrible lies she had woven....* To have to arrive looking like a ragamuffin seemed like the outside of enough.

Grimly she blinked her tears away. She refused to cry over this. If nothing else, her tears would leave tracks on her dirty cheeks, making it obvious that she had been crying. *And no doubt* he *would think that she had been crying because of him.* She grimaced as her thoughts turned to the obnoxious man who had virtually abducted her.

He was uncouth, low and thoroughly maddening. He had treated her reprehensibly. No man of breeding would have grabbed her so roughly or pinned her to the ground like that. She remembered the bold way his eyes had lingered over her breasts, revealed by the thin, wet material of her dress. It made her blush, even sitting there alone in the dark carriage, to think of the way his legs had clamped around hers, of how intimately his body had been pressed against her—and of the shocking movement his body had made as he looked at her. It had felt so strange—almost exhilarating, even at the same time that it was utterly improper and infuriating.

She shifted on her seat, pulling her sodden dress away from her. She was growing more and more uncomfortable by the moment. The mud was continuing to dry on her, and her clothes were sticking to her flesh. Worst of all, her wet garments were quite cold, so that she was shivering almost continuously. She wanted to drape her cloak around her to help keep off some of the cold, but she hated to get mud all over the inside of it. Still…she could hardly just sit there and catch a chill. She was eyeing the cloak uncertainly when she became aware of the fact that the carriage was rattling over cobblestones. With a suppressed cry, she pushed aside the curtain and looked out to see that they had entered the village.

Within moments, they were turning into the yard of the Blue Boar. Camilla let out a sigh of relief. Though she had tried not to let herself think about it, she had been worried that the stranger would not really take her into the village at all, but, realizing the dangers of her being able to identify him, would abandon her on some dark and lonely road…or worse.

Now, with a cry, she jerked open the door of the carriage even before they came to a complete stop and jumped down from it. "Boy, see to the horses," she called to the ostler, who had started across the yard toward their vehicle. "And look to my coachman, too. I fear we may have to send for a doctor."

The ostler came to a dead halt, goggling at her, but Camilla did not notice. She was already hurrying to the front door, her only thought to get safely inside before the stranger atop the chaise could catch up with her.

As soon as she stepped inside the public room, all conversation came to a halt, and everyone swiveled around to stare at her. Camilla stopped short, dismayed at being the focus of so many sets of eyes. In her relief at reaching the Blue Boar, she had forgotten about her appearance, but now those stunned expressions reminded her of just how she looked. Her hand went to her mud-encrusted ringlets, and she glanced down at her wet gown, pressed to her body in a most improper way, one sleeve completely ripped away. A wave of deep red washed up her face to her hairline.

The keeper of the inn, a large, bluff man, started toward her from his post at the tap. Camilla saw him and was swept by relief. "Saltings! How glad I am to see you!"

She took a step or two forward, then stopped as he said, "Here, now, miss, what do you think you be doing? Coming in here like that! This is a decent inn, it is, and we've no use—"

"Saltings!" Camilla exclaimed, shaken. "Don't you recognize me?" Tears of humiliation sprang into her eyes. This seemed the last straw, the perfectly awful end to a perfectly awful day—that Saltings, who had known her all her life, should mistake her for a common doxy. *Was he actually going to toss her out?*

The man stopped and peered at her. "Do I know you?"

"It is I! Camilla Ferrand!" Tears flooded her eyes. She could not hold them back, and they spilled over, coursing a trail through the smear of mud on her cheeks.

"Miss Ferrand!" he repeated, his jaw dropping. "Sweet Lord, what happened? What are you doing here this way?"

He went to her, gently taking her arm and steering her toward the smaller private room of the inn, then stopped. "Oh, dear, no, there's a gentleman there." He took another glance at Camilla beside him, muddy and disheveled and struggling to hold back her tears, then at the rest of his customers, all staring avidly.

"Well," he said with a sigh, "there's nothing for it. You can't stay out here, that's for certain."

He rapped sharply on the door to the private room and pushed it open when a man's voice inside answered. "I beg your pardon, sir," Saltings said, ushering Camilla inside the room. "I'm sorry to disturb you, but we've got a bit of a problem here. There's a lady here, and, well, it wouldn't be right for her to be sitting outside with the common crowd, sir."

Camilla looked across the room, fighting to contain her tears. The gentleman sitting beside the fire—for it was just as obvious that he was a gentleman as it had been that the stranger on the heath earlier was a ruffian—rose to his feet, his eyebrows lifting in astonishment. He was dressed impeccably, from the crease of his simple yet elegant white neckcloth to the tips of his polished Hessians, and his hair was dressed in a similarly subdued yet fashionable style known as the Brutus.

He took one swift look at Camilla's muddied state and said, "Precisely, Saltings. You are right. The lady must have the private dining room. The only thing is, I am expecting a visitor— Ah, there he is now. And looking, I might add, quite as if he had shared this young lady's adventure.''

Camilla swung around at his words. ''You!'' she exclaimed with loathing.

There, in the doorway, stood her tormentor.

2

The man gave Camilla a look that left little doubt that he shared her feelings. She straightened, bolstered by his irritation. It was some comfort, at least, to see that he was as filthy, wet and bedraggled as she.

"What the devil are you doing here?" the man asked roughly. "Am I never to be rid of you?"

"I might say the same about you."

"I take it that you two have met," said the gentleman by the fireplace, his voice as smooth and suave as if they were all standing in a London drawing room.

The stranger from the carriage ride grunted and moved into the room. Camilla said icily, "I am afraid that we were not *properly* introduced."

"Ah, Benedict." The gentleman sighed. "I fear you are ever lacking in manners." He moved forward toward Camilla. "Allow me to correct his oversight. I, dear lady, am Jermyn Sedgewick. And this is, ah, Benedict, uh…"

"How do you do, Mr. Sedgewick? I am pleased to make your acquaintance," Camilla replied formally, trying to ignore the absurdity of the polite greeting in contrast to her grubby state of dress. She cast a flashing glance toward the other man. "I am sorry I cannot say the same about meeting Mr. Benedict."

Mr. Sedgewick opened his mouth to speak, then closed it. He cast a grin toward Benedict. "I see you have made your usual charming impression."

Benedict's only reply was a noise resembling a growl. He turned away from both of them, striding over to the fire and holding out his hands to it. Mr. Sedgewick ignored him as he spoke to the innkeeper. "Well, Saltings, I think what we need here is a hot rum punch. Why don't you bring us a bowl of it? I'll do the mixing."

"Of course, sir."

Saltings bowed out of the room reluctantly. Camilla knew that he had been hoping to hear the details of what had happened to her and Benedict.

Sedgewick turned toward Camilla. "Now, Miss...?"

"Forgive me. Here you have been so kind, and I haven't even told you my name. I am Camilla Ferrand."

"Miss Ferrand. It is a pleasure to make your acquaintance, even under such deplorable conditions. Please come over here by the fire and warm yourself. I am sure you must be quite chilled." He guided her toward the fire and into the chair beside it.

Camilla sank into the chair, grateful for its softness and for the warmth of the fire. She leaned forward, soaking up the heat. Benedict looked at Camilla, and his mouth twisted in a grimace. He withdrew to the other end of the fireplace, turning away from her and planting his elbow on the mantel. Sedgewick glanced from him to Camilla and back again, but he made no comment. The silence stretched out awkwardly.

At last there was a knock on the door, and Saltings bustled in, followed by the tap boy, carrying the inn's best silver punch bowl and a trayful of ingredients. They set their loads down on the sideboard, and Saltings fussed around for a bit before Benedict pointedly opened the door for them and gestured a dismissal.

"Now, then," Sedgewick said, advancing on the punch bowl. "This will fix you right up, Miss Ferrand. Normally, of course, it is not what I would consider giving a young lady such as yourself, but considering the chill of the night and the ordeal you've gone through, I think it will be just the thing to set you up."

He began to mix the punch expertly, adding rum, sugar and lemons until he decided that the hot drink had just the right taste. He handed one silver cup of the mixture to Camilla, and she took the steaming drink gratefully. She had never had as strong a drink as this, for, as Mr. Sedgewick had pointed out, it was not considered a fit drink for women. However, Camilla considered herself no slave to tradition, and she was rather pleased to have the opportunity to sample a little of the sort of drink men consumed. It had a slightly unpleasant taste underlying the fruity sweetness of the punch, but, all in all, it was not as strong or as bad as she would have thought, and it was blessedly warm. The liquid rolled down her throat, warming it all the way, and burst fierily in her stomach. She finished off the cup and decided that she felt better already.

"That was excellent, Mr. Sedgewick, thank you," she said, and he graciously refilled all their cups.

"Now, Miss Ferrand, you must tell me how you happened upon Mr., uh, Benedict."

Camilla cast a stormy look toward that individual. "He abducted me."

"Oh, God," Benedict said callously, turning his back to the fire to warm it. "Not that again."

"I was almost killed," Camilla added, crossing her arms over her chest and glowering at Benedict.

"Benedict!" Mr. Sedgewick stared at the other man in astonishment. "What in the world happened?"

"She exaggerates. It was nothing." He waved a hand dismissively. "We were shot at."

"Shot at?" Sedgewick repeated incredulously. "You call that nothing?"

Benedict shrugged. "No one was hurt. They were some distance away, and I don't think any of them could hit the side of a barn, anyway."

"No one was hurt!" Camilla cried, raising her face from her hands. "What about my driver? I think you killed him!"

Benedict rolled his eyes. "I knocked him out," he explained patiently to Mr. Sedgewick, then added to Camilla, "The reason he stayed out so long is that he'd been nipping at a bottle all evening. He was drunk. 'Tis no wonder you were lost."

"Lost?" Sedgewick repeated. "My girl, you have had a dreadful day."

Tears started in Camilla's eyes as she thought about just how dreadful the day had indeed been, even before Mr. Benedict came along to persecute her. "You've no idea, sir." Her voice roughened, and she stopped, trying to blink back her tears. "I think—I think this is the worst day of my life!"

And suddenly, surprising even herself, she burst into tears.

Sedgewick stared at Camilla, his face showing all a gentleman's horror at being confronted with a sobbing female. "Dear lady," he began feebly, "pray, don't... I'm sure it cannot be that bad."

"Oh, it is!" Camilla cried, covering her face with her hands. "You just don't know. It is too, too awful!" Tears poured down her face.

"Well, it's not a tragedy," Benedict pointed out brutally. "I am sure you have been lost before, and will be again. We were never in any real danger. I told you."

"Oh!" Camilla would have liked to shout at him that she was not absurd enough to collapse into sobs because her carriage had gotten lost, but she could not stem the tide of her tears enough to answer. At any other time, she would have been ready to sink through the floor with humiliation at giving way like this in front of two strangers—especially when one of them was as obnoxious and rude as Mr. Benedict. However, tonight, she was too weary and distressed to care.

"Shouldn't have given her that rum punch," Benedict told Sedgewick. "She's bosky."

Sedgewick cast him an impatient glance. "Don't be absurd."

Benedict shrugged. "I'm not. She's in her cups."

"I am *not* in my cups!" Camilla flashed, raising her head and glaring at him, her irritation at his rudeness cutting through her emotional outburst. She wiped angrily at the tears wetting her cheeks. "I am merely tired and...and overset. Everything is just...just ruined!"

Benedict cocked a supercilious eyebrow. "A party canceled? A beau marrying another?"

Camilla jumped to her feet, her fists clenched by her sides, letting out an inarticulate cry of rage. "How dare you! How dare you trivialize my...my... Oh, I hate you! My grandfather is dying!"

She burst into tears again and threw herself back into the chair. Sedgewick cast the other man an admonishing look, and even Benedict had the grace to look abashed.

"I am sorry," he said stiffly. "I had no idea...."

"Dear girl," Sedgewick began, going over to her and reaching down to take one of her hands and pat it. "I am so sorry. If there is anything I can do..."

"There is nothing anyone can do," Camilla said when her spurt of tears had subsided. She brushed the tears from her cheeks, once again disturbing the smears of mud, and drew a ragged breath. "He is old, and his body is failing him. He had a fit of apoplexy several months ago, and ever since then he hasn't been able to leave his room. His doctor——" She swallowed hard. "His doctor said he hadn't long to live, but he has kept hanging on." She offered a watery smile. "He was always the stubbornest of men."

"I am sure he's had a long, full life," Sedgewick said comfortingly.

Camilla nodded. "He has. And I—I've almost resigned myself to his death. It's just— Oh, I've made the most awful mess of everything." She gulped back her tears and raised large, beseeching eyes to Sedgewick. "Truly, I didn't mean to. I did it all for the best, but now...well, now I have to tell him the truth. All of them. And I am so afraid it will kill him."

The man frowned. "I am sure it cannot be that serious."

"It is. I—I lied to him, you see."

At her words, Benedict let out a noise of disgust
and said with withering sarcasm, "Naturally."

Camilla whirled toward him indignantly. "I did it
for the best!"

"That is what they always say," he retorted. "Deceiving you and then pretending that it's for your own
good."

"Hush, Benedict. Don't mind him, Miss Ferrand.
Our Benedict has a warped view of the human condition."

Benedict grimaced but did not reply, and Camilla
turned back to Mr. Sedgewick, ignoring the other man.
"I *did* do it for the best," she reiterated. "I was trying
to give him some comfort, to make his last days better.
But I never thought that he would tell Aunt Beryl!"

"Well, of course not," Sedgewick agreed, confused
but sympathetic.

"But I haven't been to see Grandpapa, not since
that first collapse, and all because I cannot bear to face
Aunt Beryl. She will ask all sorts of penetrating questions, you see, and would want to know where *he* is.
It would be impossible. And now Lydia is there, and
of course she can't carry the burden of the lies. It's
not that she can't lie to Aunt Beryl, for Lydia is capable of the most perfect whoppers, all the while looking completely innocent." Her tone indicated a wistful
envy of the said Lydia's ability. "The trouble is that
she gets carried away by them and winds up saying
so many things that she gets all tangled up. So I had
to come. And I have to tell them the truth."

"You are not making the slightest bit of sense," Benedict pointed out rudely.

"Benedict…"

"No, he's right. I'm all muddled." Camilla put a hand to her head and sighed. She gazed at Sedgewick for a moment, then gave a little nod, as if coming to some sort of decision. "You can be trusted, can you not? I mean, you would never tell another soul, would you?"

"Of course not!" The man looked offended that she could question his integrity even that much. "But you must not tell me if it makes you uneasy."

"No, I feel as if I must tell someone or burst. I have been thinking about it all day, driving down here. All day—truth is, I've thought of little else for weeks. I don't know what to do, how to extricate myself from this tangle I've created."

"You have my word of honor," Sedgewick assured her solemnly, "that anything you say will not go beyond this room. Feel free to tell us."

Camilla cast an uneasy glance toward Benedict, who grimaced and muttered, "Trust me, Miss Ferrand, I shall not be telling your girlish secrets all over London."

Hastily Sedgewick put in, "I will vouch for Benedict. He will not say anything. Now, tell me, what is this problem you are wrestling with so?"

Camilla hesitated, glancing toward the punch bowl. "Do you think… Could I have a bit more of that punch? It is so warming."

"Of course." Sedgewick politely took her cup and ladled more of the spicy brew into it, also refilling his and Benedict's cups.

"You are going to wind up with an intoxicated female," Benedict warned him dryly, taking his own cup and drinking from it.

"Don't be nonsensical," Camilla retorted. "I have neber, uh, *never,* been intoxicated in my life."

"Hush, Benedict. Now, Miss Ferrand, please proceed."

She took a sip of her drink, drew a deep breath and began. "Well, as I told you, Grandpapa was taken with apoplexy, and the doctor put him in bed and said he hadn't long to live. Of course, I posted down to Chevington Park as soon as I heard."

"Chevington Park?" Sedgewick repeated, surprised. "You mean...your grandfather is..."

"The Earl of Chevington." Camilla nodded. She was looking down at the cup in her hands and so did not see the swift glance that her benefactor cast toward Benedict. "Yes. My mother was his daughter.

"My parents died when I was a child. So I was raised by my grandparents, as well as by my Aunt Lydia—Lady Marbridge, that is. She was married to my uncle, the heir to the Earl, but he died when their son Anthony was just a child. So it was quite kind of her to take me on, as well. We all lived at the Park with my grandparents. I suppose that is why I am so close to my grandfather. My grandmother died a few years ago. I came to see my grandpapa as soon as I learned that he had been taken ill. The doctor said we should all be very careful not to upset him, that it would damage his health, maybe even send him into another fit. But I could not keep him from worrying about me. He was so very anxious, you see, because I am not married. He kept saying that I needed a husband to take care of me, which is, really, the most absurd thing, because I am quite capable of taking care of myself.''

Benedict made a muffled noise, and Camilla turned to look at him sharply. He gave her a bland look in return and gestured for her to continue.

"As I was saying, he was fretting himself tremendously. You see, Grandpapa is rather old-fashioned, and he is convinced that I ought to be married.''

Sedgewick cleared his throat deprecatingly. ''Well, it is the usual thing for a young lady to do.''

"Yes, but, you see, I am not the usual young lady. I don't wish to be married.''

''Indeed.''

''Yes.'' She nodded vigorously. ''Marriage, you see, is an institution designed for the benefit of men, and I see little advantage for a woman in marrying.''

''I beg your pardon?''

''Well, it's true. Men, after they marry, are still free to do as they please, the rulers of their households, whereas their wives have no freedom at all. They are expected to obey their husbands and raise heirs and keep the house in order. And nothing else. They have no rights and no freedom.''

Sedgewick smiled faintly. ''Come now, Miss Ferrand, surely you overstate the matter.''

''Do I?'' She straightened, looking at him with narrowed eyes. ''A woman's property becomes her husband's as soon as they are married. She, in fact, is considered his property, a chattel. He has the right to discipline her, to restrict her movements, even to beat her if he wishes. She cannot vote.''

''Vote? Good Gad, you wish to vote?''

"I don't see why not. But that is beside the matter. The point is, whether I wish to or not, I *cannot*. I have had an excellent education, and my understanding, I think I may say without contradiction, is not small. Yet the stupidest fellow is allowed to vote, simply because he is a man and owns property, whereas I am not."

"God help us," Benedict commented dryly. "A bluestocking."

Camilla shot him a look that would have blighted a less sturdy sort. "I fail to see what is so reprehensible about a female of intellect and education. No doubt you are the sort who thinks that women should tend to their knitting and not speak unless spoken to or have a thought in their heads that does not pertain to dresses and hairstyles."

"No, Miss Ferrand, actually, I have had quite enough of empty-headed females." He gave her a small bow, a faint smile on his lips conveying the distinct impression that he included her among that number.

Sedgewick turned the conversation back to its original track. "So that is why you have not married, Miss Ferrand?"

"Yes. I see no reason to give any man control over myself or my property. I am a person in my own right, and I shall remain so as long as I do not marry. Therefore, I am twenty-five years old and a spinster, and while I am quite happy in that condition, it has worried my grandfather for years. After he was taken ill, it plagued him even more. He would tell me how he could not bear the thought of dying and leaving me unprotected. And no matter how I tried to tell him that

I was fine, that I had the property my mother and father left me, so I am quite able to live independently, he would not stop fretting about it. He told me it was an unnatural sort of life I was leading, living on my own, even though I have a companion, so it is perfectly respectable. But he wanted me to have children and a man to take care of, and all the things that he said were right and natural for a woman." She paused, then sighed and confessed, "So I told him that I was engaged."

Benedict let out a short bark of laughter. "Oh, that's rich—the defender of women's rights, pretending that she has snagged a husband."

"I was trying to keep him from worrying!" Camilla snapped. "Of course, *you* would never think of such a thing as trying to save someone pain or worry."

"Whatever your reasoning," he pointed out mildly, "'tis still a lie."

"Fine words from a thief!" Camilla retorted hotly. "Or smuggler, or whatever you are. You don't hesitate to steal carriages and kidnap people, or to knock a man senseless or draw an innocent bystander into a fight, but you draw the line, of course, at telling a small fib to ease the mind of a dying man!"

"Benedict…" Sedgewick shot him a quelling look. "Pay him no attention, Miss Ferrand. Benedict has little use for us ordinary mortals and our petty problems. It's perfectly understandable that you would have told your grandfather that story, so that he could die more peacefully."

"Thank you." Camilla smiled at him gratefully and took another sip of her drink. It no longer felt like fire as it rolled down into her stomach; it merely sent a pleasant warmth spreading throughout her, lifting her spirits a little. She felt better already, she thought, and she realized that confession must indeed be good for the soul.

"You are a very understanding gentleman," she told Sedgewick with a warm smile. "I am so glad I told you. You see, I didn't want to lie to Grandpapa, but it seemed a small enough thing to do to make him happy. He was so sick that he didn't ask me much about the man or how we had met." She smiled faintly. "He didn't even lecture me on the impropriety of becoming engaged without the man coming to ask for my hand from him first. He was quite happy about it, and after that he rested more quietly. Then he began to improve a little, and soon he began to feel much better. Before we knew it, he was cursing his valet and wanting to get up and go downstairs, and ringing a peal over the doctor's head for not letting him. The better he felt, the more he asked me about my fiancé, and it became most awkward. Of course, I had to make everything up, and I felt so awful about lying to him. I regretted ever having told him, but I couldn't tell him that I had invented the whole thing. I was afraid it would upset him so that he would have apoplexy again. Finally, I could not bear it any longer, and I fled back to Bath. But then I kept getting letters from him asking about my fiancé, wanting to know when I was going to bring him to Chevington Park to meet him. I have been trying ever since to figure out a way to get out of it."

"Just tell him the fellow cried off," Benedict suggested callously. "That will put an end to the matter. It is quite believable. If your escapade tonight was any indication, you would give any man adequate reason to get out of an engagement.''

Camilla swung on him. ''You have the gall to blame *me* for what happened tonight? Anyway, my fiancé is not the sort of man who would 'cry off' an engagement, as you so vulgarly put it.''

He let out a bark of laughter. ''That's rich. Since your fiancé exists only in your imagination, I would imagine that he can do anything you wish.''

''I mean that the sort of man I have told my grandfather he is would never do such an ungentlemanly thing. You cannot understand that, no doubt, but most gentlemen have a code of honor.''

''Oh, aye, that's a bit out of my reach, miss,'' he replied, adopting a thick accent and tugging at an imaginary forelock like some dim-witted farmhand. ''Not being used to Quality, like.''

''Do shut up, Benedict,'' Sedgewick said mildly. ''Obviously she could not tell her grandfather that either of them had broken off the engagement, because the old gentleman is not supposed to be upset.''

''That's it exactly,'' Camilla agreed, pleased to see that he understood. ''Grandpapa is still in ill health, and the doctor says not to disturb him. He says it is a miracle that he hasn't gone already. So I kept putting him off about when Mr. Lassiter and I were going to come to Chevington.''

''Mr. Lassiter?'' Benedict asked.

''My fiancé.''

''Ah, yes, of course.''

''Would you let her get on with the story, Benedict?'' Sedgewick asked. ''I still haven't heard about Aunt Beryl. That is what I'm waiting for.''

"Her!" Camilla said with much disgust, her lip curling. "She decided that Grandpapa needed her care to improve, so she moved to Chevington Park, girls and all. Aunt Lydia says she just took advantage of the fact that Grandpapa is too sick to kick her out. Well, he can't, very well, when she came there on an errand of mercy. But I am sure that she has been driving him mad. And it put the housekeeper's nose out of joint, as if she couldn't take care of the house unless one of the family was there to keep an eye on her. But that's neither here nor there. The point is, Grandpapa told Aunt Beryl that I was engaged. I never dreamed of his doing that. Of course, when I told him the lie, I didn't expect him to even be alive a few days later."

"I see. And Aunt Beryl's knowing it puts a whole different light on the matter, I presume."

"Oh, yes." Camilla shook her head sadly and took another sip of her drink. Despite the awful situation she was in, she was beginning to feel quite mellow. "Aunt Beryl is the worst of my relatives. She has two of the most insipid daughters, whom she is always trying to marry off, and it has been a source of great pleasure to her that *I* have not married before either of them. However, she is always afraid that I will yet tie the knot before she unloads her brood on some poor, unsuspecting men."

"Haven't you told her of your philosophical position against marriage?" Benedict asked, his lips curling in an amused way that Camilla found quite irritating.

"Of course I have, but she doesn't believe me. She thinks that I am simply making excuses for being an old maid, and that I would jump at the opportunity to marry, just as her daughters would.''

''An understandable misapprehension, considering the fact that you are pretending to be engaged.''

Camilla frostily ignored Benedict's interruption, speaking only to Sedgewick. ''Aunt Beryl didn't believe it—that I was engaged, I mean. Apparently she and Grandpapa had quite a quarrel about it. Lydia learned all about it when she went down to Chevington Park. The doctor was so angry that he told Aunt Beryl not to bring the subject up again with Grandpapa. But Lydia writes me that the two of them keep sniping at each other about it. Aunt Beryl makes pointed remarks about the fact that I have not brought my fiancé to visit. Lydia says that Grandpapa defends me.'' Tears sprang into her eyes at the thought of her grandfather's loyalty. ''Oh! I feel so wretched! I have lied to him, and I cannot bear to think what he will think of me when he finds out. Because he must find out. Lydia wrote me that I have to come. Grandpapa keeps asking for me. She is right. I must go. I have to be with Grandpapa. I am afraid that it won't be much longer before he—''

She broke off, her throat clogging with tears. Sedgewick reached out and patted her hand. ''There, there, my dear.''

Camilla smiled at him waterily. ''You are very kind. None of this is your problem, and you have been the kindest of men to listen to me.''

''But what are you going to do?'' he asked.

''I must tell them the truth.'' She sighed. ''Lydia thinks that we can stave off Aunt Beryl's questions and barbs, but I don't see how. I am certain that she

will ask me all sorts of things about my fiancé that I
won't be able to answer. Things one should know. She
will want to know what family he belongs to and how
he is related to this person or that. I would be bound
to get caught in a lie, and that would be even worse
than telling everyone that I am not engaged. And what
sort of excuse can I give for his not coming with me?
I mean, it is a family crisis, and he wouldn't let me
travel down here all by myself. But I don't think that
I can bear to confess that I lied about it all and have
Aunt Beryl look at me in that pitying, superior way
she has. And Grandpapa—what if it upsets him so that
he dies? It is just too awful to contemplate.''

She stood up abruptly, setting her cup down on the
table with a clatter, and began to pace agitatedly about
the room. ''If only I could think of some way out of
it! I have been cudgeling my brain for days. All the
way down from London, I could think of nothing else.
But I came up with nothing...nothing!''

There was a long moment of silence, then Sedgewick said quietly, ''What if I thought of a solution?''

Both Camilla and Benedict swung toward him in
astonishment.

''What the devil—'' Benedict began.

''What?'' Camilla asked, hope rising in her face.
She started toward him eagerly. ''Do you mean it?
Have you really thought of a way out of my predica-
ment?''

He nodded. ''Perhaps. If you are willing to risk it.''

''I would do anything!'' she exclaimed rashly.
''Just tell me what it is!''

''What you need to do is arrive at Chevington Park
tonight with a fiancé.''

"What?" Camilla frowned, confused. *Had the fellow not understood what she had been telling him?* "How could I— Who—"

Sedgewick smiled and nodded toward the other man in the room. "Benedict will be your fiancé."

3

Camilla gaped at Sedgewick.

Across the room, Benedict expressed her fears more forcibly. "For God's sake, Jermyn, have you run mad?"

"Not at all. If you will think about it, you will see that it is the perfect solution."

"I see that it is perfect insanity," Benedict retorted. "If you think that I am going to become engaged to that…that…"

Camilla turned to look at him, her eyes sparkling dangerously. "To that *what*, Mr. Benedict?"

"Come, come, Benedict, you are usually not so slow," Sedgewick told him lightly. "Of course, I don't mean *actually* engaged. I am talking about a pretense of it. You will ride to Chevington Park tonight with Miss Ferrand. In the morning, you shall meet her relatives, talk to her grandfather and so forth. You stay a few days, then you say that you have to get back to the city, and you leave. The Earl will be reassured and happy, the dragon of an aunt will be routed, and you…well, you will spend a few days at

Chevington Park, which I understand is an elegant country house.''

Benedict narrowed his eyes and started to speak, then pressed his lips tightly together. He turned away, growling, ''You are as silly as she is. It is impossible.''

''Why? You are well able to *act* the part of a gentleman, aren't you?''

Sedgewick's gray eyes twinkled. ''A trifle rude, perhaps, but then, some lords are.''

''Oh, I don't need a lord,'' Camilla stuck in. ''Simply a gentleman will do.''

Benedict turned on her. ''Don't tell me that you are actually considering such a harebrained scheme!''

Camilla had had no intention of agreeing to Mr. Sedgewick's plan. However, Benedict's sneering tone made her decide that it was worth thinking about after all. Her chin came up, and she glared back at Benedict defiantly. ''Why not? It would suit my purposes. And however rough your manners are, you *do* speak like a gentleman. We might be able to pull the wool over everyone's eyes for a few days—as long as you avoided talking to everyone as much as possible. I will pay you for it, of course. Wouldn't that be a better way of making money than thievery? And it will answer my problem. It will make Grandpapa happy, and then, later, I can just pretend that I realized that we should not suit. Or better yet—'' her face brightened ''—I shall say that you died! That would be perfect.''

''Perhaps for you.''

''Well, only insofar as my family is concerned, of course.''

''It would be a trifle awkward, don't you think, if

they happened to meet me again a few months from now?''

"Don't be absurd. Why should they meet you?''

"I could run into one of them on the street in London. I *am* free to walk in London, despite my lack of gentility.''

"Oh. Well, in that case, I suppose I shall have to stick to the story that we broke it off.'' She sighed. "Pity. The dying story would have been much more dramatic.''

"You're right,'' Sedgewick agreed, his expression disappointed, though his eyes twinkled merrily. "However, I suppose we shall have to be content with the plainer tale.''

"Would everyone kindly stop talking this nonsense?'' Benedict burst out. "I am not going to pretend to be your fiancé. I can't believe that you would even consider it. It is obvious that you are drunk.''

"I am not!'' It was true, Camilla acknowledged to herself, that she felt very warm and cheerful, and that her mind was a trifle, well, fuzzy, but she had merely been relaxed by the rum punch. It had not influenced her thinking. "I am open-minded enough to see the value of Mr. Sedgewick's idea. It would work admirably for both of us. You are simply too stubborn to go along with anything that anyone else says.''

"I am glad that *someone* appreciates my endeavor,'' Sedgewick said lightly, taking out his snuffbox and expertly flipping it open with one hand. "Pinch, my dear Benedict?''

The other man let out an inarticulate growl. "Obviously I am the only person in this room with any sense.'' He stalked toward the door and opened it, then turned back. "It doesn't matter what you two bedlamites cook up, because *I* am not going along with it!" With that parting shot, he walked out, slamming the door behind him.

Sedgewick and Camilla stood for a moment, looking at the door, then turned toward each other. Sedgewick gave her a long, considering look, then asked quietly, "Are you willing to do it?"

Camilla gazed back at him, wide-eyed. *Was she?* This plan would no doubt shock a conventional female like her aunt down to her toes. However, Camilla had always prided herself on not being conventional. She was independent and generally unafraid to tackle any situation. Of course, it was odd that a stranger like Mr. Sedgewick was so willing to help her out of her troubles, but just because a man went out of his way to be kind, that did not mean that she should reject his help. The worst aspect of the plan was having to be around such a rude, insufferable man as Benedict for several days. However, she was quite competent and reasonable, and she was sure that she would be able to manage both the situation and him. Fate had dropped this opportunity into her lap, and she would be foolish not to take advantage of it.

"Yes," she responded firmly. "I am willing."

Sedgewick gave her a small smile. "Then I will go talk to Benedict. In the meantime, you may use this parlor to, um, freshen up."

Camilla almost giggled at the inadequacy of his polite words to describe the daunting task that lay before her. She was caked all over with mud, and she could not imagine how she would ever get it all out of her hair and off her skin without taking a complete bath.

"I shall tell the maid to bring in a pitcher and basin. I'm sure you have a change of clothes in your post chaise." When Camilla nodded, he went on, "I'll have my man fetch your bags, then, so you will be able to get into some clean clothes."

Camilla nodded. "Thank you."

"No trouble at all." He started toward the door, then hesitated. "You might want to fortify yourself with another cup of punch, as well."

Benedict walked no farther than the bench in front of the inn and sat down on it to light a cigar. He had no doubt that Sedgewick would be following him in a moment. For all Jermyn's exquisite manners, he was like a dog with a bone when he got his mind set on something, and Benedict was sure that he was not about to give up easily on his latest idea.

He had barely gotten his cigar lit when Jermyn came out of the inn and strode over to the bench. Sedgewick stood for a moment, looking down at him. Benedict blew out a cloud of smoke, studiously ignoring the other man.

"Well?" Jermyn asked at last. "Would you like to explain why you are refusing such a golden opportunity?"

Benedict cocked his head to look at him. "Golden opportunity? For what? Making an even bigger hash of things? Wasting what precious time we have? Good Gad, Jer, I think you *have* gone mad."

"At least I'm not blind. Or is it hopeless? Have you given up?"

That remark brought Benedict surging to his feet. "No man, not even you, can accuse me of giving up."

"Oh, give over, Rawdon," his friend retorted equably. "I know better than anyone how little likely you are to give up. When everyone had given you up for lost there in the Peninsula, I was the only one who was certain that you would find your way back to your own lines—and bring back your comrades, as well, even though you had caught two balls in your leg. After all, I was the one who had had to suffer to the bloody end through every ghastly childhood escapade you dreamed up. However, I cannot understand why you are so unwilling to do this."

Benedict goggled at him. "You have come unhinged, Jer. Anyone could see that it's utterly impossible. Pretend to be engaged to that...that hoyden? It wouldn't last a day. We would be at each other's throats in a half hour. No one could believe that we are wanting to marry each other."

"Why not? She's an attractive woman...underneath that mud, I mean."

"How can you tell? Hell, it's not her attractiveness. I'll grant you that she has a *pleasant* face."

The other man groaned. "Pleasant? Didn't you see those eyes? Blue and sparkling..."

"And a passable figure."

"Now, I know you haven't changed that much. No matter what Annabeth did to you, surely you can still appreciate a damn fine figure."

"Oh, all right. Yes, she has a most delectable body." Benedict's voice roughened faintly on the words as he remembered how that body had felt as it slid through his hands, the brief moments when his fingers had brushed over her ripe breasts as they struggled. "And no doubt she has skin like an angel beneath all that mud. But that is beside the point. It is not her physical appearance that is the problem. It is her personality. We have been at each other like hammer and tongs from the instant we met.''

''You think there are not husbands and wives who are the same way? You must have lived too sheltered a life in the military.''

''Of course I've seen battling couples. But surely they were not like that when they were first betrothed.''

''Nonsense. There are some who simply love to fight. Remember Capston? He and the baroness couldn't get through the day without a disagreement, but he was mad about the woman.''

''Capston was mad, period.''

Sedgewick shrugged. ''So? These people don't know you. How are they to know that you are not mad, also? Besides, there are other reasons people marry, you know, besides compatibility. There are bloodlines, wealth, titles—''

He stopped abruptly, casting a guilty glance at Benedict. ''I'm sorry. I didn't—''

''Yes,'' Benedict retorted flatly. ''I am well aware that there are those who marry for wealth and titles. And it is precisely because of my experience, Jermyn, that I do not want to get involved in this. Do you think that I could trust my safety and the safety of all our agents to a woman?''

Sedgewick sighed. ''Not all women are like Annabeth. Not all would sell their souls or their bodies for a title.''

''Oh, Annabeth did not break our engagement simply because I had lost the title. There was also the estate.'' He smiled grimly. "And I know that not all women are like her. There are some whose price is much lower—and doubtless some who would look even higher. But I will not put my faith in a woman again, much less give my secrets and my life into her hands. Least of all a hellion like that one.''

"But there is no need to! That is the beauty of it. She need know nothing about us. Or about our little project. She needs a fiancé for her own purposes. She is too busy worrying about her problem to wonder what you are doing or why you are willing to do this for her.''

Benedict snorted. "She would not wonder why I was willing. She thinks I would do anything for money.''

"You haven't done a great deal to give the girl a good impression of you," his friend pointed out. "And that's all to our advantage. Thinking you are a scoundrel, she will not question your hiring yourself out as her fiancé. She will never dream that you are a spy in the midst of her family. You do not have to trust her. She will be as deceived as the rest of them.''

Benedict looked at his lifelong friend. Jermyn's bland good looks and impeccable manners had always hidden an active and scheming brain. It had usually been Jermyn who came up with the tricks they pulled as lads, though it had just as usually been the dark, willful Benedict who was blamed for them, while the blond, angelic Jermyn was forgiven for going along with his mischievous friend. Benedict often thought that if the war with Napoléon had not come along, giving Jermyn a chance to turn his devious, imaginative skills to the task of defeating the enemy, Sedgewick would have wound up in Newgate—and doubtless would have somehow inveigled Benedict to be there with him.

"And you see nothing wrong in deceiving an innocent young woman in this way? In planting a spy in her household and embroiling her in a vipers' nest of treachery and murder?"

Jermyn pulled back, one hand going to his chest in a dramatic fashion. "Benedict...you think that I would harm this young woman in any way? I wonder that you should even want to claim my friendship."

"There are times when I do not," Benedict retorted bluntly. "And don't put on that innocent air with me. I think that you would do anything necessary to find out what has happened to our agents and to save our 'little project' from being destroyed."

"Wouldn't you?" Jermyn raised a cool eyebrow. "My dear friend, I have worked long and hard to establish those men in France, and their services are invaluable to our government. Knowledge is priceless. It is what wins wars. Right now, we are utterly without knowledge."

During the past four years, while Benedict was with the army on the Peninsula, fighting Napoléon's armies directly, Jermyn had been in the Home Office, battling the French on a secret front. He had established a network of spies within France, calling the project Gideon and planting men, both Englishmen and French émigrés, inside the other country, whence they kept him supplied with news of the enemy. Rumors, stolen documents, the mood of the people, financial and political conditions, news of troop movements and morale, of supplies and problems—all were funneled out of France and into Jermyn's office. For the past few months, since Benedict was forced to leave the army because of the injuries he had suffered in battle, he had joined his friend in his dark, desperate conflict.

Benedict knew how invaluable their work was, and, though he chafed at being relegated to a passive, waiting role in the government offices, he had given it his usual full devotion. And, like Jermyn, he knew just how catastrophic was the danger that was now threatening the spy ring—and, by implication, England itself, for the destruction of the Gideon network in France would create a huge hole in the whole war effort. The army, the government, would once again be without the knowledge it so desperately needed. Worse, there was always the possibility that the French might be sending in spies or saboteurs of their own through the very channels that Jermyn, through the Gideon network, had created.

"You are right," Jermyn went on implacably. "I would do almost anything to keep that network of agents in France intact and unknown, to keep them from being hunted down and killed. Those are my men out there, Benedict, and it is my responsibility to keep them safe, just as it was your responsibility to bring your comrades back to safety. You didn't let your wounds stop you, and I am afraid I cannot allow the prospect of some minimal danger to one woman stop me."

He stopped and sighed. "I know that sounds callous. But what would you have us do? Lose this chance? Benedict, this is a golden opportunity. You can get inside Chevington Park. You will be accepted as an insider, one of the family. They will talk to you.''

''Yes, but it hardly seems likely that anyone in the Earl's family is connected with the smuggling.''

When Jermyn set up the spy ring, smuggling had seemed the logical way of bringing messages and people into and out of England. With trade with France barred legally, only the illegal trade in French brandy and tobacco from the United States offered an opportunity for passage in and out of France. The smugglers had been operating for centuries quite successfully, and it required only paying the smugglers to get them to bring in a few letters or human cargo, as well. Richard Winslow, one of Jermyn's friends and co-workers, had been their connection to the smugglers who operated in the area of Edgecombe. Unfortunately, to keep news of the operation from getting out of the notoriously leaky Home Office, only Winslow had known who his contact among the smugglers was.

The flaw in this scheme had become obvious a few weeks ago, however, when Winslow had died, apparently by his own hand, taking the secret of the smugglers to his grave. Both Jermyn and Benedict had been astonished that the serious, dedicated Winslow had killed himself, thereby endangering the spy ring, but they had not been suspicious until a week later, when the messenger they were awaiting from France did not arrive. They did not know whom to contact in Edgecombe, so they could only wait and worry as weeks passed without word from him.

Growing ever more suspicious, they began to look into Winslow's death again. On closer inspection, they had realized that the suicide note did not exactly match

Winslow's handwriting, though it had been a very good copy. In the face of that, certain inconsistencies about his death that they had dismissed before now loomed large, and they became convinced that Winslow had been murdered, rather than being the victim of his own melancholy.

They continued to receive no messages from France, and they became even more convinced that their messengers were being killed, as Winslow had been. There was a traitor working against the network. Their fears were further heightened by a message from a known French spy that had been intercepted on its way to France. One terse line in the message had conveyed the fact that "we have a man in place in Edgecombe, and we will pick them off one by one." It was clear that Gideon was in danger.

Unfortunately, they were still in the dark about the identity of the French agent at work in Edgecombe. The Frenchman who had sent the messages fled before he could be arrested, and his whereabouts were unknown. Moreover, they did not even know how to get to their friend among the smugglers to warn him about the danger. Only Winslow had sent the messages or directed the agents where to go. Only Winslow knew the identity of the man with whom he had dealt.

It was for this reason that they had come to Edgecombe over a week ago: to gather information about the smugglers and hopefully discover not only whom they should contact, but also what had happened to their agent and who was trying to harm Gideon. Unfortunately, in the time they had been here, they had learned almost nothing. Jermyn had tried mingling with the villagers, but none of the locals would talk to

him about the smugglers. However law-abiding the
citizens were, the smugglers were, after all, their own,
and they protected their own. Benedict, on the other
hand, had kept a low profile, wandering the heath and
shore for signs of the smugglers or their contraband,
investigating caves and trails and spending every evening for a week lying in wait for them in the likeliest-
looking places. He had discovered as little as Jermyn.

"No one in Chevington's family is likely to be one
of the smugglers, that's true," Sedgewick admitted
now. "However, you know we have discussed the
possibility that Winslow's killer was someone he was
at least acquainted with, another 'gentleman,' perhaps."

Their suspicions had been aroused by the fact that
the murder took place in Winslow's study late at night.
The doors and windows of the house had been locked,
none of them forced, and there had been no sign of a
struggle. The servants had heard nothing except the
gunshot and had admitted no one into the house that
evening. Lord Winslow, in fact, had not even been at
home until late in the evening, and no one was sure
when he had come in, as he had told the servants not
to wait up for him.

Sedgewick and Benedict surmised that the killer
must have entered the house with Winslow or been
admitted by him. It would seem likely, therefore, that
the killer was someone he knew—or at least someone
who had appeared sufficiently like a gentleman that
Winslow had had no suspicions about letting him into
his house.

"Yes, I know." Benedict sighed. They had been

over this ground many times since the man's death.
"Still—the Earl of Chevington?"

"It could be someone connected with the family, or
someone who would come into contact with them. The
social life of Edgecombe must revolve around the Earl.
Anyone with any pretensions of gentility must call on
them. Besides, if you are engaged to the Earl's granddaughter, you will have entrée to everyone, not just
the gentry and the family. The servants will talk to
you, the villagers. You're bound to be able to find out
something about the smugglers."

"You can't be sure of that." Benedict sighed.
"They are the most closemouthed group I have ever
met."

"Not once they have accepted you as one of their
own," Sedgewick pointed out. "The Earl is regarded
with love and respect by the people around here. I've
found that much out. They have a tremendous loyalty
to the Chevingtons. Why, I'd lay you odds that that
young woman in there could find out in a few well-
chosen questions what you and I have been idling here
trying to discover for over a week." At his companion's dark look, he waved a quieting hand. "No, no,
don't worry, I am not suggesting that you enlist her
help in asking the questions. I am merely saying that
if you are known to be her fiancé, they will answer
you, too—not as readily, perhaps, but far more quickly
and easily than they have answered me so far."

"That would not be difficult, since you and I have
learned virtually nothing. Otherwise I wouldn't have
been out on that damnable heath again this evening.
And I would have found them tonight, too," he burst

out irritably, ''if it hadn't been for that blasted girl! They were right there. They fired at me.''

''Trust me. Once you reflect on it calmly, you will see that running into Miss Ferrand was a godsend.''

His companion snorted derisively. ''This is absurd. This time your scheme simply will not work.''

''Why not? At the moment, *you* are the only obstacle.''

''Well, to begin with, what if one of these people recognizes me? I mean, we do move in the same circles. I might have seen them at parties. What if one of them says, 'Hallo, Rawdon,'' when my name is supposed to be Mr. Emerson, or whatever it was she made up.

''Lassiter, I believe,'' Sedgewick supplied. ''It's very unlikely. You have been out of the country for four years, and you weren't Lord Rawdon when you left, you were still plain Benedict Wincross, with another heir between you and the title. You have been back only a few months, and you know as well as I do that you never go to parties. Besides, these people have been rusticating down here for the past few months. Miss Ferrand said so. They would not have been anywhere in London to see you. And even if someone did realize who you were, you could always make up some faradiddle about a secret engagement. Secret engagements are always handy things.''

''Particularly for those who don't have to participate in them,'' Benedict said sourly. ''Since having the whole scheme blown sky-high by someone recognizing me doesn't bother you, what about the fact that we are placing our trust in this chit about whom we know nothing? There isn't a chance in hell that she won't somehow give the game away."

"She has every reason not to. She wants her family to believe that you are her fiancé as much—or more than—we do. She will do her utmost to maintain that illusion."

Benedict grimaced. "Even with the best goodwill, she can still make a mistake."

"She seems a bright enough girl. Not lacking in spunk, either. I can't picture her giving it away through fear or timidity."

"No." Even Benedict had to give a reluctant grin. "There's little likelihood of that. Still, I doubt she is accustomed to such deception."

"What?" His friend looked at him with comic dismay. "Is this Benedict Wincross speaking? The man who swore to me four years ago that all women are steeped in treachery?"

Benedict had the grace to flush. "They are taught to deceive from the cradle, and you know it. I warrant that even Bettina, the best of women, has led you a merry dance from time to time."

Sedgewick chuckled, seeming not at all disturbed by this description of his wife. "Indeed, that she has. Thing is—I rather enjoy following your sister's steps, you see."

"It is the grand scale of the deception that I doubt she could maintain. False smiles and a few sweet lies are a far cry from maintaining a fiction for days before all one's relatives. Moreover, this woman seems more—direct, shall we say?—than most."

"Perhaps. But, still, I think she is clever—and saving oneself from the tooth-and-claw of a vicious aunt is no mean motivation.''

"Perhaps she is capable of such pretense, but how the devil am I supposed to act moonstruck about a woman whose every word seems designed to raise my hackles? I have not been with that woman for two minutes running without wanting to wring her neck.''

"Just look at her as you did at Annabeth,'' Jermyn retorted unfeelingly. "For God's sake, Benedict, this playacting is vital to the existence of our network. You cannot let that whole group of men, all our efforts, be destroyed just because you don't like a woman.''

"Dammit, this isn't a mere whim of mine! This trumped-up story will not work!''

"What if it does not? We know nothing now, and our entire network is in grave danger of being destroyed. Not to mention the fact that we obviously have a very clever enemy among us who could be bringing in more enemies through the very channel we established. How will it be any worse if you are discovered to be an impostor? How much less could we know? How much more could our network be destroyed? How much more danger could our country be in?''

Benedict gazed back at him for a long moment, caught by his argument. Finally he said in a truculent voice, "I don't want to waste my time when I could be out looking for the smugglers.''

"We both know this way of looking for them will be faster and easier.'' Sedgewick paused, then raised an eyebrow. "Or is it that I'm wrong— Perhaps you are dragging your heels not because you dislike the woman...but because you like her too much? Is that why she stirs you up so much? Is that why you are so determined to avoid being around her? Because she makes you feel things you thought were long dead?''

''Don't be an idiot,'' Benedict said roughly, tossing his cigar down on the driveway and grinding it out savagely. ''Bloody hell! All right, I will do it. But, by God, Jermyn, you better be right about this. Otherwise, Gideon will be lost.''

He turned without another word and strode back into the inn.

Still feeling cheered by the warm drink within her and by Mr. Sedgewick's sympathy, Camilla turned to the almost herculean task of setting her appearance to rights. She could well imagine what both her aunts would say if they saw her looking like this.

As soon as the maid brought in a pitcher of water and a basin, as well as rags and towels, she stripped off her filthy clothes and scrubbed away at the mud with a wet rag. When she had managed to rid herself of nearly all of the dirt, she put on clean undergarments from her trunk. As she dressed, she thought about the inevitable gossiping the servants of the inn would indulge in. No doubt by tomorrow it would be all over the village that Lady Camilla had arrived here last night looking like a hoyden, covered with mud and with a strange man in tow.

It would really be better, she realized, if that loathsome Benedict person did agree to pretend to be her fiancé. At least it would explain his presence in her carriage. If she told the real story, Aunt Lydia would go into near hysterics about the danger she had been exposed to, and Aunt Beryl would find it a golden opportunity to lecture her on her foolish, heedless ways and the danger into which they could lead her. It was enough to make her hope that Mr. Sedgewick would be able to talk Benedict into it.

Of course, it would be awful having to pretend for several days that she was in love with him and wanted to marry him—indeed, it was daunting to think of even having to be in his presence that long. She was quite sure they would have difficulty not getting into a roaring argument every few minutes. Mr. Benedict was, after all, the most irritating man she had ever met.

No one would expect them to bill and coo, of course; that was not the sort of behavior encouraged by people of her station in life. Even engaged couples were usually chaperoned and stayed a chaste distance from each other. There was none of the public hand-holding or kisses such as Camilla had seen the parlor maid, Lizzie, and the butcher's son engage in. No, if there were a kiss or embrace exchanged, it was usually done in secret.

However, they would be expected to be together a lot of the time, and it would probably be thought odd if they did not take a few quiet walks alone together. She remembered the sort of warm glances that had been exchanged between her friend Henrietta and her fiancé, Malcolm. There had been something in Malcolm's eyes when he looked at his future wife that even now, when she thought about it, made a faint flush rise in Camilla's cheeks. He had not been crude, but seeing him, no one would have been mistaken as to his feelings for Henrietta. Even Camilla, the avowed opponent of marriage, had breathed a few wistful sighs over those looks.

It was that sort of signal—the whispers with heads close together, the sighs, the looks across a roomful of people—that let everyone know that a couple was in love, and an engaged couple who never indulged in such behavior would look a trifle odd.

Still, as long as the two of them maintained that they were engaged, who would have the nerve to dispute them? They might be labeled cold, and someone as suspicious as her aunt might wonder about them, but the sheer audacity of pretending to be engaged would be enough, she thought, to convince even that woman that they were telling the truth.

Sedgewick's scheme made sense...in an outlandish sort of way. Once he talked Benedict out of his stubborn refusal, surely Benedict would see the advantages of being paid money for nothing more difficult than living in a nice house and pretending not to dislike her for a few days. And surely she could endure Benedict's presence for the same length of time, knowing that it would ease her grandfather's mind...not to mention put Aunt Beryl's nose out of joint.

On that pleasurable reflection, she called in the maid, and the two of them tried to wash the mud out of her hair. It was no easy task to do in the parlor, with only a pitcher of water and a washbasin to work with. Camilla bent over the basin while the maid poured the pitcher of water carefully and slowly over her hair. It took four pitchers of water and much carrying and emptying of the basin before the water ran through it cleanly. Camilla did not even bother with trying to lather it with soap. She would take a good, soaking bath once she got home. For right now, all she needed was the semblance of cleanness. At least one could see that her hair was black now. So she wrung out her wet hair as soon as it was no longer caked with mud and knelt before the fire to brush out the tangles while the maid left the room to pour out the dirty water one last time.

She thought nothing of it a few moments later when the door opened again, for she assumed it was the maid, who had scurried in and out of the parlor several times already as she helped Camilla to clean up. However, when she heard the thud of boots upon the wooden floor, she swung around with a low cry.

It was Benedict who had entered the room, and he turned toward her now at the noise she made. For an instant they froze, staring at each other. Camilla was dressed in only her chemise and petticoats, not having wanted to get her dress wet while she washed and brushed out her hair. Her damp hair lay like a dark cloud over her shoulders and down her back, and her eyes were huge dark pools. Her skin was warmed by the golden glow of the firelight. Her breasts swelled up over the top of the chemise, and the lace-trimmed white cotton cupped the full globes. She made an entrancing picture there, curled in front of the fireplace, her ripe curves clothed in chaste white, her hair down like a child's, thick and luxuriant, inviting his touch. She seemed at once innocent and sensual, a woman to stir desire.

A blush surged up Camilla's throat into her face, and she raised her hands to her shoulders, covering her luscious breasts. "Sir!"

He stepped back, a little jerkily, as though pulling himself from a trance. "A thousand pardons, Miss Ferrand." He made an elaborate bow, then added with great irony, "How fortunate that we are engaged, else your reputation would now be in shreds."

"Then…you have agreed?"

"Yes, I have agreed to Sedgewick's scheme, God help me." He turned and strode to the door, where he looked back at her. "I am going up to Sedgewick's room. He hopes to make me look the part of a gentleman. You had better lock this door if you don't want any more unexpected guests."

As soon as he left, Camilla darted to the door and turned the heavy key, as he had suggested. She turned back to the room, pressing her hands to her flaming cheeks to cool them. She thought of the look in the man's dark eyes, the way they had run rapidly down her figure, and she shivered, once again feeling that odd quiver deep in her abdomen. For a moment she wavered, wondering if she should cry off from their agreement. There was something about this man that seemed dangerous.

But then she straightened her shoulders and marched across the room to the chair where her dress lay. She pulled it on and fastened the neat little row of buttons up the front. *She would not let this ruffian scare her away from her purpose. She would pretend she was going to marry him, and she would do such an excellent job at it that no one would suspect the truth.*

She wrapped her still-damp hair into a knot at the base of her skull and pinned it securely, then pulled on her gloves and tied a chip-straw hat on her head. It would hide her wet hair, and the cape in the post chaise would cover the wrinkles in her dress that came from being packed in a trunk. That ought to do in the

dim light of candles. As late as it was, she hoped that
Aunt Beryl would not even be up to see her enter the
house.

She went to the door of the parlor and opened it.
The public room beyond was empty now, except for
Mr. Sedgewick, who turned and smiled at her. "Ah,
splendid. Miss Ferrand." He came forward to take her
hand and raised it to her lips. "You are even lovelier
than I had realized. It would be clear to anyone but
your dragon of an aunt that if you are unmarried, it is
entirely through your own choice."

"What a pretty compliment." She gave him a little
curtsy.

"'Tis no less than the truth." His gaze moved past
her and fastened on the staircase beyond. "Here is
your fiancé. And looking more the part, I must say."

Camilla turned toward the stairs. It was all she could
do to keep her mouth from dropping open. Gone was
the rough-clothed, muddy lout of earlier in the evening, and in his place was a man who was every inch
a gentleman. He had obviously bathed and shaved. His
dark locks, still damp, had been ruthlessly combed into
order. He was clean-shaven, and his cravat was
starched and snowy-white, tied in a simple yet elegant
fall. Though his breeches and coat were plain black
and his waistcoat a conservative dark-figured one, they
were undeniably expensive and well cut, and his boots
were polished until they held a mirror gleam.

"Mr. Sedgewick," Camilla breathed. "What have
you wrought? But, surely, you cannot wish to give up
your clothes."

Sedgewick cast a look at Benedict, his eyes twinkling, and said, "Don't give it another thought, dear lady. I was happy to do so."

"I should think so," Benedict put in sourly, effectively terminating any hope that *he* might have changed with his clothing, "considering that I—"

Sedgewick cut in. "Yes, yes, I know—you earned them. So you told me earlier." He turned back toward Camilla. "Do you think he will do, Miss Ferrand?"

"Yes. Although I had not given anyone a hint that my fiancé had such a *bearish* personality."

"Ah, well, 'tis something it would be quite natural to hide."

"Let us go," Benedict growled. "The man's already taken down my portmanteau. Your portmanteau, I should say, Sedgewick." He turned toward Camilla, hand out. "The money?"

"What?"

"I believe we had an agreement?"

"Oh! Well—" She cast a helpless glance toward Mr. Sedgewick. "What should I pay him?"

"I'm not sure." He frowned at Benedict. "What do you usually get for such a thing?"

"I have never done such a thing." Benedict thought for a moment. "I'd say a hundred quid."

"A hundred pounds!" Camilla exclaimed.

"Benedict! I say!"

Benedict raised one amused eyebrow. "A man's got to live, hasn't he?"

"But that's more than a servant would make in...in years!" Camilla protested.

"Ah, but you couldn't take a servant in to meet your family, now, could you?"

"It is only a few days' work."

"It's not the time, though, is it? It's my keeping our little secret. I'll take fifty pounds, and not a penny less."

"Oh, all right. I have money in my reticule in the chaise. But I haven't that much there. The rest of my money is in my trunk...." Her voice trailed off as she thought about the fact that she would be alone in the dark night with this man. *What was to stop him from knocking her over the head and taking all her money? Certainly not her coachman, whom he had already rendered unconscious once tonight.*

Her face must have given away her thoughts, for Benedict grinned evilly. Mr. Sedgewick hastily put in, "Don't worry, he would not dare take your money and run. Remember, I will have seen the two of you drive off, and if anything should happen to you, he would be hunted down immediately."

"Of course. Thank you." Camilla smiled at Sedgewick, who smiled graciously back, then turned to give Benedict a scowl.

Sedgewick escorted them out of the inn, and the innkeeper hurried out to see her off, too. "There now, my lady, I've replaced that fool of a driver of yours, and I'm sending a boy with a lantern, too, to light the way. Don't you and your man worry a bit." He leaned forward, grinning, and whispered, "'Twill make your grandfather happy to have you marrying, my lady, and there's no doubt about it. A fine strapping gentleman, too, if I may say so. We'd been wondering a bit why he and that other one were hanging about, but now I see that he was only waiting for you to arrive."

"Thank you, Saltings." Camilla felt a twinge of guilt. She hated deceiving people, and she realized that this was only the next of many times in the chain leading from the lie she had told her grandfather.

Sedgewick handed her up into the carriage, and Benedict climbed in after her, sitting down on the seat across from her. Sedgewick closed the carriage door, and with a sharp cry from the driver and a slap of the reins, they started forward.

Camilla looked at the stranger across from her and wondered what she had gotten herself into.

4

Camilla picked up her reticule and dug into it, finding the roll of banknotes she had stuck there earlier. Carefully she counted out twenty-five one-pound notes and handed them across the carriage to Benedict.

"Why, thank 'e, my lady," he told her, again affecting a thick lower-class brogue and tugging at his forelock like a peasant.

"It is only half the money," Camilla said crisply, refusing to let him draw her into irritation. "You will get the other half when you have finished your role."

"Afraid I might run off as soon as we get there?" he asked in his normal voice, the usual sardonic smile playing about his lips. "I suppose that would be rather embarrassing."

Camilla ignored his words. "What are you?" she asked. "An actor? A sharp?"

"You surprise me. An Earl's granddaughter, so familiar with gambling cant?"

"I've heard enough of sharps and flats and the sort of gambling dens that innocents are drawn into. They use well-spoken apparent gentlemen, don't they, to lure the young men in?''

"So I have heard.''

"You are not one of them?''

He shook his head. "I thought we had established that I was a common thief.''

"I am not aware that we had established anything about you,'' she responded coldly. "The only thing that I am certain of is that I do not trust you.''

"No doubt you are a wise woman.'' Again his dark eyes glinted with amusement. "But, then, a trustworthy man would hardly suit your purpose, would he?''

Camilla looked at him, nonplussed by his words. *He was right. A scrupulously honest man would never have agreed to such a charade as this.* The fact did not reflect well on her, she realized, since she was engaged in the same deception as he—worse, really, since it was her own family that she was deceiving.

She looked away from him, doubt sweeping over her for the first time. The warmth that the rum punch had brought her had gradually melted away, and there was a small, insistent throbbing at the base of her skull that betokened the beginnings of a headache. *Had she really been inebriated, as this man had claimed earlier? Had she made a foolish, drunken decision that she would regret tomorrow morning?*

She cast a sideways glance at him, wondering what she was doing, bringing a thief right into her family's home. *Was she simply being weak, deceiving her grandfather this way? Was she doing all this merely for the sake of her pride?* Doubts assailed her.

"What?'' he asked in a smooth, oily voice. "Having second thoughts, my lady? Wondering if your course is less than honorable? Or is it doubt about letting a thief have access to the treasures of Chevington Park? Perhaps you should have thought of that earlier, before you invited the viper into your bosom, so to speak.''

"Don't be absurd," Camilla said boldly, managing to keep the tremor out of her voice. "Even you would not be so stupid as to steal something, when it would be so obvious who had done it. When I could identify you."

"As what? Mr. Lassiter, was it?"

Her eyes flew to his, startled.

"That's right," he went on. "You don't even know my name, do you?"

"But…is it not Benedict?"

"Aye…my first name."

"Your first name! But I thought Mr. Sedgewick meant your last name. What is your surname, then?"

"Why, Lassiter—what else?"

She merely looked at him, wide-eyed, momentarily bereft of words.

Suddenly, startling her even further, he reached across the carriage and grabbed her, pulling her across the carriage and into his lap. One arm went around her shoulders, the other around her waist, pinning her arms very effectively to her sides.

"What are you— Stop it! Let go of me at once!"

"You seem to have forgotten one other little thing in your rush to fool your family. A fiancé, you know, has certain expectations."

He bent, and his lips fastened on hers. They were hard, almost bruising, pressing into her soft lips with an insistent force. Camilla gasped in surprise, and he seized the opportunity to slip his tongue inside, amazing her even more. She had been kissed only once or twice, and then only by gentlemanly beaux overcome by a moment of ardor. But she had never felt anything like this. His mouth seemed to feed on hers, hungry and urgent, demanding that she give in to him.

Just as suddenly as he had begun, he stopped, raising his head and gazing down at Camilla for a long moment. His face was flushed, his chest rising and falling rapidly, and there was a glitter to his dark eyes. Camilla stared back, mesmerized, for once unable even to speak. She thought for an instant that he was about to kiss her again, but then he abruptly set her back on the seat across from him.

"Remember that," he told her darkly, "the next time you decide to pretend some man is about to become your husband."

Anger flooded Camilla, wiping away her astonishment, as well as the stab of fear she had felt a moment earlier. "How dare you!"

"I dare anything," he returned flatly. "Do you think I care that you are a supposed lady, or that your family is respected? You know nothing about me, least of all my character. You were a fool to agree to this."

"Then perhaps I should end it right now!" Camilla's cheeks flamed with color. "Why don't we stop, and you can get out and walk back to the inn?"

"Oh, no, my lady, we made a bargain, and I intend to see it through to the bitter end. Are you planning to renege on it?"

Camilla drew herself up proudly. "I never go back on my word. But don't get the idea that you can claim any fiancé's rights. I am paying you good money, and if that is not enough for you, then I suggest you leave right now. For you are not going to get anything else." Her fierce gaze would have melted iron.

Her words seemed to amuse him, more than anything else, for he only smiled faintly and murmured, "You don't scare easily, do you?"

"Is that what you were trying to do? Frighten me?" She gazed at him in perplexity. "To what purpose?"

"'Tis better not to go into a situation blind."

"So you were testing me?" Her mouth twisted with exasperation. "Well, I can promise you, Mr.... whatever your name is...that if there is a weak link in this plan, it is not I." She looked at him pointedly. He returned her gaze without expression, and after a moment, she drew herself up in her most prim, governess-like manner and said, "I believe it would be best if, instead of indulging in juvenile tests, we settled down to make certain of our story. Now, your last name is Lassiter, as you have said. I think that we could use your own name, Benedict, as your first name. That way, if I slip and say it, it won't seem odd. I have never spoken of you as anything but Mr. Lassiter in my letters home, so they don't know what your given name is."

He nodded agreement. "Tell me, where do I live? How do I spend my time?"

"You live in Bath. Your parents have a small estate in the Cotswolds. You are a gentleman of leisure, and you write."

"I what?" His expression turned pained. "I hope you don't mean poetry."

"Oh, no. You are a very scholarly gentleman. You

are interested in ancient history, particularly the Romans. You have written several articles, and are working on a book.''

''Good Gad, you mean I will be expected to converse on the subject?''

''Oh, no,'' she assured him airily. ''Grandpapa generally dislikes scholarly subjects. I just thought it sounded like an admirable thing to be interested in.''

He grimaced and went on, ''All right. Now, what else should I know about this paragon?''

''You are a most kind and well-mannered man— *there* is where you will need to work on your role. Mr. Lassiter would never dream of pummeling a coachman or wrestling a poor defenseless woman to the ground.''

''Sounds like a dull dog to me.''

''He is *not!* He is a superior gentleman.''

''Well, your description makes me wonder why any woman would want to marry him.''

''You obviously have no understanding of women.''

''So I've been told.''

''Mr. Lassiter respects women, and he believes that women are as intelligent and as capable as men.''

Benedict cast her a sardonic look. ''Doing it rather too brown, aren't you? Don't you think he is a little too perfect to be believable—intelligent, gentlemanly, a man who prefers a woman to be a bluestocking?''

''No. I wouldn't have agreed to marry him otherwise. He will be perfectly believable, as long as you act that way.''

''You may be stretching the limits of my acting ability.''

"*You* are stretching the limits of *my* patience. Now, will you kindly pay attention and do what you are supposed to?"

"I shall try my humble best," he promised sardonically. "Pray go on. Tell me about my most excellent qualities."

They spent the remaining minutes of the journey in conversation about the fictitious Mr. Lassiter, with Camilla trying to remember everything she had written her grandfather about the man.

Finally, just as they passed through the gates to Chevington Park, Benedict thought to ask, "Do I look like him?"

An odd look crossed Camilla's face. "What?"

"Do I resemble this chap physically? Surely you must have described him."

"Well…I certainly did not picture him looking like you," Camilla admitted. "He would not be so large and so…physical." Her brow wrinkled. "But I'm not sure I said anything to Grandpapa about his size. I might have said he was of average height."

She looked at him doubtfully. Benedict's six feet would hardly be called average. But at least she had not mentioned whether his shoulders were wide or whether his long legs filled out his breeches to perfection. She tried to remember exactly how she had pictured her imaginary fiancé, but she had some difficulty. She had not really thought that much about his looks, only about his characteristics, and besides, the actual man sitting in front of her kept intruding on the image she tried to conjure up in her brain. He had an irritating habit, she was finding out, of dominating whatever scene he happened to be in.

"I said his hair was brown." Camilla looked at Benedict's short, thick black locks. "That should be close enough." She paused. "However, I think I said his eyes were gray." There was no possibility that anyone could have mistaken this man's gleaming dark eyes for gray. "Well, he probably won't remember, anyway."

"Hopefully."

At that moment the carriage pulled to a halt in front of the house. Camilla pushed open the door before the lantern boy could get to it to open it, and stepped out. Benedict followed her. Camilla looked up at the venerable old house, warm affection on her face. Benedict followed her gaze. It was a graceful house, built in the shape of the letter E, and the white of its native stone gave it a warmth that was enhanced by the lights that blazed beside the massive front doors and poured out the windows.

"Oh, dear." Camilla belatedly noticed the multitude of lights. She had been hoping that her family would have given up on her and already gone to bed, so that she and Benedict would not have to face all of them now. Obviously that was not the case.

As if to emphasize that fact, the double front doors were opened wide and held by two liveried footmen, and a rotund man dressed in sober black came rushing down the wide stone steps toward them, a grin stretching across his face.

"Miss Camilla!" he cried. "It's wonderful to see you."

"Purdle!" Camilla flew forward and gave him a hug. "You shouldn't have waited up."

"As if I could go on to bed, not knowing where

you were, and leave you here to be greeted by the footmen?'' The beaming man looked affronted by the idea.

''No,'' Camilla agreed. ''I can see that you could not.'' She turned toward Benedict. ''Dear? Do come here and meet Purdle. He is the butler, and has been running all our lives for years. Purdle, this is Mr. Lassiter. He—''

''Yes, yes, I know!'' He grinned broadly at Camilla's companion. ''The Viscountess has told us all about him. Congratulations, sir. Much happiness, miss. 'Tis a wonderful thing. And, I must say, His Lordship is very happy. The news has picked him right up. He's looking forward to seeing you, too, though I'm sure that comes as no surprise to you, miss. He wanted to stay up to greet you himself when you came in, but the draft the doctor gave him put him right to sleep after supper. The doctor said it was too much excitement for him. 'Course, the Earl will be mad as hops tomorrow morning, when he wakes up and finds out he missed your arrival.''

Benedict eyed the butler in fascination as he ushered them up the steps and into the house, talking without ceasing. He had never seen a butler quite like this one, beaming and chattering like a magpie. Of course, he reminded himself, he might have known that nothing and no one connected with this girl would be normal.

''It looks as though everyone else is still up,'' Camilla said, a little questioningly, as Purdle swept them through the wide front hall.

''Oh, yes, the whole family,'' he agreed, not noticing the way Camilla's face fell. ''Well, except the young master, of course.''

"Anthony?" Camilla named her cousin, who at eighteen, was the old Earl's heir and the closest to her of anyone in her family. When her parents died, his mother, Lydia, had raised Camilla, and the two of them had grown up like brother and sister.

"Yes. He retired early this evening."

"Anthony?" Camilla repeated in disbelief. Her cousin was the liveliest of souls, always getting into some mischief or the other. He would be the last person she could imagine going to bed before everyone else, especially when she was expected tonight. "Is he sick?"

"Oh, no, miss. He's, well, he's been retiring earlier the past few months. Since, um, Mrs. Elliot came to visit."

"Ah." It was clear to her now. Anthony abhorred Aunt Beryl, perhaps even more than Camilla did. She always seized every opportunity to lecture him about his duties as the future Earl and to opine about the fact that her own husband had been the second son and therefore Anthony would inherit instead of her own sons, who were, by implication, much more worthy of the honor and position than Anthony.

"Precisely. No doubt you will see him soon enough."

"Yes. I am sure I will." She was certain that Anthony was not asleep; she would slip down the hall to his room once the others were in bed.

"Here we are." Purdle stopped before a double set of doors that stood open, leading into the blue drawing room, a large, formal room that was rarely used by her grandfather. Camilla was sure it was by Lady Elliot's command that it was being used now. Though

Lydia was higher in rank, being the dowager Viscountess and the mother of the future Earl, Camilla had no doubt that she had let Aunt Beryl take the reins of the household. Lydia was intimidated by the older woman's poisonous tongue, and, moreover, she had little liking for running things, anyway. Aunt Beryl, on the other hand, lived to command.

Purdle stepped inside the room, addressing Aunt Lydia. "My lady, Miss Camilla has arrived."

He stepped aside for them the enter. Camilla drew a deep breath and looked up into Benedict's face. He smiled down at her, transforming the harsh lines of his face into handsomeness and startling her so that for an instant she could not move. Then she realized that he was assuming a loverlike expression for their charade. She tried to adjust her face into the same sort of look as she tucked her hand into the crook of his arm.

They stepped inside the room and stopped abruptly. It seemed as if the room were filled with people, and every eye was on them. For a moment the faces were an unrecognizable blur. Everyone in the room froze where they were, staring at Camilla and Benedict.

Then the multitude of faces resolved into several distinct people. The two young women were Aunt Beryl's daughters, Amanda and Kitty. They had fair, painfully curled blond hair and vague-colored eyes that seemed about to pop out of their heads. Kitty was plump, and Amanda was as thin as a stick, but both were incessant gossips and gigglers, and Camilla was usually bored to death by their company within five minutes. Aunt Beryl, with the same pop eyes and fair hair, though starting to go gray, as her daughters, was seated in one of the wing-back chairs near the fire, a shawl thrown around her shoulders to ward off the chill to which the low neckline of her evening dress exposed her.

The other older woman—though it took a second, longer look to realize that she did not belong to the same generation as Aunt Beryl's daughters—was Aunt Lydia. Lydia was possessed of a creamy complexion upon which much care and many unguents were lavished, and her figure was as slender as if she had never borne a child. With her Titian red hair and vivid blue eyes, she was still one of the reigning beauties of London, and no one who did not know her would have guessed that she could have a son who was eighteen years old. She was staring at Camilla and Benedict as if she had never seen Camilla before.

These four women Camilla had expected to find at Chevington Park, though she had hoped that Aunt Beryl and her daughters would have gone on to bed by the time she arrived. What she had not expected to find here were the three men: her cousin Bertram, Aunt Beryl's oldest son and one of the leading dandies of London, as well as two young men whom she had never seen before in her life.

"Aunt Lydia," Camilla said, smiling and starting toward her aunt with outstretched arms.

"Dear girl," Lydia murmured, rising to her feet and reaching out to enfold her niece in a graceful hug, all the while staring at Benedict with a peculiar look on her face.

"Camilla." Aunt Beryl rose ponderously, though she did not extend her arms for a similar hug.

Camilla curtsied to her politely, exchanging greetings with her aunt and cousins. Her gaze flickered curiously toward the two strangers, but she hurried on, eager now to get her lying over with. She turned toward Benedict, holding out her hand toward him. To her relief, he started toward her with alacrity. She realized with amazement that he looked every inch the gentleman...and quite handsome, too. Amanda and Kitty were gazing at him with their mouths open.

Camilla drew breath to introduce Benedict, but before she could speak, Aunt Lydia flashed one of her sparkling smiles at Benedict and walked past Camilla, saying brightly, "No, you've no need to tell us, Camilla. We all know that this must be your *husband*."

Her aunt's words were followed by a complete silence. Camilla gaped at Lydia. Aunt Beryl's shrewd eyes flickered from Camilla's stupefied face to Benedict's.

"How do you do, Mr. Lassiter?" Lydia went on, as if she had said nothing out of the ordinary. "I am Viscountess Marbridge. Camilla's aunt."

Benedict recovered well, smiling at the Viscountess and giving her an excellent bow. "How do you do, my lady? It is a pleasure to make your acquaintance."

He turned toward Camilla, and a look of pure fury flashed from his eyes. He was certain that she had played him for a fool, had for some strange reason maneuvered him into this situation.

Lydia, too, looked at Camilla. "Oh, dear," she said, pouting prettily. "I hope I haven't completely spoiled your surprise."

"Oh. No, of course not," Camilla responded faintly.

Lydia started across the room toward them. Benedict, smiling warmly down at Camilla, curled his hand around Camilla's wrist and squeezed it in a most un-loverlike grip. Bending close to her ear, he whispered, "What the devil do you think you're doing? Whatever you hope to trap me into, I promise you, it won't work."

Camilla could not control the irritation that flashed over her features. "I have no idea what's going on," she whispered back, baring her teeth in what she hoped would pass for a smile. "I know nothing about this."

Benedict's eyes told her that he would like to pursue the point further, but by that time Aunt Lydia was upon them. She took Camilla's hands in hers, squeezing them significantly. "I know you wanted me to keep the news a secret, but I was simply so elated when I received your letter that I could not resist telling everyone the news. Please say you will forgive me."

"Yes. Certainly." Camilla had recovered her poise and her senses well enough to know that she had no choice but to play along with her aunt's outrageous statements.

"So unexpected," Aunt Beryl put in, and Camilla could feel Aunt Beryl's eyes boring into her.

She forced herself to meet her other aunt's gaze, hoping that she looked adequately calm and in control. "Yes, wasn't it?"

Lydia went on, "I am sure you must be very tired after your journey." Squinting at Camilla, she leaned closer to her and whispered, "My dear, is that *mud* on your neck?"

Camilla put a hand to her neck. "Yes, I am rather tired," she agreed, seizing on the opportunity to get out of this room and be alone with her aunt. "My— our coachman got lost."

"How dreadful. You must go up to your room and rest." Lydia took her arm, starting toward the door, but Aunt Beryl's voice stopped her.

"Now, now, Lydia," Aunt Beryl said in a jovial tone. "We won't allow you to steal Camilla away like that. Will we, girls? We are simply agog to hear all the details of the wedding. It isn't often that something so…unexpected happens. And you must meet Mr. Oglesby and Mr. Thorne."

"What? Who?" Lydia asked vaguely, then turned toward the two young men whom Camilla did not recognize. "Oh, yes, of course." She led Camilla and Benedict toward the mantel, where Cousin Bertram and the two young men stood.

Camilla followed her reluctantly. She had no desire to have to make polite chitchat with strangers. All she wanted was to get her featherbrained aunt alone and find out why she had pushed this outrageous pretense on Camilla.

But Aunt Lydia was rushing on, saying, "Camilla, Mr. Lassiter, this is Edmund Thorne, a, ah, friend of mine from London. He has been so kind as to visit us the past few weeks."

Mr. Thorne was a stocky young man with a starched cravat so high that he looked as if it might choke him at any moment. His brown hair was arranged in seemingly careless curls that Camilla suspected he had spent hours getting just so.

He bowed deeply over her hand, saying, "Fair Diana—for Aphrodite, you see, can be no other than Her Ladyship."

"I beg your pardon?"

"But no." He put out a hand dramatically, as if to stop something. His other hand went to his brow. "Ah, yes, I see it. But of course—the fair Persephone. I feel the muse upon me. Lady Marbridge is Demeter, so filled with joy at seeing her daughter again at last— though, of course, no one could believe that Her Ladyship is old enough to be your mother. More a sister."

Beside her, Benedict made an odd strangling noise, which he turned into a cough. Cousin Bertram raised his quizzing glass and studied Mr. Thorne.

"Really, Mr. Thorne," Bertram said dryly. "They would hardly be Demeter and Persephone then, would they?"

"But such a nice thought, Mr. Thorne," Lydia assured him kindly. Turning to Camilla and Benedict, she added, "Mr. Thorne is a poet, you see."

"Ah." Benedict nodded. "No doubt that explains it."

"Allow me to introduce Mr. Terence Oglesby," Cousin Bertram began, clearly dismissing the boring subject of Edmund Thorne.

Cousin Bertram was a dandy, and it showed. From the top of his hair, coiffed in a style known as Windswept, down to his tasseled boots, rumored to be polished in a special blend of champagne and bootblack, he was the very picture of the man of high fashion. While he did not indulge in the most excessive of styles, such as enormous boutonnieres in his lapel or coats so padded at the shoulders and so nipped in at the waist that his silhouette resembled that of a wasp more than a man's, it was obvious that he considered his clothes as his art. It took him almost two hours in the morning to dress, for he often used as many as ten fresh cravats before he had one arranged to his liking, and the fit of his coats was so nice that it took his valet, as well as his butler, to ease him into it. Indeed, it was said about one of his coats that his valet had to slit it partway up the back to get him out and sew him back up in it when he put it on.

His companion was dressed in similar finery. However, Terence Oglesby obviously had no need of fine accoutrements in order to be noticed. He was, quite simply, the handsomest man that Camilla had ever seen. Everything about him was golden—his skin, his hair, even the pale sherry brown of his eyes—and his broad-shouldered, slim-hipped figure required no enhancement from his clothes. He smiled now at Camilla and bowed over her hand, and Camilla had little doubt that he had entrée into many of the best houses of London.

"Have you been here long?" Camilla inquired politely.

Oglesby merely smiled and turned toward Cousin Bertram, who answered, "Oh, a few weeks now. London's gotten dreadfully boring, full of hungry mamas pushing their daughters on the Marriage Mart. So Terence and I decided to rusticate for a while."

Knowing that Bertram lived to be seen, and thrived in the social scene of London, Camilla had grave doubts about the truthfulness of his explanation. The truth more probably was that his notoriously tightfisted father had cut off his allowance after he plunged too deep at cards or got himself far in debt to the moneylenders.

Accurately reading the speculation in Camilla's

eyes, Cousin Bertram sent her a wink, as though to confirm her suspicions.

"Now, stop monopolizing your cousin, Bertie," Aunt Beryl scolded playfully, her mouth stretching in the grimace that she employed as a smile. "Come over here, Camilla. And bring Mr. Lassiter. We want to hear all the details of the wedding. Don't we, girls?"

Camilla hesitated, her heart sinking. There was a glint in her aunt's eyes that told Camilla the woman did not believe that she was married. She could understand why. She knew that she must have looked as if she had been slapped in the face when Lydia called Benedict her husband. *What* had *Lydia been thinking of?* Now Aunt Beryl was going to quiz her for all the details of a wedding that she knew nothing about, and Camilla could not imagine how she was going to invent them without tripping herself up.

Much to her surprise and relief, Benedict reached out an imperious hand and took her arm, stopping her. "No, my dear. I am afraid I must exercise a husband's right and not allow you to indulge in a cozy gossip with your cousins this evening. You are much too tired."

Camilla turned to him, gaping. He had spoken in the tone of one used to command, and there was on his face a haughty look that brooked no denial. He appeared for all the world as if he were the one born to generations of Earls, rather than she. He turned toward Aunt Beryl with an expression of hauteur and faint condescension that was precisely the attitude that would impress and quell her, no matter how much it might make her bristle with indignation.

"Mrs. Elliot, I look forward to talking with you

tomorrow. But right now I must insist that we retire. Poor Camilla has had a very tiring day, I'm afraid— the exigencies of traveling, you know—and I fear that her constitution is far more delicate than she would like us to believe. No doubt she would, if left to her own devices, weary herself in satisfying your curiosity. Fortunately, she now has a husband to take care of her. And I must insist that she retire for the night.''

He smiled benignly at Camilla, and she shot him back a look that should have wounded. Instead, it only made a small light of suppressed amusement flicker in his dark eyes. She would have liked to tell him what he could do with his ''husbandly rights'' and his talk of her ''delicate constitution,'' but right now it suited her own wishes too well to be taken away from Aunt Beryl.

So she smiled up at him with sickening sweetness and batted her eyes, cooing, ''Whatever you say, dearest.''

She found her reward in the flummoxed expression that stamped her aunt's face—as well as in the involuntary twitch of Benedict's lips that told her he wanted to laugh at her antics. He had such nice lips, too, she thought, firm and well cut, with just a hint of sensual fullness in his lower lip. She found herself looking at him for a moment longer than was necessary, and only the quizzical look in his eyes brought her back to her senses and made her turn away.

''Of course,'' Aunt Beryl countered. ''That is most understandable. I have put you and your husband in your old room, Camilla dear. I am sure you know the way.''

Camilla stiffened. ''The same room?''

She stopped as she realized how idiotic her words sounded. Of course a husband and wife would have the same room. She looked at Lydia, hoping for a way out, but her aunt was mute, her eyes wide with horror.

"Uh, that is…I—I assumed that we would have two rooms. Connecting rooms." A flush rose up her face.

"Newlyweds?" Aunt Beryl said, and tittered, raising a hand to her mouth. "But, my dear, how odd." Her eyes were avid with curiosity.

Camilla's blush deepened. "Um, well, yes. I mean, 'tis not uncommon. There are…well…" She stumbled to a halt, casting a desperate look at Benedict.

Benedict took over smoothly. "What my wife is trying to say, is that there are special circumstances. Unusual ones, which make it far better if we have separate rooms." There was a long pause, and then he went on, "In short, I am afraid that Camilla snores. It makes it very difficult for me to sleep."

Camilla let out a strangled noise, and Benedict turned toward her blandly. "Yes, my dear?"

There was a muffled laugh from the direction of Kitty and Amanda, and Cousin Bertram seemed to have suddenly acquired a cough. Camilla thought with great delight of boxing Benedict's ears. There was nothing she could do or say. She had wanted him to say something to get her out of the dreadful situation; she could hardly deny his words now.

"Oh, my." Aunt Beryl looked from Benedict to Camilla, and Camilla could see a flash of triumph in her face as she went on, "But, dear girl, separate rooms are rather difficult right now. What with all the guests we have, there is so little space available. Why, to give you two connecting, or even adjoining, rooms, we would have to open up the west wing, and you know how your grandfather detests that. And it could not possibly be done tonight. The servants are all in bed.''

Camilla gritted her teeth. She could hardly insist, in the face of what Aunt Beryl had said. It was obvious that the woman did not believe this story of a marriage—and that was no wonder. It was all one lie built upon another, and each one more outrageous than the last. She thought about giving up and telling the truth, admitting to her aunt that it had all been a lie. It would be easier than trying to maintain this charade. But then she thought of her grandfather's happiness when she had told him that she was engaged, and how he would react when he found out it had all been a tissue of lies. His disappointment in her would be hard enough to bear, but worse than that, his anger and distress might well be enough to call on one of his attacks.

So she clamped back the words that wanted to rise from her throat. Pulling her lips back into a smile, she said, ''Of course. It isn't that important. Benedict exaggerates sometimes, don't you, darling?''

Bidding the others good-night, Camilla put her hand on Benedict's arm, and they left the room.

5

"What the devil is going on here?" Benedict growled at Camilla once they were safely out of earshot of the drawing room.

"I don't know," Camilla moaned. "Obviously Aunt Lydia must have told them I was *married* to Mr. Lassiter, but I cannot imagine why. What am I going to do?"

"Well, nothing at the moment, except try to act normal. Your aunt Beryl is already suspicious enough. Your carrying on about getting two rooms didn't help any."

"What did you expect me to do?" Camilla flared. "We can't sleep in the same room!"

"No? Then what can we do? Do you want to go back in now and tell Mrs. Elliot that you have made the whole thing up? That I am not your husband? That you never even had a fiancé? That you lied to your grandfather? To her? That your other aunt lied to everyone, as well? Do you want her running in to spill that load of news to your grandfather?"

"What an awful muddle I've made of everything."

"You have to make the best of it now," he told her unsympathetically. "At the moment, I think that means being my loving little wife. We shall decide how to deal with the rest of it later." He took a firm grip on her arm and propelled her across the hall, toward the stairs. "Where is your bedroom? Up here?"

Camilla nodded, irritation at his high-handed attitude rising in her. "Just a minute. What do you think you're doing? You are not in charge here."

"Obviously, neither are you," he retorted, inexorably leading her up the stairs. "As for what I am doing, I am getting us up to a room where we can close the door and hash this out without worrying about servants or relatives hearing us."

Camilla grimaced. She could hardly argue with his reasoning, but the way he was assuming command rankled.

"Camilla! Psst!"

Both of them turned to see Lydia at the bottom of the stairs, following them. She waved to Camilla to stop and hurried up after them. "Oh, my dear," she cried softly as she neared Camilla, holding out her hands toward her. "My little love, can you ever forgive me? I am so, so sorry."

Her big blue eyes sparkled with tears, and her flushed face bespoke her agitation. Camilla took her hands and squeezed them.

"Of course I can forgive you. Anything. You know that."

Others, such as Aunt Beryl, called Lydia a "fribble," and Camilla had often enough bemoaned her aunt's vague, haphazard ways, but there was no one with a warmer heart, and Camilla loved her dearly.

"Thank you. You don't know how that relieves me. I was worried that you would hate me."

"I could never hate you." Camilla took her arm and led her down the hall to her bedroom, Benedict following behind them. "But I don't understand what is going on. Why did you say he was my husband?"

They reached the door of Camilla's bedroom and walked inside. A small fire burned in the fireplace, and an oil lamp was lit, giving the room a soft golden glow.

"It was terribly bad of me." Lydia caught her lower lip between her teeth, looking chagrined and absurdly youthful. She was only thirty-seven, and over the years had retained her good looks. "If I had only thought about it, I would have realized that it might cause trouble. But I simply could not stand it anymore. You know how Beryl is."

"Well, I don't," Benedict put in bluntly. "My good woman, what are you talking about?"

"Why, the reason I said you were Camilla's husband. It was because of Beryl. She was driving me quite mad—all those sly digs and innuendos. She was convinced from the first that it was all folderol, though how she could tell, I'm sure I don't know. Your letters sounded so convincing that sometimes even *I* thought that you really had gotten engaged. But she would make remarks in that *insinuating* voice of hers— You know what I mean. So vastly irritating. Your Uncle Varian always used to say he wanted to pinch her lips shut whenever she began to talk that way."

"Yes, Aunt," Camilla said, trying to bring her back on track. "But what happened *this* time?"

"She kept asking why you were so vague about

your wedding plans. She said it didn't sound natural, a bride-to-be not bubbling over with news of her trousseau and her dress. Well, that is true, but I can quite understand why you wouldn't think of putting things like that in your letters, my love, since you have no interest in marrying. I should have thought of it, for that is exactly how I was when Varian and I were engaged, always talking about my dress and flowers and—''

"Mrs. Elliot..." Benedict reminded her flatly.

"Oh. Well, one day she said, in that silly jesting way of hers that isn't joking at all—you know what I mean. Anyway, she said, right there in front of the Earl—I am positive she meant to do it that way—that she thought you didn't mean to marry at all, because you hadn't set a date. She didn't go so far as to say that you had made the whole thing up, although I'm certain that's what she wished to say, for she knows that the Earl won't listen to her speak an ill word about you. That is why she always couches her statements in that pseudolaughing way. But she said, with a false little titter, that she thought you must be getting cold feet, and she reminded him how you had always been so set against marriage. 'So unnatural in a gel that age.'" Lydia imitated her in-law's drawn-out vowels and nasal tone to perfection, even adding the way Aunt Beryl had of lifting her chin and stroking down her throat.

Camilla had to chuckle. "So you, of course, decided to tell her that I had already married."

"I didn't mean to. But she was looking at me in that way, you know, and I opened my mouth and somehow it just came out. I told her I had gotten a letter from you, and that you and your Mr. Lassiter had gotten married two weeks ago.''

Camilla let out a low groan.

''I'm sorry, Camilla, but once I'd done it, what could I do? I didn't think it would do any harm. It seemed no worse for you to pretend to be married than to pretend to be engaged. And it was so pleasant to see Beryl sitting there with her mouth opening and closing.'' She paused, then added, a trifle resentfully, ''I never dreamed you would actually bring a man with you. I thought you would arrive by yourself, with some excuse why Mr. Lassiter could not come. And since we would only be talking about him, what difference would it make whether he was your fiancé or your husband?''

''Of course,'' Benedict agreed. ''A mere trifle.''

Lydia smiled at him, pleased by his understanding, and said, ''Exactly. I am so glad to hear you say so.'' She turned to Camilla. ''Where did you find him? I don't understand how you managed to come up with him.''

''I paid him,'' Camilla told her bluntly.

Lydia's eyes widened. ''You mean you can buy a husband?''

''Actually, she only bought a fiancé,'' Benedict stuck in. ''Now that I am a husband, perhaps I should charge more. What do you think, Camilla?''

''I think this is scarcely the time for humor.'' She turned back to her aunt. ''I didn't mean that I purchased a husband, Aunt Lydia. I meant that I am paying him to pretend to be my fiancé.''

''How odd,'' Lydia said thoughtfully.

''But that doesn't matter now. What is important is

the fact that Aunt Beryl thinks we are married—and she put us in the same bedroom!''

Lydia moaned. "This is terrible. Your reputation will be ruined! Whatever are we to do? Oh, drat my wretched tongue!''

"It's all right, Lydia. Don't worry about it. We will manage to scrape by.''

Lydia continued to look distressed. "But, Camilla, that just won't do. You can't— I mean— If anyone found out—''

"No, please, my lady," Benedict said suddenly, coming forward and taking Lydia's hand. "Don't upset yourself. Camilla, you are taking this jest too far.'' He smiled down into Lydia's eyes, exerting a charm that Camilla had heretofore not witnessed. "Lady Marbridge, you must forgive Camilla. She is teasing you because she is a trifle peeved at your stealing her thunder.''

Lydia wrinkled her brow, looking confused.

"What are you talking about?" Camilla snapped. "Stealing my thunder?''

"Yes, dear. You see, my lady, Camilla was wanting to surprise you. She thought it would be such a good joke, after all this pretense about a fiancé, when she arrived here already married. All I can think is that you must have a sixth sense, my lady, to have thought of it. The fact is, Camilla and I really *are* married.''

Camilla gaped at him, momentarily bereft of speech. Lydia's face, on the other hand, after an instant of confusion, lit up. "But how wonderful!''

She swung toward Camilla. "My dear, this is perfect! Everything is all right. I shan't have to worry anymore. What a relief! And your reputation is safe now. This is the best news I could have had."

In the face of Lydia's delight, Camilla found that she could do nothing except give her a sickly smile. "Yes, isn't it?"

"Do you think I really did sense it? I can't remember that ever happening before—although, now that I think of it, there was that one time when Anthony had caught a cold, and even though I was in London, I was quite sure that there was something wrong with him. Then the next letter from Mrs. Blakely said that he had been ill, and it was almost exactly when I had been worrying about it."

"Yes, I remember, but I don't think—"

"But how—" Lydia went on, her mind drawn back to the entertaining topic of her niece's marriage. "When—and why didn't you tell me about it?"

"Now, now, Aunt," Benedict said smoothly. "I hope I may call you that now, for I quite feel as if I know you, I have heard Camilla talk about you so often and with such warmth—but may we save the questions for tomorrow? Camilla will love to sit down with you and tell you the whole story."

"I am sure it must be dreadfully romantic," Lydia hazarded.

"Yes, indeed. It is most romantic. But Camilla is very tired right now. It was a long and wearing trip, in truth."

"Yes, of course. I won't say another word." Lydia gave her niece a roguish smile. "But I won't be able to sleep a wink for wondering, you sly thing." She hugged Camilla impulsively and planted a kiss on her cheek. "Till tomorrow, sweetheart."

"Good night, Mr.—" Lydia paused, frowning. "But surely you are not really Mr. Lassiter?"

"No. But for the moment, no doubt, it would be better to pretend it is so."

"Yes, of course." Still beaming, Lydia gave them a playful waggle of her fingers and left the room.

As soon as the door closed behind her, Camilla swung toward Benedict. "What in the world do you think you are doing? Are you mad?"

"No. In fact, I am trying to bring a little order into this mad situation. You are going to have to make up a story for your aunt. I am certain that you can think of one that is suitably romantic. And I suppose you will have to have me die now. One cannot cry off from a marriage."

"*You* think! *You* prefer! How can you presume to tell me what to do? Or to change my plans? My story? Mr.—Benedict." Using his first name did not have quite the ring of authority over him that she wanted. However, she found it almost impossible to call him by the pretend surname she had given him. "I think you are forgetting that you are my employee."

"How could I forget that?" he responded dryly. "You remind me of it constantly."

"Well, you certainly do not act as if you are aware of it. *I* am the one who will make the decisions about what we do, not you. It is, after all, my plan."

"Well, actually, it was Sedgewick's. You and I, as I remember, merely drank the punch and listened."

Camilla flushed and tried to remember how many cups of that punch she had drunk. Three? Four? To drink even one was unladylike behavior. The more she thought about it, the more she was inclined to believe that she had been under the influence of the drink when she agreed to this scheme. *No wonder they called it demon rum.*

"Yes, it was Mr. Sedgewick's scheme, of course," she said primly, "but it was *my* story to begin with, and I am the one who hired you. That means that you follow my orders, not tell me what to do."

"If you think that I am going to let a snip of a girl run my life, you are sadly mistaken," Benedict retorted, dropping his teasing manner. He took her chin between his thumb and forefinger and looked straight down into her eyes, saying in a cold voice, "You may be paying me money, and it may be your idiotic little story that we are playing out here. But I am in this thing, like it or not, and as long as I am, I plan to make sure that it goes as smoothly and cleanly as possible. You and your aunt have obviously already created a tissue of lies that everyone, including Mrs. Elliot, could see through. I am sure that the only one who is convinced of the truth of it is your poor sick grandfather, who no doubt chooses to be deluded."

Camilla drew in her breath sharply, but he put his hand over her lips.

"No. Hear me out. If you have any sense at all, which is something I rather doubt about your aunt Lydia, then you saw tonight that Mrs. Elliot did not believe your story. The girls look like ninnies, so perhaps they do. I am undecided about the dandy and the other two men—though I cannot believe that anyone could be quite as foolish as that poet fellow appears. The important thing is that your aunt does not believe you. And unless I am gravely in error, she would love nothing more than to prove to your grandfather that you are lying. So it is up to us to make sure that she does not have any opportunity to do so.''

"Of course. That is what I intend to do. It is why I hired you. But that has nothing to do with your suddenly acting as if you were in charge.''

Benedict released an exasperated sigh. "I don't intend to be part of a botched operation. If we are going to do this, then we are going to do it right.''

"Are you saying that *I* cannot do it right?'' Camilla inquired icily.

He ignored her tone, saying reasonably, "No, not that you *can't*. But up until now you *have not*. I hope that you are capable of doing so, because if you are not, we're doomed.''

Camilla was so flooded with fury that for the moment she could not speak.

Benedict went on as if nothing were wrong, "We cannot continue with you and your aunt saying the first lie that pops into your heads. We have to have a story and stick to it. That is number one.'' He held up his hand, starting to tick off the numbers.

"I agree. But that does not mean that you are the one to make up the story. And why did you tell Aunt Lydia that whopper about our being married? We don't need to fool her. She already knew the truth. It just makes one more lie we have to tell.''

"No. It means one less opportunity to get tripped up. If she knows the truth, she's likely to slip up and say something to Mrs. Elliot that will reveal that you are not married. If she thinks we really *are* married, then she cannot. It's that simple. And tell her to absolutely not make up any more lies on her own. Tell her that if she does, you will deny what she said, and she will look remarkably foolish."

"I can't say that to her! She's like a mother to me! She helped raise me after my parents died, even though she was barely more than a bride herself, with a baby son to raise."

"I am sure she is a wonderful woman," he replied disinterestedly. "She is also featherheaded."

"You don't even know her!"

"One doesn't need to know her. It's obvious. Only a nincompoop would have told Mrs. Elliot you were married, knowing that you weren't even really engaged."

"I thought it was rather clever of her to give us that hint, though, when we first came in the drawing room."

"It would have been more clever to have waylaid you before you reached the room and told you the whole of it. At least that way you wouldn't have looked like a landed trout when she called me your husband."

"You are the most insulting man I have ever met."

"No doubt. But that has nothing to do with what we're talking about."

"It certainly does. I don't want Aunt Lydia to think that I actually married someone as boorish as you."

"Tell her I have lots of money. That always makes up for a great deal of boorishness. Besides, just think how pleasant it will be when you can tell everyone that I have died."

"Perhaps we could arrange an accident tomorrow," Camilla said pointedly.

A smile flashed briefly across his face, surprising

her. "At least you have a sense of humor. That will help." He paused. "Well, are you willing to do those things? To tell Lydia to keep quiet and to not inform her about me or the charade we are playing?"

"But what will I tell her? Why wouldn't I have told her about you before? And why would I have gone through all that pretense about a fiancé if I were planning to marry you?"

"I don't know. You are the one who is so creative. Maybe it was very sudden. Or tell her you had to keep our love a secret for some reason. We thought there was no hope for us or something. Say I was betrothed to someone else."

"So I kept silent about my feelings, even with Aunt Lydia. Hmm, I suppose it might work. I could say that was why I refused to ever marry, that I wanted no one if I could not have you. But then your fiancée died, and you were free."

"What is this morbid fascination you have with killing people? Just say the poor girl realized what a boor I am."

Camilla grimaced. "I told you, I cannot have a boor for a husband. You are simply going to have to pretend to be pleasant. Anyway, I have a much better idea. I shall say that you lost your fortune, and she, the girl you were betrothed to, cast you off because you were penniless." She paused. "Why are you looking at me that way?"

"What way?" His voice was guarded.

"I don't know. You just looked...odd."

"I was stunned by your aptitude for embellishing any story with melodrama."

"Well, it makes it much more interesting. I mean,

her just deciding that you wouldn't suit is so... ordinary.''

''Ordinary is the most believable,'' he pointed out. ''Not to mention the easiest. Why don't you stick to plain lies? Tell Lydia that you and I were in love, but I was promised to another, and then this fictitious girl broke it off, and you and I were free to marry. Because of your grandfather, we decided to get married without delay, knowing how it would please him.''

''All right.'' Camilla sighed and turned away. For the first time since they had entered the room, she actually became aware of it—the soft light, the intimate setting...the large, postered bed that dominated the room. She swallowed hard. *She was going to spend the night alone in this room with a strange man. Not only that, everyone in the house, even Aunt Lydia, thought that he was her husband.*

Camilla cast a nervous glance back at Benedict.

''Don't worry,'' he said roughly, interpreting her look. ''Your reputation will not be damaged, not as long as we convince everyone that we are married. There is nothing wrong with sleeping with your husband, and once you 'do away' with me, you will just be a widow, and no one will ever know.''

''Except me. And you.''

He regarded her for a moment, then said, ''Are you suggesting that I might take advantage of the situation?''

''It had occurred to me.'' She faced him resolutely.

''Don't worry,'' he told her bluntly. ''I have never yet taken an unwilling woman, and I don't plan to start now. Least of all with you.''

Camilla drew a sharp breath at the casual insult, her

eyes flying to his face. He chuckled, his brows going up questioningly. "What? Would you rather think that I will be lusting after your lily-white body the entire time we are together here? Well, I am sorry to disillusion you, but I will not. I prefer a woman with more experience. Coy virgins are not for me."

"I see," Camilla said sharply. "Then you prefer a woman who sells herself?"

"All women sell themselves. It is just the price that varies. Personally, I prefer an honest whore to the sort of pristine miss who teases and lures a man, all the while keeping her legs locked, until he's willing to put a ring on her finger and his goods in her purse."

Camilla stared at him, amazed. "I hate to think how you acquired that view of women."

He gave a small, humorless laugh. "From experience."

Camilla turned away. She went to the window and pushed aside the drapes, gazing down into the moonwashed garden below. "How can you do this?" she asked slowly. "How can you pretend to be married, when you have such a view of women?"

He was silent for a moment, then said, "For money. Don't you remember?"

"I don't mean why did you agree. I meant, how could it be possible for you to act like a married man, feeling as you do?"

He looked into her eyes, and there was a long silence. "I can remember." His voice was hoarse, and he cleared his throat. "I can remember the fool I was before."

Something about his voice sent a sympathetic pain

through Camilla's chest. "You must have loved her very much."

"There was nothing there to love." His face and tone were as cool and hard as glass. "I think we are straying from the subject. Our problem is convincing your aunt Beryl that we are married. To do so, we must sleep together in this room. She will not believe that you would risk such scandal if you were not married to me. I give you my word that I will not seduce you or force you."

Camilla's cheeks pinkened at his blunt words. "But what will you— I mean, where will you sleep?"

He glanced around the room and pointed toward a door. "What is in there?"

"It is the dressing room." Camilla's face brightened. "Oh! It is rather large. I remember when I was sick, Nurse used to bring a cot down and sleep in there, so that she could hear me if I called."

"Is there a cot in there now?" He opened the door and stepped inside, surveying the room.

"No. She had one of the footmen bring it down. I don't know where it came from—the attic, perhaps. I could have one brought in."

"No. Too blatant. We must not give Aunt Beryl any reason to doubt the union. Perhaps, after a while, we could have a 'lovers' spat' and you could kick me out onto the cot." He came back into the room and walked over to the fainting couch that stood against the opposite wall. "But for the moment, I think this would be the best place for me to sleep."

Camilla looked at it doubtfully. "It is too short for you. You wouldn't be comfortable."

He cocked an eyebrow at her. "Perhaps *you* would

rather sleep there? No? I thought not. Just give me a
blanket and pillow, and I will be fine. Believe me, I've
slept in far worse places.''

"All right.'' Camilla started toward the bed to get
the pillow, but he caught her wrist as she turned away.

"Wait. That's not all.''

"What do you mean?''

"I mean that we haven't finished talking.''

"Why not?''

"Sleeping together in this room is not enough to
convince everyone that we are married. When you
were speaking to me just now, you didn't meet my
eyes. You did not smile. You treated me as a stranger,
not as a woman treats her husband.''

Her eyes widened. "I didn't realize....''

"I know. That is exactly what will trip you up.
Whatever you feel about me, however little you like
me or think me worthy of you, you must look at me
as you would look at a man you loved.''

"I—I am not sure how that is.'' Camilla could feel
a flush rising in her face.

He looked disbelieving. "You mean to tell me that
you have never been in love? Or at least thought yourself in love?''

"I would think, from your words earlier, you
wouldn't believe a woman capable of feeling it,'' Camilla reminded him wryly.

"I've often wondered.'' He allowed himself a small
smile. "No doubt I spoke too hastily. There are
women who love, I know.'' He thought of Bettina,
and the way she looked at Jermyn. "I have a sister,
and when her husband enters the room, her face glows
as if the sun had come back into her life.'' His voice

was low and a little wistful. "She smiles up at him with a look in her eyes as if..." He shrugged. "I'm not sure...as if they were the only two in the room. At a party, they always drift back together, as though they cannot stand to be apart."

His words stirred Camilla. She thought of loving a man like that, of feeling as if every fiber of her being were being drawn to him. "How does he look at her?"

"As if he could consume her."

"Is that how you want me to look at you?" Camilla gazed up into his face, softened a little now, and darkly handsome. She wondered how it would feel to look at him as if she loved him, to have him return the look. It made her feel strange and breathless even to contemplate it.

Benedict made no reply for a moment. Her words had sent a strange, piercing yearning through him, a coiling of desire as strong as if she had touched him. Her blue eyes were huge and dark in the dim light. He remembered the feel of her soft flesh beneath him as they had rolled in the mud this evening, the sexual intimation as he had sat up, pinning her beneath him. He thought of sleeping on the couch not ten feet from her bed.

Benedict swallowed and stepped back, saying gruffly, "Yes. As much as you are able. We are supposed to know each other intimately. It is presumed that we have deep feelings for one another. It is patently false if our eyes rarely meet or we turn away from each other."

"Yes. Of course. I understand that. I...I will endeavor to look at you—in that way...." She trailed off, embarrassed, looking everywhere but at him.

But Benedict did not notice, for he had turned away and started pacing, as if deep in thought. "We must spend a good deal of time together, also," he went on. "Newlyweds are forever in each other's company." He had not thought of this when he agreed to the masquerade. It would certainly limit his movements. But he would have to find a way around that. The most important thing was to make the marriage seem real; if everyone thought it a sham, they would be suspicious of him, and he would have difficulty learning anything.

"All right." Camilla did not like the idea of being around Benedict all the time, but she could see the logic of his words. He was right in saying that there would be no scandal in their sleeping together as long as everyone thought they were married. Therefore, it was much more imperative than before that they give no one cause to suspect that they were not married. They had to put on a good act.

"We can go walking together. You can show me the beach."

Camilla nodded. "We can go riding around the estate."

He paused, tapping his forefinger thoughtfully against his lips. "What else?" His head came up sharply. "Oh, yes. A ring."

"A ring?" Camilla drew in a breath as she realized what he was talking about, and she looked down at the blatantly bare ring finger of her left hand. "Oh, dear, I had not thought about that."

"I thought about the lack of an engagement ring, but I hoped that we could somehow scrape through. But you must have a wedding band."

"Of course." She thought for a moment. "I have rings, but Aunt Beryl has probably seen them all, and none is really suitable for a wedding ring."

Benedict sighed and reached inside his coat, fumbling with the chain of his watch. After a moment, he slid off a small ring and refastened the chain. He strode forward, holding out the ring on the palm of his hand. "Here. You had better use this."

Camilla's eyes widened. It was a beautifully engraved gold ring, centered with a bloodred ruby. She reached out and took it between her fingertips, bringing it closer to examine it. "But...it's beautiful!"

Benedict raised an eyebrow. "I hope you did not assume that I was a thief without taste."

"Oh." Camilla's delight in the ring's beauty lessened. "You stole it."

"You may tell some romantic tale about it. Say it belonged to my beloved grandmother and that is why I gave it to you for your wedding ring."

Camilla nodded, her eyes beginning to gleam as she slipped the ring on her finger. Benedict groaned. "For mercy's sake, don't make it too complicated. And," he added scowling, "whatever you do—don't you dare lose it."

"I won't. I promise." Camilla held her hand up, admiring the workmanship of the ring. *It really was beautiful. It would be quite easy to weave a romantic tale around it.* She wished she did not know that it didn't belong to him.

There was a knock upon the door, startling them both. Camilla glanced at Benedict and called to the visitor to come in. The door opened to reveal a young girl dressed in the plain gray dress and starched white apron of one of the maids.

"I'm Millie, miss, I mean, mum. I'm one of the upstairs maids."

"Yes, of course, Millie. You are one of Rose's sisters, aren't you?"

The girl flushed with pleasure at being recognized. Mrs. Elliot never knew her name, despite the fact that the woman had been here for several months. "Yes, mi—uh, mum, I am. Mrs. Blakely, she said I was to come and be your abigail."

"How kind of her," Camilla murmured, but a cold chill ran down her spine at the girl's words. Millie was here to help Camilla undress and get into her nightclothes. It was a service she was accustomed to and needed, for her bodices usually fastened with a long row of buttons down the back. Millie would not think it was odd to help Camilla undress with Camilla's husband standing there in the room. *But she could not change into her nightgown in front of a man!* She could not allow him to see her in her undergarments.

Camilla glanced over at Benedict. The amused glint in his eye told her that he was quite aware of her predicament. She knew that there would be no help coming from that quarter. No doubt he would find it quite funny to see her humiliated.

"I, uh…" Camilla glanced around her, trying to think of some excuse. She supposed she could insist on going into the dressing room to change, but it would look odd. They had just agreed to put on a convincing show of being married, and her hiding to undress would certainly damage that.

"Why don't you take down my hair first?" Camilla suggested, and walked stiffly to the vanity table. She sat down in front of the mirror, and Millie obediently came up behind her and began to unpin Camilla's hair. Camilla's mind raced, trying to think of a way out of her predicament.

Benedict lounged on the couch on which he had proposed sleeping, watching her lazily. Camilla knotted her hands together in her lap. Perhaps if she sent the maid down to the kitchen to get a cup of warm milk for her, she could talk to Benedict and convince him to leave the room while she finished undressing.

She cast a quick sideways glance at him. He was watching Millie brush out her hair now, and there was a warmth in his eyes that did strange things to Camilla's stomach. *Why was he looking at her like that? What did it mean?* His eyes made her jittery; they were no longer amused. Of course, he had said that they must look at each other differently, as if they were in love. *That must be what he was doing.* However, it made her nervous, and she wished he would stop it.

Millie finished brushing out her hair. The maid's hands went to the top button of Camilla's dress. Camilla tried to say something to stop her, but her throat was suddenly dry, and only an odd noise came out.

"My dear." Benedict rose lithely from the sofa and strolled over to the vanity table. "If you will excuse me, I believe I shall step outside for a cigar before we go to bed." He smiled on her benignly. "I know how much you hate the smell of it."

Camilla glanced at him, amazed. "Thank you."

He reached down and took her hand and raised it to his lips. The touch of his lips across her skin sent a shiver down through her. ''Anything for you, my darling. You know that.''

He walked out the door, and Camilla went limp with relief. She glanced up at the maid then, afraid that she had noticed her reaction to her supposed husband's departure. But Millie was paying not the slightest attention to her. Her hands had fallen away from Camilla's dress, and her eyes were fixed dreamily on the door through which Benedict had departed. She released a long sigh.

''Oh, mum, what a handsome man he is. And so polite...''

''Yes, thank you, Millie.''

Millie returned to unbuttoning Camilla's dress, but her irrepressible tongue did not stop. ''Everyone in the servants' hall is so happy for you, Miss Camilla. They been talking of nothing else ever since Her Ladyship told Mrs. Elliot about it. And tonight—when you come in with him, well, you can imagine, they were *that* excited. Such a fine gentleman.''

Camilla squirmed a little inside with guilt. She wished everyone was not so excited about her supposed marriage. It made her feel like a wretch. For the first time, it occurred to her what outpourings of sympathy she would get when her pretend husband ''died.'' The thought made her feel even worse.

She hurried through her undressing, afraid that Benedict might walk back in, right at the worst moment, though she did take time for a quick bath to rid herself of the last vestiges of mud. When Millie seemed inclined to linger and talk, she practically shooed her out the door. Millie smiled knowingly at this behavior, and Camilla realized with a blush that Millie thought she was eager for Benedict's return.

She closed the door behind the girl and turned the oil lamp on the small bedside table down to its lowest, then hopped into the high bed. She wanted to be in bed and at least pretending to be asleep by the time Benedict returned.

As it turned out, she had quite a while to wait. She tossed and turned and squeezed her eyes shut over and over again, but sleep did not come, only boredom and a growing curiosity over where Benedict was and what he was doing. She was on the point of wondering whether he had gotten cold feet over the whole project and decided to scale the garden wall when at last she heard the scrape of a bootheel in the hall outside and the door to her room opened quietly. She closed her eyes immediately, watching through her lashes as Benedict eased into the room and shut the door softly behind him.

He glanced toward her, then crossed the room almost stealthily. It occurred to Camilla that perhaps he had intentionally waited until he thought she would be asleep before he came back to the room. She wondered if he had done it to be thoughtful or simply because he did not want to have to talk to her again. She suspected it had been for the latter reason. He carried a single candle with him, which he set down on the small table at one end of the fainting couch. He shrugged out of his jacket and folded it, carefully laying it across the back of a straight chair. Camilla's chest tightened as she realized that he was about to undress.

She closed her eyes tightly at the thought. But she

could not resist opening them a narrow slit again. It occurred to her that she was violating his privacy as he had not violated hers, but she shoved the thought aside. It was not as if he were going to take off all his clothes, she told herself. *Surely he would not lie on the couch naked.* Nor could she quite picture him undressing and pulling on a nightgown such as her grandfather wore. But if, perchance, he did, she would close her eyes.

Benedict removed his cuff links and set them aside, then rolled up his sleeves, revealing tanned, muscled arms. He sat down on the couch and began to pull off his boots—a gesture so masculine and at the same time so intimate that it stirred an odd sensation deep in her abdomen. His hands were large and long-fingered, their movements supple. Camilla remembered the strength of them around her arms, and the way they had slipped over her body as she and he had struggled in the mud, touching her in places where no man had ever touched her—and not entirely by accident, in her opinion. His muscles moved beneath the skin of his arms as he tugged off the boots.

Camilla's mouth felt dry as dust. His boots were off now, and he stripped off his stockings and wiggled his feet appreciatively, leaning back against the couch with a sigh. His fingers went to work on the intricacies of his cravat, and after a moment, he pulled off the long strip of white cloth and dropped it on the floor. His waistcoat he removed more carefully and placed with the jacket. He stood and began to unbutton his shirt.

Camilla knew that she should stop watching now, but she could not close her eyes. They were riveted to his chest as the sides of his shirt fell away, button after button, revealing a swath of flesh all the way down to his trousers. He peeled the shirt back off his shoulders and dropped it on the chair. Camilla's eyes traveled over him, from the bony outcroppings of his shoulders down the length of his chest, smoothly padded with muscle, to his narrow waist. Camilla had never seen a man's naked chest before, and she could not control her curiosity enough to look away or close her eyes. She stared at the dark circles of his flat masculine nipples and at the dark, curling hairs that grew in a vee down his chest, narrowing into a thin line as it drew near his stomach. A dark line curved around his lower rib cage on the right side; she realized that it must be a scar.

Benedict turned away and walked over to the fireplace, and Camilla studied his back. The muscles were thick along his shoulders and back, curving to the bony outline of his spine. Camilla was aware of a curious desire to touch his back, to feel the contrast of hard bone and smooth muscle beneath the skin.

He squatted beside the fire and stuck the poker into the coals, sending up a shower of sparks and making the coals burn a bright red. He was half turned from Camilla, and she could see the play of the firelight on his face and chest, lighting his skin with a golden glow. She pressed her legs together tightly, aware of an unaccustomed warmth between them.

When he had the fire adjusted to his liking, Benedict rose and turned, starting toward Camilla's bed. Camilla barely suppressed a gasp, and she squeezed her eyes shut. She lay tensely, listening to the approach of his soft footfalls. He was almost there, she could sense his presence, but she did not dare to open her eyes. He stood beside the bed for a long moment. Her heart raced. *What was he doing? What was he going to do?* He leaned forward, and it was all Camilla could do to keep from shrinking away from him.

He stretched over her. She could feel the heat of his body, sense his bulk. Her throat tightened; she could scarcely breathe.

He picked up the pillow on the other side of her and straightened up. Tucking it under one arm, he pulled a blanket from the bed, as well, and started toward his couch. Camilla's taut muscles went limp.

He turned back to look at her and, in a mocking whisper, asked, "Well, Miss Camilla? Did you see enough to satisfy you?"

He had known she was awake and watching him!

Her eyes flew open. He was standing two feet from her bed, his eyes alight with amusement, a smile curving his lips. Heat flooded her face, and she was glad for the concealing dimness of the room. In that moment, she hated him. She picked up the closest thing at hand, a pillow, and, with an unintelligible shriek, she threw it at him. He laughed, ducking and lifting an arm to deflect the soft missile. He blew out the oil lamp burning beside the bed, then turned and walked back to his couch, still chuckling to himself.

He pinched out the candle, and the room was plunged into darkness. Camilla lay in the darkness, still flooded with humiliation, and thought furious thoughts about him. It was even worse when, in a few minutes, she heard the slow, steady sound of his breathing and knew that he had fallen asleep, while she lay wide awake and thoroughly humiliated.

She tossed and turned, trying to find a comfortable spot, but it seemed hopeless. She was still awake some time later when the door to her room opened stealthily, and a man crept into the room.

6

For an instant, fear paralyzed Camilla. Then the man turned toward her bed, his candle casting light on his face, and she recognized him. She started to speak, but in the same instant Benedict came off his makeshift bed in one smooth motion, a drawn pistol in his hand.

"Stop right there," he barked.

The other man jumped, startled. "Ow! Damnation!" He let out a string of oaths. "You scared the devil out of me. Burned myself with candle wax." He peered across the room at Benedict. "Who the bloody hell are you, anyway, and what are you doing here?"

"I might ask you the same question," Benedict retorted. "Who are you, and what are you doing in my wife's bedroom?"

"Your wife!" the other man ejaculated, staring.

"Oh, hush!" Camilla said to the room in general, scrambling out of bed and running across the room to the young man. "Anthony!"

"Milla!" He grinned and opened his arms, catching her as she flung herself at him. He lifted her up and hugged her tightly.

Benedict, surveying them sourly, lowered his pistol and waited.

The young man set Camilla down with a final squeeze, saying, "Careful, you're going to light your hair on fire. Lord save us, what sort of game are you at now?"

Camilla giggled. "Shut the door and come in and I'll tell you." She turned as he went to the door to do as she said. "Oh, Benedict, do put that gun away. 'Tis not a thief, only my cousin, Anthony."

Benedict put the gun down but continued to look at Anthony with disapproval. "What's he doing creeping into your bedroom at this time of night, anyway?"

"Who *is* this man?" Anthony countered indignantly. "And what in the name of all that's holy is he doing in your bedroom, Camilla?"

"Well…" Camilla grinned, a look of mischief coming over her face. "Actually, he *is* my husband."

"What?"

Camilla laughed at his outraged expression. "I'll tell you all about it. I promise you. But first come over here and let me look at you. I swear, you've grown at least two inches since I saw you last."

She lit the oil lamp, turning it up, and pulled Anthony into the circle of its light. Its glow revealed a young, gangly man, already grown to a man's height, but with the narrow leanness of youth. His face was square-jawed and handsome, his eyes a pale blue, and his hair a fine blond cloud of curls. He would have looked angelic, had it not been for the spark of mischief that usually lay in his eyes and the burgeoning muscles of his arms and shoulders.

"I was disappointed when we got here and Purdle

said that you had retired,'' Camilla told him, smiling. "I was sure you must be sick."

Anthony groaned. "I can't stand sitting around with Aunt Beryl after dinner, making polite chitchat and listening to Kitty and Amanda murder Mozart. It's even worse now that Mama has arrived with that puppy Thorne in tow, always spouting off poetry to her eyes and such. Why, do you know, he wrote an ode to her brow the other day. *Her brow!* Now, I ask you...what can one say about a forehead? Then there's Cousin Bertram, with all his airs, and that silent chap with him. It's enough to drive a fellow straight into a megrim, I'll tell you." He looked aggrieved, thinking of the many wrongs he had to endure. "But, wait, you are not getting me off the subject that way. We were talking about *him.*" He scowled in Benedict's direction.

"She told you," Benedict said blandly. "I am her husband."

"You can't be."

"Why not?"

"She's never said a word about you."

"Why, hasn't Lady Marbridge told you that Camilla is now married?"

"But that's just some flummery of hers," Anthony protested. "It isn't *true.*"

"Stop teasing him," Camilla told Benedict, then turned to Anthony. "Of course it isn't true. Benedict is merely *pretending* to be my husband."

Anthony stared at her, thunderstruck. Benedict let out a low growl. "Camilla, I thought we agreed..."

"But that was not to tell Aunt Lydia. Anthony is different. I promise you, he can be trusted with a secret. He's kept hundreds of mine over the years. And he tells bang-up lies.''

''What a recommendation,'' Benedict said dryly.

''Well, it is. He could always tell whoppers with the straightest face.''

''Yes,'' that worthy young gentleman agreed, ''it was always *you* who got us caught.''

''That's not true!'' Camilla protested.

Anthony arched an eyebrow. ''Oh, no? What about that time we hauled the pig up the stairs to—''

''Oh!'' Camilla's eyes flashed, and she set her hands on her hips. ''You dare to throw that up to me? It was *you* who insisted on doing it, and then we couldn't get him down again!''

''How was I to know he would balk?''

Benedict interrupted them. ''Children, please... Could we get back to the subject at hand? I'd like to find out whether Mr....uh...''

''Oh. I'm sorry. Anthony, this is Mr., uh, Lassiter. Benedict, this is my cousin, the Viscount Marbridge. He is Aunt Lydia's son.''

''I see.'' Benedict executed a slight bow toward the younger man. ''Lord Marbridge. Pleased to make your acquaintance.''

Anthony bowed back, his face still stamped with suspicion. ''Yes, well, that's all well and good, except that I know your name's not Lassiter. He is the chap Camilla made up.''

''Yes, and I am he. A figment of Camilla's imagination.''

''He is pretending to be my husband,'' Camilla explained.

''And he is staying in here?'' Anthony's voice rose

in outrage. "A man who is not your husband is sleeping in your bedroom? Good God, Camilla, what do you think you are doing? Your reputation will be ruined."

"I told you," Benedict said wearily, shooting Camilla an exasperated glance. "You're going to bring us both down if you persist in telling everyone what we are really doing."

Camilla was a little surprised at her easygoing cousin's consternation. In general, Anthony was the most adventurous of young men, always off on some lark or other. "I never thought that *you*, of all people, would try to put a damper on my scheme. After all the things you have done..."

"This is different."

"Yes, it's me having an adventure instead of you." Camilla crossed her arms over her chest and lifted her chin pugnaciously.

"That's not it, and you know it!" Anthony protested. "Anyway, I certainly never brought a girl into my room."

"There is nothing wrong with it, and no one will know that he isn't my husband unless *you* blather it about."

"You know I would never rat on you." Anthony looked indignant at this slur upon his honor. "But—" He glanced over at Benedict, who was watching their exchange with interest. "Oh, dash it! Camilla, this is most peculiar, and I cannot help but think that you are getting yourself into trouble."

"I am afraid that Miss Ferrand is already *in* trouble," Benedict pointed out. "She hasn't been out of it from the moment she started concocting all these lies. Let me remind you, Lord Marbridge, the whole house knows that Camilla and I went into this bedroom as husband and wife. It is too late for her to back out of our deal now. Her reputation would be in shreds. The only way she can save it is if we convince everyone that we are married.''

''I said I wasn't going to tell, and I won't. Word of an Elliot. It's just—well, I wish you had talked with me about it first, Milla. That's all.''

''I probably would have if I had had time. But I didn't.''

''Speaking of Miss Ferrand's reputation,'' Benedict put in. ''Do you make a practice of visiting her bedroom in the middle of the night?''

Anthony goggled at him. ''You mean— You aren't suggesting that I— Good Gad, man, that means nothing. Camilla and I have known each other forever. No one would think anything wrong of it.''

''I suspect there are quite a few ruling ladies of the ton who would find long acquaintanceship no excuse for such intimacy.''

Anthony's face turned red with anger, and he took a step toward Benedict, doubling his fists. Camilla caught his arm, flashing a speaking look at Benedict. ''Really, must you be so disagreeable with everyone?''

She turned toward the door, tugging at her cousin's arm. ''Come along, Anthony. Let us visit someplace else.''

''You are going to gossip in the hall? That should be enlightening to your family.''

''No one is up this late except *us*,'' Camilla assured him. ''Anyway, we won't talk in the hall. We shall go up to the nursery. It's where we always hatched our schemes, isn't it, Anthony?''

Anthony did not reply, but he went with her without protest, though he did pause at the door to cast a threatening look back at Benedict. Unfortunately, Benedict was turned away, calmly remaking his bed on the fainting couch, and did not see it.

The nursery was on the third floor and consisted of a large room where the children had studied and played, as well as several bedrooms for them. Not as high as most of the servants' rooms on the fourth floor, it was still far away from the larger adult rooms.

Anthony had chosen to remain in his bedroom there as he grew older, rather than move down to the second floor and a room more befitting his age and station in life. It was well-known that Aunt Beryl disliked climbing stairs, and their cousins would rarely think of venturing up to the realms of childhood. Even their grandfather, before he grew ill, and Aunt Lydia had preferred to visit Anthony in their own rooms or one of the drawing rooms downstairs. His room was plain to the point of severity, but Anthony barely noticed the lack of luxury and considered it a sacrifice well worth it.

Camilla followed her cousin up the back stairs and into the large schoolroom. She glanced around with fondness as Anthony used his candle to light an oil lamp and bring the room into greater light. She had grown up in this house, and the nursery held many memories for her. There were still a trunk of toys and shelves of her and Anthony's favorite books, as well as a table of tin soldiers arrayed for battle, but Anthony used the room now for his studies, so there were also the more recent additions of an adult-size table and chairs. It was here that the cousins sat down.

"How is Grandpapa?" Camilla asked, knowing that only from Anthony would she get an entirely straight and unvarnished answer.

He shrugged. "Better, I think. He was excited all day, waiting for you to arrive."

"I am sorry I was late. My coachman lost the way. We had to go back to the inn and get a new coachman and a boy to lead the way."

"He was certain you would be bringing a husband with you. How did he know?"

Camilla shook her head. "Just hope on his part, I think. I had not written that I was bringing Benedict. Heavens, I didn't even know it until tonight. I came here prepared to confess my whole stupid lie. I didn't even know that Aunt Lydia had turned my fiancé into a husband."

Anthony grimaced at her words. "I told Mama she shouldn't have said that. But by then, of course, it was too late." He frowned. "I never liked anything about the idea from the beginning. I mean, it's too difficult a thing to pull off. I figured you were bound to run aground with it."

Camilla made a show of crossing her fingers. "So far I have not."

Anthony scowled even more darkly. "You're deeper in a quagmire than ever. How did that fellow in your room come into this? Who is he—and don't tell me Mr. Lassiter, for I know that's a bouncer."

"No. Of course he's not Mr. Lassiter. His name is Benedict." She could not bring herself to admit that she did not know the man's last name. "I met him tonight."

"Tonight!"

She nodded. "When I got lost."

Anthony groaned. "Camilla! And you talk about me being impulsive! Whatever possessed you to pretend he was your husband?"

"I only hired him to be my fiancé. It wasn't until I got here that I found out Aunt Lydia had promoted him to husband. I wouldn't have done it if I'd known that. But once I came in here with him and Aunt Lydia called him my husband, what could I say? I couldn't embarrass her in front of Aunt Beryl and Cousin Bertram and everyone else by saying she was lying."

"No, of course not." Anthony understood Camilla's reasoning very well. He had dealt with his volatile, scatterbrained mother often enough. "But how did you meet him? Why did you decide to hire him to playact as your fiancé? I never heard of such a thing."

"Frankly, I didn't think of it. That was Mr. Sedgewick's idea."

"Who?"

"The other man at the inn." She began to relate the whole story of meeting Benedict and Sedgewick, beginning with their original confrontation on the foggy heath and proceeding through to their agreement in the private room of the Blue Boar. She was careful to leave out some of the details, which she knew would only inflame Anthony's budding protective instincts. Even so, her story was punctuated by his exclamations of disbelief and dismay.

When she reached the end of the tale, Anthony let out a groan and laid his head down on his arms on the table. "Camilla! How could you even consider such a thing, much less agree to it? If that isn't the most harebrained thing I ever heard of! How do you expect to carry it off?"

"We managed tonight. Tomorrow we will be better prepared. We've already discussed it, you see. We can ride around the estate. That will get us out of Aunt Beryl's clutches, as well as making it seem we want to be in each other's company. And we can work on all the details of our story. Where is your vaunted sense of adventure? We shall carry it off—if you will help."

"Of course I'll help. It's just—I don't trust that chap, Milla. You don't know a bloody—excuse me— a blessed thing about the man. Where he's from, what he does for a living. Nothing. It sounds havey-cavey to me."

"What does?"

"The whole thing. Those two men, meeting him out there in the fog, his friend being at the inn. How do you know the whole thing wasn't planned?"

"Planned! How could they possibly plan my getting lost and running into him, or my telling them about the lie I made up?"

"Well, maybe not planned," he conceded. "But why were they there, that's what I want to know. Why would a gentleman be hanging about the inn in Edgecombe, I'd like to know. What's he doing associating with this fellow? And how does it benefit this Sedgewick chap for you to pretend to be married to Benedict?"

"He did it to be kind, not for benefit."

"Yes, but one doesn't just travel the countryside looking for lost people to befriend, does one?"

"No, I suppose not."

"I mean, if I had come upon a chit with a story like yours, I might have felt sorry for her, but I wouldn't have volunteered to be her fiancé." He sighed, staring thoughtfully at the opposite wall. "I can't imagine why you agreed to it, either. You must have been bosky. They gave you that rum punch to befuddle your thinking so you would say yes."

"I was not drunk!" Camilla snapped, ignoring her own doubts upon the subject earlier. "I cannot believe that *you*, who have thrown yourself from one foolhardy thing to another your whole life, are taking me to task for doing something impulsive."

Anthony gave her an irrepressible grin. "Didn't you know? I have become quite staid—nothing but studies and books now."

Camilla's suspicions were immediately roused. "What are you into now, you wretched boy?"

He assumed a wounded air. "Nothing! How can you think I am?"

"Because I know you," Camilla retorted.

Anthony chafed under the restrictions of living at Chevington Park under the watchful eyes of his tutor and the many old family retainers. Their grandfather had not allowed him to go off to school, declaring that he would learn much better here with his tutor, but both Camilla and Anthony knew that his real reason was much simpler: He could not bring himself to let go of his grandson just yet. Because he loved his grandfather, and because the old man's health had not been good for some years, Anthony had accepted the edict with as much grace as he could. But Camilla knew how much the doting and cosseting of every member of the household wore at Anthony—and how often it led to him throwing off the traces and getting involved in some prank or adventure. It had been quite a while since she heard Aunt Lydia bemoaning Anthony's latest scrape, which Camilla suspected meant that he was due to get involved in something soon, if he had not already.

"You needn't worry about me," Anthony told her. "Anyway, you are just trying to pull me off the subject. We were discussing *your* pranks, not mine."

"I haven't pulled any pranks."

"Ha! What do you call pulling the wool over everyone's eyes about that chap down in your room? You know what I think?" He proceeded to inform her, without waiting for a reply. "I think he's a thief. He and his friend both. That's why they were so eager for him to play the part of your fiancé. He wanted to get inside Chevington Park and look at all the valuables."

"Oh, Anthony, what nonsense! If you had met Mr. Sedgewick, you would realize that. He is obviously a gentleman."

Anthony snorted. "Or at least he was able to fool you into thinking he was. You said yourself you thought Benedict was a highwayman at first. What was he doing out there if he wasn't looking for coaches to rob?"

"I don't know. But he didn't try to take anything from *me*."

"You aren't wearing any jewelry. It's obvious that you are a young girl traveling, no doubt from family member to family member, not someone who would be carrying a large amount of cash.''

Camilla lifted her chin, rather disgruntled by his description of her. "I had money in my reticule."

"He wouldn't know that from looking at you. He doesn't know you are a woman of independent thinking and her own fortune."

Anthony grinned, and Camilla rolled her eyes at his teasing. "He was watching some other people."

Anthony's grin dropped from his face, and he said cautiously, "Some other people? Who?"

"I don't know. But they fired at us. Benedict was quite angry with me because I held up a lantern. I think that is what let them know he was there. He must have been hiding there in the dark, spying on them."

Her cousin was silent for a moment, then said, "Why would he be skulking about at night like that unless he was up to no good?"

"I have no idea. I don't know what any of them were doing, although it did occur to me that either he or they might be smugglers. You know, being out late at night like that and not carrying any lights."

Anthony nodded. "You're right. But why would he be watching them? Perhaps he thought he could steal from them, but they wouldn't have money, just brandy and such." He straightened, enlightenment dawning on his face. "Unless he is from the excise office."

"What? You mean, you think he's trying to catch the smugglers in action?"

"Why not? They're always after them. Trying to plant spies, to catch them bringing in the goods."

"But if he were doing that, why would he agree to

come here and pretend to be my fiancé? It would be a waste of his time."

"Not necessarily."

"But the smugglers don't live here!"

"Of course not. But we are close to the shore. It would give him a place to stay, a reason to be here, where he could keep a better watch on things."

"I don't know. Perhaps you're right." Camilla could believe Benedict a thief far better than an excise man. Excise men were bureaucrats, men who tallied up numbers for a living, not hard-muscled sorts who could drive a carriage to a hand or knock out a brawny driver with a single blow. Nor could she see Benedict accepting authority well enough to work for the government. He obviously hadn't the slightest notion of how to take orders.

"You have to admit, it was damned peculiar the way he pulled that gun on me. I mean, there he was asleep when I came in—and it wasn't as if I was banging about, either. I was quiet. And then he was up in a flash, that gun in his hand as he rose. Those are not the actions of an ordinary man."

Camilla nodded. She, too, had been taken aback by Benedict's even owning a pistol, much less his ready response with it. "You're right. Benedict is anything but ordinary." She sighed. "But, however much you might deplore it, he is in this with me. I cannot confess to Aunt Beryl now."

"I should say not!" Anthony looked shocked. "She would run straight to the Earl, no matter how sick he is, and tell him the whole of it. *She* wouldn't care if he had another bout of apoplexy because of it. She thinks if she can make Grandpapa angry with you, he will leave money to her brood instead of to you.''

"Is that why she's so certain that I am not really engaged? I mean, married?"

"Yes. She thinks it's something you made up so that Grandpapa will leave you more money." He shook his head in disgust. "Addlepated notion. It don't make any sense. If Grandpapa thought you were married and all set in life, he'd be likely to leave you *less* money than if he thought you single and all alone in the world."

"He's leaving almost everything to you, anyway. Everyone knows that."

"And don't think Aunt Beryl doesn't do a slow burn over that. However, even she realizes that there's nothing she can do about the entail. Still, she'd love to get her hands on the money that isn't entailed."

"Yes, but I've heard him say countless times he will leave most of that with the land because you will need it to keep the estate in order."

Anthony nodded. "I'm sure he will leave all his grandchildren some amount, but the bulk of it will go with the estate. Still…there's no reasoning with Aunt Beryl when she's got the bit between her teeth. So you're right, we have to keep her from finding out the truth about your Benedict. All the same, I don't like your having to be around him. Especially in the same room." He scowled. "It's madness! What's to stop him taking advantage of you?"

"We have already discussed it. He assured me that I was not the sort of woman he was attracted to, anyway."

"What? The devil you say! The man has a lot of gall. I've a mind to give him a sound thrashing."

Looking at her cousin's slender, youthful frame, Camilla doubted that Anthony had much chance of thrashing Benedict. However, she was tactful enough not to point this out, saying only, "I don't think that would help our masquerade, Anthony. Benedict is right—if we want to convince Aunt Beryl that he and I are married, we have to stay in the same room. There is no other way. We can't raise any suspicions, and that includes you attacking Benedict or doing anything else that you would not do if he really were my husband. And it is imperative that we convince her. Otherwise, not only will Grandpapa find out, but my reputation will be in shreds."

"I know," Anthony agreed reluctantly. "But I intend to keep my eye on that chap. If he takes even one step out of line..."

"He won't."

Fortunately, Anthony had grown up accepting Camilla's authority, since she was several years older than he, and he made no further protest. Their talk turned to their grandfather and his condition and what had been happening at Chevington Park. By Anthony's account, absolutely nothing had gone on for months, and not all her questions could pry out anything other than a deadly-dull dinner party a few weeks earlier at their cousin Harold's manse. Her cousin's lack of complaints made Camilla uneasy. It was unusual for Anthony to put up with such boredom, and she was not sure whether he was not telling her the whole truth or whether he had indeed been enduring the dullness and was now reaching the point where he must break out. She had told her grandfather more than once that he was courting disaster by keeping Anthony so close to home, with only his studies to occupy him. A sedentary tutor was no fit companion for a lively eighteen-year-old boy.

Finally she gave up on worming any information out of Anthony and bade him good-night. Back in her own room, she found Benedict asleep, and this time he did not leap to his feet, gun in hand. Camilla crawled into bed, expecting another bout with insomnia, but, to her surprise, she fell deeply and almost instantly asleep.

She did not awaken until the next morning—when Benedict jumped into bed beside her.

7

His leap was a smooth dive over Camilla's sleeping form and onto the bed beside her. He barely grazed her, but the movement brought her instantly awake.

"What—" she began furiously, but Benedict wrapped his arms around her and squeezed her to his chest, cutting off her words.

"Hush!" he whispered against her ear. "The maid."

At that instant it registered on Camilla that she could hear a gentle rapping at the door, and now the door creaked as it eased open. Camilla lay still in Benedict's arms, her eyes tightly closed, as Millie tip-toed into the room and set a tray down on the small table beside the bed. Camilla tried to make her breathing slow and shallow, as if she were asleep, even though every nerve in her body was alive and tingling. She was acutely aware of Benedict's bare chest against her face, the curling hairs tickling her skin. She had never seen a man's bare chest before last night, let alone felt it pressed against her. His arms were like iron around her, holding her tightly, lest she make a movement that would give them away. His male scent filled her nostrils; his heat seeped into her body.

"Miss Camilla. Uh, Mrs. Lassiter," Millie stage-whispered. When Camilla did not respond, the maid leaned closer to the bed. "Missus, please, wake up."

Benedict opened his eyes, his arms loosening around Camilla. Camilla took this as her cue to stir and "awaken," also.

"What the devil do you want?" Benedict asked the maid gruffly.

"I'm sorry, sir." Millie looked pitifully abject. "Truly I am. It's just that the Earl is up, sir, and he's asking to see you. He's very eager to see you and Miss Camilla. I mean, the missus."

"Oh." Camilla understood now why the maid had had the audacity to awaken them. She knew her grandfather, and his orders brooked no argument. "Grandpapa ordered you to wake us up and bring us to his room."

"Yes'm." Relief flooded the girl's plain face at Camilla's ready understanding. "That's it. I brought you tea and toast."

Camilla nodded. "It's all right, Millie. We aren't angry with you."

"We aren't?" Benedict asked sourly.

Camilla wanted to shoot him a look that was just as sour, but instead, she smiled at him with great sweetness, saying, "Now, dearest, I told you how my grandfather is. Millie isn't to blame. I am sure he commanded her to awaken us."

To her surprise, Benedict smiled back at her, his dark eyes alight with affection. He leaned over and kissed her lightly on the lips. "Of course, my love.

Your smile can sweeten even my sour disposition. Forgive me.''

"Of course." She tried to act as if she were used to that loving look in his eyes, to his warm, firm lips touching hers. She drew a steadying breath.

"Shall I iron out a dress for you, ma'am?" Millie asked now, going to the dressing room. "I only hung them up last night. I haven't pressed them yet."

"Yes. Uh, the sprig muslin would be fine."

Millie bobbed a quick curtsy and disappeared into the large dressing room. She emerged a moment later with the dress in question and left the room, promising to be back "quick as a wink."

When the door closed behind her, Camilla sagged with relief. "Sweet heaven! How did you know she was about to come in?"

"I am a light sleeper. I heard her rattling about with the tray out in the hall, setting it down so she could knock on the door, and I realized what she was about. Sorry if I startled you."

He sat up, pushing aside the cover. Camilla realized that he was lying on top of her bedcovers. He had brought the blanket with him as he leaped over her onto the bed, spreading it hastily over them. She glanced at the bed beside her and saw that he had brought his pillow, too. *A very efficient man, even in an emergency.*

"Is your grandfather so fearsome, then, that everyone jumps at his command?" he asked, searching the drawers for his clothes, which the maid had unpacked the evening before. "Even waking us up and dragging us out of bed?"

"He can be something of a tartar. He's used to getting his way, you see. He assumed the Earldom when he was only twenty-two. That was nearly sixty years ago, so it is almost as if he has been in command his whole life. Besides, he comes from a more autocratic time. He's rather old-fashioned in his ways.''

''I see. Then I suppose we had best not keep the old fellow waiting, had we?''

He pulled on a clean white shirt and buttoned it up. Then he began to unbutton his breeches, and Camilla realized that he intended to strip them off and put on fresh ones right there in front of her. With a gasp, she scrambled off the bed and into the sanctuary of the dressing room. While she was there, she pulled off her nightgown and put on her chemise and the single petticoat that she could wear with the modern slim-lined skirts that were fashionable nowadays.

Millie found her in the dressing room when she returned with Camilla's dress, and if she found it odd that Camilla was whiling away her time there, she was in too much of a hurry to say anything about it.

When she emerged from the dressing room, Camilla found Benedict fully dressed, even his cravat tied to perfection. He was waiting for her, lounging on the couch on which he had passed the night, looking both bored and aristocratic. He looked so much the picture of the refined, faintly contemptuous gentleman that so many young men of fashion strove to attain that Camilla had to smother a smile.

He rose when she entered the room and swept her a bow. ''How lovely you look, my dear—as always.''

Even though she knew that the compliment was only another part of the image he was trying to create, Camilla could not restrain the flush of pleasure that rose in her. It was always nice to hear a compliment, she reasoned. *It had nothing to do with the fact that Benedict was the one who had given the compliment to her.*

She sat down in front of the vanity, and Millie quickly brushed through her hair and twisted it up into a simple Grecian knot atop her head, finger-curling a few strands of hair around Camilla's face into soft dangling curls. With that, she was ready, and they set forth down the wide hallway to the Earl's bedroom, her hand formally on Benedict's arm.

With each step, the bundle of nerves in Camilla's stomach grew larger and tighter. She hated the thought of lying to her grandfather, even if it was to make him happier. She wished that she had never blurted out the stupid fib in the first place.

They stopped in front of the door to his bedroom, and Benedict looked down at her. "Nervous?"

She nodded. To her surprise, he laid his hand over hers, where it rested in the crook of his arm. It was a comforting gesture, and the last thing she would have expected from this man.

"Don't be," he told her in a low voice. "I'll be there to help you out. And, remember, don't explain too much. Real life is full of contradictions and mistakes. Only lies are perfect and smooth."

She nodded her understanding and gave him a small smile. He rapped lightly at the door.

A moment later, the door creaked open to reveal a stooped man who looked older than time. He was bald except for a fringe of white hair that ran around his head level with his ears, and his skin was a network of lines. But his eyes were bright with intelligence, and when he saw Camilla, he broke into a wide smile.

"Miss Camilla! I should say, Mrs. Lassiter. Come in, come in," he said in a loud voice, and stepped back, holding the door open for them. "You are a sight for sore eyes. His Lordship will be so happy to see you."

"Hello, Jenkins." Camilla beamed back at the man, raising her voice, as well. "It's good to see you. You are looking quite well."

"Thank you, ma'am. It is kind of you to say so. My arthritis has been acting up a bit, but not enough to complain." He then proceeded to complain about it all the way across the floor to the large testered bed beside the window. Since his steps were slow and shuffling and the room was large, they were privileged to hear a rather lengthy description of the condition of his various joints.

An old man sat up in the huge bed, a dark green velvet cover across his lap. Despite being in bed, he was dressed in a snowy white shirt, with a starched cravat tied beneath his chin and a heavy green satin dressing gown embroidered with Chinese dragons over the shirt. His hair, unlike that of his old valet, was a thick shock of white, worn longer than was now fashionable and clubbed back into an old-style queue. He was freshly shaven, and his skin was ruddy. He had blue eyes, paler than his granddaughter's, and though they were hooded with age, their gaze was sharp. There was a distinct downward turn to one side of his mouth, and when he spoke or smiled, that side of his face did not move as much as the other, a sign, Benedict assumed, of the man's earlier apoplectic fit.

"My lord," Jenkins announced in stentorian tones, "here's Miss Camilla to see you."

"Yes, I can see that, you old fool," the Earl grumbled. "Stop shouting. *I'm* not deaf."

"Very good, my lord." The valet seemed not to mind the other man's stricture. Indeed, Benedict wondered if the old fellow had even heard it.

The Earl waved at the servant in dismissal, and Jenkins began his slow, shuffling way back to a chair in the opposite corner of the room. The Earl held out his hand toward Camilla, and she quickly went around to the side of the bed and took it, leaning forward across the mattress to kiss his cheek.

"How are you, Grandpapa? Still growling at everyone, I see."

He made a "humph" noise but held on to her hand, motioning for her to sit on the bed beside him. "Better than I can convince any of these fools of, I'll tell you that. Of course I growl at them, otherwise they'd all be convinced I have one foot in the grave."

"You? Never!"

The old man's eyes twinkled at her, and he reached up to pinch her cheek between his forefinger and thumb. "You always were a saucy one. I like that. Never could abide the fragile, meek sort. Your mother was one of those. Could hardly believe she was my daughter. Lucky thing Ferrand found her. She was so mousy I didn't think anyone would come up to scratch."

"Grandpapa! You're talking about my mother!"

He shrugged. "I know that. She was *my* daughter. Doesn't mean I can't speak the truth about her. At least she smiled. That's more than I can say for that damned Beryl. What the devil she's doing here, I don't know. I never could abide her.''

"She came because you were sick," Camilla pointed out.

"Well, there you have it—exactly why she shouldn't have come. If you don't like someone when you're well, how can you stand them when you're sick? I ask you. Seems a damnable thing to me. No doubt she reasoned that I would be too ill to kick her out." He scowled. "Or else she's trying to hurry my demise, the way she's starving me.''

"Starving you!"

He nodded. "Got Cook feeding me pap. Said I shouldn't be eating so much red meat. Got me on bread and water, practically. Told Purdle and Jenkins not to bring me any more liquor, except a little wine with dinner. Now, I ask you, what's that except trying to do me in? Damned woman.''

"I can't imagine any of the servants obeying her against *your* wishes." Camilla knew how much the housekeeper resented her aunt's interference, and she also knew how loyal all the household was to her grandfather.

"She's got them all convinced it's going to kill me if they let me eat what I want or have a glass of brandy after dinner." His face reddened with anger. "Damn doctor told them to follow her orders. I told the fellow what I thought of that. Kicked him out and told him never to come back, but he still keeps showing up here. Damn leech.''

An affectionate giggle escaped Camilla's lips. "He's the only doctor in Edgecombe. You *have* to see him.''

"So everyone keeps telling me. But it's him keeping me sick, I tell you. He won't even let me get out of my bed and go downstairs, unless the footmen carry me down there and set me in a chair. Felt like a damn fool, I'll tell you." Dismissing the subject of his doctor, the old man swiveled his head and scowled at Benedict from under his bushy white eyebrows. "Is this he?" he barked. "Come here, boy, where I can see you."

He waved toward the side of the bed where Camilla sat and where the window let in the warm glow of the morning. Benedict obediently went to stand beside the bed and executed a polite bow toward the old gentleman. It wasn't an elegant bow, such as Mr. Sedgewick or Camilla's own cousin Bertram made, but then, she knew, her grandfather would think someone who gave him such a bow was a frippery fellow, a "court card," as he would say.

"Papa, this is Benedict Lassiter. Benedict, this is my grandfather, the Earl of Chevington."

"Good morning, sir," Benedict said. "I am glad to see you in good health."

"Well, what do you have to say for yourself, young man?" the Earl demanded gruffly. "What do you mean whisking away our girl without even asking me for her hand?"

"Oh, Grandpapa..." Camilla moaned. "You know I don't believe in such antiquated customs."

Both the Earl and Benedict ignored her comment. Benedict looked the old man straight in the eye and said, "It was wrong of me, sir, and I must beg your forgiveness." He smiled, and the stern lines of his face lifted and changed. "But, you see, I could not wait, not for a woman such as Camilla. I am sure you understand that. I trusted that you would not judge me ill, despite my impatience, that you would let me prove my worthiness to you after our marriage.''

''Humph. A very pretty speech, I must say.''

Camilla, staring at Benedict in amazement, had to agree. It was straightforward, yet respectful to the Earl, and subtly suggested a strong affection for Camilla. Despite the Earl's rather slighting words, she knew that he approved of what Benedict had said, and she wondered how Benedict could have guessed that this was the tack he should take with her grandfather. *Perhaps it was because the two men were alike.*

The thought startled her, and she immediately discounted it. The old Earl was nothing like this man pretending to be her husband. Her grandfather was a man of strong principle, one who would never waver from his duty, a nobleman in the truest sense of the word. He might be autocratic and old-fashioned, but Camilla knew that there was no one she would trust more, no one she would be more likely to turn to with a problem—or, at least, that had been the case until he became ill. How could she even think of comparing him to this man who was perhaps a thief, certainly someone willing to give up his own identity in order to get a little money, and who was even now calmly lying to the Earl? *It was absurd!*

It was just something about the expressions on their faces, she thought as she looked at them. That was what had made her think that somehow they were alike. Benedict was a tall man, a commanding presence, just as her grandfather was, and he had that rather arrogant way of looking at one, as if he expected everyone to do as he said. With her grandfather, it came from years of breeding, of training, of being regarded with the awe and respect that was afforded the Earl of Chevington. She wondered how Benedict had acquired it. *Was he that good an actor?* It made her wonder if perhaps he was not from the lower classes, as she had assumed. He might be an illegitimate son, she surmised, or maybe even a man from a good family who had fallen into disgrace, or from a family that was genteel but poverty-stricken. It seemed to her that surely he must have grown up around aristocrats, to be able to imitate the look, the stance, the attitudes, so easily.

She remembered Anthony's suspicions. A penniless son of a good family might easily have become a bureaucrat such as an excise man. Or he could be in the army, she supposed. After all, it was always the army that was trying to catch the smugglers and put an end to their activities. Could Anthony be right, and there was some other, deeper motive for his willingness to pose as her husband? He would bear watching, she decided.

"Do you think that a few charming words will make me give you my blessing?" the Earl went on belligerently.

"I had not thought about it," Benedict replied. "Frankly, sir, it does not matter to me whether you give our marriage your blessing. However, for Camilla's sake, I do hope that you will do so. She will be far happier."

"Stop being such a sham, Grandpapa," Camilla interjected. "You and I both know that you are pleased

I am married. It is pointless trying to intimidate Benedict."

"Mmm." The Earl regarded him unblinkingly for a moment, then said, a little grudgingly, "I suppose I must welcome you to the family."

"Thank you, sir."

"Do you play chess?" the Earl asked hopefully.

"Oh, Grandpapa...no. You aren't going to make Benedict play chess with you, are you?"

"It would be no hardship," Benedict said quickly. "Indeed, sir, if you would like to, I would enjoy a game of chess very much."

Chevington let out a laugh of glee. "Jenkins! Get out the chess set. Mr. Lassiter, pull up a chair." He pulled himself straighter in his bed and rubbed his hands together. "Wonderful. I haven't had a game since I don't know when. None of these people will play with me. Well, except Anthony, but he's too fidgety. Drives me mad, always jumping up and pacing about while I'm trying to think. The rest of them think I'll have another fit if I play—not that any of them are any good. I'd as soon play with a child as have to play chess with Lydia. And Beryl's even worse, always prosing on about something or other."

Camilla looked from her grandfather to Benedict worriedly. "Grandpapa, are you sure you should?" She was not afraid that a game of chess would excite her grandfather so much that he would have another fit of apoplexy, but she did not like the idea of his spending that much time with Benedict. There was so much more possibility of a slipup.

"For heaven's sake, girl, don't turn into a ninny like all the others. I am not going to pop a blood vessel over a game of chess. Why don't you run on along and visit with your aunt? Lydia's been most anxious to see you.''

''Uh, well, I thought I might stay and watch.'' Camilla liked even less the idea of Benedict being trapped alone with the old man. Her grandfather was a clever man, no matter his age or his present infirmity. She had seen him trip up more than one person who thought that his wits were no longer sharp because of his condition.

''Don't fuss,'' the old man ordered peremptorily. ''We shall be fine. I promise I won't interrogate the fellow. Much.'' He winked at Benedict.

Jenkins brought the set and put it on the bed, and Benedict began to set up the pieces. Camilla lingered beside him, trying to think of a reason to stay. Benedict looked up at her and smiled.

''I will be all right, my dear. You would only be bored if you stayed. I'm sure you and the Viscountess have a good deal to talk about.''

Camilla remembered then that she had promised to tell Aunt Lydia this morning all about her supposed marriage to Benedict. She felt even less like leaving. However, with both her grandfather and Benedict practically shoving her out the door, she could hardly stay here. With a sigh, she leaned over and kissed her grandfather on the cheek, promising to come back and visit with him that afternoon.

When she had walked out of the room, Benedict turned to the Earl. ''Now, I presume, is when I should tell you about my finances and what sort of allowance I am giving Camilla.''

The Earl waved his hand, dismissing the topic. "Can you take care of her?"

"Yes."

"And will you squander her money?"

"Her money is and shall remain her own, to do with as she will," Benedict answered truthfully. "I am not even aware of how much she has."

The old man looked surprised, but only shook his head. "All these modern ideas... Well, she is a self-sufficient little thing, always has been. 'Course, old Marlin will take care of her, right and tight. He's been my agent for years, and his father before him." He paused, studying Benedict. "Do you gamble? Drink? Chase after other women?"

"No. I neither gamble nor drink to excess, and I am no libertine." Benedict tried to repress his indignation at the questions. It was, after all, the old man's right to pry into his affairs if he was married to his granddaughter.

The old man cackled. "Don't like being asked questions, do you? Well, neither would I, if I were in your shoes. But I'm not, and my only concern is my granddaughter. I won't ask you if you love her. Foolish notion. In my day, people didn't go about spouting off about *love*—leastways, not where marriage was concerned. You married for family and property, and if you were lucky, you liked your spouse well enough." He shrugged. "Well, it don't matter whether you love her now or not. If I know my girl, you will soon enough."

Benedict could think of nothing to say in response.

"Well, let's get to it," the Earl went on impatiently,

as if it were Benedict who had been delaying the game, and waved toward the board.

They began a game. Benedict found himself enjoying it more than he would have thought. The old man still had his wits about him, and he took the first match from Benedict. Benedict came back and won the second.

"We shall have to play again," the Earl said, settling back among his pillows and grinning. "You're the only person here who will give me a decent game."

Benedict bowed his head in recognition of the accolade and started to rise. Chevington waved him back down. "No. Sit. I have something else I want to say to you." He glanced around the room. "Jenkins?"

"Yes, my lord?" Benedict had forgotten about the old servant, but he came forward now to pick up the chess set.

"Take that away and go find yourself something to do," Chevington commanded.

Jenkins frowned. "But, my lord..." He glanced from the Earl to Benedict and back again. "Are you wanting to sleep? Shall I see Mr. Lassiter out?"

"No, dammit, I have no desire to sleep. That's all I ever do. And Mr. Lassiter can find his own way out, I'm sure. I want to talk to him—alone."

"Of course, my lord," Jenkins said frostily, pulling himself as straight as he could stand. He shuffled away with the chess set. Chevington watched him put the set away in its cabinet, then shuffle on to the door, turning back for a last look before he went out and closed it behind him.

The Earl let out his breath in a noisy sigh. "I'll hear

about that for a week, I'm sure. Worse than a wife.''
He shook his head. ''Ah, well, can't be helped.'' He
turned toward Benedict and studied him for a moment.
''I have to talk to you.''

''Yes, sir?'' Benedict straightened, alerted by something in the man's tone.

''First—'' the old man pointed a long, bony finger
at him and fixed his piercing gaze upon him ''—can
you keep a secret?''

''Of course.''

''Even from Camilla?''

''Why, yes, if need be.''

''Good. Then open that window.''

Benedict was glad to do so. The room was overly
warm, and he had felt stifled most of the time he was
there. He pulled the casement window back, letting in
a soft stirring of pleasant spring air. He turned back
toward the bed, but the old man gestured toward the
mahogany wardrobe standing on the other side of the
window.

''Go open the second drawer,'' Chevington instructed. ''And reach to the back, under the clothes.''

Benedict did as he directed, and his hand fell upon
a small box. He pulled it out and carried it back to the
bed. Chevington, smiling, opened it to reveal several
cigars nestled inside. The Earl released a long sigh of
pleasure and pulled out one of the cigars. He rolled it
between his fingers and ran it back and forth beneath
his nose, breathing in its scent.

''Ah...nothing like a good cigar to help a man
think...or talk, or just about anything.'' He proffered
the box to Benedict. ''Care for one?''

''Thank you.'' Benedict reached forward and took

one, while the Earl pulled out small scissors from the table beside his bed.

"So you're not going to scold me for smoking a cigar?" the Earl asked as they went through the ritual of snipping off the ends and lighting their cigars.

"No, sir. I would think it is your decision to make."

"Good for you. They yammer at me if I even mention a smoke or a glass of brandy. But I say, what good is it to keep on living if you have to live like this?"

"You have a point." Benedict thought of living his days cooped up in one room without a single vice to lighten his time. It was enough to make him shudder.

They sat together in companionable silence for a time, puffing at their cigars. After a while, Chevington said casually, "Military, aren't you?"

Benedict glanced at him, a little surprised. "Why, yes, as a matter of fact, I was. Light Horse. I served in the Peninsula until a few months ago."

The old man nodded sagely. "Thought you had the bearing. What made you leave?"

"A ball in the thigh." He did not mention the other two, more minor wounds. "Worse was the infection—couldn't get back to my lines right away. Laid me up for weeks. I cashiered out. There were...personal matters I had to see to, also."

"So is that how Camilla met you—convalescing in Bath?"

Benedict nodded. He had been speaking about his real past, but he could see that it meshed nicely with Camilla's tale. "Hard to remain unhealthy when she's about."

Chevington puffed thoughtfully on his cigar. Finally he said, "I think that you are just the man I need."

"Indeed, sir?" Benedict wondered where this could be going.

"Yes. Ordinarily, of course, I would take care of it. But they've got me so laid up here that I haven't been able to. Things are slipping from my grasp."

"Your estate, sir? I would think your heir would be the one you should talk to."

"No. Not the estate. The farm agent's a good man, and he keeps me informed. Marlin's the same. I don't worry about investments and such. And Anthony's just a pup. I can't expect him to handle it. Besides, I'm afraid he's— Well, I shall let you find out for yourself. You see, that's the problem, I don't know enough. I don't know anything."

"About what?"

"About what's going on here." He frowned in frustration. "I don't know what it is, but there's something wrong. Something damned havey-cavey. And I'm afraid of what's going to happen."

8

Benedict's pulse quickened, though he was careful not to show any excitement. "I'm not sure what you mean, sir. What makes you think something is wrong?"

"I hear things. I can't get out and around and see for myself, but I have plenty of friends here, and they visit me. And Jenkins and Purdle keep me up to date about what's happening in the Park."

"What *is* happening?"

The old man pursed his lips, struggling to put it into words. "There is a feeling around the place, an edginess. There's something different. It has to do, I think, with Nat Crowder's death."

"Nat Crowder?" Benedict asked, confused. "Who is he?"

"A local man. A steady sort, good provider. The sort of man you could deal with. He was a cabinet-maker, not superior. But he was a damned good smuggler. He died a while back, and ever since then...well, there's just been something odd." The Earl looked up at Benedict. "Maybe you don't understand about the smuggling. Outsiders often don't. They think that the men are all a band of criminals.'' He shrugged. ''Well, I suppose they are, for that matter, but they are not bad men. Not all of them. Locals look at it differently. It's something that has gone on here for years—generations, for that matter. The Crowders have been smugglers, I think, clear back to Nat's great-grandfather. But to the people around Edgecombe, it's considered an honest enough occupation. Who are they hurting, after all? If the damn taxes weren't so high, no one would have to smuggle.''

It was an old and common argument, Benedict knew. In the past, the taxes on both tea and tobacco had been so high that an ordinary man could not afford the goods unless they were smuggled. He knew that people spoke of Sam the smuggler just as they would Sam the baker or Sam the tailor. Even the rector of his church had purchased smuggled tea and thought nothing wrong of it. Why, the colonists had even revolted at being forced to pay the tea tax.

''Still, there is a difference, don't you think, when you're talking about smuggling in liquor from France when we are at war with them?'' Benedict argued. ''Then it's a betrayal of your country.'' As soon as he said the words, he felt hypocritical. After all, he and Jermyn had made use of the very same smugglers for Gideon.

The old man snorted, obviously enjoying a good argument. ''As if a man is going to give up his brandy because Boney's on a rampage. Besides, the smuggling works both ways. We're sneaking English cotton into France despite the emperor's embargo on English goods, and they can't get enough of it. There's no harm there, is there—thwarting Bonaparte and his attempt to cripple England's trade?''

Benedict smiled. "I can scarcely argue with that."

"Of course not. It all works out. Anyway, what I'm saying is that smuggling is accepted hereabouts. Nobody likes the government coming in and telling us what to do. Outsiders' interference isn't appreciated."

"But I am an outsider," Benedict pointed out. "And you are asking me to interfere, aren't you?"

Chevington shook his head. "You're not an outsider if you're a member of my family, which you are now. Especially not if I let it be known that I have approved of you, that you are acting under my aegis, so to speak."

"You are a powerful man, it seems."

He shrugged. "I am Chevington, of Chevington Park," he said simply. "The people look to us. To me."

"I'm not sure what it is you want me to do."

"Find out what's going on. Just talk to people. Talk to Purdle, ask around in the village."

Benedict nodded. "This Nat Crowder..." Benedict tried to keep his voice casual. Inside, his heart was racing. He had heard nothing about this in the village. But a dead smuggler might very well have a great deal of significance. "How did he die?"

"No one knows. He was found at the bottom of the cliffs one morning, his neck broken. He knew those cliffs like the back of his hand."

"Mm. Seems suspicious. You think someone killed him?"

The Earl shrugged. "Those cliffs are treacherous, and a fall can happen at any time. Who is to say what happened? But it makes me uneasy. It is said that Nat's death made the smugglers leaderless. Yet they continue operating. I think they have a new leader.''

"Who?''

"I don't know. I've heard no names. I have no information about him at all. I think he is feared. I also think that there are very few who know who he is.''

"Is that usually the way it is?''

"No. As I told you, it's practically a local institution. The smugglers are all from around here, and they talk. Everyone talks. Usually it's pretty much common knowledge who is involved with the smuggling, even who the leader is. As it was with Nat Crowder.''

Benedict nodded thoughtfully. "Tell me this, why do you want to know? What do you plan to do with the answers if I can find them?''

"I told you. The Chevingtons have always taken care of Edgecombe. I consider it my responsibility.''

Benedict considered the old man. He was sure that the Earl did feel a responsibility to the locals, whom he no doubt considered "his people.'' It was a feeling he himself had about the area of Lincolnshire where the Rawdon country estate lay. His uncle and grandfather had held the belief even more strongly. Still, he could not keep from thinking that there was something more behind Chevington's concern. It seemed to be a problem that worried him unduly. *What did it really matter to him if there was a power struggle among the smugglers, or even a new leader?*

However, Chevington said no more, simply looked at him. Finally Benedict nodded. "All right. I will see what I can find out for you.''

They finished their cigars, and Benedict put them

out, tossing the butts and the ashes into the bushes below. Then he replaced the cigars in their hiding place and closed the window.

"Come back," the Earl commanded, a twinkle in his eye. "We'll have another game."

"I will."

Benedict walked out into the hall and, finding only the offended Jenkins sitting there waiting, he made his way downstairs to the public rooms. He found Camilla in a sitting room that was smaller and more comfortable than the formal drawing room where they had met her family the evening before. She looked up at him and smiled, and he was struck anew, here in the daylight, by how very pretty she was. Her skin was cream and rose, dewy-fresh, and when she smiled, her face seemed to light up. His eyes fell to her breasts, emphasized by the high waist of her dress, their creamy tops hidden by the modest ruffle of lace. It was not difficult, he realized, to look as if he were a new bridegroom. The first thing he felt upon seeing her had been a swift rush of desire.

"Ah, there you are, my dear," he said, tamping down the feeling and coming across to bend over her hand. He turned to her companion. "Viscountess."

"Good morning, Mr. Lassiter," Lydia answered sweetly. "Camilla has just been telling me about your marriage. A most affecting story."

He felt sure it had been. He wondered what the story was. He cast a look toward Camilla, hoping for help, but she merely smiled. "I see," he finally replied, which, while hardly truthful, was vague enough, he hoped, to do for any contingency.

"Yes. Your poor mother, so sad."

"Yes." He sat down on the couch beside Camilla and gave her aunt a smile that he hoped was both pleasant and sad as he wondered what tragedy Camilla had seen fit to inflict on him.

"But I must say, I find you admirable to stay by her side throughout it all."

"Thank you. I could have done no less."

"Of course not." Lydia beamed on him. "I told Camilla she could have trusted me with the whole story long ago. But, then, I know how you young people are. And, of course, with your wicked uncle, I can understand how you might not trust one's relatives."

"Mm-hm," he murmured, completely at sea. He sat forward. "My lady, if you will excuse us, I had hoped that I could persuade Camilla to show me the gardens."

"Of course. They aren't in full bloom yet, but, then, I am sure you will enjoy them anyway, as long as Camilla is with you."

"Indeed."

He stood up, offering Camilla his arm, and she rose lithely to take it. There was a twinkle in her eyes that told him she was enjoying his confusion. However lovely she was, she was equally annoying, he reminded himself.

Just as they started toward the door, Camilla's dandyish cousin languidly entered the room. "Ah, my dear coz. And Mr. Lassiter," he drawled. "My goodness, everyone seems to be up before me. They say it's the country air—so refreshing. Personally, I find I rarely sleep well in the country. All that noise, you know, owls hooting, roosters crowing... There's such an inordinate number of birds around."

"I am sure it must be very trying for you, Cousin Bertram," Camilla said sympathetically. "You must tell Aunt Lydia all about it. Benedict and I are just going out for a stroll in the garden."

"Ah, yes, exercise. That's another tiresome thing about the country. People are forever tramping about, it seems. Well, I won't keep you from your bucolic amusements." He moved out of the doorway toward Lydia, then stopped, studying them, one finger up beside his mouth. "You know, Mr. Lassiter, I keep having the oddest feeling that I know you. Have we met before?"

"I doubt it," Camilla interjected hastily. "Benedict lives in Bath."

"All your life?" Bertram's expression indicated disbelief that one could actually live in Bath for that long.

"Yes," Camilla answered.

"No," Benedict replied at the same time.

Benedict put his free hand over Camilla's on his arm and squeezed it, smiling down at her. "Now, dear, I haven't *always* been in Bath. There was, ah, the family estate."

"Yes, dear," Lydia added. "He must have resided with his uncle."

"You are right. How silly of me."

"Of course," Benedict went on, "my life did not really begin until Bath, where I met you."

He heard Lydia let out a soft, fluttering sigh behind him. Cousin Bertram, on the other hand, looked faintly ill. With a polite nod to him, Benedict swept Camilla out of the room before Cousin Bertram could begin to ponder the idea that he had seen Benedict before.

"Do you know him?" Camilla whispered as she guided him through the house to the door leading into the gardens.

Benedict shook his head. "I didn't recognize him. I suppose he could have seen me before."

"Cousin Bertram acts like a fool, but he's actually quite smart. If he does know you, I am sure that he will come up with it. You never worked for him, did you?"

Benedict shook his head.

"Or stole anything from him?"

"Why do you persist in this belief that I am a thief?" Benedict asked, exasperated.

"I don't know. Perhaps it is because you stole my carriage."

"I did not steal it. I merely drove it."

"Without my permission."

He shrugged off this minor point. "I could have met him when I was younger. I don't remember him. I have been out of the country the last few years, so—"

Camilla drew in a breath, her eyes rounding. "You mean you had to leave the country?"

He frowned. "Your opinion of me is gratifying. No, I did not *have* to leave the country. I was in the army. As I told your grandfather. So whatever this 'affecting' history is that you have given me, you had better work that into it."

"Oh, dear, this is getting complicated. Well, if it comes up, I shall just tell Lydia that you joined the military after you thought I no longer loved you. Why do you look at me like that?" Camilla stepped away from him uneasily.

"Like what?"

"As if you might put your hands around my throat and squeeze."

"Don't be absurd. I just wondered what possessed you to say such a thing."

"Well, I had to come up with some explanation for why we married so quickly and why Aunt Lydia had never even heard of you."

He sighed, opening the door for her, and they stepped outside. "All right. Tell me what sort of a sorry past you have given me. I am sure I no doubt played the fool in it."

"No—although you were duped, of course."

"Of course."

"So was I." They started along the graveled path leading into the formal flower garden. "I told Aunt Lydia that we met in Bath many years ago, when I went there with the Barringtons. Those are some cousins of my father's, and Aunt Lydia never sees them, for they are dead bores. So I knew that they were perfect, for Lydia will never check out the story, and I was seventeen at the time I went there with them, which is a perfect age to fall madly, hopelessly, in love, don't you think?"

"Ideal," he replied dryly.

"I thought so. Anyway, we met there, and we fell in love. But you could not ask for my hand, you see, because you had to stay with your mother, who had consumption."

"Good Gad."

"I was too young, anyway. So we said we would wait. But in our hearts we felt as if we were engaged. Only then your uncle—"

"Ah, the wicked uncle."

"Yes. He did not want you to marry me, so he intercepted our letters and concealed them from us. We each came to believe that the other one no longer loved us, since we never got any letters, and of course I was heartbroken. I refused to marry, because no other man ever measured up."

Benedict chuckled. "How could they?"

Camilla made a face at his quip. "Only, unknown to me, you, too, did not marry, still carrying the flame of passion for me in your heart."

"I was such a nodcock that this whole time I never thought to come to London and check with you? Ask you why you stopped writing and whether you no longer loved me?"

"Of course not. You could not have, obviously, for that would have ruined my whole story."

"So I am not only lovesick, but a fool?"

"No! You were very noble. You knew that your fortune was not grand and you had no title, so you felt you were not truly worthy of me, although, of course, none of that mattered to me."

"Ah, better and better. Foolish, tied to my mother's apron strings, and now penniless and baseborn, as well."

"No, not baseborn. I never said that. Nor penniless, either. Aunt Lydia would not really approve of my marrying you if our stations were that disparate. She is romantic, but not completely impractical."

"I am relieved. Tell me, if we were at such a standstill, no longer communicating and never seeing each other, how did we ever get married?"

"Oh, that is because I moved to Bath last year. You see, when I turned twenty-four, I knew that I was quite old enough that, being unmarried, I would be considered a spinster. And, having my inheritance, I could live on my own, with a companion, of course. So I hired a companion, an in-law of my father's sister.''

''Not one of the boring Barringtons.''

''Oh, no. They, *unfortunately*, are blood relatives. Drucilla is much nicer and only related to me through my aunt's husband. We took up residence in a sweet little house in Bath.''

''This part of the tale, I assume, is true?''

''Yes.''

''I am surprised your grandfather allowed you to do such a thing.''

''He did not like it, I assure you. But I am a grown woman, and it was all perfectly respectable. And since I was living in London with Aunt Lydia at the time, he really could not stop me. He wrote me letters, of course, threatening to come up and bodily move me back here, but Aunt Lydia and I were able to soothe him enough in our letters that he did not do so. Of course, he continued to write and tell me I was a terrible influence on Anthony, who was now wanting to come up and live with me, to provide safety for me. As if it would have been respectable for my cousin and me to be living there together with no older relatives! Otherwise, I would have begged Grandpapa to let him, for he is so terribly bored here. I worry about him.''

''I worry about you. I do not think I have ever met such a female in my life.''

''Probably not,'' Camilla agreed judiciously.

''I don't think you would know the truth if you met it driving to Newcastle. You have told so many falsehoods since I've met you that I have no idea how you even keep them all straight.''

"It *is* getting difficult,'' Camilla admitted. "But you were the one who wanted me to develop another lie to tell Aunt Lydia about our marriage. I had intended to tell her the truth.''

"Then there's the way you went off and lived by yourself, as if you were a widow or something! Twenty-five is not an established spinster, my dear girl, and even if it were, you should hardly be living on your own, with only a hired companion. One would think you have no relatives, instead of quite a few loving ones.''

"But loving relatives can be the worst. They can make you feel simply smothered, you know.''

"No. I am afraid I don't. I, you see, have only the wicked uncle.''

A little gurgle of laughter escaped her lips. "Do you really have an uncle?''

"I did have. But he is dead now—and when he was alive, he was a good fellow who would never have dreamed of interfering with my love life.''

Benedict stopped, pulling Camilla to a halt with him. Putting his hands on her arms, he turned her to face him and smiled down at her as if they were having an ordinary conversation. *No, not quite that. He was looking at her as if…as if he were hungry.*

"Don't pull away,'' he told her quietly, all the while gazing at her in that odd, unnerving way. "Your aunt Beryl is in the bay window, watching us. No! Don't look. Keep looking at me.''

"Why?''

"And smile at me, as if I had told you you are beautiful."

She could not keep from softening into a smile at his words.

"Good. That's it. Now...we are going to put on a little show for your aunt."

"To convince her that we are married?"

"Quick girl. Yes. So please don't pull away or slap my face."

His face was lowering to hers. Camilla felt her breath coming faster in her throat. She knew that he was going to kiss her, yet still she asked, "Why?"

"I am going to kiss you." His lips brushed lightly over hers, soft as a hummingbird's wings. "Kiss you as if I had lain between your legs."

She gasped at his words, and then his mouth covered hers.

His lips were gentler than they had been last night in the coach, but still firm and insistent. They moved on hers, digging deeper, pressing her own lips apart. Then his tongue flicked out, teasing at her lips, and it slipped inside her mouth, moving with velvet softness around her own tongue. His arms went around her tightly, pulling her hard against his body. Camilla trembled, glad for the support, yet even more unsettled by the feel of his hard body against hers. Her fingers curled unconsciously into his jacket, clinging to him in the maelstrom of sensations that enveloped her.

Finally he raised his head and looked down at her. Camilla, aware of a deep pulsation within her abdomen, hoped that he would not release her now, or she might fall. Breathlessly she asked, "Is that enough, do you think? To convince her?"

A sensual smile curved his lips, and he answered huskily, "No, I think she should see at least one more."

He bent his head toward hers once more, and this time Camilla went up on tiptoe to meet him. He let out a low groan at this evidence of her eagerness, and his lips sank into hers hungrily. He kissed her deeply, fully, as if he would consume her, but Camilla, a little to her surprise, was not at all frightened by his hunger, only stirred in a most delightful way. Every nerve in her body was suddenly alive and sizzling, and heat blossomed low in her abdomen. She had never felt this way, never even guessed that such feelings existed. Her arms went around his neck, and she kissed him back, her tongue twining around his.

Benedict's hands moved down her back, curving over her hips and pressing her up into him. Camilla was aware of something hard against her, pushing urgently. He lifted her almost off her feet, rubbing her abdomen against him. Moisture flooded between her legs, thick and hot, and there was a deep, pulsing ache there. She realized with some amazement that what she yearned for was to feel *him* there. She was flooded with heat at the thought, embarrassed and excited all at the same time. She wondered if he knew what she was feeling, what she was thinking. It would be humiliating for him to realize that he had such power over her, and yet...there was such need pouring through him, so much so that she felt a tremor pass through his arms, that she knew she had this heady power over him, as well.

He tore his mouth away from hers and trailed hot, greedy kisses down her throat. Camilla shivered at the delightful sensation, and she lolled her head back, offering up her soft white throat to him. He made an inarticulate noise, and his hand slid up and around her body to cup her breast. A fierce white heat speared through her at the intimate touch, and she moved against him unconsciously. He mumbled something against her skin, his hot breath tickling her. Camilla let out a soft sigh, melting against him as his hand caressed her breast. His mouth moved lower, onto the quivering top of her breast. Camilla's hand slid up and into his hair. Heat enveloped her, and she found it hard to think. She felt as if she were slipping away, sliding down into a red-hot maelstrom of desire, and she had no idea where it would end.

9

"Camilla! Where are you?" A male voice came booming across the yard, plunging Camilla and Benedict back into stark reality.

Camilla gasped, stiffening. Benedict's head came up, his dark eyes glittering.

"I'll kill him." He grated out the words. "Who the devil is it?"

"Cousin Harold," Camilla said with a groan, pulling away and smoothing her dress back into place.

"Bloody hell! How many cousins do you have?"

"Too many. There is only one more of the Elliots, but he is in the army, so hopefully we shan't see him."

"With our luck, his regiment will come to town tomorrow." Benedict turned aside, combing his fingers back through his hair in an impatient gesture.

"Halloo!" came the booming voice again, and now a tall man came around the corner of the box hedge. He was dressed in severe black and wore a low-crowned hat. Around his neck was a white clerical band.

"Good God! Your cousin's a clergyman?"

Camilla nodded. "Grandpapa gave him the living at Edgecombe." She raised her hand and waved toward her cousin, forcing a smile to her face.

Benedict drew a deep breath and released it slowly, tugging on the lapels of his jacket to straighten it. He turned back to her, his face under control, and cast an assessing glance down her. He stepped forward and, with a proprietary air, retied the ribbon adorning her neckline, which had come loose during their heated embrace. His eyes for a moment glowed with their earlier heat, and his mouth softened sensually. His gaze went to her breasts, the nipples still pointed with arousal. As his hand pulled away from the ribbon, he brushed his knuckles across one nipple.

Camilla drew in her breath sharply. He glanced back up at her face. Her lips were rosy and faintly swollen, and just looking at them sent desire spearing through his gut again. "There's no hiding that you have been well and thoroughly kissed."

"Benedict!"

There was no time to say anything else, for by this time the vicar of Edgecombe was upon them. He swept his hat from his head, executing a creditable, if somewhat stiff, bow. "My dear cousin!"

He came forward, ignoring Benedict, and grabbed Camilla's hands.

"Hello, Cousin Harold." Camilla tugged vainly at her hands. "It is so nice to see you. May I introduce my husband, Mr. Benedict Lassiter?"

Harold looked shocked and, to Camilla's relief, dropped her hands as if they had burned him. "Your what?" He turned toward Benedict.

"Husband," Benedict supplied helpfully. "How do you do?"

"But— I thought—"

"Didn't your mother tell you?" Camilla asked.

"Why, yes, she did say something about it, but, frankly, I thought it was all one of Aunt Lydia's little faradiddles."

"Oh, no. Benedict is quite real," Camilla assured him.

"This is so—so surprising." He looked at Camilla, saying earnestly, "You know that I had always cherished the hope..."

"Ah, Cousin Harold." Camilla smiled winningly. "Don't try to pretend you meant any of those blandishments you were always giving me. Why, everyone knew you were merely being gallant. The two of us would never have suited. I am far too frivolous."

"Only because you are still young. I am convinced that in time you would have settled down and..." His eyes dropped down to her full breasts, then skittered away. He cleared his throat. "Um, well, become a proper wife and loving mother."

"Indeed, I am sure she will be," Benedict interjected, taking Camilla's hand and tucking it into his arm possessively. His hard eyes bored into the other man's. "Why don't we return to the house, where we can have a more comfortable visit?"

"Oh, yes," Camilla agreed quickly as they started to walk back into the house. She was a little surprised by Benedict's obvious antagonism toward the other man. "I am sure everyone else wants to see you, as well. Indeed, I am quite surprised that Aunt Beryl allowed you out of her presence so soon after your arriving.''

''She did not know I was here. As soon as Purdle told me you were in the garden, I rushed out to see you.'' He paused, considering. ''It would have been more dutiful of me, no doubt, to have gone first to visit my mother. However, since she has been living here for some months now, we see each other several times a week, and I do not think it is slighting her to go to you first.''

''No, I am sure it is not,'' Camilla agreed, for her cousin's always sober face was set in even grimmer lines than usual. ''I know that your mother would say that you are her most dutiful son.''

''Since Graeme is always off with the regiment and Bertram thinks of no one but himself, I cannot feel that that is the highest recommendation.''

They returned to the sitting room, where Cousin Bertram and Lydia still sat, now joined by Anthony.

''Hello,'' Camilla announced merrily. ''Look who we came upon in the garden!''

She was not sure which of the occupants of the room looked up at them with most horror. Anthony glanced quickly around, as if seeking escape, and Lydia turned a reproachful gaze upon Camilla. Cousin Bertram merely sighed in a resigned way.

''Hallo, brother dear,'' he said languidly, rising to execute an elegant bow. ''So we are to have the pleasure of your company again. I had not realized it was so near time for luncheon.''

Camilla had to press her lips together to keep from giggling. Harold was well known for dropping in right at the time for a meal, though no one was entirely sure

if this was due to his parsimoniousness or to the quality of his housekeeper's cooking.

Harold's eyes narrowed at his brother's comment,
but he replied blandly, "Is it that late? I was unaware
of the time. I have been out all morning visiting the
sick of the parish."

"Of course."

Harold greeted Anthony, managing to annoy him by
clapping him heartily on the shoulder and calling him
"son." Harold had decided since Anthony's own father had died that it was up to him to act in a father's
stead to Anthony, giving him frequent advice and even
more frequent lectures on the wickedness of his ways.

"How are your studies?" Harold went on to ask
Anthony, sitting down beside him.

"Fine."

"I shall have to ask you a few questions later to
make sure of that," Harold told him in a ponderously
playful manner, wagging his forefinger at him. More
seriously, he turned to Lydia and said, "You know, I
am not completely convinced that Mr. Forbes is an
adequate tutor for Anthony. Last time I talked to Anthony, it seemed to me that his Greek was woefully
lacking."

"Lacking what?" Lydia returned sweetly.

"Mr. Forbes is an excellent tutor," said Anthony
belligerently, despite the fact that his usual views on
the aforesaid Forbes were that he was an "old bore"
or a "stuffy bagwig."

Harold patted Lydia's hand in an avuncular way,
though he was in fact much younger than she. "My
dear Viscountess, I know that you find the subject of
Anthony's studies confusing, but you must see that it

is vastly important to the boy's future. How can Anthony assume his place among his peers with a country education? I have thought time and again that he should have been educated at Eton, as all of us were.''

Anthony shut his mouth, looking frustrated. For once, Harold's opinion happened to coincide with his, and he could not argue with him, no matter how much it pained him not to do so.

"Perhaps I should take it up with the Earl...."

"No!" Lydia and Camilla exclaimed in almost the same breath.

"You will give him apoplexy again if you start arguing with him, Cousin Harold," Camilla told him bluntly. "You know he cannot abide your telling him what to do."

"Camilla, you wrong me. I would never think of telling a man as old and respected as my grandfather what to do. It would be a gross impertinence."

"You are right there," Anthony stuck in.

"However, I am sure that the earl would not be averse to listening to a reasoned argument regarding the future Earl's education."

"Then you don't know Grandpapa."

He smiled at Camilla indulgently. "Dear Camilla, I must differ with you in that regard. You forget that I have held this living for some years now and have visited our grandfather often. I know him very well indeed. I think I can say with assurance that the Earl values my advice regarding Anthony."

Camilla could see from the expression on Anthony's flushed face that he was getting close to being unable to keep a lock on his tongue. She cast about for something to divert Harold from the present course of his conversation.

To her surprise—and relief—Benedict spoke up. "I am sure the Earl does value your advice. I find him to be a very sensible man."

"Yes, of course," Harold agreed, adding a caveat. "Although he can be a trifle careless about certain virtues."

"Really? Well, I must admit that when we were talking earlier, he did seem somewhat lenient about the practice of smuggling."

"Smuggling!" Anthony exclaimed. "What the dev— I mean, why on earth were you discussing smuggling?"

Benedict shrugged. "The conversation simply turned that way. I cannot remember why. We were, of course, deploring it."

"I am sure Grandpapa never said anything so poor-spirited," Anthony contested hotly.

Benedict's brows rose lazily. "But, surely, smuggling *is* illegal."

"Of course." Cousin Harold pursed his lips disapprovingly and sent a stern glance in Anthony's direction. "But far too many people, including people who should be setting an example for their inferiors, are too permissive—one could even say *supportive* of such activities."

"You mean, the locals support the smugglers?"

Harold shrugged expressively. "It is well known around here that many a case of brandy is left on certain doorsteps on certain nights."

"Really, Harold," Cousin Bertram drawled, raising the quizzing glass that hung from his waistcoat by a ribbon and focusing it on his brother. "Do stop prosing on so. We are discussing liquor, not murder."

"That is precisely the sort of attitude I mean," Harold said stiffly. "Young Anthony is even worse. Really, Aunt Lydia, the boy needs more control."

"Not from you!" Anthony rose to his feet, then subsided with ill grace at a quelling look from Camilla.

"One would think," Harold went on, "that with the death of Nat Crowder, everyone would have realized that the wages of sin are death. But it seems to have made no one regret their actions, or even think about them."

"Nat Crowder?" Benedict asked innocently.

"Yes. A local chap, found dead a few weeks ago. Rumored to be one of the smugglers, even the head of them. The sort of end that comes to people like that."

"People like what?" Anthony was white-lipped with anger. "Nat was a good man. At least he wasn't a pharisee who went about beating his chest in public."

"He was a criminal," Harold retorted flatly.

"This man was murdered?" Benedict interjected. "Because he was a smuggler?"

"He was found at the bottom of a cliff with his neck broken," Anthony said. "That does not mean he was murdered."

"It does make it likely," Cousin Bertram put in. "No one knew the cliffs around here any better than Nat."

"You knew him?" Benedict asked.

"Oh, yes, when we were boys. He was much the

same age as I. We would often play together when I was down here visiting. Don't you remember, Harold?"

"Of course I remember. Just because we used to play blindman's buff together doesn't mean I approve of what Nat grew up to become."

"Gave me quite a start, his dying like that," Cousin Bertram said reflectively. "I mean, well, makes you think, doesn't it?"

"It ought to make you think about what you are doing with your life," Harold told his brother darkly.

Bertram lifted his brows in feigned astonishment. "Really, brother, one might think that you disapproved of me."

Harold let out a snort.

"But what about Nat Crowder?" Camilla asked, trying to steer them away from the conflict that seemed to be springing up on every side. *Really, Cousin Harold managed to rub everyone the wrong way.* "Why was he murdered? What did it have to do with smuggling?"

"Nothing," Anthony said sourly. "It was probably caused by something else entirely."

"Perhaps it was a struggle for power," Benedict suggested.

"Someone else trying to take over the smuggling ring?" Camilla nodded. "That makes sense."

"Then who is the new head of the smugglers?" Bertram asked. "That would seem to tell us who the murderer was."

"No one knows," Harold answered, shrugging.

"But everyone apparently knew that this Crowder fellow was the ringleader," Benedict pointed out.

"Yes. But I have heard nothing about anyone taking his place."

"Who would tell the village vicar anything like that?" Bertram asked disdainfully.

"You would be surprised how many rumors find their way to the door of the church. My sheep often bring their troubles to me."

Bertram rolled his eyes.

"Harold, dearest!" Aunt Beryl sailed into the room, holding her hands out to her youngest son. Camilla had long thought that Harold was her aunt's favorite child; they were, after all, so much alike in their sanctimonious, bossy ways. "I just now learned that you were here. Why didn't you send a message straight up to me?"

"Dear madam, I hope you will pardon me when I tell you that the news of my fair cousin's arrival drove all other thought from my head. I hastened at once to greet her."

"You naughty boy," she said with a roguish look, first at him, then at Camilla. "But I know how you young people are. Always more interested in each other than in seeing one's poor old mother." She smiled archly and waggled a playful forefinger at Camilla, as if she had been engaged in some youthful hijinks.

Camilla gazed back at her in amazement. Though Aunt Beryl had always disapproved of Camilla, she had nourished the hope that Harold would prevail on her to marry him. Camilla did, after all, have a tidy little inheritance. But Camilla could hardly believe that the woman actually seemed to still be encouraging a romance between her and Harold. *Did she not believe*

Camilla's marriage was real, even after that scene in the garden today?

"Indeed?" Benedict asked coldly. "Precisely what do you mean, madam?"

Camilla turned toward him. Benedict's voice was like ice, and his face might have been the model for a disdainful aristocrat. Even Aunt Beryl seemed at a loss in the face of his disapproval.

She gaped at him for a moment, then went on in a flustered way, "Well, ah, that is, I was merely teasing Harold a little. He and Camilla have been close since childhood."

Camilla's brows went up at that gross overstatement. Cousin Bertram sighed and began to twirl his quizzing glass, looking at Benedict.

"Really?" Benedict drawled. "How odd that Camilla had not mentioned him to me."

Aunt Beryl and Harold both looked affronted at this statement, and Camilla hastened to say soothingly, "Now, Benedict, you know that I told you about all my relatives."

"Did you?" Benedict replied in a bored way. "I fear I have forgotten."

Aunt Beryl's face hardened, and Camilla could see from the way she looked at Benedict that she was growing to dislike him as much as she did her niece. Camilla hoped she would not say anything, for Benedict seemed to be in a wretched mood, and she feared that he might give her aunt a set-down.

At that moment, however, Mr. Thorne walked in, breaking the mood of the scene. His hands were clasped behind his back, and his forehead was wrinkled in thought. Anthony, who had been watching the brewing confrontation between Benedict and Aunt Beryl with interest, let out a groan at Thorne's arrival. Thorne looked up and glanced around in surprise, as if he had not been aware of where he was. Then his eyes fell upon Lydia, and he smiled rapturously.

"Ah, fair Diana," he exclaimed, going to her and bowing low over her hand. "I have been composing a verse this morning. You are my inspiration. How fortunate that I have found you."

"Have you?" Lydia returned vaguely. "Isn't that nice?"

Anthony jumped to his feet, looking as if he had been goaded beyond his endurance. "I am going to my room to study."

Lydia looked at him in astonishment. Harold nodded and beamed approval.

"Good lad! I am glad to see that my words had some effect on you."

Camilla had to smother a laugh at the frustration on Anthony's face. She knew that he was almost tempted to stay in the room, rather than have Harold think that his advice had had any influence on him.

"I told my tutor that I would come back," Anthony said ungraciously. He turned toward Camilla suddenly and said, "Milla, won't you come, too? Mr. Forbes is eager to see you again."

Camilla did not betray her surprise that Mr. Forbes had expressed any opinion about her at all. Instead, she stood up, glad for an excuse to leave her aunt and cousin. "Benedict, dear..." She ignored Anthony, who was turned with his back to the rest of the room and was winking at her madly. "Would you like to meet Anthony's tutor?"

She was offering him an escape from Cousin Harold's stultifying conversation, as well as Aunt Beryl's entrapping questions, so she expected Benedict to leap at the chance. Instead, he smiled and said, "Thank you, Camilla, but why don't you go along by yourself? I would enjoy visiting further with your cousin Harold."

"Of course." She tried not to look as astounded as she felt.

As she and Anthony walked out the door, she heard Cousin Bertram saying to his brother, "Doesn't Mr. Lassiter look familiar, Harry? I've been trying to think all morning where we've met before. Where did you go to school, Mr. Lassiter?"

Camilla smiled to herself, thinking that it served him right for staying.

"I can't believe that you asked him to come with us!" Anthony hissed once they were out of hearing distance of the sitting room. "Didn't you see me winking at you?"

"Of course I did. And you looked quite silly, too."

"Silly be damned. I didn't want him with us."

"I know you don't like Benedict, Anthony, but I am at a loss to understand why. You don't even know the man."

"Do you like him?"

The question took her aback. "Of course not." She shook her head and repeated, "Of course not. I was worried about what Aunt Beryl might trick him into saying. That's the only reason I wanted him to come with us. I cannot understand why he would not seize the chance to leave."

"Because he wanted to try to get more information out of them. Didn't you see?"

"No. What are you talking about? What kind of information could he possibly get out of Aunt Beryl or Lydia?"

"Gossip, that's what. And Cousin Harold's the main one, not my mother or Aunt Beryl. Didn't you hear Benedict asking about the smugglers?"

"Yes."

"Well? Don't you see? It proves that he is an excise man, just as I told you last night. As soon as he brought up that smuggling thing, I knew it."

"Was he the one who brought it up?" Camilla asked as they reached the staircase and started up it. "I thought it was Cousin Harold."

"Oh, Cousin Harold couldn't keep from spouting off about it, of course, in that brainless way of his. But it was your Mr. Lassiter who worked the conversation around to it in the first place. And now he's going to wring every last bit of information out of them that he can. Thank heavens Harold is such a self-important fool. He will act as if he knows everything, when he knows nothing about it at all. He could not misdirect the man more if he tried."

Camilla looked at her cousin oddly. "What does it matter? Why do you care whether he finds out anything? Personally, I would much prefer that he is an excise officer than a thief, which was your other surmise. If he is a customs man, at least we aren't in any danger."

Anthony glanced at her quickly, then away. Camilla came to a halt, realization dawning on her. "Wait!"

She reached out and took Anthony's arm, pulling him to a stop beside her. "Anthony! Are you—"

She glanced all around, then dragged him down the hall and into her room. When she had shut the door firmly behind them, she turned to him, hands on hips. Anthony fidgeted, looking anywhere but at her.

"Anthony Lionel Fitzwilliam Elliot!" she said fiercely, keeping her voice to a whisper, as if they might be heard even inside this room. "Are you involved with the smugglers?"

He set his jaw, still not looking at her, which was answer enough.

"Anthony! I cannot believe this of you! What about your mother? What about Grandpapa? If he finds this out, it will kill him!"

"It's not that bad. Grandpapa doesn't condemn them. Why, he even buys from them," he answered sullenly, crossing his arms over his chest.

"Don't be absurd. Buying brandy, or even feeling sympathy toward the smugglers, is a far cry from actually participating in smuggling! What if you get caught? Even Grandpapa will not be able to save you. Not if you're caught red-handed and hauled off to jail. Think of your family, Anthony. Think of the disgrace. The future Earl of Chevington, caught smuggling!"

"I won't get caught. I'm careful."

"Oh, Anthony, you *never* think you will get caught."

"Usually I'm not."

"All it would take would be one time. It will be the end of you. The ruin of all of us." She turned away and began to pace. "Why? Why did you do this? It can't be for the money."

"Of course not. I just did it for a lark one night. Jem was doing it, and he was telling me about it."

"Jem Crowder?"

Anthony nodded, and Camilla groaned.

"I should have known. You and he have always gotten each other into mischief."

"They needed an extra hand. So I said, sure, I'd go along, and I went. And, oh, Camilla, it was such fun!" His handsome face lit up, betraying how much he was still a boy, no matter how large he had grown. "So I asked if I could do it again, and you know Nat, he was always a stand-up chap, and he let me. I've been doing it ever since."

Camilla put her face to her hands. "Anthony, Anthony…"

"Come on, Milla," he said coaxingly, going to her and wrapping his hands around her wrists, pulling her hands from her face so that he could look down into her eyes. "I am not the only one who's gotten into scrapes. Who is it that's managed to work herself into a masquerade of marriage? You let your tongue get away with you, and now you're in a terrific jam. If anyone finds out, you will be completely disgraced. Just like me."

Camilla flushed. She could not deny his words. She *was* just as bad as he was, getting herself in such a fix. "You're right," she admitted. "I have gotten myself into a mess, and it's going to be the very devil to get out of it. But at least, if I am caught, I won't be hanged for it. If you are caught—"

"I won't be. You know the 'gentlemen'—" he gave the smugglers their local nickname "—haven't been caught."

"Not recently. But there have been those in the past who were. And you know what happened to them. I couldn't bear it if anything happened to you! The whole family would be ruined. Your mother could never again go back into Society. And Grandpapa—"

"I know. I know," he said wretchedly, his shoulders slumping. "Oh, Milla, I know I should not have done it. It was just that it was such fun, such excitement, and Chevington Park is so deadly dull."

Camilla heaved a sigh. "I know you are bored. I told Grandpapa he ought to at least send you to school. I understand that he didn't want you to go into the army. You are the heir, after all, and after your father's death, he was desperately afraid of losing you, too. But it would have been much better for you at Eton, where you could have been around other boys, not spending all your time here, bored and lonely and letting Jem Crowder talk you into things."

"Don't blame Jem. He's a good fellow."

"A good fellow who is likely to end up on the gallows," Camilla retorted. "Anthony, surely you see that you must stop. Don't you? You cannot go on with this."

"I know. I will end it. I will tell Jem, and—and when they can find someone to replace me, I will quit."

Camilla sighed. She supposed that she would have to be content with his promise, although she would have preferred that he quit right now, cleanly, and not wait for them to replace him.

"Anthony…" she asked after a moment, "do *you* know anything about Nat's death? Was it because of the smuggling?"

He frowned and shook his head. "No. I don't know anyone who knows what happened or why. Even Jem knows nothing. Nat was just found dead one morning."

"Is there a new leader? Do you think he killed Nat?"

"I don't know. I've never seen him. Everyone wears masks or kerchiefs over their faces. That way none of us can turn the others in if we get caught. Of course, some of them I know by their voices or the set of the bodies, but there are plenty whom I don't recognize. And I don't ask questions. It isn't wise." He paused, then went on, "There must be someone making plans and giving orders. Everything runs more smoothly now than it did when Nat was alive. But I never hear anyone say who should do what or where or when we go. I just get the word from Jem, and I think that's the way it is with most of the men. Someone tells someone else, who tells another. The thing is..."

"What?"

"They're talking now about swearing blood oaths. You know, taking an oath not to leave the ring and not to betray it. Having a ceremony, you see, and committing yourself to it."

"This is something you think the new leader advocates?"

He nodded. "One of the men started talking about it, but I know he didn't think it up. He is too stupid. Several of the others think that it's a good idea. To insure loyalty."

"What would happen if you left the ring, then?"

He looked away from her. "They're talking about swearing to the death."

Camilla turned white. "You mean they would kill you if you left?"

He nodded slowly. "But we haven't sworn anything yet. And none of them know who I am, anyway, except Jem, and he would never tell."

"Oh, Anthony, think!" Camilla exclaimed. "If you can tell who some of the other men are by their voices or their size and shape, don't you think that you are easily recognizable to them? Who else among them has hands like an aristocrat? I dare swear that you haven't a callus on your palm."

She grabbed his hands and turned them palm up. "Look. And what about your speech? Who else among them talks like you?"

"I'm not a fool, Camilla. I wear gloves, and I change my manner of speaking. I copy Jem. You know I can take on the accent. You've heard me. I wear clothes I borrow from Jem. They don't know me."

She gave him a long look. "There are other things you can't disguise. Your build, for instance. I'm sure that you and Jem are together always. Everyone knows that the two of you have been friends all your lives. Maybe you wear Jem's shirts, but he's far too short for you to wear his trousers. You think any of them have trousers of that cut and material? There must be one or two of them who are sharp enough to put two and two together, no matter what you've done to hide it."

Anthony looked a little nonplussed, and he rubbed his chin thoughtfully. "I hadn't thought of that. You might be right. But they're all loyal to us. They would never turn me in.''

"Hopefully not. But it's not a good situation.''

He sighed. "Yes, I know. And you're right. I will give it up. I promise.'' He looked a little wistful. "But it was jolly good fun, Milla.''

"I am sure it was.'' She smiled at him. "I will talk to Grandpapa and try to convince him that you need to spend some time away.''

"Maybe a trip to London!'' Anthony's eyes sparkled at the idea. "That would be smashing!''

"Yes, it would.''

Anthony hesitated, suddenly serious again. "And you won't tell Lassiter, will you?''

"No.'' Camilla was aware of a curious longing to unburden herself to Benedict. However, if there was a chance that Anthony was right and her "husband'' was an excise man, then he was the last person she could tell about Anthony's escapade. "You are right. We shall have to be very, very careful to keep it a secret.''

"Keep what a secret?'' asked a masculine voice from the doorway.

Camilla gasped and whirled around. There in the doorway stood Benedict, looking at them questioningly.

10

Camilla stared at Benedict. *How long had he been there? How much had he heard?*

"What?" she asked, stalling for time as her mind raced furiously.

"What is it you have to keep secret?"

"Oh, that." Camilla gave a little chuckle. "Nothing, really, just a...something that Anthony doesn't want Aunt Lydia to hear about. He's, ah, wanting to purchase a horse."

"Yes, that's right," Anthony jumped in. "Mama worries—you know how mothers are. She's afraid that the horse is too wild." He added in a realistically sulky voice, "She treats me like a baby."

"Now, Anthony, dear, she is just concerned about you. You are her only child, after all."

"I wish I were not," he retorted in a heartfelt voice.

Benedict glanced from one of them to the other. Camilla wondered if he believed them. She had been so rattled at seeing him there that she had reacted badly, she knew. But at least Anthony had been convincing; she hoped that would be enough to make

Benedict believe the story. *If only she knew how much of their conversation he had heard!* If he truly was an excise officer, as Anthony surmised, it would be disastrous for him to have heard the whole, or even a good part, of what they had said.

"I am surprised to see you here," Camilla said brightly. "I thought you were staying behind to talk to Cousin Harold." *Had he merely said that in order to skulk along behind them and spy on them?* She was feeling more and more distrustful of him.

"Yes. We talked. But it's time for luncheon, and I decided to come tell you. You see, ah, the vicar and Mr. Thorne were discussing poetry."

Camilla giggled at the pained expression on Benedict's face. "I understand."

"I should think so!" Anthony overlooked his distrust of Benedict in an upsurge of fellow feeling. "That chap Thorne is a dead bore."

"I can't think why Aunt Lydia invited him down here."

"She didn't. Mama may be flighty, but she's not a sapskull. She said the fellow just showed up on her doorstep when she was leaving and insisted on escorting her to Chevington Park. He has been hanging around her for months now, professing his undying love and all that sort of tripe." Anthony grimaced. "He told her that he could not allow her to travel all this way without anyone to protect her. As if Batters, who's driven her everywhere for over fifteen years, and George weren't enough protection. Not to mention her maid and the driver of the second coach with her luggage. She tried to talk him out of it, but he kept jawing, so finally she agreed. Once they got here, she couldn't very well not invite him to stay for a visit. It wouldn't have been polite. How was she to know the leech would live here a month?"

"A month! He's been here that long?" Camilla asked, astonished.

"Yes. Mama tried to hint to him that he needn't remain any longer, but he just said that he could not leave her to face this 'family tragedy' all alone."

"It's a wonder you haven't kicked him out."

"I would have." Anthony looked grim. "But Mama is too soft-hearted. She thinks he must be short of funds, that he wanted to escort her because he was fleeing his creditors. So she's reluctant to toss him out. She says she has been in the same position sometimes when her allowance ran out. I don't know. Maybe she is hoping he will drive Aunt Beryl away. If he could, even *I* would be in favor of his staying."

"Have your cousin and his friend been here all that time, too?" Benedict asked. "It seems an awfully full house."

"Too full," Anthony agreed darkly. "Those two have been here even longer than Mr. Thorne, though, thank God, neither one is as big a gudgeon as he is. Cousin Bertram's not too bad. At least he's not prosy like Cousin Harold and Aunt Beryl. But that other one, Oglesby—he's a strange one."

"Really? In what way?"

Anthony, who was not one to analyze his thoughts, wrinkled his brow. "I'm not sure. There's just something odd about him. Besides his clothes, I mean. I can't stomach pink waistcoats on a man, can you? Cousin Kitty and Cousin Amanda, of course, think he's the handsomest thing ever, and the two of them have been flirting like mad with him.'' A small grin flitted across his face. '''Course, he merely looks bored by them, so he can't be entirely lacking in good sense.'' He shrugged. "Perhaps it's merely that he's quiet. I rarely hear him say anything. But, somehow, I don't know, he seems…out of place.''

"Out of place?'' It was Camilla who asked him the question this time, her curiosity aroused by Anthony's answer.

"I can't explain it, Milla. Spend a little time around him, and you'll see what I mean.''

Benedict said nothing more, deciding that he had asked as many questions as he could without arousing Anthony's or Camilla's suspicions. He still wondered what the two of them had been talking about when he opened the door. Camilla's explanation had been feeble, he thought, and there had been that flash of panic in her eyes when she turned around and saw him standing there. She had specifically said that they must keep something a secret from him, and she had obviously been fearful that he had overheard what they were discussing. He wished that he had opened the door a few moments earlier.

He found it difficult to believe that either Camilla or Anthony was the person he was seeking. Anthony, after all, would become an earl upon his grandfather's death. Perhaps a hotheaded, adventure-seeking young man might be foolish enough to risk all that for the excitement of smuggling, but his very youth argued against his being the mastermind of the destruction of Gideon. As for Camilla, however odd her actions might be, she was a lady. Moreover, she had only just arrived in Chevington Park after several months away.

Their mystery, whatever it was, was probably rather innocuous—some family secret, or the location of something valuable that they did not want known by an outsider. Still, Benedict would have felt better if he had known what it was.

There was no use pressing the point, however. He had to pretend that he believed them. "Well, I imagine that luncheon is ready now. Shall we go down, my dear?" He offered Camilla his arm.

"Thank you. Coming, Anthony?"

Anthony scowled. "With Thorne and Cousin Harold and all of them there? I think not. Mrs. Blakely will send one of the footmen up with my food."

With those words, he left them, heading for the back stairs leading up to the nursery. Benedict watched him go, saying casually, "Your cousin doesn't have a room on this floor?"

It was odd for a family member—the future earl, no less—not to be staying on the same floor with all the others, where the pleasantest rooms were.

"No. He sleeps in his old room upstairs." Camilla took his arm, and they started strolling toward the stairs.

"You mean, in the nursery?"

That fact struck him as even odder. *What eighteen-year-old boy would want to stay in the rooms labeled for children?*

"Yes. It's easier, he says. He and his tutor can use the schoolroom for his studies, and he likes his old bedroom. Personally, I think it's just because it's easier to avoid all the adults that way. There is no one else up there, so he can do as he pleases."

Benedict suspected that Camilla had hit the nail on

the head with her supposition. The lure of being left
to his own devices would appeal to any adolescent
male; it would be heaven-sent for one bent on mischief. He wondered what sort of view the third-floor
nursery windows would have. He thought that it might
be an excellent place from which to look for signals
indicating that there was a ship to be unloaded that
night.

"Perhaps I ought to visit with Anthony a bit," he
suggested casually. "Get to know him a little better.
It might allay his fears about me. Perhaps we could
go out riding."

Camilla glanced at him, surprised. "Why, that's
very thoughtful. It would be nice if you could reassure
him that you are not going to 'take advantage' of me.
He feels that because he's a sort of brother to me, he
should protect me."

"Someone should," Benedict agreed.

"I beg your pardon?"

He looked down into her flashing eyes. The words
had slipped out without his thinking. Obviously they
had aroused her ire. "Well, it's true. If you were mine,
I wouldn't allow you to be running about on the heath
alone at night."

"It is a good thing that I am not 'yours,' then, isn't
it? That attitude is precisely why I decided never to
marry. As if a woman could be your possession, a
slave to do your bidding, with no will or mind of her
own."

A faint smile curved his lips. "I think that is something no one will ever accuse you of. However, that
was not precisely what I meant. I meant 'mine' as in
related to me, dependent on me. I know that the last

thing one can expect from a woman is loyalty or obedience.''

"Two very different things, sir,'' Camilla pointed out tartly. "Obedience is what one expects from a child or a servant. Loyalty is what is freely given by a thinking, autonomous adult.''

"Well, neither of them is a virtue I have found in women.''

"Then you have made a poor choice in the company you keep.''

"Obviously,'' he agreed grimly.

"That is the problem with most men—they choose a woman because she is beautiful to look at, rather than for the qualities that count, such as her intelligence or loyalty or courage.''

He thought of Annabeth's pale beauty, and the venal heart it had hidden so well. But he could not resist challenging Camilla. "I would have thought loveliness one of the primary qualities one would seek in a wife.''

"There. You see?'' Camilla came to a stop, putting her hands on her hips in exasperation. "That is just like a man. Will a pretty face provide you witty conversation at the dinner table or a thoughtful discourse beside the fire? Of course not. Does it make a sour disposition easy to bear or a dull mind less boring?''

"Well, it would make it more pleasant to look at your companion through life.''

"Ha!'' Camilla's voice dripped scorn. "If all she is is pleasant to look at, within a few months you won't even be there to see her. You will have been driven mad by boredom and will spend all your hours at your club.''

Benedict could not help but chuckle, thinking of one of his friends, to whom this exact fate had befallen. Enamored of a fragile blond-and-white beauty, he had married her, only to find once they were alone together, without chaperones, friends and family, that the poor girl had no conversation and little wit. She had the same dimpling smile and sweet expression that had bewitched him, but when they talked, there was nothing to say. He had, indeed, taken to spending most of his time with his friends at the club.

"There, you see? You've seen such marriages, haven't you?"

"Yes, I have," he admitted.

"Then admit that what I am saying is right. If a man chose a wife for her mind or her conversation, he would be much more likely to be happy."

"Passion plays no part?"

Camilla looked at him, feeling suddenly as if she had stepped onto treacherous ground. Her usual answer in the past would have been a contemptuous dismissal of such a base appetite as passion as reason for marriage. However, remembering how she had felt this morning, when Benedict kissed her, she could not be so scornful.

Her eyes went involuntarily to his lips, and he gave her such a knowing smile that Camilla longed to hit him.

"I think it a flimsy foundation," she told him primly, "for a lifetime of devotion."

"Flimsy?" Something flickered in the dark depths of Benedict's eyes as he reached up and twined one of the wispy curls that framed Camilla's face around his finger. "I would have said that it is a very strong thing, passion."

Camilla could think of no answer. Indeed, she could scarcely breathe.

"It hit me like a fist this morning," he went on in a soft, conversational tone.

Camilla drew a shaky breath. He was going to kiss her again, she thought, and she realized with astonishment how much she wanted him to. The thought seemed to break her trance, and she pulled back abruptly.

"We'd best go, or we shall be late." She whirled and started quickly toward the stairs again.

With a soft, rich chuckle that sent a quiver through her, Benedict matched her pace, saying, "Of course, madam. At your service."

Camilla was surprised—and, she told herself, relieved—that Benedict made no advances toward her over the next couple of days. He did not come up to their room at the time she was undressing and bathing; indeed, he did not come in until after she had finally fallen asleep. Nor did he spend much time with her at any other point. When she inquired where he had been, he responded vaguely.

But Anthony was quick to give her his opinion. "Snooping! That's what he's doing," he sputtered angrily. "Looking here and there, talking to everyone. I've seen him all over the house. Lord, he has probably been exploring the west wing, too. The man is up to no good, I tell you."

"Oh, hush. You sound like a suspicious old priss." However, Camilla had to admit that she was rather curious, too, as to where Benedict had been and what he had been doing.

"Well, why else would he be talking to all the servants?" Anthony pointed out reasonably. "I went down to the servants' hall last night to cajole a little snack out of Cook, and I heard one of them say that he was in Purdle's room, talking to him."

"He was talking to Purdle?" Camilla's eyebrows sailed upward. "But, Anthony, Purdle would never say anything to him. Besides, what does he know?"

"Nothing to any purpose. But he spies on me. Him and Jenkins both," Anthony said bitterly.

"Oh, now, Anthony…"

"They do. For Grandpapa. Oh, they don't mean any harm, I know that. But sometimes it's enough to drive me mad. I have to sneak out of the house if I don't want one of them questioning me."

"Even so, Purdle would never reveal family business to a stranger."

"Well, they don't think he's a stranger, do they? They think he's your legal husband."

"Still, that's not enough to make Purdle say anything that might harm you."

"Oh, you don't know. They always say it's for my own good. That they're worried about me. It's enough to make a fellow wish he were an orphan."

"You don't mean that. But I understand. I really do. All that 'taking care' of one can make one feel smothered."

"Exactly. I knew you'd understand." Anthony smiled at her, but continued to pace agitatedly. "Can't you do anything about him?"

"Who? Benedict?"

"Yes."

"What are you suggesting? That I get rid of him?"

"It's what I'd like to do. But I know there's no chance of it. Just watch him, keep him on a shorter leash. He's supposed to be married to you. Can't you make him do things with you?"

"All right, all right. I will try."

So it was that the next morning Camilla put on her riding habit when she got up and went downstairs in search of Benedict. She found him in the breakfast room with Mr. Oglesby. If he was trying to worm anything out of Mr. Oglesby, Camilla thought with a smile, then he was having rough going. She had tried to talk to the man after dinner the evening before, and he had hardly said a word.

"Camilla!" Benedict arose with a smile and came over to brush a kiss against her cheek. Camilla was not sure if he was putting on an act for Mr. Oglesby, who had also risen politely at her entrance, though more slowly than Benedict, or if he was genuinely glad to see her.

She breathed in the elusive scent of his masculine cologne and replied, a little shakily, "Benedict."

He led her to the seat beside him, pulling out her chair for her.

She nodded at the other man at the table. "Good morning, Mr. Oglesby."

"Mrs. Lassiter," he replied, a little stiffly. "How are you this morning?"

"Quite well, sir." She realized with a bit of surprise that this statement was the truth. She was in an absurd situation, one that would be ruinous to her reputation if she was found out, and yet she was in excellent spirits.

Benedict solicitously dished up a plate of food for her from the long breakfront, while Camilla vainly attempted again to engage Mr. Oglesby in conversation. He spoke only in answer to questions, and then largely in monosyllables, not rudely, but with an air of discomfort. Camilla could not decide whether he was very shy or very dull.

"I find the country air quite refreshing myself," Benedict said, joining in her effort to converse. "A pleasant change from the city. Are you from the city, Mr. Oglesby?"

"Yes, yes, I am." Mr. Oglesby shifted a little in his chair.

"London?"

"Yes."

"Of course, there's little of the excitement of London here," Benedict went on.

"No. There is not."

"We reside in Bath," Camilla put in.

"But I have lived in London in the past," Benedict said. "Perhaps we might have some acquaintances in common."

"Oh...I...I wouldn't think so."

"What part of London do you live in?"

Oglesby looked even more uncomfortable. "Mm, well, near St. James Place."

"Then you must live close to Cousin Bertram. Is that how you met?"

He gaped at her for a moment, then said hurriedly, "Yes, yes, that's right. Happened to meet walking down the street one day. Down St. James, in fact."

Oglesby stood up, giving them a stiff smile. "I beg your pardon, but I must leave now."

Camilla looked at his plate, where half his food still remained. He followed her gaze, and color rose in his face. "I...ah...I'm afraid I must not have been as hungry as I thought. If you will excuse me..."

He sketched a bow toward them and left the room. Camilla watched him go, then turned back to Benedict. "Odd."

"What is, my dear?"

"Mr. Oglesby. Didn't he seem awfully nervous to you? What do you think was the matter?"

"I don't know. Perhaps we are an imposing couple."

Camilla grimaced. "Nonsense. We were only trying to make conversation."

"Perhaps he felt that we were interrogating him."

"What else can one do but ask him questions? He won't say anything but a direct answer to a question— preferably in one word."

"Perhaps he feels...mm...intimidated."

"Intimidated? But why?"

"Some people are awed by things that do not faze the granddaughter of an Earl."

"What do you mean?"

"I mean this house." He nodded toward the end of the long table, which was centered by a huge silver epergne, then at the heavy mahogany sideboard, with its load of glittering silver dishes, and the liveried servant standing by to fill one's glass and cup or to serve something from one of the chafing dishes. "Not everyone is used to living on a country estate, nor to conversing at breakfast with an Earl's family."

"*You* seem to have no problem," Camilla pointed out tartly.

He grinned. "No. But I overcame my inhibitions long ago. It's easier for scoundrels, you know, to be at ease in any company."

There was something about the twinkle in his dark eyes that made Camilla wonder all over again if she had been wrong about his low birth. The whole time he had been here, there had been no slip in his speech, no mistake made in his attitude. His manners did not have the elegance of Mr. Sedgewick's or her cousin Bertram's, it was true, but there was in him the air of someone who acted as he chose, not because he did not know better. He showed none of the awkwardness that had been so apparent in Mr. Oglesby.

"Purdle tells me that he is 'not quite a gentleman,'" she said, putting aside for the moment the question of Benedict's own qualifications.

"What? Why?"

Camilla shrugged. "I'm not sure. That is all he said. Purdle had that look on his face that he gets when he's talking about certain people—those who don't fit his ideas of what is proper or genteel. He's a terrible snob." It occurred to her that Purdle had made no such comment about Benedict. Of course, he thought Benedict was her husband, but Purdle usually had his ways of making his opinion subtly known.

"I have generally found that a butler or a valet is much better at dividing the 'Quality' from the riffraff than the aristocracy are."

"Well, it seems very odd that Bertram brought him here. Cousin Bertram is something of a snob himself.

He always surrounds himself with the best—his clothes, his furnishings, his possessions.''

"Your cousin must be a wealthy man, then."

"Actually, I don't think so. He is his father's heir, of course, but not Grandpapa's. Anthony will inherit everything from Grandpapa. Uncle William is wealthy enough, I suppose, but I don't think he gives Cousin Bertram a generous allowance. I suspect that Cousin Bertram is down here avoiding his creditors, like Mr. Thorne.''

"He is a man of some wit, your cousin."

"Yes. You would hardly guess that he is Graeme's or Harold's brother, for neither of those two could be said to have a facile intellect.''

"Graeme Elliot?" Benedict asked, startled. "He is your cousin?"

"Why, yes." Camilla looked at him oddly. "Do you know him?"

"No. No, of course not. It is just—I was astounded at the existence of yet another cousin.''

"I told you about him yesterday. He is a lieutenant in the Hussars.''

"Ah, yes, the Army man."

"Those are only my Elliot cousins, though. I have another whole batch on my father's side. Those are the ones that you know.''

"What? The ones *I*—oh!" He remembered the presence of the liveried servant at the sideboard. "Oh, yes. The ones you were traveling with when we first met." He smiled, his eyes glinting with amusement, and he reached across the table to take her hand. "Tell me, my love, do you think of those days with fondness, as I do?''

"I am sure that I remember them with fully as much joy as you."

His smile broadened. "I cherish the knowledge that our esteem is mutual."

Camilla rolled her eyes and pulled her hand away. "I had thought we might go riding today," she said. "I could show you around Chevington Park. Would you like that?"

"Indeed I would," he answered honestly. It would provide a perfect opportunity for him to investigate the area. He had explored the house and grounds on foot yesterday, but he wanted to move farther afield. "I had thought to ask your cousin Anthony to take me on a tour this morning, but I understand that he left bright and early this morning and has not returned."

"I am sure Anthony would love to ride out with you another time, especially if you have an urge to see the limestone caves along the shore."

"Caves? You have some here on this estate?"

Camilla nodded. "They are everywhere here, some big, some small. Of course, Lydia and Grandpapa absolutely forbade Anthony and me from going inside them."

"Which no doubt guaranteed that you explored them."

Camilla chuckled. "Yes. Unfortunately, there is nothing very exciting in any of them. Anthony and I were always hopeful of treasure, but we never found any. He says that there are interesting formations farther back in one of them, but I have never gone that far."

"That sounds like a sight not to be missed."

They finished their meal, and Benedict went up to

change into riding clothes. Then they set out to explore the estate. The head groom, after a look at Benedict, put him up on a gray gelding, her grandfather's last acquisition for the stables, one that he had never had an opportunity to ride before he was laid low by his illness. Camilla almost protested, unsure how well Benedict could ride. But when she saw him mount the horse, she clamped her mouth shut on the words. He rode like one born to the saddle, controlling the animal easily with his muscled thighs and the most delicate of touches on the reins.

They rode to the cliffs at the edge of the ocean, where they reined in their horses and sat looking out.

"What is that?" Benedict asked, surprised, pointing across the water at a small hump of land rising out of the sea.

Most of the small island was covered by the ruins of an old building. Some walls still stood, as well as the remains of a turret, but much of the stone lay in tumbled heaps.

"That is Keep Island. The ruins are what is left of the original keep. It was the home of the Earls of Chevington for many, many years and quite a stronghold at one time, I believe. The water protected it, of course, and then there were stout, high walls with six towers, and inside them, the keep itself. It was abandoned long ago, though. It proved not to be very sociable or convenient in later times. They used nearly all the stones from the walls to build Chevington Park. What was left was scorched some years later by a fire—started, I understand, by my grandfather's father when he was a lad. As you see, we have always been a little prone to getting into trouble."

He smiled at her sally but turned his attention back to the ruins. "It looks very secure, but somewhat impractical. How did they get to it? I mean, it's too small for there to have been a village or for them to have raised crops or livestock."

"Ah, that's the beauty of it," Camilla replied, grinning. "It is an island only when the tide is high. When the tide is low, there is a strip of land that runs from the beach across to the island. So it is really an oddly shaped peninsula. When the tide rises, the causeway is covered up."

"How convenient."

"Yes. You can reach it by boat at any time. Anthony and I have often rowed across. But boats were much easier to defend against. Even when the tide was low, you had only that one narrow bridge of land on which enemies could ride across. It was never taken."

"When did they abandon it?"

"They started Chevington Park during the reign of Elizabeth and finished when James I was king. The keep's advantages were no longer very necessary, and they grew tired of the inconvenience. Besides, I imagine it would have been a damp and windy place to live. And the Chevingtons prospered greatly under the Tudors. They could afford to build a more luxurious, grander residence."

"I would like to visit it." It occurred to him that the ruins of the keep might be an excellent place for smugglers to store their loot. "It looks interesting."

"It is," Camilla replied cheerfully. "Sometime, when the tide is low, we can walk over. It isn't far, really, and walking is the easiest way. Would you like to see one of the caves?"

"Certainly."

"We are rather close to one of them. Anthony would be a better guide, but I shall do my humble best."

"I am sure that will be quite enough."

"Flatterer."

Camilla swung down off her horse, saying, "We have to lead them down to the beach. The path is narrow."

Benedict dismounted, too, and they walked down the steep trail to the beach. At the bottom they stopped, looking out across the narrow strip of sand to the pounding ocean. Camilla glanced up at her companion. He was staring moodily at the water.

"Who was she?" Camilla asked, surprising even herself with her boldness.

"Who?" Benedict looked at her blankly, for his treacherous first love had been the farthest thing from his mind at that moment.

"The girl who hurt you so. The one who has given you such a dark view of females."

"Oh." Benedict shrugged. "Her name was Annabeth." He tried to summon up her face, but he could not quite remember it clearly. Camilla's dusky curls and mischievous blue eyes kept imposing themselves over any picture of Annabeth's pale beauty.

"What happened?"

He started to dismiss her question with an icy retort; that was what he had done any other time anyone was impertinent enough to ask. He had never told anyone the full story, not even his sister or Sedgewick, though he suspected they had pieced together most of it. But, strangely, the walls did not come up inside him as they usually did, and he realized with a start that he did not mind telling Camilla.

"My uncle—the one I really *do* have—was an old man. He and his wife were childless, and, though she was younger than he, she was considered too old to bear a child. I was my uncle's heir. Then, amazingly, his wife became pregnant. Of course, given her age, no one expected her to give birth without complications. I met Annabeth shortly after I heard of my aunt's pregnancy, and we became engaged a few months later. Annabeth insisted that we keep it a secret. I didn't understand why, but I was too happy and foolish to care. To everyone's astonishment, my aunt carried the child to full term, and the child was born healthy. Then Annabeth told me that she could not marry me. When I pressed for a reason, she said that it was because I would no longer inherit from my uncle, since he now had a child of his own."

Camilla drew in her breath sharply. "She threw you over because you wouldn't get the money?"

He nodded. "Precisely. Of course, I understood then why she had wanted to keep the engagement secret. I think she had not known when we first met that my aunt was pregnant. Then, when she found out, she had put too much time into the project to just drop me, and she was hopeful that my aunt would lose the child. So she hedged her bets. She waited to see what the outcome of the pregnancy was. If my aunt had miscarried, or the baby had been born dead, Annabeth would have made the engagement public. But when my aunt bore the heir, Annabeth was able to break the engagement with no entanglements, since no one had known about it."

Impulsively Camilla curled her arm around his and squeezed it, leaning her head against his arm tenderly. "I'm sorry."

An odd quiver ran through Benedict at her affectionate gesture. He half turned, and she went naturally into his arms, wrapping her arms around him and hugging him. He held her tightly for a moment, struck by how good it felt and how little the memory of Annabeth hurt now. When she pulled back a moment later, he was reluctant to open his arms and let her go.

"I mean," Camilla said, stepping back and looking up at him, "that I am sorry for how bad you must have felt. But not sorry that she broke off the engagement. You know, you were lucky there. You should feel glad."

"I should?" He raised his eyebrows.

"Why, yes. What if you had remained your uncle's heir, and she had made the engagement public? Then you would have had to marry her—and you would not have found out what she was really like until you were tied to her for life. That would be much worse than having your heart broken, don't you think? To live with a woman so cold and deceptive?"

Benedict had to chuckle. He had hated the memory of Annabeth for years, had relived their time together and cursed her for the heartbreak he had felt. But he had never, in all this time, considered the matter from this angle. Trust Camilla to turn everything on its head.

"You're right," he told her. "You are absolutely right. I am a lucky man."

Camilla watched his face lighten with amusement,

and she liked the way it looked. It pleased her to have made him smile. "You should laugh more often."

"I shall endeavor to work on it."

They rode their horses down the beach until they reached the mouth of the cave. Tying the horses to a low, weather beaten gorse bush, they ventured inside. Benedict had to duck to go through the entrance, but inside, the ceiling rose several feet above his head. Lit only by the sunlight coming through the entrance, the cave was dim, and they could not see to the back wall.

"It's too dark inside to go any farther," Camilla commented. "If you come back with Anthony, you will have to bring lanterns. It extends some distance."

She turned toward him and saw that he was looking at her, not their surroundings. "What? Why are you looking at me in that way?"

"What way?" His voice came out low and husky. Ever since her impulsive hug on the beach, he had not been able to stop thinking about taking her in his arms again. He wanted to feel her soft body against his again. He wanted to taste her mouth as he had the other day. He took a step forward.

Camilla's breath caught in her throat. There was something about the tone of his voice, the look in his eyes, that made her knees feel suddenly weak. "I'm not sure. As if you were..." *Hungry.* "...ah, thinking about..."

"About what?" He took another step closer, his eyes still intent on her face. He looked down at her, so close to her that she could feel the heat of his body, yet not touching her.

"I—I'm not sure." Camilla could hardly speak or

even think. She felt caught, trapped by the heat in his eyes.

"I was thinking about you." His hand came up, and he brushed his knuckles slowly down her cheek. "About how beautiful you are."

"Indeed, sir," she said with a breathless little giggle, trying vainly to reestablish the former tone of their conversation, "'tis too dark in here, I would think, for you to see anything."

He smiled slowly. "I can see that you are beautiful in sunlight or in shadow. You make it difficult to concentrate, Camilla."

She could have retorted that he had the same effect on her, but she could not summon the wit or the energy to speak. She could only look up at him as he reached out and curled his hands around her arms. He pulled her closer to him. Camilla went, unresisting. Benedict's gaze dropped to her mouth, then lower still, to the soft swell of her breasts beneath the riding habit. He remembered the feel of the soft mounds beneath his fingers the other day in the garden, the taste of her lips, and he wanted to experience it again.

He knew that he was behaving like a fool. They were in a cave that was a perfect hideout for the smugglers, and instead of paying attention to it, he kept letting his eyes go to her. Worse, his thoughts seemed to stay there, too. It had been that way all morning—indeed, ever since their embrace in the garden. All the time he was talking to the servants or looking around the house and grounds, his mind had kept straying from smugglers back to kisses and clear blue eyes and a body as soft as her tongue was sharp.

Moreover, what he was thinking of was impossible.

Camilla was not the sort of woman whom he could have and then leave, no seller of flesh, nor a dissatisfied wife or lonely widow who was interested in a casual affair, the only sort of women whose company he had allowed himself the last few years. No, she was an unmarried girl of good name, a virgin, no doubt, and despite the fact that she had gotten herself into this compromising situation, he could not in good conscience take advantage of it. To sleep with her would be to commit himself, and that was something he had vowed never to be so foolish as to do again.

But at this moment, he was having difficulty remembering his promises. There was something so entrancing about the white column of her throat…and that errant black curl that clung to her cheek…the softness of her arms beneath his hands. He realized that unconsciously his fingers had begun to caress those arms.

He told himself that he should leave, walk out of the cave and back to their horses. To stay here was insane…dangerous.

"To hell with it," he murmured, and leaned closer.

11

Camilla took a shaky step backward but came up against the wall of the cave and stopped. He moved closer still and braced his hands against the wall on either side of her head. He ached to lean into her, to press his suddenly hard, throbbing flesh into her softness. Only a remnant of good sense kept him from doing so.

"You have a curious effect on me," he murmured, taking the straying curl between his fingers and gently rubbing it. The silken feel of it sent tendrils of heat curling through his abdomen.

"I do?" Camilla's voice came out breathless and high. All she could think about was how close he was and how she would like to trace the sensual curve of his lower lip with her finger.

Acting on the impulse, she reached up and ran her forefinger along his lip. It was smooth and warm, and the feel of it sent a shiver straight down through her. Benedict's eyes darkened, and he bent toward her until his head was almost touching hers. She could read the passion in his eyes, and it stirred her.

He placed his lips where her curl had lain against her neck. Gently he nuzzled her skin, and shivers darted through her. Her breath caught in her throat, and she was aware only of the heat of his body so close to hers, the tingling of her skin where his lips touched it, the strange flowering of heat between her legs. His hand came up and cupped her breast. His thumb found and caressed her nipple through the cloth of her bodice. The little point elongated at his touch, engorged and hard, and her other breast ached for a similar touch. As if he knew, his other hand slid down and found her breast and began to gently knead it.

His mouth explored her throat at length, teasing and caressing, even gently nipping with his teeth, and with each new sensation the fire between Camilla's legs grew. She moved her legs a little apart, hoping to ease the heat. Feeling her movement, Benedict slipped his knee between hers, opening them more. Then, to her surprise, he put his hands beneath her hips and moved her up and forward, seating her firmly on his thigh.

Camilla gasped at the shock of pleasure that ran through her. He rocked her gently upon his iron-hard leg. She felt as if her loins had turned to flame. She whimpered, unconsciously moving her hips with the rocking of his hands, and moisture flooded between her legs. Benedict let out a low sound of satisfaction, pressing her even harder against him. He raised his head and sealed her mouth with his, tongue and lips taking hers with an almost savage ardor.

He filled her senses. She could not think, could scarcely breathe, rocked as she was by delightful sensations. She could not contain small animal noises of passion, but Benedict swallowed them with his kiss.

His lips sank deep into hers even as he pressed his leg harder against the very root of her desire. Camilla thought she might faint, yet her arms clung to him, pulling him more tightly against her. It was not enough, she knew; she wanted something more and harder. The very gate of her femininity ached and pulsated.

Now his mouth left hers, and her head lolled back against the cool rock wall. Her chest rose and fell heavily. He unbuttoned the top few buttons of her bodice and pulled it down, shoving down her chemise, as well, and exposing one lovely white orb. Benedict groaned and bent to take it in his mouth. He suckled on it, somehow both easing and increasing Camilla's ache. She dug her fingers into his scalp, murmuring, "Please, please," over and over in a sensual cadence, though she did not even know what it was she asked for.

Sensation was building between her legs, so delightful it was almost painful. She longed for something, felt as if she were racing toward it, and yet it remained maddeningly out of her reach. She moved frantically against his leg, unable to control the little moans and pants that escaped her throat. She felt as if she were tumbling out of control toward something that she could only guess at.

Outside the cave, one of the horses whickered, followed by the indistinct murmur of a man's voice. The sounds penetrated the haze of their desire. Camilla stiffened. Benedict groaned and stepped back, fighting to regain control. Outside, there was a masculine laugh and the scrape of a bootheel.

Benedict grabbed Camilla's hand and moved deeper

THE EDITOR'S "THANK YOU" FREE GIFTS INCLUDE:

▶ Three of "The Best of the Best"
▶ A lovely Picture Frame

PLACE
FREE GIFT
SEAL
HERE

YES! I have placed my Editor's "thank you" seal in the space provided above. Please send me 3 free books and a Picture Frame. I understand I am under no obligation to purchase any books, as explained on the back and on the opposite page.

183 CIH A2RF (U-BB4-97)

NAME

ADDRESS   APT.

CITY   STATE   ZIP

Thank you!

Offer limited to one per household and not valid to current subscribers.
All orders subject to approval.

THE BEST OF THE BEST™: HERE'S HOW IT WORKS

Accepting free books places you under no obligation to buy anything. You may keep the books and gift and return the shipping statement marked "cancel". If you do not cancel, about a month later we will send you 3 additional novels, and bill you just $3.99 each plus 25¢ delivery per book and applicable sales tax, if any.* That's the complete price, and—compared to cover prices of $5.50 each—quite a bargain! You may cancel at any time, but if you choose to continue, every month we'll send you 3 more books, which you may either purchase at the discount price...or return to us and cancel your subscription.

*Terms and prices subject to change without notice. Sales tax applicable in N.Y.

into the darkness of the cave. They turned a corner. Beyond them lay only impenetrable blackness. They had to stop. Camilla slumped back against the wall, still stunned by the force of the emotions that had moved through her.

Benedict looked down at her. She had not made a move even to straighten her clothing, so her bodice still hung off one shoulder, cupping her bared white breast and pushing it saucily upward. Even in the dim light of the cave, he could see that the nipple was red and swollen from his kisses, gleaming wetly, beckoning him. Benedict swallowed hard, forcing back the desire that surged up in him anew.

There was a man's voice again, echoing so that Benedict knew he had entered the cave. "There must be someone here," the man was saying, his voice laced with disappointment. "The horses must belong to someone."

There was the yellowish glow of a light beyond the curve in the wall, and Benedict surmised that the man and his companion must have brought a lantern with them.

"Doubtless. Perhaps it is Camilla. The stable boy said that she and her husband had ridden out this morning." His voice rose as he called out, "Camilla! Are you in here?"

Camilla sighed. "Cousin Bertram," she whispered. "We'll have to go out and meet them."

Benedict nodded, wishing Camilla's cousin were at the devil. He reached out and pulled her dress into place, his fingers brushing tenderly over her breast as he covered it. There was nothing he wanted so much as to linger there. It seemed the purest form of hell to have to pull himself back into some semblance of order and venture forth to meet Camilla's foppish cousin.

He turned away, breathing deeply, as Camilla called back, "Bertram? Is that you?"

She smoothed her hair into place and pressed her palms against her hot cheeks, praying that what they had been doing would not be too obvious. She plastered a welcoming smile on her face and edged around the corner. She let out a forced chuckle when she saw her cousin and his friend Mr. Oglesby.

"Oh, my, you will think us foolish indeed," she said, walking toward her cousin. Benedict followed behind her, smiling grimly. "When we heard voices, we thought it might be the smugglers or such, and we hid farther back in the cave."

Benedict cast her a sharp look at her words, but said nothing.

"Smugglers!" Bertram exclaimed, bringing his hand up to his heart theatrically. "Oh, my. Why, Terence and I never thought of that, did we?"

The taciturn Mr. Oglesby did nothing but shake his head.

"I see you brought a lantern," Camilla chattered on. She was so nervous she could not seem to stop talking. *What if Cousin Bertram guessed what they had been doing? Was the dim light of the cavern enough to conceal the heightened color in her cheeks and the state of her hair and clothes? What if one of her buttons was undone or the skirt of her riding habit was hiked up?* She did not dare to check anything, though her fingers itched to do so. So she kept on talking, hoping with her chatter to distract the other men's attention. "We were not so wise. We decided to explore the cave on the spur of the moment. Obviously you planned your expedition."

Bertram looked at her oddly, but said only, "Yes. Mr. Oglesby had expressed an interest in the local caves, so I undertook to show them to him."

"And you brought a lunch, as well." Camilla looked at the wicker basket and blanket in Oglesby's hands. "How delightful!"

Bertram smiled stiffly, and the other man seemed to find something of great interest on the cave's wall. "We thought we might spend quite a bit of time exploring the cave, so we had Cook pack us a lunch. Would you care to share it, perhaps? I am sure there is ample for all of us."

"Knowing Cook, I dare swear there is," Camilla agreed gaily. "But we would not dream of imposing ourselves on you. Would we, Benedict? Besides, I am not really dressed for exploring."

Benedict agreed, nodding and smiling as he steered her around the other two and out into the sunlight. Camilla sagged against the cliff in relief. "Oh, God," she said with a sigh, "what idiots we must have appeared."

A giggle rose to the surface, and she quickly clapped her hand over her mouth. But the nervous tension she had felt was quickly dissolving into laughter as she thought of the absurdity of the situation. "Oh, what we must have looked like!" she cried out softly, and began to laugh again.

Benedict grabbed her arm and quickly walked her toward their horses. "Hush! They will hear you."

"I cannot help it," she whispered back, struggling

to stifle her giggles. "They are no doubt laughing at us, too! When I think of what the expressions on our faces must have been when we came around that corner! Cousin Bertram is too well-bred to betray anything, but I am sure he must have thought we were mad."

"I suspect your cousin Bertram has seen enough of the world that he had a pretty fair idea of what was going on," Benedict retorted dryly.

Camilla's cheeks flamed anew with embarrassment, and she brought her hands up to them, as if to hide them. "I don't know how I shall ever look him in the face again!"

"Well, we *are* married," he pointed out as he tossed her up into her saddle. He mounted his own horse, and they started to ride away. "There would be nothing wrong in newlyweds sneaking a few kisses away from a crowded house."

"Except that we are not really married. And it is still embarrassing to know that he is imagining what we were doing—or worse." She was aware suddenly, as she had never been before, of the motion of the horse beneath her. Her fear and embarrassment over Cousin Bertram's arrival had driven it away momentarily, but the hot ache between her legs had not completely gone away, and she could feel it building again as they rocked along. Desperately she sought for something to say to take her mind off her physical self. "Did you see poor Mr. Oglesby's face? He kept trying to look at anything but us. I would have felt sorry for the man if I hadn't been so busy feeling sorry for myself. No doubt he thinks Bertram's family is a scandalous lot."

"Yes, I would say he was embarrassed, although a wooden countenance appears to be the man's usual expression."

Camilla chuckled. "You are right. I should not be so unkind, I know, but Mr. Oglesby seems such a dull sort of friend for Cousin Bertram. Bertram is such a convivial man. He craves company, and he can always be counted on by a hostess to brighten up a party. I can't think how he became friends with such a silent man as Mr. Oglesby."

"Perhaps it gives him more chance to speak."

Camilla shrugged. "Well, Oglesby is not the sort who is usually Bertram's friend. I have met some of them, and they are generally a silly, frippery lot—more concerned about the cut of their waistcoats than anything else, and most voluble about their inanities, too."

"Interesting." He was silent for a few more minutes as they rode back toward the house. Then he asked casually, "Is Bertram much given to caving?"

"Bertram?" Camilla laughed. "Hardly. It would muss his clothes, you see. I can't remember when I've ever heard of him going into the caves. Even when we were children, he had little liking for it. No, I am sure that their going there would be Mr. Oglesby's doing. And carrying a picnic lunch, yet! They must be planning to spend some time there."

"Mm-hm."

"Odd sort of a place to choose to have a picnic," Camilla went on. "I mean, it's damp and cool, and nothing to sit on but hard rock."

"Doesn't sound very inviting."

"There's only one reason that I can think of to go there."

Benedict looked at her, intrigued. "Really? And what is that?"

Camilla grinned impishly. "Why, to get away from Aunt Beryl, of course."

"Of course. I should have thought of that."

He smiled back at her, and a rush of pure desire swept through her all over again. *How could this man make her feel this way?* No other man had ever had such an effect on her. This afternoon in the cave, when he kissed and caressed her, it had been the most exciting, most breathtaking, thing she had ever known, and somehow she had been positive that there was something waiting for her along that path, something earth-shattering—if only she could reach it.

She wondered if this feeling was what she missed by refusing to marry. Maybe other women routinely experienced this. Aunt Lydia? Aunt Beryl? Her mind boggled at the thought. She could not imagine her prim aunt swept up in throes of passion, no matter what the provocation.

Camilla sneaked another glance at Benedict. *Perhaps it was just him.* Not a routine thing a woman felt with a man, but what a woman felt with just this one man. She looked at his hands on the reins. They were gloveless now; she didn't know what had happened to his thin leather gloves. *Had they wound up on the cave floor during those wild, wonderful moments?* She looked at his long, supple fingers, at the backs of his hands, lightly sprinkled with dark hair. His hands were slender, yet strong, and they handled the horse firmly, capably. She remembered those same hands on her body, caressing her breasts, capable still, and oh, so gentle. Just thinking about it, she felt her nipples flame with heat and harden.

She looked away, her eyes going to his broad shoulders and then sliding down his straight back. They strayed to his thighs, which were clamped around the horse, muscled and taut. Camilla swallowed and turned her head away. She was being a fool, she told herself. *She would not,* absolutely *would not, let him see what effect he had on her.*

When they reached the stables and the groom came running out to take their horses, Benedict bowed and begged her pardon, saying that he thought he would take a walk around the estate before tea time. Camilla readily agreed. There was something in her that desperately wanted to remain in his company, but at the same time she wanted very much to be all alone to examine her feelings. So she turned and hurried into the house and upstairs to her room.

She closed and locked the door and flung herself facedown across her bed. Her thoughts were a jumble; a wild mixture of sensations tingled through her. There was still a pulsation between her legs. Unconsciously her hand stole down her body and slipped in between her thighs. She pressed against the throbbing flesh, closing her eyes as she recalled how it had felt to have his thigh there, rubbing against her, both soothing and increasing the ache. Her hand seemed a very poor substitute for him.

Camilla groaned and rolled over. *Whatever was the matter with her?* She had never had such wild, licentious thoughts or feelings before. She hopped off the bed and rang for Millie. She had to do something; if she lay there thinking and remembering much longer, she was sure that she would go mad. When the maid came, she had her draw a bath. Then she bathed and washed her hair and dried it out by brushing it in front of the fire. By the time she was through with that, she was congratulating herself that she had gotten her unruly emotions under control again. She dressed in the most severe dress she had brought with her and had Millie wrap her hair up in a plain bun.

Satisfied that there was nothing about her of the wild woman who had returned from their excursion, she went up to visit her grandfather.

"Good Gad, girl, what have you done to yourself?" were the old man's first words when she walked into the room. "You look like a nun."

Camilla rolled her eyes. "Oh, Grandpapa."

He motioned for her to sit on the bed beside him and took her hand. He studied her face for a moment, nodding to himself in satisfaction. Finally, he said, "Well, you may have taken it into your head to dress like a dried-up old spinster, but I've got eyes enough to see you don't feel like one."

Camilla looked at him blankly. "What do you mean?"

He chuckled. "Don't be coy with me, missy. It's obvious that your young man has put a sparkle in your eye."

"Oh!" Camilla felt herself blushing. "Grandpapa, really!"

"Anyone can see that there's that certain spark between the two of you. Not many couples have it. It's no wonder you married him so quickly."

Camilla squirmed, wishing that her grandfather

would drop the subject. But, naturally, the old man was like a dog with a bone.

"I like him. You made a good choice, Milla."

"Thank you, Grandpapa."

"He came by to see me this morning. Did he tell you?"

"No." Camilla felt a little uneasy.

"Yes. We had a good talk the other day, and he's dropped in to see me a couple of times."

"What did you talk about?"

"Oh, this and that. Nothing you need worry about. I can trust your young man."

"Trust him? Grandpapa, I don't understand." Camilla's brows rushed together. "Why would you need to trust him? What did you trust him with?"

"Now, now..." He patted her hand reassuringly. "He is just doing a little business for me. Nothing for you to worry about. That's what you've got a husband for."

Irritation rose in Camilla. "I don't need a husband to take care of my affairs. Is that what you talked to him about? My business? My funds?"

"Don't get your dander up, girl. We didn't talk about anything like that. That's more Marlin's place, to be talking with him about your moneys."

"No one need talk to him about it!" Camilla retorted, eyes flashing. "It is my money, and no concern—" She halted, realizing her mistake. Of course her husband would know about her financial affairs. As soon as they were married, her money would have become his. It was one of the many things wrong with the institution of marriage and for which she felt such contempt. "Of...of yours or anyone else's," she finished, trying as best she could to salvage her statement. "*I* told Benedict about my finances. He agreed that I should continue to handle them—along with Marlin, of course."

Her grandfather's mouth dropped open. "What nonsense is this?"

"He is a very modern husband, Grandpapa. He...he believes that my money should remain mine, and I...I shall leave it to our younger children someday. He has ample property."

"Ah, I see. That is probably a wise choice. However, I don't know what good can come of you managing your own moneys. Your grandmother never could keep her clothes allowance in order, let alone invest funds."

"Well, I am not Grandmama. She was very good at herbs and such, and nursing people back to health. I am good at this. She did not need to invest her funds, but I have been doing so with Marlin for years now."

Her grandfather scowled. Her direction of her own funds had been a source of argument between them since the day she turned twenty-one, and she suspected that the Earl was rather disappointed that her finances had not only not suffered under her guidance, but had actually made a substantial profit.

Finally he said, "Well, if that is the way the two of you choose to go on, I suppose it is none of my concern."

Camilla could barely keep her mouth from dropping open. She had never expected to hear such a statement from her grandfather, who had always thought it not only his right, but his duty, to meddle in her life. She realized with some chagrin that his change in attitude was not due to her or to any recognition on his part that she was capable of making good decisions, but was solely because he liked the man who was pretending to be her husband. *If only he knew what the man really was!*

But, then, what was he? She realized that she knew as little about him as her grandfather did. *And what was this piece of business that the earl had entrusted to him?* Camilla knew that if Benedict betrayed the Earl or took advantage of him in some way, it would be her fault.

As soon as she left her grandfather's room, she charged down the hall to her bedroom, hoping to find Benedict alone there. She was determined to have a talk with him. She swung open the door and strode inside, then came to an abrupt halt.

Benedict was indeed in the room. He was sitting in the slipper bathtub in the center of the room, water up to his chest. Camilla stared at him. She felt as if her stomach had fallen to her feet. She opened her mouth and closed it, but no sound came out. Finally she let out a little shriek and whirled around, raising her hands to her face. "I'm sorry. I— I didn't realize—"

"It *is* your room," he pointed out reasonably. She could hear him standing up in the tub. "I was almost through, anyway."

"I'll leave." It was evidence of how slowly her mind was working, she realized, that she had not left the room immediately.

"No need," he replied easily. "It won't take me a minute to dry." Within moments, he went on, "All right, you can turn around now."

She did so, slowly, unsure whether she could meet

his eyes after the embarrassment of their encounter. She forgot the embarrassment when she realized that he was still clad in only his trousers. His powerful chest and shoulders were still bare, the skin gleaming and taut over his muscles.

"Ah…" Camilla cleared her throat, trying to re-gather her scattered thoughts. Benedict turned and picked up his shirt. Camilla found herself watching the play of his muscles across his back.

Benedict turned back and raised his eyebrows ques-tioningly. "You had something you wanted to say to me?"

He was enjoying this, Camilla realized in irritation. *It hadn't rattled him in the slightest, hadn't made him think of their passion this afternoon.* She set her jaw.

"What did you talk to my grandfather about?"

"What do you mean? When? We have talked about several things. You, of course. How his weakness ir-ritates him, the influence that the Elliots have in this part of the country." He trailed off, looking at her as if he hoped that he had satisfied her peculiar request.

"I am talking about this 'business' he had with you." She moved closer to him. The clean scent of his soap clung to his skin, distracting her. She turned away, trying to concentrate. "What was this busi-ness?"

"Business? My dear, how could I have any business with your grandfather? I had never seen him before yesterday."

"He told me you were taking care of some business for him. And don't call me 'my dear.' You have no need to put on a show of affection here. No one can hear you."

He looked startled. "I hadn't realized that I was putting on a show." A sardonic smile curved his lips. "I must have grown so accustomed to thinking of you as my beloved wife that I have some difficulty dropping the role."

Camilla's lips tightened. "Don't be absurd. I want to know what Grandpapa told you. Did he ask you to do something for him? If you take advantage of his trust in you, I swear that I will—"

"Will what?"

"I don't know. But I will see that you pay for it, I promise you that."

"I would not take advantage of your grandfather." He felt a twinge of guilt as it occurred to him that he had done exactly that, using the old man's permission to talk to the servants for his own ends of discovering what had happened to his agents. "I like the old gentleman. He is the last of a dying era."

"He believes you to be my husband. It is only because of that that he entrusted you with information. If you have any decency, you will not use your knowledge to hurt him in any way."

"I have no interest in hurting your grandfather. What do you think I am going to do, anyway?"

"I have no idea. I don't know what he told you."

"If the Earl did not tell you, then I must assume that he did not want you to know," Benedict pointed out calmly. "I can hardly betray his confidence by revealing it to you."

"You are saying that he trusted you, a total stranger, more than he trusted me." She could not hide the tremor, part fury and part hurt, that ran through her voice.

Benedict took an unconscious step toward her, his hand reaching out as though to soothe her. "No, do not think that. Camilla, he loves you very much."

"We are not speaking of love but of trust. Confidence."

"It is not that he does not trust you. It is simply that he does not want to burden you with it. He feels that a man—"

"Would handle it better," Camilla finished bitterly. "Yes, I know. He does not feel that I can even handle my own life better than a strange man can. That is why he was so eager for me to marry. He thinks I need a keeper."

"Someone to take care of you," Benedict amended. "Not a keeper."

"What is the difference?"

"Well, I— Do you never feel the need for someone else's help? Are you that self-sufficient?"

"Help, yes," Camilla responded stiffly. "But not someone to think for me and act for me."

Benedict smiled faintly. "I think it would take a very brave or very foolish man to try to do that."

Her eyes flashed. "You are right about that, at least. But such foolishness seems to be a trait quite common to men. Like Harold—always telling me how I should conduct myself or what I should say. And then he had the audacity to think that I would actually tie myself to him!"

"Your cousin Harold is a fool. You cannot say that most men are like him, I hope."

"No. But whenever they start hanging about me, tossing pretty compliments my way, likening me to a rose—"

He chuckled. "That, at least, is an apt comparison. Beautiful, but full of thorns."

"Ha! The similarity is more that they want to cut me off and stick me in a vase of their choosing."

"Then you should see my house. No roses in vases. They are all growing riotously outside. Wild—for that is how I like them."

Camilla raised her head sharply. His voice was low and rich, and his words stirred her. He was looking at her in a way that stirred her even more. "What—what do you mean?"

"I mean that you cannot judge all men by a single standard."

He put his hands on her bare arms and slid them upward. Camilla's knees turned to wax, and all the fiery sensations that she had so determinedly buried earlier came alive again, skimming through her.

She pulled away. "No."

Light flared in his eyes, and he started to go after her, but he pulled up. "You are right. I'm sorry. We must dress for dinner."

She had not gotten the answers she wanted, but Camilla was not going to press the point. She knew that she was lucky to have escaped so easily from him just now; Benedict was capable of much more determined pursuit.

She turned away and went to the dressing room to choose the dress she would wear this evening. Oddly enough, she found that she did not feel lucky. She felt...disappointed. *Obviously Benedict had not been as affected by what happened at the cave as she had been.*

Camilla looked through her evening gowns, and her

eyes fell on one of deep royal blue satin that complemented her eyes well. Its neckline was lower-cut than that of most of her gowns, but right now that suited her mood. In fact, she thought that she would not tuck into it the lace fichu that she usually did. And her hairstyle would have to be changed, as well. She rang for her maid and set about getting ready.

By the time she was ready, Benedict had left the room and was waiting in the hall, leaning against the wall with an air of great patience. When Camilla opened the door and stepped out, she was gratified to see that he straightened immediately, his dark eyes lighting with an unholy flame. His gaze raked down the front of her dress, and she saw his hands tighten at his sides. Camilla felt somehow vindicated. Gracing him with a smile, she took his arm.

Dinner was unusually tedious that evening. Camilla had difficulty keeping her mind on the conversation, which was dominated by her aunt Beryl, and it did not help matters that every time she glanced across the table at Benedict, she found him gazing at her. The meal was followed by a stultifying hour in the music room. The men were mercifully absent for the first few minutes, off enjoying a cigar and brandy in the study. But they soon joined the women, and Camilla discovered that if there was anything worse than having to listen to Aunt Beryl's daughters play insipid piano pieces, it was having to listen to them under Benedict's unswerving gaze.

Just having him watch her, his eyes drifting from her hair to her lips to her breasts to her legs, made her feel so warm that she was afraid she was flushing bright red in front of everyone. Camilla plied her fan to cool her heated face and tried to ignore the questions that hovered at the back of her mind: *What was going to happen in their room tonight? Would he try to seduce her? And if he did, how would she respond?*

When at last Aunt Beryl raised her fan to hide a yawn and announced that she was ready to go to bed, Camilla rose with alacrity, saying that she was rather tired herself. Aunt Lydia cast her an odd look, for usually Aunt Beryl's retiring was the signal to break out the cards or launch into more interesting conversations. But then she smiled knowingly, her cheeks turning pink, and Camilla found her own face reddening in response. She glanced at Benedict, who had also risen and come forward to offer her his arm. He smiled at her in a way that denoted not amusement, but a sort of sensual satisfaction, and when she placed her hand on his arm, he brushed his other hand over hers.

They followed Aunt Beryl and her daughters up the stairs, neither Camilla nor Benedict speaking. When they reached the bedroom, they found her maid there waiting for her. Camilla tossed her fan and gloves on the vanity table, sneaking a glance at Benedict out of the corner of her eye. He was standing by the bed, his gaze fixed on her, his expression unreadable. Millie came forward and began to unbutton the multitude of tiny buttons down the back of her dress. The two sides of the bodice peeled away, exposing the smooth white expanse of Camilla's back.

Benedict made a muffled noise. Camilla glanced at him. He was standing with one hand wrapped around the post of the bed, his whole body rigid and his eyes blazing in his set face. Suddenly he turned, as if wrenching himself away from the bed, and strode out the door.

Camilla turned away. She told herself that it was for the best, that Benedict had done the right thing. But her words could not get rid of the disappointment that filled her.

Benedict marched rapidly down the long hall, away from Camilla's room. He thought he might very well go mad at any moment. He had told himself that he could be with Camilla this evening and not make love to her, but at the last minute he had had to bolt. When her maid unbuttoned the back of her dress and the sides fell away, revealing the sweet curve of her spine, something in him had snapped. He had known that he had to get away or he would fall upon her like an animal.

He came to the stairs and stopped, clutching the rail and trying to decide what he was going to do. Instead, he found himself thinking about Camilla. He remembered this afternoon, when he had stepped back from her, and the way she had looked—her face flushed with the heat of passion, her lips soft and swollen, slightly open in shock, and that one sweet white breast exposed, cupped and lifted by the neckline of her bodice, the nipple damp and rosy from his mouth, pointing eagerly toward him.

Just thinking about it made him almost groan aloud. His manhood was stiff as a board, and his skin felt as if he had been stripped and doused in burning pitch. There was nothing he wanted to do at this moment but turn around and go right back to her bedroom.

But *that*, he knew, would be insanity. He could not

defile a woman under his protection. It would endanger his mission, violate his principles, and constitute a hundred other sins—none of which he could recall at the moment for the abominable thrumming of his blood through his temples. *Why did she have to smell so good and taste so sweet, like the ripest, most succulent fruit?*

He had tormented himself all through supper with the most lurid sexual fantasies. He had imagined pulling Camilla onto the long table in front of everyone and tearing off her clothes, then feasting on her as he had feasted on her breast earlier. He'd daydreamed about her sliding out of her chair and crawling under the table to him and unbuttoning his trousers, caressing and playing with his manhood until it was full and hard, quivering with eagerness, and then taking him into her mouth and bringing him to climax. He had thought of seating her on his lap and letting her ride him, or of pulling her down to the floor and throwing up her skirts and plunging into her right there. He had imagined taking her on every piece of furniture in the dining room, and later in the music room—and in every conceivable position. As a result, he had spent a highly uncomfortable evening.

The last straw had been when he stood there, rooted to the floor, while the maid began to undress her. He knew he could not take any more of this torture without giving in to his desires. That was why he had to occupy himself in some way until Camilla was safely in bed and asleep—and, hopefully, divert his own mind from these tormenting imaginings.

He drew a long breath and let it out. After a few more minutes, feeling somewhat calmer, he started down the hall to the Earl's room. It was not late; he and Camilla had gone up to bed early, when Aunt Beryl did, so he was hopeful that the Earl's valet might yet be up. He had not talked to Jenkins yet; he knew, ruefully, that he had been putting it off because the old servant resented him for the Earl's sending him away whenever Benedict came to visit.

Well, it had to be done, and now, he supposed, was as good a time as any.

A soft tap on the door brought Jenkins to it. The old man frowned as he stuck his head out and whispered, "His Lordship is asleep, sir, and cannot be disturbed."

"I understand. But it is you I wanted to speak to."

"Oh. I see." Jenkins hesitated, and Benedict felt sure he would have liked to refuse, but years of training won out. He reached back inside the room for a candle, then slipped out the door, closing it softly behind him and motioning for Benedict to follow him. He led him down the hall to the next door, which he opened, and ushered Benedict into the room.

It was a very small chamber, with only a narrow bed, a chair and a small chest of drawers. Benedict surmised that it had formerly been a dressing room, a guess borne out by the side door opening into what must be the Earl's bedroom. Punctiliously polite, Jenkins offered Benedict the straight-backed chair and sat down himself on the edge of the bed. His face gave nothing away, but the rigidity of his posture made it clear that he would have preferred to be elsewhere.

Benedict smiled at him. "His Lordship thinks very highly of you," he told him.

Jenkins gave a small nod. "Thank you, sir."

"I am sure that is why he asked me to talk to you. Did he tell you?"

"He requested that I speak freely to you, yes, sir."

"The Earl seems quite worried about this smuggling ring. I told him I would do my best to help him."

Jenkins struggled for a moment to hold on to his stiff distrust, but his concern for his employer overcame him, and he leaned forward, looking worried. "He has been somewhat bothered by it, sir, for several weeks. It worries him constantly, and the doctor says that is not good for him. But nothing I can say soothes him. He—he trusts you. He told me that Miss Camilla chose well. Can you help him? Will you do something about it?"

"I shall do all I can," Benedict promised readily. "But at the moment, I am still fumbling in the dark. I talked to several of the servants, including Purdle. The main thing I have learned from them is that there appears to be a new leader of the smugglers, but that no one knows who he is. Do you think that is true?" Benedict had been unable to tell whether no one actually knew or they were merely refusing to talk to an outsider, no matter what the Earl had instructed them.

"I think it is the truth. I have not heard anyone even hint that they knew who he was. There are one or two men who seem to be his henchmen, closer to him than the others. One of them often gives orders. But the orders have to come from someone else. He is too stupid to act on his own."

"You know this man?"

Jenkins shrugged. "Yes, but I find it doubtful that even he has seen the man's face. No one but a fool would let this fellow know who he was, and the new leader is no fool.''

"I could talk to him nonetheless. Who is this man?''

The valet hesitated for a moment, then shrugged. "If the Earl says to trust you, then I must. His name is Evans. He is a drunken lout who lives in the village. His wife died long ago—they say she was lucky. But you will get little out of him, I think.''

"What else do you know about the new man? Some have said that he talks as if he was from around here.''

Jenkins grimaced. "Or *tries* to copy the accent, anyway.''

"Are you saying that he is not from the area?''

"That I do not know. What I am saying is I've heard that he tries to talk like one of the locals. But sometimes his accent slips or he uses too fancy a word. In short, there are those who say he is Quality.''

12

Benedict straightened, his heart suddenly racing. It was what he and Sedgewick had talked about time and again—the possibility that the man they were looking for was from the upper classes, someone Richard Winslow would have readily invited into his home, even into his inner sanctum, his study.

"A gentleman? Are you sure?" he asked carefully, trying not to give away his excitement.

"No," Jenkins admitted. "Not sure. I'm just saying there's some suspicion."

"Is there anything beside the slips in his speech?"

"Well, I heard that one man got a glimpse of his hand one time, and it looked like a gentleman's hand, white and uncallused."

Benedict sat back, looking at the man. "How do you know so much? Even Purdle didn't tell me this."

Jenkins returned his gaze without wavering. "Purdle is a fine man, Mr. Lassiter, but he is not from here. He came to work for the Earl some thirty years ago. He's from Sussex originally, I believe. My family, on the other hand, has been here as long as the Chevingtons—perhaps longer.'' His blue eyes twinkled. ''I have connections, perhaps, that Purdle does not.''

''I see.'' Being an outsider, it seemed, was a stigma that was rather difficult to overcome among these people. ''Then perhaps you can tell me this, too, why is the Earl *so* upset? *So* worried?''

Jenkins's expression was perfectly blank. ''I beg your pardon, sir? I'm afraid I don't know what you mean.''

''I think you do, and I think you know why, too. The Earl seemed uncommonly perturbed by these local disturbances, more so than I would assume a man in his position would be.''

''His Lordship is a very good landlord, sir. He likes to know what is going on among his people.''

''But that doesn't cause the kind of anxiety I saw in his eyes. I think both you and Purdle know, but Purdle would not tell me. However, I am hoping that your concern for the Earl is greater than your immediate loyalty to your employer. I must know everything if I am to help him.''

Jenkins sighed and looked away. He seemed to come to some decision, for he turned back to Benedict and said, ''You're right. He is quite worried, sir. It's, well, it's Master Anthony. His Lordship is afraid that he has joined the smugglers.''

Benedict, who had been leaning forward, intent on drawing the answer out of the old man, now sat back with a sigh. ''That is what I feared.''

''There's nothing wrong with the boy,'' Jenkins assured him earnestly. ''He is a wonderful lad, full of life and fun. He always has been. It's just that, well, sometimes, he doesn't think. He has been a trifle spoiled, perhaps, and he gets bored here. His Lordship cannot bear to let go of him, you see.''

"Better to do that than to let him sink the family with his mischief.''

Jenkins winced at his choice of words, but said only, "Yes, I tried to convince His Lordship to let him go up to Oxford now that he is eighteen, but he would not hear of it. And as for the army, which is what Master Anthony wants to do...well, it doesn't bear thinking of.''

"Why do you think he is involved with the smuggling ring?''

"Purdle and I have seen him sneaking out at night. It isn't the first time he has done so, by any means, but it's been much more frequent of late. Every time we have seen him sneaking out, the next morning our delivery of brandy is on the doorstep.''

Benedict sighed. "Everyone turns such a blind eye to the smuggling here. It's no wonder the boy was intrigued by it.''

"Mayhap, sir, but for an Elliot—a future Earl, no less—to be involved in it...! Why, it would break His Lordship's heart if anything were to happen to that boy. That would be even worse than the scandal. And God knows the scandal would be bad enough.''

"Yes, well, we must make sure that there is no scandal.'' He paused, then continued cautiously, "Anthony is a smart lad, and daring. He could turn his frustrated yearning for the army into another sort of campaigning. Could it be he who is the gentleman leading the smugglers?''

"No!'' Jenkins's face flushed red with anger. "Never. You don't know Master Anthony like I do, or you would not say that. It is one thing to help out for a lark. But he would never, ever, murder anyone.''

"Soldiers kill. You say he has a longing to be a soldier.''

"On command. For his country. Yes, then the lad could kill, I suppose. And he would do so to protect his family or, indeed, any innocent person who was threatened. But he has a good heart. He would never kill anyone for gain. Especially not Nat Crowder. Nat was Jem Crowder's brother, and Jem and Master Anthony have been friends since they were little tykes. It'd be almost like killing one of his own family. Worse, really, if you were talking about the rector, whom he cannot like.'' Jenkins stopped abruptly, looking embarrassed. "Oh. Pardon me, sir. I should not have said that.''

"Perfectly understandable. I have visited with the Right Reverend Harold Elliot, you see.''

"Yes, sir.''

"Well, thank you, Jenkins.'' Benedict rose from his chair.

"Anything to help ease His Lordship's mind, sir. If you don't mind my asking...have you told Miss Camilla about this?''

"No. The Earl told me to keep silent.''

"Ah. Very good, sir.'' Jenkins looked relieved. "I was hoping that was the case. I fear Miss Camilla would get in a regular taking if she was to find out about the young master's escapades.''

Benedict suspected that, far from not knowing about them, Miss Camilla was probably neck-deep in them, from the way he had seen the two of them whispering together like conspirators. However, he said nothing to disillusion the aging servant, just bade him good-night and walked back down the hall to his own room.

The room was silent when he walked in. A lamp burned low on the table, lighting the room dimly. In the faint golden light, he could see Camilla's sleeping form on the bed, as well as his own couch, a blanket and pillow thoughtfully left upon it.

He walked to the sofa and began to undress, glancing over now and then at Camilla's recumbent form. She was turned on her side, away from him, and all he could see was the dark cloud of hair above the covers. He wondered if she was really asleep. He thought of a pair of fine blue eyes and of the way her lips had yielded sweetly beneath his.

A few days ago, the pretense of marriage had seemed like nothing but a nuisance, and sleeping in the same room with her had been a fine jest on her for creating such a pretense in the first place. Tonight, sleeping fifteen feet away from her bed did not strike him as particularly funny.

Mentally cursing, he lay down on the couch and wrapped the blanket around him. He adjusted the pillow beneath his head and closed his eyes. But sleep would not come. He kept imagining what it would be like to go to her bedside and pull back the cover, to look at her lying there in her nightgown. The gown would be white, he knew, and he could picture it rucked up around her legs, exposing her shapely calves and thighs. He would be able to see the dark circles of her nipples beneath the thin material, the soft swell of her breasts and hips. He thought of tracing her sleeping face with his forefinger, of touching her forehead and cheeks and lips, of trailing his finger down over the velvet softness of her throat.

Benedict turned his head into his pillow to stifle a groan. He was so suddenly, poundingly hard he felt as if he might burst, yet he could not stop thinking about her. About kneeling beside the bed and taking her nipple into his mouth, cloth and all, and pulling gently. When he pulled away, the wet cloth could cling to the hard pink bud, inviting his return. He thought of sliding his hand down her body to the apex of her legs, slipping in between them and stroking until she was hot and damp with pleasure. He could hear her moan, feel her thrusting up against his hand, wanting more.

This was insane! He bit into the pillow and wrapped his arms around his torso, willing himself under control. So he lay, wide awake, refusing to give in to his desires, through much of the seemingly interminable night.

He did not drift off to sleep until the pale light of dawn began to show around the edges of the drapes. Then, just as he was finally sliding down into the darkness, the creak of the door brought him wide awake.

Benedict turned, his hand sliding down to his boot, beside the sofa, and the knife that was strapped inside it. He pretended still to slumber, watching through slitted eyes as a man tiptoed across the room toward where Camilla lay sleeping.

The man crossed in front of him, and Benedict relaxed, recognizing the slender form as that of Camilla's cousin Anthony. He started to sit up and comment on the young man's unusual visiting hours, but he restrained himself. The wiser course, he knew, would be to watch and find out exactly what had brought the young Viscount here at this hour of the morning.

Anthony leaned over the bed and shook Camilla's shoulder. She came awake with a low cry, and Anthony quickly clapped his hand over her mouth.

"Shh…Camilla, it is I."

Camilla recognized Anthony's voice, and, blinking the sleep from her eyes, she could see his features now in the dim light. She pushed his hand away irritatedly.

"What in the name of heaven are you doing?"

"Waking you," he answered reasonably, still in the same low whisper. "Get up. I need you."

"Why?"

He shook his head and turned to look over his shoulder at the couch where Benedict slept. Camilla followed his gaze and understood. He was afraid that Benedict would awaken, and he did not want him to know why Anthony was here. She nodded her understanding and slid quietly out of bed. She stuck her feet into her slippers and wrapped the heavy dressing gown around her, all the while keeping a cautious eye on the sleeping form on the sofa. With Anthony on her heels, she stole out of the room.

Outside in the hall, she strode across to the long, narrow table where Anthony had left his candle and turned to face him. "All right. Now what is going on?"

"Shh," he cautioned her again. "You'll wake everybody up."

"Oh. You mean the way you woke me?"

He grinned sheepishly. "All right. I'm sorry. I wouldn't have done it, Milla, except that it's an emergency."

"Isn't it always?"

"No. I really mean it. There is another man's life at stake here."

"What?" Camilla straightened, all teasing erased from her voice. Her eyes flew instinctively toward her door across the hall.

"No, not him," Anthony said impatiently, picking up the candlestick in one hand and taking her by the arm with the other. He started down the hall, pulling Camilla along.

"Then who?" Camilla asked as she hurried along beside him.

"I don't know."

"Anthony, you aren't making any sense. Are you bosky?"

"No!" he answered indignantly, forgetting his stricture to be silent. "I haven't had a drop to drink since a cup of wine at dinner last night...where, I must say, you and Mr. Lassiter were acting most peculiarly."

"Don't be silly." Camilla was grateful that the dim light of the hallway hid her rising blush.

"*I* was not the one being silly," he replied significantly. "The two of you were making sheep's eyes at each other all night. And don't think that I am the only one who saw it. Mama was going on about it for ages after you left last night. Even that cipher Thorne noticed it. He kept blathering on about love in bloom."

"Oh, no, really?" Camilla choked back a gurgle of laughter.

Anthony gave her a jaundiced look. "You wouldn't have thought it was so bloody funny if *you* had been the one who had to endure his poesy."

"I'm sorry. Poor Anthony. You are quite right. I am sure I would have been bored out of my mind."

He nodded, vindicated. They had reached the top of the stairs by now, and Anthony stopped to pick up a small case there. Camilla recognized the worn cloth bag immediately. It had belonged to her grandmother originally, and for years it had contained the bandages and ointments required for household emergencies.

Camilla eyed it now with misgiving. "What are you doing with that?"

"I told you, a man's life is at stake. Now would you stop asking questions and come on?"

His words frightened her, and she followed him quickly down the stairs. They slipped out of the house by the solarium door and hurried across the garden. The horizon to the east was lightening, turning the whole sky a dull gray and giving them enough light to see clearly as they made their way along the path toward the beach. They went down the cliff trail as quickly as it was possible to traverse the steep path, and when they reached the sand, Anthony led her at a trot toward the long spit of land that led across the water to Keep Island.

"Hurry up. The tide is rising," Anthony told her as they started across the narrow strip of land.

Camilla could see that indeed it was. There was a path of land no wider than a foot between the two sides of the ocean, and even as they walked across, the water was beginning to crash over it.

"You're going to strand us on the other side!" Camilla protested, following him and watching her step, so as not to slip and wind up in the water. The water on either side grew quickly deeper as they advanced over the spit of land, and she had no desire to receive a dousing in the chilly predawn ocean.

"Don't be daft," Anthony replied in a brotherly fashion. "I took my boat over here earlier. I just came back to get you on foot because it was faster."

The hulking ruins of the keep grew ever clearer in the increasing light. The first rays of the sun struck its eastern walls, turning them the same warm color as the stones of the present-day Chevington Park. But nothing could disguise the bleakness of its tumbled walls or the black marks left by fire.

Behind them, the water began to wash over the lower central section of the land bridge. They reached the island and climbed up the crumbling stone steps to higher ground and hurried on into the ruins. They did not look back. And so they did not see the figure standing on the cliff on the other side, a hand shading his face, watching them.

Frustration surged up in Benedict. He had had to stop to dress before he followed Camilla and Anthony, and it had eaten up precious time, as had the fact that he strayed a little off course and lost sight of them for a few minutes. By the time he reached the top of the cliff, they were almost all the way across the spit of land to Keep Island.

He headed down the path to the beach at a reckless clip, stumbling once and almost falling. He ran across the sand to the bridge to the island, but he had not gone ten feet onto the path before he saw that it was impossible.

He stopped, his breath going out of him in a rush. With a quiet curse, he turned and walked back to the beach. He stood for a long moment, looking out over the narrow waterway to the island. Camilla and her cousin had disappeared into the ruins of the keep. He wondered what had sent them rushing madly over there in the dawn. *Had it been a planned excursion? Or an emergency?* He had the gnawing feeling that old Jenkins's suspicions were true, and that young Anthony was involved in smuggling. *But apparently Camilla was involved in it, too.*

His heart thudded in his chest, making him feel slightly sick. It was absurd that Camilla could be in a smuggling ring. Still, he was learning rapidly that Camilla was a warmhearted creature who would do almost anything to help the ones she loved. And she was not one to count the risks. What she did, she did wholeheartedly. If her beloved cousin needed her...

Benedict's mouth twisted. *Just how much did she love her cousin? What would she do for him? And was it smuggling they were involved in, or something else...something worse?* Black emotions swirled within him.

He turned and stalked back toward the house.

Anthony led Camilla through the large room, open to the sky, that had once been the great hall of the keep. The inner walls were down, mere piles of rubble over which they had to climb, and only one of the outer walls was completely intact. They walked across the grassy area and around another pile of rubble. They were sheltered from the wind by the remains of the outer wall as they made their way to what had once been the kitchens of the keep, though little remained now except the massive fireplace. By now Camilla had a good idea where they were going, an idea that was confirmed when Anthony led her straight toward the ruins of the back wall of the kitchens. They skirted a pile of large stone blocks and ducked behind them. A spreading bush grew there, and Anthony pushed aside its branches. He squatted down and crept under and behind the bush. Camilla watched him in exasperation, her hands on her hips.

"Anthony! I'm not crawling around in the cellars. I have gotten too old for it. What do you have down there? Why can't you just tell me about it?"

"No, you have to see for yourself." Anthony turned back toward her, pushing aside the branches so that she could enter.

Camilla bent down, looking at the square wooden door set into the ground beneath the bush. The wood was old and weathered, but still thick and sturdy. An iron ring was set into it on one side, and now Anthony curled his hand through the ring and tugged sharply. The door came up, though not easily, its rusty metal hinges squealing.

Camilla had found the door when she was a child, playing in the ruins, and later she had shown it to Anthony. They had often scared themselves silly by climbing down into its dark depths with their lanterns and exploring. The door had been set in the stone floor of the kitchens. Though many of the stones had been dug up and hauled across the water to pave the driveway of Chevington Park, and grass had grown up over much of what had once been the floor, the door down into the cellars had remained, its edges hidden by the grass. Camilla and Anthony had torn the grass away in those long-ago days when they played here, but

Camilla would have supposed that the grass had reclaimed it. Instead, the grass had been neatly cut away all around and lay in a pile beside it.

Camilla cast Anthony a suspicious look. "Anthony! Have you been using the cellars for the smuggled brandy?"

"No! I swear—I would never show this to anyone outside the family. I haven't told a soul about the cellars or this door. But it seemed an excellent place to hide— Well, you will see."

He was already swinging down into the hole, searching for the rungs of the ladder with his feet. He scrambled down the ladder. "Wait." His voice came back muffled. "I have a light down here."

After a moment, light flared into life below the door. Camilla peered down into the hole. Anthony stood at the bottom, holding a lantern in one hand and gazing up at her. Beside him stood a sturdy wooden ladder, obviously not the same worm-eaten relic she and he had ventured down as children.

Camilla sighed. She knew that a woman her age ought to behave with more dignity. But she could not resist the siren lure of the dark mystery below. Hiking up her nightdress and dressing gown, then rolling them at the waist, she anchored them securely with the belt of the dressing gown. With her legs unencumbered to the knee, she crawled backward into the hole, searching with her foot for the first rung of the ladder.

The way down was not as long as she had remembered from her childhood, and soon she was standing on the ground beside her cousin. Anthony grinned at her boyishly and raised his lantern, giving her a better view of the room. They were in the earthen cellar where once the cooks had stored their foodstuffs. It was empty now, except for a few rotting barrels.

Anthony started off toward the low doorway in the far wall, and Camilla followed him, remembering how they used to explore down here, unwinding a spool of yarn behind them, like Theseus in the labyrinth, so that they could find their way back. There was a network of other rooms spreading away from here, some large and some small. Anthony had always claimed that if they searched far enough, they would come upon the dungeons where prisoners had been kept in the Middle Ages. They had never found them, but, then, their nerve had never lasted long enough for them to go very far.

Camilla wondered if Anthony had explored the cellars more thoroughly during the past few years. It seemed like exactly something he would do.

"Don't tell me you have found your oubliettes and torture chambers," she said teasingly as they crossed a long, narrow, low-ceilinged room.

"No," Anthony confessed with a grin. "I've tried, though. I am afraid our ancestors were more interested in storing things than in holding prisoners."

"A boring lot."

"Yes, weren't they?"

"Anthony...where are we going?"

"Just a moment. We're almost there. I couldn't go very far."

"What do you mean?"

He entered another room and turned to his right. Another, even lower, door opened into another room. Unlike the rest of the cellars, the room beyond was not dark. A low golden light burned within. Camilla blinked in surprise. *Why had Anthony left a light burning here?*

Anthony bent over, almost in half, and walked through the doorway, and Camilla ducked down, following him. As she came through the door, she could see the whole small room at a glance. She gasped and stood up too quickly, striking her back on the doorway.

"Anthony!"

A man lay on the floor before them, taking up half the space of the room. He was lying on his back on a blanket spread on the ground, and another blanket lay on top of him, though he had pushed it down so that it covered only his legs. A coat, rolled up, served as a pillow. He was dressed in dark, rough clothing. He was of medium height, with pale skin and light brown, curling hair. His face was flushed, and there were drops of moisture on his forehead and upper lip. His eyes were closed, and he lay still, his chest rising and falling in slow, shallow breaths.

Camilla stared at him. Even though Anthony had said that a man's life was at stake, she had taken his words as exaggeration. She had not been prepared to find a man down here in the cellars, much less one who was obviously quite ill.

"Anthony, who is he? What is he doing here?"

"I don't know who he is. He is down here because I brought him here. It seemed the safest place. I found him on the beach, you see, and I didn't dare take him home. This was the only other place that was close, where he could be sheltered from the elements."

Camilla went forward and dropped down on her knees beside the man. She was no expert on medical matters, but over the years the minor cuts and scrapes and ills that had occurred at Chevington Park had usually fallen to her. Lydia had never had the temperament for treating illness, and since the servants were accustomed to looking toward the mistress of the house for treatment, from long years of doing so with Camilla's grandmother, Camilla had taken on the burden after her grandmother's death.

She curled her fingers around the man's wrist. His pulse was tumultuous, and his skin was fiery to the touch. "This man has a high fever, Anthony. You need to take him to the doctor."

"No. At least, not yet. Please, Camilla, can't you try to do something for him? Grandmama always said you were good at it."

"That was with colds and minor fevers and such. What happened to him? Why is there a bandage here?" She pointed to his shoulder, where a white bandage peeked out from beneath his shirt.

"That's not the only one," Anthony said grimly. He reached down and unbuttoned the man's shirt, revealing another white bandage that was wrapped around his rib cage. He pushed up the stranger's sleeve to show another long strip on his arm. Camilla noticed that there were several other red scratches on his arms and hands, not bad enough to be bandaged.

"Anthony…what happened to him?"

He shook his head. "I don't know. I wasn't there." He glanced at her and saw the frown on her forehead. "No, don't go thinking I was involved in this. I just found him the other day. He was lying on the beach, bleeding. It looks like he was stabbed to me. All these scratches and everything. And the one on his chest is long and shallow, as though someone had tried to stick a knife in him, and it hit the bone and slid along it.''

"Please.'' Camilla swallowed against the bile that rose in her throat at Anthony's description of his wound.

"Oh. Sorry. I forget sometimes that you are a female.''

Camilla shot him a darkling glance. "Why, thank you.''

"You know what I mean. You've always been a real game 'un.'' He hunkered down on the other side of the wounded man. "I found him near the Point, where there are so many jumbles of rocks. You know?''

Camilla nodded her understanding.

"He was hiding back in some rocks. I only noticed him because Bumper was with me, and he went nosing over there. I went to see what interested him so, and there was this chap. He was unconscious, just lying there with a pistol beside him. I picked it up, and it smelled of gunpowder, so he had obviously fired it. And he had just as clearly been cut up. I splashed a little water on him, and finally he came round.''

"Then he hasn't been like this the whole time? He was conscious for a while?''

"Yes. He didn't have the fever when I found him. He had just passed out from losing so much blood. When he saw me, he looked scared, but I assured him that I wanted to help him. He saw I meant him no harm. He told me that he had been attacked. Someone had been hiding amongst the rocks and jumped out at him. He said they struggled, but he managed to pull out his gun, and the fellow took off. He fired it at him, but he didn't think he hit him. I looked around a bit, and I could not see a trail of blood, so I think he was right.''

''Anthony! You talk so lightly of such things.''

Her young cousin shrugged, and suddenly Camilla was aware of how little he was still a boy. Somehow, when she wasn't looking, he had changed into a man, with a man's frame and a face that had seen something of life. She realized all over again how foolish it was of her grandfather to keep him shut up here at Chevington Park.

''Well, I've seen a few cuts before, and once Jem's cousin— Well, never mind about that. The thing is, I had to do something to help the fellow. At first I couldn't think where to take him, but then I remembered the keep and the cellars, and I thought they would be an excellent place to hide him.''

''I don't understand why you didn't take him to the doctor. Or back home. Even Aunt Beryl wouldn't turn away an injured man. And the authorities should know about his being attacked. They could be out looking for the man who tried to murder him. You should have gone to the magistrate. In fact, we ought still to go to him.''

''John Hamersmith?'' Anthony let out a brief, contemptuous bark of laughter. ''Do you honestly think he would be able to deal with a murderer running loose about the countryside? You know he always just ran to Grandpapa whenever he had a real problem. And he's never had to deal with something like attempted murder. Why, the biggest thing that's happened here was Boly Baker stealing Mrs. Runford's hen.''

Camilla sighed. She knew that that was true. Mr. Hamersmith was a ditherer, and she, for one, would not want to place her own life in his hands. "No, I guess you are right."

"I was afraid that if this man's attacker knew that he was still alive and around here somewhere, he would try to finish the job. It would be better if I kept him secret until he was well again."

"But what...what if he dies?" Camilla asked quietly.

He stared at her for a moment. "I—I don't know. I guess then we would have to tell someone. The magistrate, I suppose. But he won't die, Milla. You won't let him."

"You have a touching faith in me," Camilla told him dryly. "So why didn't you bring me down here to help him when you found him?"

"For one thing, I knew you would make a great fuss about it, just like this," he retorted. "Besides, at the time, he wasn't feverish. He even managed to walk most of the way here with my help. I thought if I bandaged his wounds and let him rest, he would be all right. But I guess the effort of getting here was too much for him. I should have gone back and gotten a horse and put him on it, but I didn't want to leave him, you see. I thought that his attacker might decide to come back in the daylight and finish him off. But he lost consciousness on me before I got him across the land bridge to the island, and I had to carry him over on my back. He woke up once when I was tending to him, but he was obviously feeling quite bad. Then, the next time I came, he had this fever. I'm afraid that he developed an infection. When I got here this morning, I realized I was going to have to have your help.''

Camilla looked at the wounded man doubtfully. ''I will try. But I'm not sure I can do anything for him.''

She opened the bag of supplies and looked through it. She pulled out a vial of dark brown liquid. ''Do you have any water?''

In answer, Anthony pulled out a jug from the corner of the room and opened a box to take out a glass. Camilla poured a little water into the glass and added a few drops of the brown liquid from the vial, then swirled it around.

''All right. Now we need to get this down him. You will have to help me.''

Anthony got behind the man and lifted his head and shoulders, holding him propped against him. Camilla lifted the glass to the stranger's lips and tilted it, saying, ''Drink.''

The man did as she said. Camilla wasn't sure if he was responding to her command or simply reacting to the glass being placed at his lips. He grimaced at the bitter taste of the mixture, however, and turned his head away.

''He has to drink it,'' Camilla told Anthony. ''It's for his fever. It will help to bring it down.''

''What is it?'' Anthony cast an uncertain look at the glass. ''It looks pretty ghastly.''

''A decoction of feverfew and some other herbs. It was one of Grandmama's recipes, and I made some for Mrs. Horton last time I was here. She said it did wonders for her.''

''All right. I'll hold his head. You pour it in.''

It was not an easy task, but after several efforts—

and with a good bit of the liquid spilled on the man's shirt—they managed to get most of it down him. Then Camilla made a paste of herbs and water. She unwrapped the bandages to reveal two red, puckered wounds. As gently as she could, she pressed the paste against them and rebandaged him.

As she worked, she and Anthony talked. "Has he said nothing else?" she asked.

"Very little. I haven't been here the whole time, obviously. You know how suspicious Purdle and Jenkins are. They are always watching me, sure I'm about to fall into some sort of mischief. And Aunt Beryl's almost as bad, wanting an explanation each time I don't come down for dinner. Besides, I was afraid his attacker might be lurking about, watching, and would notice if I spent much time here. So after I bandaged him, I left him a jug of water and some bread and cheese I'd brought over from the Park. I didn't see him again until the next morning. He woke up then, but he was clearly feeling rather rough, and I didn't want to press him. He seemed wary about answering my questions. I could tell he didn't completely trust me."

"After you had saved his life?"

He shrugged. "He has a right to be suspicious. After all, someone did ambush him. He doesn't know but what I saved him only for purposes of my own. I asked him what his name was, but he said that it was better I didn't know."

Camilla shook her head as she carefully applied the herbal paste to his wounds. "This is most mysterious. Anthony, I cannot help but think that you are involved

in something you should not be. I wish we had someone we could turn to.''

Anthony nodded. ''I do, too. I wanted to tell Grandpapa, but he is far too sick. I wouldn't tell that dolt
Cousin Harold anything. And Cousin Bertram would
probably just say, 'Oh, my,' and disapprove of how
the bandage spoils the line of the shirt.''

Camilla smiled. ''That is probably true.'' She
paused, then began, ''What about—''

''No! I am not going to that Benedict chap with
this!'' Anthony burst out. ''He can't be trusted with
it. Why, we don't even know his last name.''

''But if he really is a customs agent, as you said,
he would know someone in authority, perhaps, someone who could do something about this.''

''More likely, he'd turn us all in. For all I know,
he is the one who stabbed this man.''

''Anthony!'' Camilla whirled to stare at him, her
eyes wide with shock. ''No! How can you say such a
thing?''

''Very easily. We know nothing about him. Perhaps
that is why he was lurking about that night you met
him. He was waiting to ambush this man. You just
gave him a better place to start from when you opened
our house to him.''

''Benedict is not a murderer.''

''How do you know?''

''I just do. It's absurd to even think it. Why would
a customs officer go about stabbing people, anyway?''

''I don't know. Perhaps he isn't one. Perhaps he is
a smuggler himself. Maybe he is the one who is taking
over the smuggling ring. Maybe he killed Nat Crowder, too.''

"That is the silliest thing I ever heard of!" Camilla retorted, her eyes flashing. "Benedict is not a smuggler or a killer! I won't have you saying such things about him."

"It isn't as if he is really your husband," Anthony pointed out. "Egad, we better hope he is not the killer or a smuggler, for then you'd really be in the suds. What if he got arrested for murder, and here's everyone thinking that he is your husband?"

"Well, they won't, because he won't get arrested. He is *not* a killer."

"I am not taking the chance and turning this man over to him."

"But if he is a customs officer, he—"

"Camilla! Don't you see? I think this fellow is a smuggler."

"What?" Camilla looked back down at her patient, then at Anthony. "But I've never seen him before. He isn't from around here."

"No. But I saw him the other night when I was helping to unload the boat."

"What? How do you know it was he?"

"He has a ring."

"What?"

Anthony picked up the man's rough coat and dug in the pocket, pulling forth a piece of twine tied into a necklace. A man's gold ring dangled from one end of it.

"Oh, my." Camilla reached out and took the ring in her hand, bringing it closer. The design was of a serpent swallowing its tail. Emerald chips glittered as its eyes. "This looks expensive."

"I would not think that he is a peasant, no."

"Was he wearing it?"

"Not on his hand. He must have known how that would stick out among the others. But once, when he bent over to pick up a barrel, it fell out from the neck of his shirt, and I saw it. He quickly stuffed it back in. Of course, I couldn't see the design, but when I found this man with the ring on a cord around his neck, I was certain that it had to be he."

"But why was he with the smugglers? He's not from around here. And he's carrying that expensive ring...."

"He could be a gentleman smuggler."

"Two at the same place?" Camilla retorted sarcastically. "I think that is unlikely."

A little reluctantly, Anthony went on. "I— Well, he was on the boat when they came to shore. I think he came with the brandy."

"Came with it? You mean from France?"

He nodded. "When I came back last night, he had a fever. He was asleep, but he was mumbling in his sleep. He said, well, I don't know what it was, but I think he spoke in French."

Camilla felt as if the breath had been knocked out of her. She sat back on her heels, staring at her cousin. "He's a Frenchman? Are you saying that this man is a spy?"

13

‴**I** don't know,'' Anthony answered wretchedly. ''I could hardly believe it when I heard it. When he spoke to me, he didn't have a French accent. But I am certain it was French that came out in his sleep.''

''Then you must turn him in!''

''But what if he is not a spy? What if I was wrong, or—or he's Belgian? And there must be Englishmen who can speak French.''

''Can, yes. I *can* myself. But I don't go mumbling it in my sleep. That is the sort of thing you do when it is your native tongue.''

''Even if he is French, it doesn't mean that he is a spy,'' Anthony went on stubbornly.

''What else would he be? We are at war with them.''

''It could mean that he is escaping from France. That he is against Bonaparte, even that Bonaparte tried to arrest him, say, and he had to flee. That would explain him being with the smugglers. He paid them to bring him over with the cargo.''

''He could have paid them to do that if he was a

spy, too. That is no proof. Anthony, this is awful.''
She looked back down at the man. "We cannot let
him run about free in England, no matter how much
compassion we might feel for him.''

"I don't think he is going to run about anywhere,
at least not anytime soon.''

Their patient did look undeniably helpless at the
moment. Camilla wavered. It seemed inhuman to give
him up to the authorities, as weak and ill as he was
right now. If they turned him in, whoever had tried to
kill him before would know exactly where he was and
could try again. And Anthony was right in saying that
the magistrate would be of little help and even less
protection to the man. *Oh, she wished that she could
ask Benedict for his advice!* She did not stop to question why she should rely so much on the opinion of a
man she had met only a few days ago.

"There's not even anything to arrest him for,'' Anthony pointed out. "All we know that he has done is
get attacked. So they might not even put him in jail.
We would probably still be taking care of him at the
house, only everyone would know about it.''

Anthony could see that he was making headway, so
he went on in a wheedling voice, "Please, Milla. Let's
just see what happens, how he does. Right now, we're
not even sure he will survive to be turned in. And it
may be that if he comes out of the fever, he will tell
us all about himself and how he got to be here. There
may be a perfectly safe explanation for his speaking
French.''

"All right.'' Camilla sighed and stood up. She had
finished rebandaging the man's wounds. "I have done
all I can do for him. That paste may help the wounds.

He will need to take this draft periodically, though, for his fever. Can you tend to him? I can't be missing all day, or everyone will wonder. Especially Benedict.''

Anthony nodded. ''Yes. I will row you over to the mainland, then come back here and sit with him today. I'll just lock the door to my bedroom and put it out that I am ill. Will you come back later, when the tide is low?''

''Yes. I will sneak away this afternoon to check on him.'' She sighed, casting a last look at the man on the floor. ''Promise that you will keep yourself armed when you are sitting with him?''

Her cousin rolled his eyes. ''Honestly, Camilla! The man is so weak he can barely lift a hand. What do you think he could do to me?''

''I don't know,'' Camilla snapped back. ''I just know that he is perhaps French, perhaps a spy—and that no one knows anything about his being here except you and I. It is a dangerous situation. If you won't have the sense to be careful, then I shall have—''

''All right, all right...'' Anthony playfully laid his hand across her mouth, chuckling. ''I promise I will always be armed around him. And I will watch him like a hawk. I have no desire to let a French spy loose in the country, either. Now, come.'' He curled his arm around her shoulders and began to steer her toward the door. ''We had better get you back to the house.''

As soon as they reached the house, Camilla hurried to her bedroom, while Anthony went to the kitchen and his room to gather supplies for his day on Keep Island. Camilla was disappointed to find that Benedict was not in the room, for she had hoped that she would be able to slip back into bed unnoticed.

Instead, she dressed and went downstairs to the dining room. She hated having to lie to Benedict, and she wanted to get the story over with as soon as possible. She paused at the doorway, looking in, and was relieved to see that he was breakfasting alone. Pasting on a smile, she sailed into the room.

"Good morning, Benedict."

He turned at her words and jumped up, his brows drawing together fiercely. "Where the devil have you been? I was beginning to worry."

His words brought her up short. She had braced herself for his curiosity, but not for worry. "You mustn't," she replied. "I was with Anthony."

He cast her a speaking look. "Oh, *that* relieves my mind greatly."

Camilla chuckled. "Anthony is quite protective of me."

"I am sure." Benedict pulled out Camilla's chair for her in an ungracious manner and waved to her to sit down. "Where were you?"

"We went out for an early-morning tramp about the estate. We often do." Camilla could not bring herself to meet his gaze as she told him her fib, so she was glad for the distraction of the footman bringing her a plate of food from the sideboard.

"Without telling me? Rather cavalier attitude for a wife, don't you think?" he asked softly.

Camilla glanced at him oddly. She leaned closer and whispered, "But I am not really your wife, am I?"

For a moment, he looked a little taken aback, but then he, too, leaned forward and whispered back, "We agreed to make it look real. Otherwise, you will make a slip.''

''*I* will!'' Camilla retorted. ''Never you, of course.''

He cocked an eyebrow at her and sat back in his chair and returned to eating. For the next few moments, the room was filled with a heavy silence.

The strained quiet was beginning to weigh on Camilla's nerves when Benedict leaned forward again and whispered, ''Don't you think your dressing gown is, ah, somewhat casual attire for a walk around the estate?''

Camilla glanced up at him, startled, and met his bland gaze. She could feel her cheeks growing warm. ''How did you know—''

''I was looking out the window—keeping an eye out for you, you see—and I saw you and Anthony returning,'' he explained.

Camilla struggled to keep the guilt out of her face. She tried to remember the exact view from her bedroom window. He couldn't see as far as the ocean, so he would not have seen her and Anthony dock the boat.

''Well, uh...you see, something had happened. That's why Anthony came to get me. He needed help.'' She was seized with inspiration. ''Medical help.''

''One would think a doctor would have been a more likely person to fetch than you,'' he offered mildly.

''Oh, no, it was old Nan Gandy. The widow of one of my grandfather's tenants. She lives in a little cottage on the other side of the woods. She was sick, and she would never see a doctor. Not even if Anthony brought him out there. She fears doctors and is convinced that they are more likely to kill her than heal her. She would never trust anyone but my grandmother to give her a potion. Grandmama was well-known locally, you see, as a healer. She knew a good bit about herbs, and she always took care of the servants and the tenants. Old Nan believes I inherited her gift, though in truth I only inherited her medicine bag and her recipes.''

"I see. So Anthony was there visiting her at dawn and discovered that she was ill and came to fetch you?''

"Oh, no.'' *Trust him to immediately latch on to the flaw in her story.* "Old Nan's great-nephew came to fetch me. He just, uh, happened to meet Anthony. Anthony, you see, had been out for an early-morning walk. He likes to do that. And Anthony told him he would bring me over to their cottage.''

"You must be very devoted to your tenants, that they know they can rouse you from your bed at dawn to tend to them.''

"Normally they would not have, of course, but she had turned quite ill. Feverish. She was out of her head with it. They were rather frightened.''

"Ah. Time was of the essence.''

Camilla nodded. It occurred to her as soon as she said it that she had worked herself into an untenable position with her story. If the family had rushed here at the crack of dawn to seek her aid, the natural thing for her to do would have been to ride a horse over to Old Nan's cottage, not to walk. She wondered if Benedict would see the contradiction in it. He did not say anything, but his steady, silent regard made her nervous.

"We walked," she offered, "because it really isn't that far and—and the woods are rather dense. It would not be much faster by horseback, what with the time it would take to wake the grooms and get a horse saddled and all."

"Of course."

Camilla realized that she was babbling. It would have been better to say nothing than to try to explain something that had not even been questioned. Usually she was better at carrying off a story than this. But she found it extremely difficult to look into Benedict's face and lie.

She wished, with a sudden, fierce pang, that she could tell him the truth. She felt confused and uncertain, and she was very afraid that Anthony had gotten in over his head with this adventure. Like Anthony, she wanted to protect the injured man, to keep his would-be killer from finding him, but, on the other hand, she was afraid that they might be aiding and abetting an enemy of England. Then, there was also danger from the man who had attacked him. *What if he was out searching for him? What if he found out where they were hiding him and attacked him again?* She thought of Anthony sitting alone with the man over in the ruins, and her heart squeezed within her chest.

Something of what she felt must have showed in her face, for Benedict said suddenly, "What? What's the matter?"

She looked at him, surprised to see worry in his eyes. She wanted quite badly to tell him her troubles, to lay the whole burden on his ample shoulders and let him deal with Anthony and the wounded stranger and the man who had tried to kill him. The idea of resting her head on his chest and pouring out the whole story sounded very appealing. She could almost feel his arms going around her, could almost hear his deep voice telling her not to worry, that he would take care of it.

Camilla sighed. She could not do that. She was growing more and more to believe that Anthony had been right, that Benedict was an excise man. It was clear to her that he was not the common thief she had at first believed him to be. His speech, his manners, his very bearing, bespoke a gentleman—not to mention the story of his fiancé and her rejection when he was displaced by a new heir. He had not received the inheritance, of course, but it showed that he was a member of a family with enough property to dispose of. *So why would the son of a gentleman, even an impecunious one, go along with her thinking him a thief, or even participate in her charade?* Perhaps need of money had made him that desperate...or perhaps he was engaged in some secret endeavor, such as chasing smugglers.

Her problem, she told herself, was that she had begun to believe her own story. Sometimes she found herself actually thinking of Benedict as her husband. It made her erroneously believe that she could trust him, could count on him. She did not dare do that. She could not hand over the fate of the stranger, much less that of her own cousin, into his hands. If she let him in on Anthony's secret, he would find out about the smuggling, too, and then the whole family would be in terrible trouble. She could not let that happen simply because of her own weakness.

So when he looked at her with concern on his features and asked her what was the matter, Camilla squared her shoulders and forced a smile to her face.

"Nothing's the matter," she told Benedict brightly. "Nothing at all."

She was lying. Benedict scowled as he urged his horse forward. The horse responded to his expert handling, as well as to the anger surging in him, and fairly flew down the road.

It would have been obvious to him that Camilla was lying even if he had not already seen her go across to Keep Island with her cousin. She had been unable to look him in the eye, and her voice had been rapid and nervous. Explanations that he had not even asked for had come tumbling from her lips. She had been lying about where she'd gone and why. And she had been lying when she told him that there was nothing wrong. *Why? Why wouldn't she trust him? Confide in him?*

He had wanted to press her on the issue, but some remnant of good sense had stopped him. He could not appear too interested in Anthony or what was going on at Chevington Park. She thought him an uninvolved party, a stranger to whatever was going on. He could not risk making her suspicious of him by appearing to be too concerned or too disbelieving of her story.

However, it galled him that she had not turned to him—worse than that, that she regarded him as someone with whom she must dissemble. He was certain that he could help her, if only she would tell him what was the matter. Benedict disregarded the fact that she had no idea who he really was or how much influence and power he had. The point was, *she had not asked him for help.*

He was in a foul mood, and had been all morning, from the moment he saw her sneak over to the island with her cousin.

Benedict would have preferred to explore Keep Island, to see if he could find what had drawn Camilla and Anthony there. However, he already had an obligation to meet Sedgewick. The two had arranged the meeting before he went to Chevington Park with Camilla, so that Sedgewick could be apprised of whatever Benedict had discovered at the Park. It could not be easily canceled.

When he reached the clearing where he and Sedgewick had agreed to meet, his friend was already there, sitting on a flat rock, waiting for him. As Benedict dismounted from his horse and tied it to a tree branch, Sedgewick strode across the clearing, smiling at him.

He greeted Benedict with a cheerful "Hallo."

Benedict mumbled an unintelligible reply.

Sedgewick raised his eyebrows a little, but forged ahead. "The masquerade still intact?"

"Yes." Benedict wondered if Jermyn had heard in the village that he was supposed to be married to Camilla. Knowing the way small towns gossiped, he suspected that it was common knowledge in Edgecombe that Miss Ferrand was married to him, not just engaged. But he was not sure that Sedgewick, being an outsider, would have heard such news. He found himself hoping that he had not.

Jermyn alone would know for a fact that the marriage was a pretense and that therefore Camilla's honor was a shambles now. Of course, Jermyn was not the sort who would spread it about; there was no one whom Benedict trusted more. Still, Benedict wished that no one knew how thoroughly her reputation was at risk.

His hopes were immediately dashed, however, when Sedgewick went on. "What's this I hear? The young miss at the Park has a *husband?*"

Benedict rolled his eyes. "Yes. It is a bloody mess. The lady in question has a featherbrained aunt who decided to embellish on Miss Ferrand's original story by telling everyone that Camilla had gotten married. Ergo, I am the fictitious husband."

"Extraordinary. But I trust you have been able to pull it off."

"We have been so far, but it has only been a few days." It surprised Benedict a little to realize that this was so. It seemed as if he had been living with Camilla forever. "If we don't carry off the pretense, Miss Ferrand will be in a pickle." He scowled at Sedgewick. "All because of your little scheme."

"Don't look so blackly at me. How was I to know her fiancé had been elevated to a husband?"

"You couldn't. But you ought to know that there is always *something* that goes wrong with mad schemes."

"Not always. We have brought off a few, you and I."

Benedict allowed a small smile at his friend's words. "I suppose."

"You look tired." Concern crept into his friend's voice. "Is the sham wearing on you that much?"

"You would be tired, too, if you'd stayed awake

half the night and then spent the dawn chasing about after—''

Benedict broke off, realizing with some amazement that he did not want to tell Sedgewick about his following Camilla and her cousin to Keep Island this morning. Jermyn would be too likely to jump to the wrong conclusion, not knowing Camilla and Anthony as he did. However foolish they might be, Benedict was certain that they could not be involved in anything worse than smuggling. He did not want to reveal their suspicious-looking trip to Keep Island until he was certain he could keep their reputations from being hurt. It occurred to him that he was beginning to think like a husband, not a stranger, but he shoved the thought aside. It was what any gentleman would do, he told himself.

Sedgewick looked at him, puzzled. ''Chasing about after what?''

''Oh, nothing. I thought I had a clue, but it turned out to be nothing. Just one of Camilla's cousins' pranks.''

''Why did you stay awake half the night, then? Looking for smugglers?''

Benedict found that he wanted even less to discuss what had kept him awake. ''It's the damn sofa I have to sleep on.''

''Sofa! You mean they haven't even given you a bed to sleep in?''

''They have put me in Camilla's room. I told you, they think we are married. I am having to sleep on a sofa in her bedroom—and if you ever let a word of this out to anyone, I swear I will...''

Sedgewick backed off, raising his hands in mock

terror. "I assure you, I shan't breathe a word of it to anyone. Whatever made you think I would?"

"Oh, I know you would not. It's just that it is such a damn coil. I feel responsible for the chit, even if she was silly enough to let you entangle her in this mess."

"Really, Benedict…"

"And the marriage isn't the worst of it," Benedict went on, building up steam as he thought of his grievances. "The damned house is filled with people—aunts and cousins and visitors. I never envisioned performing to such a large audience. One of the fellows keeps insisting that he knows me."

"What? Who?"

"Camilla's cousin, Bertram."

"Bertram Elliot? A dandy?"

"Of the first order."

"I know him. A complete lightweight." Sedgewick dismissed him. "He will give you no problem. He is more concerned with the cut of his coat than affairs of state."

"But not more concerned than he is with gossip, I warrant, or social standing. What if the fellow recalls who I am?"

"You are right," Jermyn admitted. "If he's likely to remember anything, it would be a person's look, or his tailor—or at which party he'd met him."

"I have no memory of ever seeing the fellow before. But I am doomed if he remembers me." He had a sudden thought of how Camilla would react if her cousin suddenly announced that Benedict was Lord Rawdon. He suspected that it would not be a pretty sight if she found out that he had been deceiving her all along. "Bertram has a friend, as well, a very quiet sort. The servants consider him 'not a gentleman.' "

"Really?" Sedgewick perked up. "The servants always know. They're a better judge than a duke. Why do you suppose someone who is 'not a gentleman' is hanging about in the country with Elliot?"

Benedict shrugged. "I don't know. Perhaps he is just some hanger-on, and Bertram doesn't realize he isn't Quality. Perhaps Bertram simply doesn't care because the fellow is so entertaining—although I cannot imagine that. Oglesby never talks. Whereas Bertram talks entirely too much. Yesterday he trapped me in the hall for ten minutes asking my opinion about his waistcoat. Nasty-looking striped thing."

"Egad." Sedgewick shuddered at the thought. "Who else is there?"

"More cousins, two girls, sisters to Bertram. The Viscount Marbridge, heir to the earldom—that is Cousin Anthony. And a poet who seems to have attached himself to the Viscountess's skirts. She is there, too—she is the cork-brained one who thought up the 'husband' story. And, of course, Bertram's mother."

"The fearsome Aunt Beryl?"

"The same. Then there is Chevington himself, who may be laid up in bed but is still sharper than most men. A tutor for the Viscount. I have yet to see him, but I'll warrant he has enough on his hands trying to keep Anthony at work on his studies without plotting to destroy Gideon. Worst of all, a parson drops in on us all too often. A brother of Bertram named Harold, whose grandfather gave him the local living. An utter, prosing bore. Fortunately, he was quite eager to spout off about the smugglers. Unfortunately, he was more concerned with the sinfulness of the practice than with details. I must say, none of the people at the Park looks very promising as a candidate for a spy.''

"We could hardly count on being lucky enough to find our man right there in the Earl's household.'' Sedgewick paused, then prodded further. "Well, man? Have you discovered anything useful?''

"I've only been there a few days,'' Benedict protested. Once again, he could hardly believe how little time it had been. It had seemed far longer—especially during the long nights when he lay awake thinking about Camilla lying in the bed across the room from him. Those hours had been endless.

"I realize that. But you know how little time we have. We have to find out who is doing this to our network!''

"You don't need to remind me,'' Benedict growled back. "All right. I talked to the Earl. He told me that he is concerned about what's happening in the area. He is especially concerned about the death of Nat Crowder.'' Briefly, he explained who Nat had been and how he had died.

"Of course. Simple way to work oneself into a smuggling ring. Get rid of the leader and take over. That explains a lot. It must have been Nat Crowder with whom Lord Winslow was working.''

"Once he and Winslow were both gone, there was no one who knew anything about the spy ring. The local men are smugglers, pure and simple.'' Benedict waited for a moment, then added, "Lord Chevington asked me to investigate.''

Sedgewick's eyes opened wide. "You can't be serious. The old Earl himself set you to the task?''

Benedict nodded. "Yes. It has made questioning the servants a damn sight easier. The other locals, too. I am riding into town to talk to a couple of them after this."

"But this is perfect. Thank God for Miss Ferrand. I could not have dreamed up a better scheme myself."

"Yes, fine for us, but what about them? I feel lower than a swine for taking advantage of the Earl this way. He trusts me. He is relying on me. And I am using him."

Sedgewick frowned, looking puzzled. "He won't be harmed. It isn't as if you are trying to do him wrong. You are simply doing what he asked you to, what he wanted done."

Benedict thought about Anthony, and Jenkins's suspicion that the lad was involved in the smuggling. He doubted that Sedgewick would think he was doing Chevington so little harm if he knew that his investigation might throw scandal on the heir to the earldom.

"The rumor is that the man we are looking for is a 'gentleman,'" Benedict said abruptly.

"What?" Sedgewick straightened, his pale eyes suddenly intent. "Are you serious? But this fits perfectly with what we had surmised before—that Winslow was killed by an acquaintance. Why do they think he is a gentleman?"

"The word is that he is educated and well spoken. Apparently he often speaks in a rough way, but some of them think that it doesn't ring true. That is what I heard from the valet."

"Then we would have to drop Bertram Elliot's friend from the list, since the servants suspect that he is not a gentleman."

Benedict shrugged. "Or perhaps it just means that they recognize that both roles are counterfeit. Maybe the real man is neither Oglesby nor a rough smuggler, but something in between, a man who knows how to act both ways, yet is not quite believable in either one."

"An actor, maybe. Or a dancing instructor, a tutor, something of that sort."

"Or a sharp."

"Yes. Winslow could have walked home with someone like that from some gambling den or other. He did have a fondness for the cards. He could have assumed that his companion was a gentleman, someone he would admit into his house, particularly if he was a little bosky."

Benedict sighed. "But it is all supposition. I know nothing substantial."

"No signs of activity on the beach?"

Benedict shook his head. "It is too soon after the last shipment. I shall have to wait." He thought of the prospect of sharing a bedroom with Camilla for several more days, even weeks, and the idea almost made him groan. He was certain he would never last that long.

"Damn!" Jermyn began to pace, frowning. "We can't spend that amount of time here. I need to be in London. And we cannot afford to leave our network hanging. We need to get word to them if there is a French spy who has infiltrated the smugglers. We must not let any more of them come in and be killed."

"I know. Perhaps I should give up this masquerade. I may have learned all I can from it. I could pretend that I was called back to Bath. I've been here long enough to satisfy Camilla's purposes.''

Even as Benedict spoke the words, he knew that he did not want to leave. Hellish as it was to sleep in the same room with Camilla, the idea of not seeing her at all made him feel suddenly ill, as if he had been punched in the stomach. Besides, he could not simply leave her in the middle of whatever predicament her rapscallion cousin had involved her in. He had to untangle the mystery and get Anthony out of the smuggling ring—if that was what he was involved in.

''No. Let's give it a few more days. We *have* to find out what is going on.''

''Why don't you go back to London?'' Benedict turned toward his friend. ''You are much more necessary to the government than I am. You can keep up the investigation into who killed Winslow there. And,'' he added, as Sedgewick opened his mouth to protest, ''you can help me by finding out whatever information you can on the people who are visiting at Chevington Park. If our quarry is one of them, there may be some bit of gossip you can dig up about him that would help. That one of them is especially in need of money, say, or has a French mother, or keeps a mistress who might be blackmailing him. Anything to indicate a possibility that he might sell out to the enemy.''

''Yes, of course.'' Sedgewick nodded eagerly. ''That's an excellent idea.'' He searched through his pockets until at last he found a stub of a pencil and a folded receipt on which he could write. ''Now, what are their names? Terence Oglesby, you said?''

''Yes.'' Slowly Benedict listed the names of everyone staying at the house, even Aunt Beryl and her two giggling daughters.

"Very good," Sedgewick said, folding up the paper and sticking it in an inner pocket. "I will pay my shot at the tavern and start for London this afternoon, then. God, it's been miserable, just sitting about and doing nothing." He turned and reached out a hand to shake Benedict's. "I will let you know as soon as I return. In the meantime, watch your back. I don't want anything happening to you."

"I will be careful," Benedict promised. He did not add that he was less concerned about being found out by the shadowy figure they were trying to unmask than he was about surviving a few more days of sleeping in Camilla's room without going mad.

14

Benedict spent the rest of the day talking to several people in town whom Purdle and Jenkins had told him he could trust, including the tavernkeeper, who greeted him with a wide grin and a demand to know why Benedict had not told him that he was the young miss's husband when he was staying there earlier.

Though the villagers were willing to open up to him, now that he had the old Earl's blessing, they were still of little help. Everyone swore that he had no knowledge of the new leader of the smugglers, other than the common rumor that he was one of the gentry.

He also dropped by to see Evans, whom Jenkins had pointed out as a henchman of the new leader of the smugglers. He was, as Jenkins had said, a drunken lout and quite stupid. Already, though it was only late afternoon, he stank of liquor. Benedict casually asked him the same sorts of questions that he had asked the other villagers, but instead of displaying the free manner of the others, this man remained guarded and silent, folding his arms across his chest and staring stolidly at Benedict with his small, piggy eyes. He alone, of all the villagers, expressed no regard for the Earl, and he alone refused to answer any of Benedict's questions, replying each time only that he "didn't know nothing."

Benedict rode home feeling weary and defeated. He had gained little information in the village. He seemed to be getting nowhere in his search for the French agent. And Camilla was involved in some skulduggery or other from which he would probably have to rescue her, something for which she would probably not be at all grateful.

Benedict let out a sigh and shifted a little in his saddle. It had gotten dark. He suspected that he would be too late for dinner at Chevington Park. Perhaps he would take a long, soaking bath, then a nap in Camilla's bed. He had had almost no sleep last night, and his spine felt permanently twisted from sleeping night after night on the couch.

He was pleased to find no one in Camilla's bedroom when he came in. Apparently she had already gone down to dinner. He took advantage of the solitude with a long, hot bath. Finally, he got out of the bathtub, his body still steaming from the hot water, and dried off. After he had tucked into a hearty cold collation Cook had sent up at his request, he fell into Camilla's bed and fell immediately, soundly asleep.

It was thus that Camilla found him later when she returned to her room. After tea that afternoon, she had gone across the land bridge to Keep Island, taking with her a few things she had slipped off the tea tray for Anthony. There had been an embarrassing moment when Bertram looked across at her at the exact moment she was easing a sweet cake into her capacious pocket. He had given her the oddest look but fortunately had said nothing.

Her patient's condition had changed little. She rebandaged his wounds and gave him another dose of the draft, then hurried back to the house, afraid that she had spent too long at the island and Benedict would be questioning her. She had, indeed, missed dinner, but at least Benedict would not be wondering why. She paused just inside her door, gazing at Benedict's form, sprawled in her bed. Her heart picked up its beat.

She closed the door behind her softly and tiptoed across the room until she stood beside the bed, looking down at him. He lay on his back, arms and legs flung wide like a trusting child. His hair was still wet from his bath, and he had the soft, damp look of one who had just bathed. His scent mingled with the smell of soap and the faintest hint of the lavender that always clung to her sheets.

Defenseless in sleep, he looked even more handsome. His chiseled lips were faintly parted; his long, dark lashes lay against his cheeks, giving him a vulnerable look. Camilla's eyes drifted down over his face and onto his throat, to the pulse that beat in the hollow, then outward to the bony outcropping of his collarbone, the wide set of his shoulders. The sheet cut across his chest, revealing his bare shoulders, but little lower than that.

Camilla leaned forward, listening to his even breathing, watching his face for signs of consciousness. Unable to contain her curiosity, she hooked a finger under the sheet and slid it farther down, exposing the wide expanse of his chest.

She looked at the dark, curling hair that dotted his chest, curving down in a vee to his navel, at the flat, brownish pink nipples and the firm pad of muscled flesh across his rib cage. He was, she thought, a perfect specimen of a man.

Her hand, seemingly with a will of its own, stretched out toward him. She pulled it back hastily and clasped it behind her back with her other hand. She stood for a moment, watching his even breathing. Her eyes slid lower still, to where the sheet and cover lay, white against his bare, tanned flesh. The bedclothes stretched across his abdomen just below his navel, resting on the upthrust knobs of his pelvis. The well of his navel was exposed, as was the thin line of hair that swept downwards.

She thought that he must be naked beneath the sheet. After all, there was no sign of clothing all the way down to his hipbones. It wasn't decent for a man to sleep like that, she told herself. *It was no wonder that it raised strange and forbidden thoughts inside her head.*

And she couldn't help being curious, Camilla reasoned. *It wasn't as if he would ever know; he was sound asleep.* Of course, she knew that was not the issue. The important thing was privacy—and acting as a decent, respectable woman should act.

She leaned closer. Her face burned with embarrassment, yet she could not seem to keep her hand from creeping out, closer and closer to him, until at last her fingertips touched the covers. With the gentlest of touches, scarcely daring even to breathe, she peeled the covers back, revealing his bare body down to his powerful thighs.

The fire in her face flamed higher. She stared, mesmerized, unable to look away. She gazed at his flat stomach, at the dips and curves of muscles, bone and skin. She looked at the thick musculature of his thighs, smooth beneath his hair-roughened skin. But, primarily, she stared at what lay between his legs: the nest of thick black hair, and the male organ that lay within it, thick and heavy. *This, then, was how a man looked?*

Camilla gulped. She had never quite imagined it like this. Though she would never have admitted it to another soul, she knew that she had thought about the subject several times. She was not sure exactly what she had expected, but the reality of it was different...and much more powerful.

As she watched, he made a noise in his sleep and rolled over onto his side. Her eyes were drawn to the sleek line of his hip and thigh, the curve of his buttock. Without thinking, she reached out and drew her fingertips down the smooth stretch of skin. Her fingers trembled; she was startled by the warmth of him, and by the shock of pleasure that ran up her arm at the touch.

She knew that she should draw her hand away, yet she could not. She curved her palm over his buttock, entranced by the different texture. *Was all of him so different, so pleasurable to touch?*

Camilla ran her hand up his side, ignoring the pounding of her heart and the frantic warning of her brain. Just for a moment, she told herself. *Just this one touch.* She moved upward, exploring the softness of his side, then the hard ridges of his rib cage. The skin of his chest was no longer smooth, but dotted with hair, the muscle firm underneath. Her thumb glided across the tiny bud of his nipple, and to her amazement it tightened at her touch.

She stopped, looking at the pinkish bud, remembering how her own nipple had hardened in response to him the other day. Thoughtfully she circled the button of flesh with her thumb, enjoying the response. She was unaware of the faint, sensual smile that curved her lips.

"Move your hand farther down and we shall both be smiling." His husky voice cut through Camilla's thoughts.

She gasped and snatched her hand back, looking up at Benedict's face. He was watching her, his dark eyes flaming with an unholy light. Camilla's face flooded deep crimson with humiliation, and, with a strangled cry, she turned and ran toward the door.

In an instant, he was out of the bed and running after her. He caught her before she reached the door, his arms going around her from behind.

"No. Don't leave. Good God, you can't leave after that!"

Camilla moaned and brought her hands up to cover her face. She knew that she would never live this down. She could not even face him again. She had done embarrassing things before in her life, but nothing like this.

"Let me go!" she cried in a low, strangled voice, pulling against his arms.

"Shh." He buried his face in her hair, kissing her. "It's all right. Don't go. Don't turn away from me."

His breath came quickly, and there was a tremor in his low voice. He kissed her neck, and his hand began to caress her stomach. Camilla shivered, unable to hide her intense response. Even the sound of his breath excited her. She could hardly believe that she could feel this way in the midst of humiliation, and the very fact that she could respond so heatedly, so animalistically, seemed yet another embarrassment.

"I didn't mind what you did," Benedict told her, so close behind her that she could feel the rumble of his voice in his chest as he spoke. She could just imagine his smug smile as he went on. "Believe me, I enjoyed it."

Camilla let out a low moan and tore away from him. She ran back to the bed and threw herself upon it, curling up into a ball, away from him. He followed. She felt the bed give beneath his weight, and he laid a hand upon her back, softly rubbing it up and down over her curved spine.

"Shh...don't take it so to heart." He stretched out beside her on his elbow, letting his low voice and comforting hand work their magic.

His hand curved down over her bottom, caressing the rounded fullness. He roamed over her buttocks, gliding up to the small of her back, then back down, over the curve and onto her thigh. Again and again, he caressed her while he murmured meaningless sounds of comfort. He moved around and up, sliding his hand onto her stomach, then cupping her breast. Camilla realized that at some point while he was caressing her, she had relaxed, uncurling from the tight ball she had been in, allowing his roving hand access to her front.

His skin was hot through the material of her dress; his fingertips seared the soft flesh of her breasts. He squeezed and stroked, arousing her nipples to hardened points. His hand moved above her neckline and slid inside the dress, pushing the material down and cupping the bare orb of her breast.

Camilla gasped at the delight of his rougher skin on the tender bud. He circled the pebbling nub of flesh, then lightly pinched it between his forefinger and thumb, pulling gently. Camilla could not suppress a groan at the new and delightful sensation. He slipped his other arm around her, taking both breasts in his hands and playing with them, teasing her nipples so that they elongated, pushing saucily against his fingertips.

He pulled his hands away, and she gasped at the loss, but before she could protest, he was sliding them up under her skirts. His fingers moved up the backs of her thighs and cupped the soft mounds of her buttocks. He dug into the soft flesh, and Camilla unconsciously moved her hips, inviting more. He answered by slipping one hand between her legs. Though she was still sheathed by her undergarment, he could feel the blazing heat of her body and the welcoming dampness.

Camilla moaned, embarrassed by the eager wetness that greeted him, but she could not stop herself from moving against his hand. Her nether lips felt huge and swollen, and she was literally aching to feel his touch upon her bare flesh.

"Please," she whispered, rubbing against his fingertips. "We must not. We must stop." Yet she knew that she could not stop, that if he pulled away from her now, she would probably scream and claw to get him back. "I cannot..."

"Don't worry." He curved over her, whispering

into her ear and sending delightful shivers through her at the touch of his breath. "I won't harm you. I will only pleasure you."

Camilla drew a ragged breath. She didn't know what he meant. But she had expended what little protest she had in her.

"Now, turn over." He stopped the pleasurable things that he was doing and tugged on her arm, turning her over on her back. "I want to see you." He began to unfasten her buttons, opening her dress all the way down.

Camilla lay quietly, letting him work on her clothes, and all the while her eyes traveled over his body. She was past shame now, entranced by the feel of his hands on her body. She gazed at his muscular body, at the organ that now hung huge and thrusting between his legs, far larger than it had been earlier, and she could feel herself flushing again, but this time with desire.

He undressed her, working swiftly and competently, pausing now and then to caress her hip or thigh or stomach, or to drop a kiss upon the hard bud of her nipple. Finally, he had her naked before him. He gazed down at her for a long time, his eyes taking in every inch of her body, and all the while Camilla grew hotter and hungrier for his touch, until she was almost ready to cry out.

He laid his hands over her breasts and began to caress her. He moved slowly, surely, taking his time, gliding his fingers over her sensitive skin. He lingered over the softness of her breasts and stomach and explored the hard ridges of her hipbones. Teasingly, he circled the well of her navel with his forefinger, then trailed it slowly down to the thatch of hair between her legs. Camilla's gasp was almost a sob, and she dug her fingers into the sheets, arching up involuntarily to meet him.

His finger delved into the slick, tender folds, opening and exploring them. All the while, he looked at her face, watching passion suffuse her features, glazing her eyes and slackening her lips. Camilla panted, digging in her heels, her body as taut as a bowstring. She was flooded with moisture, quivering with desire. Something hot and hungry coiled deep in her abdomen. She thought that she could feel no newer or greater sensation.

But then he bent and touched his tongue to her nipple, and she knew that she had been wrong. Hot and wet, his tongue flicked back and forth across the tight bud, lashing it lovingly. With each little stroke, the knot in her abdomen tightened even more. He took the nipple into the warm, wet cave of his mouth and began to suck. Camilla let out a shuddering groan. Every pull of his mouth sizzled straight down to the swollen, pulsing center of her desire, where his fingers were still busily at work.

She writhed beneath him, aching for release from the delightful torment. His mouth trailed downward. His tongue circled her navel. Camilla dug her heels into the bed, straining up against him. Benedict raised his head and looked down at her quivering, lush body. His eyes roamed slowly upward to her flushed face. He watched her intently as his thumb found the tiny hard nub at the seat of her passion and gently stroked it. Camilla moaned, shocked and amazed at this newest, even more intense, pleasure. Her body trembled, caught on the threshold of something she had never dreamed of.

Benedict smiled, and his thumb pressed harder. Camilla cried out as she tumbled over the precipice. She convulsed around him, her legs clamping together as a flush suffused her chest and neck.

Finally, with a soft sigh, she relaxed. Camilla looked up at him and smiled shyly, filled with the most complete satisfaction she had ever known. "Oh, Benedict…"

He pulled his hand away slowly, trailing it down her soft thighs. Camilla glanced down and saw his throbbing, engorged manhood. "Oh!" She looked back up at his face anxiously. "But, Benedict, aren't you… Don't you…?"

He smiled. "Yes. I am, and I do." It took a great deal of effort for him to merely lean over and plant a brief kiss on her soft lips. "But don't worry. It will be all right. I promised not to dishonor you, and I won't. That was entirely for your pleasure."

"Yes, but…"

"Shh." He shook his head. "I will be all right."

He bent and kissed her again, this time letting some of his restrained passion show, but after a long moment, he pulled away. "Now, close your eyes and go to sleep."

"Will you stay here with me?"

He nodded. "Yes. I will stay here."

Camilla smiled, a little fuzzily, still wrapped up in the warm cocoon of her afterglow, and obediently closed her eyes.

Benedict swallowed hard and turned away, struggling to retain control. Her innocent questions had almost been the undoing of him. He had been mad, he knew, to do what he had done. He would pay for it the rest of the evening. He should have walked away, left the room, but he had been unable to resist the temptation. *But at least he had had enough strength not to take her.* There had been a few moments there when he was not sure he would be able to restrain himself.

He lay back down and closed his eyes, throwing his arm across them. He let out a slow, shuddering breath, then drew another, slowly willing himself into a calmer state.

He thought about Camilla and the situation they were in. He thought about his honor and hers, and the old man in the room at the end of the hall. He thought about her foolish cousin and her loyalty, about the passion that had thrummed in him the past few days and the way she had dissolved in pleasure beneath his touch. It was a long time before he slept.

Camilla lazily drew her needle through the fabric, stretched tight by the embroidery hoop, her mind only half attuned to her aunt's light prattle. She had been in a dreamy state all morning. She had awakened early, feeling blissfully happy and refreshed. She had lain for a short while, looking at Benedict as he slept and wondering if she would ever again feel what she had felt the night before. Just thinking about it made her nerves start to sizzle.

Quickly she had jumped out of bed and dressed. The last thing she had wanted was for Benedict to wake up and find her mooning over him. It miffed her a little that he had been perfectly in command of his desires and emotions while being able to so completely destroy her control. *Not, of course, that she had not been a very willing participant in that loss of control.*

The tide had already been up, so she had not gone across to the island. Instead, she had wandered down to breakfast and then into the less formal sitting room. With her thoughts still on the night before and with nothing better to do, she had picked up a partially done embroidery of a pillowcase. Before long, Lydia joined her. Since she wanted to talk at length, as she had ever since Camilla had arrived at the Park, about Benedict's courtship, the conversation had severely taxed Camilla's powers of imagination.

Fortunately, Mr. Thorne had come in and distracted her aunt, saying, "Ah, if only I had the power to paint a portrait of you now, madam. A veritable Arachne."

"But she wove, did she not, rather than sewing?" Camilla asked with great innocence. "And, if I remember correctly, she wound up as a spider."

"A spider!" Lydia exclaimed. "Really, Mr. Thorne, I think I prefer not to be compared to a spider."

The young man looked chagrined. "I meant the woman before the jealous goddess changed her, of course. I would rather cut my tongue out than offend you."

"Well, I don't really see how that would help," Lydia protested mildly, and Camilla had to press her lips together tightly to keep from laughing out loud at the admirer's offended expression.

Camilla returned to daydreaming as Mr. Thorne and Lydia continued to talk, primarily about acquaintances they had in common and a London Season about which Camilla knew little.

Then Benedict strolled into the room, and suddenly every nerve in Camilla's body was awake. She wasn't sure how she had known he was there. He had, as usual, made almost no sound, and she had been looking down at her needlework. But somehow she had sensed his presence, and she looked up to find him standing in the doorway, watching her.

A blush immediately mounted in her cheeks. "G-good morning, Benedict."

"My dear." He came into the room, greeting Lydia and her swain politely, then took up a seat beside Camilla on the sofa. "How are you this morning? I trust you slept well."

Camilla's blush deepened. "I— Uh, very well. I mean, it was good. I liked—" It seemed as if everything she said pulled her deeper into the morass of double meaning, so she stumbled to a halt.

He smiled, and Camilla's eyes were drawn to the curve of his lips. He had a lovely smile, she thought, but even better than his smile was the way his lips felt on hers. She remembered them on her body, loving her breasts, and all other thoughts went out of her head.

"I thought today would be a perfect day for us to picnic at the old keep," he went on.

"What?" Camilla looked up at him, her eyes as wide and startled as a doe's.

"Keep Island," Benedict explained. "You said that we would explore it one day, and I thought today would be ideal. We can take a picnic lunch with us."

"Uh..." *Why had he seized upon this idea?* It

seemed to her that he had an uncanny sense of what she would most like *not* to do. "But the tide is in," she protested lamely.

"We can take a boat, can we not? I can row across so narrow a strip of water."

"Oh, yes!" Lydia exclaimed delightedly. "That sounds like just the thing. So romantic."

"Eating among the ruins?" Camilla countered doubtfully. "I've been there many times," she told Benedict, "and it is really nothing remarkable."

"Oh, but think of the past," Mr. Thorne put in, obviously horrified that she did not appreciate the keep's Gothic charms. "The heroics, the evil deeds. Dungeons and fair damsels in distress."

"I think it was rather more drafty than exciting living there," Camilla pointed out practically. "I don't think there were any dungeons—or any damsels in distress, for that matter."

"Don't be so practical," Benedict said cajolingly. "*I* have never seen it, so it seems quite interesting to me."

Camilla realized that if she protested any more she would make everyone suspicious, so she forced a smile and said, "Yes, I suppose we could go."

Her patient, she reminded herself, was hidden away below ground. There was no reason to think that Benedict would get a glimpse of him. Of course, there was the entrance to the cellars. If he found that, he might want to go exploring down there. But, hopefully, she could dissuade him, could convince him that the old cellars were unsafe.

She sent a note to Cook, telling her to prepare a picnic basket, and went upstairs to change into a dress more appropriate for clambering around among rocks and ruins. Carrying the basket of food, they walked down to the Park's dock, where Camilla was relieved to see Anthony's small boat moored. They took the rowboat and made their way across the smooth waters to the island.

Camilla dutifully led Benedict up to the ruins and showed him where the great hall and the other rooms had been. Benedict, to her dismay, seemed bent on poking his nose into every nook and cranny. Struggling to keep a smile plastered to her face, she catered to his whims, showing him around every pile of rubble. When they were in the old kitchen area, near the door down into the cellars, she was careful to keep her eyes away from the scraggly bush that hid the square wooden door in the ground behind it, and was equally careful not to appear nervous or anxious to leave.

The longer they roamed the grounds, the more Camilla wondered if Benedict suspected something. He had been very suspicious yesterday morning about where she had been. *Had he seen her going to or leaving the island? Or had he spied Anthony coming over here? If he really was a customs agent, as Anthony thought, then perhaps he thought that the smugglers worked out of the ruins.* She supposed that that would be a logical enough guess. She decided to try to hint him away from that idea.

"You know," she said as they wandered back toward the grassy, sunny spot where they had decided to dine, "the locals are all terrified of the ruins." She watched him carefully to gauge his reaction.

There was nothing but mild interest on his face as he replied, "Really? Why?"

"There's a local legend that it's haunted. I suppose it started because it's such a desolate-looking place now, though most of the stones were removed for building the new house, not because of any real destruction."

"It certainly looks a likely place for ghosts." He spread out a blanket for them to sit on, and Camilla began to unpack the basket.

"I suppose that is why they believe they're here."

"What sort of ghosts?"

"All kinds. Some say there is a woman whose child died, and she walks along the gallery, which is no longer there, and wrings her hands and wails. Then there's a woman in white—isn't there always? Mysterious lights. I don't know what else. None of it's true. I mean, we have lived right across from it all our lives, and we've never seen anything. But the villagers are all scared of it."

Camilla slid a sideways glance at him. She could not tell from his expression whether her words had made any impression upon him.

Cook had outdone herself with the luncheon, perhaps carried away with the idea of the romantic getaway for the newlyweds, just as Aunt Lydia had been. After lunch, they sat and talked, gazing across the water, toward the cliffs opposite them and, beyond, Chevington Park itself. As they sat, Benedict put his arm around her shoulders. Camilla could not keep from letting out a little sigh of pure pleasure and leaning against him. *How sweet it was to sit this way with him.* Unexpected tears gathered in her eyes. She wondered how something that felt so good and sweet could also be so painful.

The good feeling came from the pleasure, the happiness of being with him, of having him close and tender. The pain, she knew, came from the fact that she loved him.

It was something she had not wanted to admit, even to herself, but it had been growing within her for days. How ironic that she had fallen in love with this man playing the role of her husband. *Was he so good an actor? Or was Benedict, a man whose last name she did not even know, the one man in the world for her? After all these years, had she stumbled in this bizarre way on a man to whom she could finally give her heart?*

It was absurd. She wished with all her heart that it was not so. But she had known as soon as the thought popped into her head that it was true—no, even before that. It had been when he put his arm around her and leaned his head against hers, and she realized that this was exactly what she wanted.

Benedict turned her chin toward him with his forefinger, and he kissed her. It was soft and warm and sweet, and Camilla wanted it never to end. As they kissed, the sweetness turned to heat, and they were straining together, arms wrapped tightly around each other. Gently he pushed her back onto the blanket, covering her with his body. His skin was searing; all the banked fires from the night before had sprung to life in him again.

A breeze caressed their bodies and tangled their hair. They kissed again and again. His hand roamed her body, scorching her through her clothes, and Camilla tentatively touched his chest. His quick, indrawn breath at her naive touch emboldened her to move her hand over his chest and back and arms, exploring the contrast of bone and muscle beneath the soft lawn of his shirt. She recalled the way he had looked naked the evening before, and the way his bare skin had felt beneath her fingers. She slipped her hand inside his shirt at the neck, and he shuddered, his mouth devouring hers.

His mouth left hers and began a trek down her throat to the neckline of her dress, leaving a line of fire in its wake. Camilla dug her fingers into his hair, caressing him. Her own hair whipped wildly around her face.

"I want you," Benedict mumbled against her throat. "God, I don't think I can take another night of this." He began to kiss his way back up to her chin.

"Then don't."

"What?" He stopped, raising himself on his elbows, and looked down at her. His black eyes burned into hers.

"I mean, I don't want that, either," she replied, a little amazed at her own temerity. But she knew, as certainly as she had realized that she loved him, that this was her one chance at love. Soon this would all be over. He would be gone, and she would be left alone. At least, she thought, she could have some memories. "I want you, too. I want to make love with you."

He swallowed hard. The wind tousled his hair. "You don't know what you're saying. Your reputation— Your future— What if you should conceive?"

"All that is my concern, isn't it?" she asked

bluntly. "As for my reputation, it is ruined, no matter what happens, if word gets out that we are not really married. And we have from the beginning planned for my future to include being a widow. As for a child, widows do have children."

"Yes. But it is harder than you imagine. This charade cannot be swept away so easily."

"Neither is it as hard as you make it out to be," she retorted, then smiled. "Do you have to fight me even on this, Benedict?"

For an answer, he bent and kissed her. When at last he raised his head, he said in a ragged voice, "This is not the time or place." In one lithe motion, he stood, reaching down and pulling Camilla to her feet, too. "We are going home."

For the first time since they had sat down to picnic, they took a good look around them. The wind that had swept over them as they lay on the ground had brought in a mass of gray clouds behind the ruins, out to sea. Even as they watched, the clouds piled up ominously, and the sky darkened.

"Oh, no. A storm," Camilla moaned. "I should have been watching."

"It is still well out to sea. Surely we can make it. The shore is not far from here."

Camilla looked uncertainly at the brewing storm. She knew how quickly storms could blow up here on the coast. But he was right; it was still a good distance away.

Quickly they packed their basket and folded the blanket, then fled back to the rocky beach where they had left the boat. They tossed in the basket and climbed into the boat, and Benedict settled down to row. Camilla wished that she could help him. Growing up by the sea, she had learned to row as a child, and was still able to, but if she manned one of the oars, her weaker strength would unbalance them, so that it would probably slow them down more than letting Benedict handle both oars.

The winds had turned the waves choppy, and they splashed into the boat now and again, forming a puddle of water that soon reached Camilla's shoes. Surprised at the sudden wetness, she glanced down. To her amazement, the floor of the boat held a huge puddle. She tore open the basket and searched through it for something with which to bail water. She came upon a bowl, and she tossed the remaining contents of it into the ocean and began to bail.

But the bottom of the boat continued to fill, far faster than she could empty it. She realized with horror that so much water could not be from the waves slopping over into it.

"Benedict!" She looked up at him, her eyes wide with fear. "The boat's leaking."

"So I see," he retorted tersely. "Rather bad one, I'd say." He turned and looked over his shoulder at the opposite shore. They were almost exactly halfway between the island and the beach.

Desperately he tried to continue rowing, and Camilla dipped out water, but they were foundering badly. The boat wallowed through the waves, moving much more slowly than it had at first. The storm was gaining on them. A wave hit them hard, washing over them, and suddenly the boat was sinking beneath them, and they were in the water.

15

Camilla's head went under the water, and she came up sputtering. She treaded water, looking around for Benedict, and let out a soft cry of relief when she saw his head bob up a few feet away from her. Quickly she kicked off her shoes. Fortunately, as was the style, she wore a narrow-skirted dress with few petticoats beneath it, but she nonetheless reached under her skirt and yanked them off, aware of how easily the sodden material could weigh her down.

Benedict moved through the choppy waves to her side, his arm going around her. She shook her head and shouted above the noise of the wind and ocean, "I'm all right! I can swim! You don't need to help me!"

He nodded, and they struck out for land. Camilla was a strong swimmer, and she had swum this far before, but never in such raging surf. The winds had kicked the waves into high, pounding walls of water that swamped her again and again. The undercurrent dragged at her, pulling her down and off course. Once she went down under a high, slapping wave, and she did not think that she could fight her way back up. She struggled, terrified, and finally popped back up above the water, coughing and flailing. Benedict fought his way to her and wrapped one strong arm around her beneath her arms, holding her up and treading water while she regained her breath.

Another wave came swooping down, but this one miraculously broke behind them and lifted them up. Camilla saw that they were much closer to shore, though a good bit farther down the beach than they had intended when they set out. The sight of the land gave them renewed strength, and they struck out again. The waves seemed to take them now, flinging them toward the shore, but this was a new danger, as well as a help, for they were being hurled straight toward the jagged rocks near the mouth of the cave. Desperately they swam against the current, as well as toward the land.

Lightning flashed across the sky, lighting the darkened day, and they saw the most joyous sight they had seen all day: a group of Chevington's servants wading out into the surf, carrying a line of rope. With renewed strength, they swam toward them. The foremost figure was Anthony, up to his waist in water. He whirled the rope around his head and threw it out. It fell in the water some feet from them, and he reeled it back in, then tossed it again.

This time Benedict grabbed it, wrapping it firmly around his arm and gripping it with his hand. His other arm went around Camilla just as firmly, and they worked only at staying afloat as they let the servants haul them safely in to shore.

Blankets were wrapped around them, and Anthony

moved to pick up Camilla to carry her to the house. However, Benedict quickly stepped forward and laid a restraining hand on his arm.

"I will carry her."

Anthony gaped at him. "But you must be exhausted."

"I am not so tired that I cannot take care of my own wife."

The younger man lifted his eyebrows at that, but he backed up, shrugging, and let Benedict lift Camilla into his arms. Camilla was tired beyond thinking, and she merely rested her head upon his shoulder with a little sigh, giving herself up to the simple joy of being safe.

He carried her into the house and up the stairs to their room, already warmed by a roaring fire. He set her down on her feet beside the tub, which her maid had ready and waiting, filled with hot water. Benedict waved Millie out of the room and helped Camilla out of her wet, clinging clothes himself. She stepped into the tub, letting out a soft moan as she sank down into the blissfully warm water. Benedict quickly removed his own clothing and climbed into the tub behind her.

She did not question his presence. She merely leaned forward to make room for him, then lay back against his chest. He wrapped his arms around her from behind and rested his cheek upon her head. They sat like that for a long time, cocooned together and wrapped in the warmth of the water.

"I thought I was going to lose you," Benedict murmured.

Camilla made a small sound of agreement.

"It scared the hell out of me," he went on. He

pressed his lips into her hair. "You know what I kept thinking? That I was going to die and I hadn't even made love to you. I realized what a damn fool I had been."

His lips moved down the side of her head, and he kissed her ear. Gently he took the lobe between his lips and nibbled at it, sending little shivers running through Camilla. She felt tired and dreamy, yet suddenly alive and sizzling, as well.

"I don't intend to make that mistake again," he said huskily, kissing his way down her neck.

He slid his hands down her water-slick arms and back up. He caressed her shoulders and back, and spread his palms out across her chest, just below her collarbone. Her skin felt like satin beneath his fingertips. His hands slid down, curving over her full breasts.

Benedict mumbled something, but his words were muffled against Camilla's skin, and she could not understand what he said. It didn't matter, though. She was lost in a world of sensation, floating hazily in the pure pleasure that his hands and lips produced in her. His fingers circled her nipples, making them tight and engorged. A low throb started between her legs, aching and persistent. She thought of the cataclysmic pleasure he had given her the night before, and her breath caught in her throat.

He cupped her breasts, seeming to weigh them in his hands, and gently squeezed them. Then his hands moved down over the flat plane of her stomach and finally delved between her legs. He caressed her thighs and hips and abdomen, returning again and again to the pulsing core between her legs. Camilla's breath turned ragged, and she melted back against him, lux-uriating in the touch of his knowledgeable fingers.

When she thought that she must explode as she had the other night, his hands, surprisingly, left her. He took her arm and turned her toward him. She instinc-tively realized what he wanted, and she turned fully facing him, reaching up to kiss him.

Their lips met and clung, for a moment gently, then with increasing heat. Their tongues clashed and twined, stoking the fires of their passion. The air was cool on their damp bodies, exposed above the water, but they did not notice it for the heat raging through them. They kissed hungrily, over and over again, straining together. His arms were wrapped around her so tightly she could scarcely breathe, and yet it did not feel close enough. Camilla wanted more. The throbbing between her legs was engulfing her. She wanted to wrap her legs around him; she wanted to feel him inside her. A whimper of pure longing broke from her throat.

Benedict surged to his feet, as if galvanized by the sound, and pulled her up with him. He stepped from the tub and grabbed a towel, wrapping it around Ca-milla. Camilla's eyes slid down his body, taking in every long, muscled inch of him. He was so power-fully male that it was almost frightening. His manhood thrust from his body, huge and ready, throbbing with desire, and even as she thought that he was far too large, that he could never fit, desire blossomed be-tween her legs, leaving her eager to feel him there.

He lifted her from the tub and set her down on the rug in front of the fire, busying himself with drying her off and, with each movement of his hands, arousing her desire further.

"Benedict..." she whispered, her hands going out to his chest.

"What?" He went still, his voice hoarse.

She did not answer except with her fingers, sliding them down over his chest, still slick with water. He stood quiescent beneath her touch, only twitching now and then or sucking in a sharp breath when she touched some particularly responsive spot. Even though his skin was still wet, he did not feel the cold. His body was like a furnace, roaring with the heat of its own passion.

Camilla's fingers traced the ridges of his rib cage and circled the small masculine nipples, delighting in the way they hardened at her touch. She slid down onto the softer skin of his stomach and caressed the hard points of his hipbones, tentatively moving closer and closer to the pulsing evidence of his desire. At the last minute, however, she lost her nerve, and her hands slid away and back over his buttocks. But that, too, was obviously pleasurable to him, for he let out a sharp little sound.

Camilla looked up at his face as her hands slid down over his buttocks and onto the backs of his thighs. His eyes were closed, and his skin seemed stretched too tight across his bones. He looked like a man teetering on the knife edge of pain...except for the full, sensual curve of his lips, which gave away the exquisite pleasure that seared him.

Experimentally, Camilla dug her fingertips into his buttocks, and was rewarded by an involuntary moan.

His eyes opened, lit by dark flames. She squeezed and stroked, her hands moving restlessly over his backside.

"Touch me," he ordered hoarsely.

Camilla knew what he meant. It was what she wanted, too, but had been too hesitant to do. Her fingertips trailed around his narrow hips, skimming over the tops of his thighs. She paused for an instant, then gingerly encircled his maleness. His member leaped wildly at her touch, and she gasped, then let out a nervous laugh.

Hesitantly she smoothed her fingertips along the shaft, intrigued by the satin skin overlying the masculine hardness. With exquisite tenderness, she caressed him. He made an odd noise deep in his throat and pulled her hard against him. His mouth devoured hers, hungry and insistent, his tongue plundering her mouth. She could feel his shaft pulsing against her skin, the hard bones of his chest flattening her breasts. His hands swept down her, digging into her derriere just as hers had with him, and she was faintly surprised by the jolt of pure lust that stabbed her.

Camilla went up on her tiptoes, clinging to him. Moisture gushed between her legs. She felt wild and desperate. She wanted to climb up him, to swallow him, to possess him to the utmost. His need was equally desperate. She could feel the tremors on his skin, his body tight as a bowstring.

Benedict pulled her down to the rug in front of the fire. The fire's glow played over their skin as Benedict stretched out beside Camilla and began to love her with his mouth. He kissed each nipple, then teased them with his tongue, lashing and circling. The little buttons of flesh responded eagerly, hardening beneath his touch. Camilla arched her back, her breasts aching for him, and he responded by cupping his hand around one and pulling the nipple into his mouth. He suckled slowly and deeply, his hand gently squeezing and caressing her breast.

Camilla's breath shuddered out, and she dug her hands into the rug beneath her. With every pull of his mouth, she felt a deep, visceral tug straight down to her womb. She squeezed her legs together, trying to ease the throbbing ache, but Benedict slipped his hand between her legs, moving them apart, and began to stroke the slick, engorged folds of flesh. Camilla groaned, bombarded by pleasure from both places. His fingertips teased and caressed the supremely tender flesh, sending her passion spiraling higher and higher.

His mouth moved to the other nipple, and, to her surprise, he slipped a finger inside her. She gasped, moving her hips against him in rhythm with his caresses, but just when she began to feel as if she were on the edge of the precipice over which she had fallen last time, he pulled back out and cupped his hand between her legs. Camilla writhed and moved against his hand, urging him to go on, but he did not, merely pressing her down and still, while his lips left her breasts and traveled down her stomach and onto her abdomen.

Her breath was coming almost in sobs now, and she pushed vainly against his hand, but he would not speed up, just continued to love her with his mouth until she thought that she would go mad with desire. Then he slipped his hands under her buttocks, raising her a little, and he moved between her legs. His shaft prodded insistently at the gates of her femininity.

"Please," she murmured. "Please. I want you... inside me."

Her words almost broke his control. He went still for a moment, struggling to regain mastery over himself. Then he guided his manhood into her. Camilla's eyes widened as he stretched her. For an instant she did not think it was going to work; then there was a flash of pain, and he slid inside. Camilla sucked in her breath, her fingers digging into Benedict's arms. She had never before felt anything like this, a delicious sensation of being stretched and filled, completely filled. She wriggled a little, opening her legs wider, as he sank deep within her.

Then he began to move within her, and she realized that what she felt before had been as nothing to the pleasure she was experiencing now. He stroked in and out in a slow rhythm, building up her passion until Camilla thought that she might scream from the mix of frustration and pleasure. He began to move more and more quickly, pumping powerfully, and the wild, sweet, dark thing that had swept through Camilla last night engulfed her again.

She let out a cry as the spasms raced through her. She held on tightly as Benedict bucked against her, his hoarse cry muffled against her neck.

Camilla wanted to laugh and cry, all at the same time and with great force. She wanted to ask Benedict a million things, but her thoughts would not stop zipping around enough for her to form a coherent sentence. Most of all, she wanted to say, "I love you." But she kept her lips clamped tight against the words. She was not so foolish as to think that he would welcome them.

* * *

Benedict gently eased out of Camilla's arms. They had fallen asleep tangled together in front of the fire, but the fire had died down and the air had grown chilly. He knelt and picked Camilla up, then carried her to the bed, where he gently laid her down and pulled the covers up over her. She sighed and smiled in her sleep, curling up on her side, but she did not awaken. He stood for a moment, looking down at her, and stroked back an errant curl from her forehead. He wondered why it had taken him so long to realize that he loved her.

He had let that witch Annabeth sour him on women, he knew. But anyone with half a brain should know, he thought, that Camilla was nothing like Annabeth. He had been stubborn and blind, and it had taken that storm and almost losing her to wake him up. Well, at least now it was much clearer to him what he had to do. He had to get her idiotic cousin out of whatever mess he had gotten himself into, and resolve the problem he had come here for. Then he would have to fix it so that no scandal could attach itself to Camilla because of this little charade they had been playing the past weeks. But first, he knew, before anything else, he must pay a visit to the Earl.

With a sigh, Benedict stepped back from his contemplation of Camilla and went over to his wardrobe. He dressed with quick efficiency, brushed a kiss across Camilla's forehead and strode out of the room.

Jenkins opened the door of the Earl's room at Benedict's knock and led him inside, announcing him to Chevington. The old man looked up and smiled.

"Well, there are you. None the worse for the wear, I trust, after your experience."

"No, sir. I think that Camilla suffered nothing more than exhaustion. I left her in bed, sleeping."

Chevington nodded, giving a peremptory wave to his servant. Jenkins quietly bowed out of the room. The Earl motioned for Benedict to come closer.

"Now, tell. me what happened. They keep things from me, not wanting to send me into another fit. It's damned annoying, I'll tell you. All they would tell me was that the storm caught you, but you and Camilla were fine. What really happened? How did you manage to get caught out in a storm?"

"We were picnicking on Keep Island. We didn't notice that a storm was brewing until late. No doubt that is my fault. I am not used to coastal storms. Grew up in Lincolnshire, you see." He hesitated, wondering just how much he ought to tell the Earl. He didn't want to frighten the old man. Though he had found the man to be much more capable of handling problems than anyone else thought him to be, still, he was not sure that the whole story wouldn't be too much for him.

Chevington frowned. "There's something else. What is it? Just say it, man. Don't worry about sending me into an apoplexy. I'm feeling much better these days. Why, I get up and walk around the room whenever I can get rid of that fussbudget Jenkins. Now, what happened?"

"I think we would have made it back before the storm broke if the boat hadn't started taking on water. Certainly we wouldn't have capsized and almost drowned, as we did."

"Almost drowned!" The old man glared. "God

dammit! I knew they were hiding something from me. 'Everything's fine,' indeed.''

"Well, we made it to shore, and we are both un-injured. The thing is...the boat had been tampered with.''

"Tampered with. How? What do you mean? Who would have done such a thing?''

"I don't know who, sir. That is what I hope to find out. As for how, I think probably a hole was cut in it. Boats don't naturally get perfectly round holes knocked in them.''

"Of course not.''

"I think he must have drilled a hole and filled it up again, put a round piece of wood in almost as big as the hole and stuck it with something sweet, probably syrup or honey or sugar, something that would dissolve in the water. I'm not sure exactly how he timed it. Perhaps he didn't. He may not have cared whether we were killed going to the island or coming back from it.''

Chevington stared in stupefaction. "I can't believe this.''

"It's true enough. I haven't told Camilla. I didn't want to scare her. I imagine she thinks the boat just sprang a leak.''

The Earl had his doubts about that. After all, Camilla had been raised on the coast and knew enough about boats not to be fooled by an intentionally cut hole. However, he wasn't one to spoil the man's illusions about his bride. Benedict would find out about Camilla soon enough.

"But why?'' Chevington asked, going to the question that concerned him the most. "Why would anyone want to harm you and Camilla? Is it connected to the smuggling, do you think?''

Benedict sighed. He was finding it harder than he had thought to go into his real reason for being here. He did not want to lose the old man's respect. ''It may be, at least in part,'' he temporized.

''Have you found out about Anthony?'' the old man went on anxiously. ''Is he involved with the smugglers?''

''I'm not sure. I haven't found any real evidence of it, just a lot of hints from the servants and townspeople. However, he is definitely involved in something odd. He and Camilla sneaked over to Keep Island the other day. That is why I insisted on going there this morning.''

''Keep Island?'' the old man repeated in a flabbergasted voice. ''What are you talking about? Why would they sneak over there?''

''I have no idea, sir. But they went there before the sun was up, and did so in a most secretive manner. When I asked Camilla where she had been, she lied to me. She told me she had been visiting an old woman named Nan, who was in ill health.''

''Lied, huh?'' Chevington seemed little surprised by that fact. ''Well, I daresay she's got something going on, then. Damme, I hope Anthony hasn't pulled her into some scrape of his. However, I can't imagine what they could be doing over there. There is nothing but ruins there. And why sneak over? They can go over there quite freely any time they like.''

''I presume they didn't want anyone to know they'd been there. It makes me think perhaps they are hiding something there.'' He paused, then went on. ''If he were involved in the smuggling, sir—might they use the ruins to hide their loot?''

Chevington shrugged. ''I suppose they could. However, you would have found it today, I would think. Everything's exposed there, nothing hidden. I would think the caves would be a much better place than the island.'' He stopped abruptly, considering, then went on. ''Well, there are the cellars.''

''Cellars, sir?'' Benedict's pulse quickened.

''Yes. The old house had cellars beneath it for storage. Quite large. During the Middle Ages they used to store great barrels of food and ale, not to mention armaments. According to the tales, there were dungeons, too, but I always doubted that myself.''

''How does one get into the cellars?''

''I'm not sure. I never went down there myself. I would have supposed the ceiling had caved in on them.'' The old man sighed. ''But if anyone had discovered a way down there, it would have been those two. They were always into trouble. Kept their nurse and governess hopping, I'll tell you.'' He paused, looking distressed. ''So he's brought Camilla into it, has he? Damn the boy!''

''Believe me, sir. I will do whatever it takes to make sure that she is *not* involved in all this.''

Chevington snorted. ''It is obvious you haven't been married to the girl long. She has always been one to do as she pleases, and she'll do anything for that young rapscallion.''

Benedict scowled. ''I am well aware of that, sir. But once I figure out what they're up to, I will make sure that she doesn't have any choice.''

''I will talk to Anthony,'' the Earl said heavily. ''I

will make him admit it. Make him agree to stop. I have been too weak. Haven't wanted to believe it." He shook his head. "Maybe I've given the boy too much freedom. That's what that tedious Beryl has been telling me for years."

"I don't know if it is that, sir."

"You don't think so?" Chevington tilted his head, looking at him with interest. "Tell me what you think."

"I think it's boredom, sir. Anthony is a lively lad, and, well, he finds his life here a trifle dull. Let me see what I can do. If I can get him out of this mess without his tarnishing the Chevington reputation, would you be willing to loosen the reins on the boy?"

"Loosen the reins? What do you mean? I have never ridden that boy hard."

"No. But you've kept him close, no doubt out of love. He is a young man of high spirits. He needs an outlet. They tell me he wants to join the army. There could be worse things for a boy like him. He would learn discipline, and he'd have a chance to use all that energy of his for a good cause."

The old man paled a little. "I cannot risk it. He's the heir."

"Other heirs to titles have been in the army. I was myself."

The old man's eyebrows lifted. "No one told me you held a title."

"I purposely didn't tell anyone. That is the other thing I came to talk to you about. But, first, promise me that you will at least think about letting Anthony leave the estate. For longer than a brief visit, I mean. If you cannot accept the army, then consider sending him off to Oxford. Or—'' Benedict took on a resigned look ''—let him come to stay with us in London.''

''London? I thought it was Bath where you lived.''

''Not in the future. Let him stay there for the Season, say. Get some town polish. I would make sure he does not get drawn into deep play or fall in with sharpsters.''

Chevington nodded. ''All right. I will think about it. I never wanted to stifle the boy.''

''I know, sir. Everything you have done has been done with love.''

Benedict fell silent. He cast a glance at the Earl, who was watching him with increasing interest.

''Well, man?'' Chevington said with obvious curiosity. ''You said you had something else to tell me. What is it? Out with it.''

Benedict drew a deep breath. He hoped he was not about to harm the old man. But he had to right this situation. He could not continue spinning lies and getting both himself and Camilla more and more deeply entrapped within them.

''The thing is,'' he began, then stopped and cleared his throat. Chevington gave him an impatient nod. ''I—I haven't been entirely open with you. Camilla and I— Well—'' He finished in a rush. ''I am not named Lassiter, and I am not married to your granddaughter.''

There was a long moment of silence. Chevington simply stared at Benedict, too stunned by his pronouncement even to be angry. ''I beg your pardon?''

Benedict repeated his words, and then, as quickly and concisely as he could, described the events of the night he had met Camilla, how she had told him and

Sedgewick about the predicament in which she had found herself, and how he had volunteered to play the part of her husband.

By the time Benedict had finished, a flush was rising in the old man's face. "Well, that sounds exactly like something Camilla would have done. She was always one to fall in with any harebrained scheme—as bad as Anthony. But who the devil are you, and why did you agree to it?"

"I am Lord Rawdon."

"Rawdon! Ha! Better come up with a better one than that, my boy. I know Lord Rawdon, and he is an old man, nearer my age that yours. Name's Sylvester, and we've played cards together."

"I don't doubt that. My uncle was ever a gambler. Fortunately for the family, he won more than he lost."

"Your uncle?"

"Yes. My father was his youngest brother. No one thought his line would inherit, but, except for Sylvester, the Wincrosses were a remarkably short-lived group of people."

"But—I thought Sylvester had a son."

"He did." A faint smile touched Benedict's lips. "Do you think to trip me up? I promise you, I know whereof I speak. In his middle years, my aunt, only a few years younger than he, produced an heir, much to everyone's surprise. While I was at war, the boy succumbed to a chest fever and died. Therefore, when Sylvester died last year, I came into the barony."

Chevington gazed at him unblinkingly for a long moment. "Perhaps you could explain to me why a lord would agree to pretend to be my granddaughter's husband."

"I know it sounds absurd."

"No more so than the rest of the story, I suppose." Chevington crossed his arms, waiting.

"I had a reason. I am here to catch a traitor."

Whatever the old man had expected, it obviously had not been this. He gaped at Benedict. "A traitor! What the devil are you talking about?"

Benedict proceeded to explain about the Gideon network and the recent problems, including Winslow's death, that had sent them to Edgecombe. The old Earl listened with rapt attention, and when Benedict had finished, he sat back with a sigh.

"Are you trying to tell me that Anthony is mixed up with treason, also? Because I don't believe it."

"No. I doubt very seriously that Anthony is in any way involved. However, someone among the smugglers must be. The odds are that it is this new leader. I will admit to you that I am hoping to use Anthony to find him. I intend to get your grandson out of it clean. I cannot, after all, have my wife's cousin on the gallows."

"But Camilla is not your wife."

"I plan to marry her when all this is over."

"I shall be interested in seeing how you bring off a wedding to a woman to whom everyone thinks you are already married."

Benedict smiled. "I have a plan."

"No doubt you do. I can see that you are a fitting partner for Camilla." He raised his hand as Benedict started to speak. "No, I don't even want to hear what it is. I believe I am growing too old for such shenanigans." He paused. "Does Camilla know all this?"

"No, sir. She thinks I agreed to help her because

she offered to pay me. She was of the opinion that I am a thief.''

The ghost of a smile played at the corners of Chevington's mouth. ''What makes you think she will agree to your plan?''

''I am confident that I can convince her.''

''Are you, now?'' The old man grinned. ''Would you care to take any bets?''

Benedict, who himself had some doubts on that score, was irritated by the other man's patent disbelief. ''She will have to agree,'' he pointed out crossly. ''Otherwise her reputation will be ruined.''

''I wouldn't use that argument, if I were you. Camilla doesn't take kindly to being coerced. Nor, I would think, to a husband who is offering only to save her reputation.''

''But I am not!'' Benedict flared. ''I love her.''

''Do you? Then I would suggest that you do what I always did with her grandmother.''

''And what is that?''

''Beg.''

Camilla awoke and stretched sensuously, very aware of her body. She glanced over at Benedict. He was still asleep, sprawled on his stomach. She reached out and tenderly stroked a hand down his hair. He had awakened her last night getting into bed, and they had made love all over again. It had been even more wonderful than the first time, if that was possible. A little pain stabbed her as she thought about the future, but she quickly shoved the thought away. There would be time enough for that later, when the bleak moment came that Benedict left.

She had no regrets about what had happened, but neither did she have any illusions. She loved Benedict, and she had wanted to experience that love in every way. But she did not expect him to return the feeling. Benedict was here for reasons of his own, and as soon as he had accomplished what he wanted, he would be gone. Camilla told herself that she was resigned to that, and she refused to let regrets about what would happen in the future spoil her time right now.

Curling a strand of his hair around her finger, she thought about staying in bed and waking Benedict by kissing him all over. It would be a most pleasant way to start the day.

But duty called her. She had neglected her patient, and she must go over to the island to see how he was progressing. She was not even sure that Anthony had been able to go back over to the island, because of the storm. She was doubly worried for the man's safety, for aside from his fever, there was the added danger of whoever was stalking him.

She would have laughed if she knew that Benedict hoped she had not noticed that their boat had been tampered with. She had realized immediately that someone must have drilled a hole in it in order to sink them. She had no idea who would have done it, but she had the uneasy feeling that it must have something to do with the man she and Anthony were hiding on the island. *Did the would-be killer know that she was helping him? Had he figured out that the man was on the island?* She did not understand the connection between causing her to drown and killing the stranger, but it seemed too coincidental to think that there were two different killers trying to murder two different people. Whatever was going on, she knew she had to see if her patient was all right.

She slipped out of bed and washed and dressed as quietly as she could, then eased out the door into the hall. She made her way quickly to the kitchens, where she wheedled some foodstuffs out of Cook before she set off for the island. It took her longer than normal to reach the ruins, for she stopped every few minutes to look around, uneasily aware that the killer could be hiding and watching her movements. The last thing she wanted was to lead him right to the man he wanted to kill. Once she thought she heard something behind her, but when she whirled around, she saw nothing out of the ordinary. Telling herself that she was letting her nerves get out of hand, she pressed on across the strip of land to the old keep.

With a last long, careful look around her, she descended into the cellars. Pulling out the candle she had brought, she lit it and made her way to the door of the room where the patient lay. Suddenly the door opened, and she jumped, almost dropping her taper in her fright.

Anthony stood in the doorway.

She let out a gusty sigh of relief. "Anthony! You nearly frightened me to death! What are you popping out like that for?"

"I heard you coming," he answered cheerfully, ignoring her crossness. "Camilla, the most wonderful thing—our man is awake!"

"What?"

"Yes. He came out of his fever." Anthony came out to her. "I came over last night and found his fever had gone down. He awakened and spoke. He didn't say much of anything, just asked where he was and who I was, things like that, and then he went back to sleep. But he is obviously much improved.''

Camilla leaned close to whisper, ''Did you find out anything about him?''

''No. Very little. I didn't like to press him, as weak as he was feeling. But I am sure that when he awakens this morning, he will feel more up to talking.''

They continued into the small underground chamber where the man lay. Camilla crossed the room to look down at him. He lay curled up on his side, blanket wrapped around him like a cocoon and one arm cradling his head. She noted with satisfaction that his color was much better this morning and his breathing no longer seemed labored.

He seemed to sense her watching him, for his eyes flew open, and he sat up quickly, wincing at the pain. He stared at her for a moment, then relaxed, saying, ''Oh. You must be the kind lady my young friend here told me about.''

''You are looking much better this morning.''

''Thank you. It is entirely due to your care, I understand.'' He started to struggle politely to his feet, but she waved him back down.

''Never mind the niceties. No point in wasting your energy.'' She set down the box she carried and began to dig in it. ''Here. I brought you some nice hot tea to drink, and some fortifying gruel.''

Anthony leaned over and looked down at the pot in the box and grimaced. ''Ugh.''

''Hush. Gruel will be quite good for our patient. He needs something warm and filling to help get his strength back.''

"It sounds delightful," the other man replied, smiling at her. "Frankly, the way my stomach feels right now, I would eat anything."

Camilla smiled back at him. He was a nice-looking young man, she thought, even with the scraggly beard that had sprouted while he was sick, and the wildly tousled hair. As if reading her thoughts, he combed through his hair with his fingers and gave Camilla an apologetic smile.

"Sorry. I must look like some vagrant."

"Nonsense. You look like a man who has been very ill for several days," Camilla corrected crisply, dishing up a bowl of gruel from the pot. "Here. Are you strong enough to hold it, or shall I help you?"

The color heightened a little in his face, and he said quickly, "Thank you. I think I'm not that bad yet."

But she noticed that his hand trembled a little under the weight of the bowl. He was far from well. He took a few slow bites. The color in his face improved, and he smiled at Camilla.

"Thank you. I feel much more the thing now."

Anthony put aside his dislike of the gruel long enough to eat a heaping bowlful. When their visitor had drunk his tea and eaten the last bite of gruel he could stuff down, he leaned back against the wall, closing his eyes.

Camilla was afraid he might slip back into sleep, so she said quickly, "Well! Now that you are feeling better, there are a few things that we really need to talk about."

His eyes opened and he looked at her—a trifle warily, Camilla thought.

"For instance, your name," Camilla went on. "We have no idea who you are."

"I know. And you are a most kind and gracious woman to give aid to a stranger like this."

There *was* something a little foreign in the inflection of his words, Camilla thought—*or was it just her imagination?*

"Thank you. But I am not looking for compliments. I would simply like to know your name."

He hesitated for a moment, then said, "It is James. James Woollery."

"I see." She found herself wondering if he had given her the compliment in order to have more time to think up a name for himself. "What happened to you to put you in such a condition?"

"Camilla..." Anthony put in. "Perhaps he isn't feeling well enough for all these questions. Anyway, I told you what happened."

"I would like to hear it from him."

"No. It is all right, Anthony," Woollery assured him. "I understand her curiosity. I only wish that I could be of more help. I was attacked, but by whom or why, I do not know. He was hiding in the rocks along the shore, waiting for me, and when I passed, he jumped out at me with a knife. We struggled. I'm not sure exactly what happened. I was cut and losing blood, but I managed to pull my pistol from my pocket, and when I did, he ran off. I fired at him, but I don't think I hit him."

"But you have no idea who he was?"

He shook his head. "He wore a kerchief around the lower part of his face, like this, and a cap pulled down low on his head. I could see nothing but his eyes, and it was quite dark. I did not recognize him, certainly. I don't even think that I could pick him out if I saw him again."

"What size was he? Large? Small?"

"Tall," he replied. "Taller than I. Strong enough."

"Did he steal anything from you?"

"No." He shifted, for the first time looking away from her. "I presume that was his intent, after he killed me, but he did not get that far."

Camilla nodded, wondering if it was mere coincidence that he had looked away just then. "It seems odd, though. Why not just tell you to stand and deliver? It seems extreme to kill a stranger to rob him, don't you think?"

The man shrugged. "I do not know what he was thinking."

"Mr. Woollery, where are you from?"

His eyebrows rose. "Well, I am from Dorset. I was on my way home."

"From France?" Camilla asked coolly.

Woollery went still. "What do you mean?"

"I mean that I know you were among the smugglers. That you came in on the boat carrying a load of brandy the other night."

"I'm sorry." He smiled politely. "But you are mistaken."

"Am I?" Camilla gazed back at him levelly. "Mr. Woollery, I am sure that you can appreciate my position. My cousin and I have helped you because we felt compassion for you, as we would for anyone injured as you were. However, we know that you came in with the smugglers. That ring of yours was seen, and it is the sort of thing that one does not easily forget.''

His hand went instinctively to the cord around his neck, but he said nothing.

''You were at the very least engaged in the activity of smuggling. But it also appears that you came here from France. You spoke French in the midst of your delirium.''

''I did?'' He looked surprised and, bizarrely, a trifle pleased.

''Yes. You did.''

''That is not difficult to explain. You see, my mother was an émigré. French is almost as much my native tongue as English.''

''That may be, but it still does not explain what you were doing here the other night, helping a band of smugglers. It does not tell me how you got here or why you are here.''

The man passed a shaky hand across his forehead. ''I know how odd all this looks. But I promise you, I am as English as you are, and I love my country just as much. I do not know the identity of the man who attacked me, nor do I know why he attacked me. As for the rest of it, well...I am sorry, but I simply am not at liberty to tell you.''

''Not at liberty!'' Camilla exclaimed.

''What does that mean?'' Anthony spoke up for the first time. ''I say, Woollery, this is hardly the time to be resting on scruples. Your life could be at stake. Or ours, for that matter. You have to tell us. What is going on?''

''Yes,'' echoed a deep voice in the doorway. ''I'd like to know that, as well. What is going on?''

"Benedict!" Camilla gasped and whirled around to face the doorway, automatically stepping between the wounded man on the floor and the man who stood in the door. *Now the fat was really in the fire.* "What are you doing here?"

"I believe that is my question," Benedict replied calmly, stepping into the room. "I followed you, my dear. I was rather interested in what kept you running out here to the abandoned keep. Sorry to arrive so late, but it took me a while to find the cellar door. I was too far behind you to see where it was, you see."

"You—you mean, you knew? The whole time?"

"I knew you and Anthony were sneaking over here. For what purpose, I was not sure. I had hoped that you would choose to confide in me, but as you did not, I took matters into my own hands."

Anthony strode over to Camilla's side and faced Benedict, his jaw set. "It wasn't her fault. It was all mine. She merely helped me when I told her what I had done."

"That I can well believe," Benedict responded dryly. "Now, if the two of you will kindly step aside and let me see who you are so assiduously hiding…"

Benedict started around them, then stopped short. "Good God."

Camilla whirled around. Their patient was staring at Benedict in much the same way that Benedict was staring at Woollery.

"James Woollery…"

"M-Major!" Woollery struggled to his feet. "Lord Rawdon!"

16

"Who?" Camilla stared at Woollery, her word echoing hollowly in her ears.

Woollery swayed, his knees buckling, and Benedict jumped forward to catch him. "Here! Anthony! Help me lower him to the ground. Camilla, fetch some water."

Both of them hurried to do as he bade. Anthony and Benedict eased Mr. Woollery to the ground and propped him against the wall. Camilla picked up the jug of water and hurried back to the others. Benedict was lightly slapping Woollery's cheeks.

"You know him?" Camilla asked in amazement.

"Yes." Benedict poured a bit of water into the palm of his hand and began to sprinkle it over the younger man's face. "James. James. Wake up. It is I, Rawdon."

"But how?" Anthony asked, puzzled. "Do you know what happened to him?"

"No. Don't you?" He glanced around. "Aren't you holding him prisoner here?"

"Prisoner! No!" Anthony looked affronted. "We

were hiding him! I brought him here to tend to his wounds and to keep his attacker from finding him again. What a thing to think!''

"That's exactly the sort of thing he *would* think,'' Camilla put in bitterly. It was becoming clear to her that Benedict had been deceiving her mightily all along. "*Lord Rawdon* obviously trusts no one.''

Benedict sent her a penetrating look, but before he could speak, Woollery's eyes fluttered open. He glanced around vaguely for a moment, then focused on Benedict. "Lord Rawdon!'' he said again in tones of awe. "What are you doing here? How did you find out?''

"So far I have found out damn little. What happened to you, Lieutenant Woollery? Why are you in this state?''

"Someone attacked me. Right after I got off the boat. I helped unload, and I started walking. I was going to go to that village.''

"Edgecombe?''

Woollery nodded. "Yes. I planned to hire a horse there. But someone attacked me. I have no idea who. It was dark, and his face was covered, except for his eyes. I managed to scare him off, and then, the next morning, this kind young man found me.'' He nodded toward Anthony. "I don't know what I would have done without him. He saved my life. He half carried me here and hid me, bandaged up my wounds.''

"We didn't know who had attacked him,'' Anthony put in. "I was afraid he might try again. The only place I could think of to hide him was here. But he developed a fever. It was touch and go there for a while. That's why I brought Camilla to him. I knew

she would be able to physic him better than I. And
look—her potions brought him out of his fever.'' He
beamed at Camilla like a proud father.

Camilla could have kicked her cousin for his cheer-
fulness. She felt thoroughly ill-used. She ignored Anthony, turning toward Benedict and asking in icy
tones, ''Who *are* you, anyway? What are you doing
here? And what right do you have to ask us any of
these questions?''

''Don't you know him?'' Woollery asked, puzzled.
''He is Lord Rawdon.'' He said it as if everyone in
the world knew the name. ''He was my major in the
Peninsular campaign. Major Wincross, then, before he
came into the title.''

''Major Wincross?'' Anthony was frowning in con-
centration. ''I've heard that name before.'' Suddenly
he looked galvanized. ''But that's— You're the man
Graeme was always talking about!'' He looked at
Benedict almost worshipfully. ''Oh, sir, I cannot tell
you how honored I am to meet you.''

''*Meet* him! You've known him for days,'' Camilla
pointed out waspishly. ''Are you talking about Cousin
Graeme? Harold and Bertram's brother?''

''Yes, of course, Cousin Graeme. Who else would
be talking about the hero of San Luis?''

''The hero of what?''

Benedict groaned. ''Please, let us not get into that
old thing.''

But Woollery was nodding eagerly. ''Yes. Yes, that
is Lord Rawdon. Who is this Graeme you speak of?
Is he with the army?''

''Yes. The Hussars. Graeme Elliot. He was forever
talking about the way this Wincross chap and his men

were trapped behind enemy lines, but somehow the major managed to avoid capture and get back to our own lines and—"

"I am sorry, gentlemen," Camilla said acidly, interrupting, "to put a halt to all this military bonhomie, but could we please return to the subject at hand—to wit, who are these two men, and what are they doing here in Edgecombe?"

Anthony looked thoroughly exasperated. "They have just told you who they are. This is James Woollery—he was a soldier, Milla, a lieutenant, not an enemy spy. And this is Lord Rawdon, the man who—"

"Yes, yes, I understand, the hero of San Something-or-Other. What I mean is, what do they have to do with the smuggling ring? And why was Lieutenant Woollery speaking French when he was unconscious? And why was Benedict down here, pretending to—"

Benedict cut in smoothly, smiling affectionately toward Camilla. "You will find that Lady Rawdon is a woman who wants answers."

"Who?" Anthony asked.

Woollery looked uncertainly from Rawdon to Camilla and back. "Sir? Is it all right to tell her?"

"Of course." Benedict waved aside his doubts airily. "You are speaking to my wife. Camilla is the new Lady Rawdon."

Camilla swung toward Benedict, her eyes shooting sparks. "What did you say? Have you gone mad?"

"Now, now, dear." Benedict smiled at her soothingly, crossing the floor to take her hand and squeeze it—hard. "We don't have to pretend with Woollery. You can admit that you know my real identity. The lieutenant is one of my own men. I do wish you had told me what you were doing over here. I could have cleared the whole thing up more quickly."

Woollery looked at Camilla apologetically. "I'm sorry, my lady, that I caused you concern. As I told you, my mother was French, and I have been in France for some time now, pretending to be a Frenchman, and, well, I must still have been thinking in the language. Sometimes it is a little difficult to switch back and forth."

"You see, Milla?" Anthony turned toward his cousin with a smug smile. "I told you it didn't necessarily mean he was a spy."

"Ah, but he was," Benedict told them. "It is just that he was spying on *them* for England. Winslow, Sedgewick and I set up the network some time ago. Winslow had some sort of arrangement with the smugglers to get our men and our information into England."

"So that's why you were unloading the brandy!" Anthony exclaimed, looking at Woollery.

"Caught, eh?" Benedict asked. "You must have gotten careless."

"It was that ring you wore on a string around your neck," Anthony explained. "I knew you couldn't be a common smuggler."

"I told you that ring would get you in trouble someday."

"But, sir, it was my good-luck charm. I couldn't leave it behind. I've worn it ever since I was a child!"

"It was no good-luck charm this time," Benedict pointed out dryly.

There was a moment of silence as all their thoughts went back to the young man's injuries.

"But what are you doing here, sir?" Woollery asked finally. "I thought you had come because I had gone missing."

"I came because some others had gone missing, as well. Someone is trying to destroy our network. We have had no word from Keswick, who should have returned three weeks ago, and no information from anyone, inside France or out. It's been dead silence." He sighed. "In Keswick's case, I am afraid that I am speaking literally."

"You—you mean, he's dead?" Woollery gulped.

Benedict nodded. "Judging from your experience, I fear so. It was only your quick reactions and Anthony's help that kept you from meeting the same end."

"This is terrible." The young man turned even paler, and he closed his eyes for a moment.

"Yes, it is. Sedgewick and I decided we had to come down here and learn something about what was going on."

"So that is why you were so—" Camilla began.

"So eager to come down here?" Benedict interrupted her, his eyes staring intently into hers. "Yes, my dear, much as I wanted to meet my new relatives, I did have an ulterior motive. And, of course, now you can understand why we had to pretend that my name was not Rawdon."

Camilla stared at him. *Why did he keep on insisting in front of this young man that they were married?* It was bad enough that her family thought she was married to him, now that he had turned out to be a lord and a war hero. But somehow she could bluff her way through it, she thought. But to be telling other people that they were married, people who knew him as Rawdon, was simply disastrous.

"Have you found out who is disrupting the network?" Woollery asked.

"The man who killed Nat Crowder!" Anthony exclaimed suddenly. "So that is why you were asking all those questions about it! I thought you were an excise officer."

Woollery chuckled at the idea, and Rawdon smiled. "An excise officer. No wonder you were suspicious of me. Just as I was suspicious that you were pulling my wife into your smuggling scheme."

Anthony looked aghast. "Sir! I would never get Camilla involved with the smuggling! It would be far too dangerous."

"Too dangerous for you, too," Benedict pointed out bluntly. "You have your grandfather worried sick about you—and Camilla, too, I'll warrant."

"But—but how does he know?" Anthony goggled at him. "Milla! You didn't tell—"

"No, I didn't tell Grandpapa that you were a criminal," Camilla retorted. "Do you think I want to kill him?" She turned on Benedict with an accusing look. "Did you?"

"No. I promise you." Benedict held up his hands, as if in surrender. "Don't pounce on me. The Earl already knew about it. It seems to have been common knowledge around the area. Did you think that Chevington, with all his friends, would not have been told about it? He asked me to help him, to find out if the gossip was really true and his grandson was about to put a blot on his family name by being caught and hanged as a thief."

Anthony's cheeks flamed red. "Sir! That isn't— Well, it wasn't like that."

"No? How was it? You were not bringing in smuggled goods?"

"Well, yes, of course I was."

"And if the soldiers or the excise men caught you, do you think that they would have let you go with merely a slap on the wrist because you were the future Earl of Chevington?"

"I…" Anthony looked even more abashed.

"Of course that is what you thought—provided you thought at all. Well, I can tell you that, had you been caught, you would have been hanged with the rest of them, or, perhaps, since you were nobility, they might have lessened the sentence to transportation. In either case, your family would have suffered the scandal. And if you were hanged, you know, your cousin Bertram would have become the Earl of Chevington. I can imagine how well pleased your grandfather would have been about that. Provided that he hadn't had another bout of apoplexy, of course."

"Benedict! Really, that's enough!" Camilla cried, seeing Anthony's crushed expression. "I think Anthony realizes what he has done."

"Does he? Perhaps he does—*now*. But I think that before this he saw it as some lighthearted lark. And you, my dear, certainly did nothing to dissuade him."

"You must not blame Camilla, sir," Anthony put in manfully. "It was all my doing. I didn't even tell her until she arrived, and then she made me promise that I would quit. And I will. I will tell Jem that I can't go out with the men next time."

"No, you won't quit," Benedict told him. "Not just yet."

Anthony stared. "I beg your pardon? But I thought you—"

"Yes, I do want you to quit. More than that, I insist on it. I have spoken to your grandfather about letting you off the leash a little. He has agreed to consider letting you go to Oxford, though I have heard you've little liking for your studies."

"Oh, I would, sir, if it meant getting out of Edgecombe."

"I think it would be just the thing for you," Benedict agreed. "But before that, you have to go out with the smugglers one last time. And you will take an extra helper with you."

"I don't understand."

"Have you gone mad?" Camilla cried. "You just got him talked out of it!"

"Ah, but this time he will not really be a smuggler. He will be working for his country. He is going to take me with him."

"You are going to find the leader!" Anthony exclaimed, his eyes lighting up. "What a bang-up adventure. You and I will capture him."

A faint smile touched Benedict's lips at the boy's enthusiasm. "Something like that."

"You can count on me, sir. You won't regret it."

"I better not," Benedict warned him sternly. "You have to obey my orders to the letter on this, Anthony. No flying off on larks of your own."

"No, sir, I won't. I shall do exactly as you say."

"I'll help, too, sir," Woollery spoke up.

"Of course. If you're feeling up to it."

"Benedict! You can't be serious!" Camilla was horror-struck. "This is even worse than Anthony's smuggling. At least all the other men doubtless looked out for him, protected him."

"They did not!" Anthony protested.

"Do grow up, Anthony. They certainly did. They would all fear Grandpapa's wrath too much if anything happened to you. But this—this is terribly dangerous. You will be dealing with someone who has killed other people—Nat Crowder, for one, and probably this Keswick man that Benedict was talking about. He obviously did his best to do in Lieutenant Woollery, as well. Why, now I see it—he is the one who put that hole in our boat, too!"

Benedict glanced sharply at Camilla. He should have known she would have reasoned out that their boat had been tampered with. A reluctant smile of admiration tugged at his lips.

"He is dangerous," Camilla went on adamantly. "If you two corner him, I am sure that he will not hesitate to kill you."

"Oh, pooh," Anthony dismissed her fears. "Don't be such a worrywart, Milla. Nothing is going to happen to me."

"Don't be so sure," Benedict told him. "I don't want you going into it with that sort of attitude or you'll get us all killed. This man *is* dangerous, and we shall have to be on our toes."

"Yes, sir."

Benedict turned to Camilla. "But one thing you don't know about *me*, my dear—I am a dangerous man, also. Rest assured that I will watch out for Anthony."

"Oh!" Camilla let out a groan of frustration. "You think that you are invincible."

"Not entirely." He smiled. "But I have gotten through some tight spots before. I know how to take care of myself—and my men. I've always brought them through."

Camilla would have liked to protest, but she knew that it was pointless. Once men made up their minds about something, especially something dangerous and foolhardy, there was no changing them.

"Then I suppose that I shall simply have to go along with you," she said calmly.

"What?" The word chorused from all three men, but only Woollery looked surprised.

"Absolutely not," Benedict pronounced, his brows rushing together sternly. "I forbid it."

"You what?" Camilla's voice was dangerously silky.

Anthony groaned, knowing that those words were like a red flag waved in front of his cousin. Quickly he jumped in, "Be reasonable, Milla. You can't go. You would be recognized in an instant. No one would think you were a man."

"I'm not much smaller than Jem Crowder," Camilla protested.

"Maybe not, but you are shaped rather differently,"

Camilla's color rose a little at her cousin's blunt words, but she said stoutly, "Nonsense. In rough workman's clothes, you won't be able to see my shape."

"There is your walk," Benedict pointed out, seeing the wisdom of Anthony's course. "The way you move, even the tilt of your head, is distinctly feminine.

And don't tell me you can heft a keg of brandy like a man.''

"That's right." Anthony nodded emphatically. "As soon as you tried to lift a heavy object, your masquerade would be over. Then the rest of us would be doomed, too."

Camilla did not like to give in, but she could see the wisdom of the men's words. She decided to try a different tack. "But how are the rest of you going to pass as smugglers? Don't you think they will notice if Anthony shows up with an extra man or two?"

Anthony nodded regretfully. "She's right about that. I don't know how you can pull this off."

Benedict looked thoughtful. "What if...some of the regular smugglers were taken ill and couldn't go—right on the very night of the run? Wouldn't the group need extra men—and quickly?"

"I suppose so."

"You know who the smugglers are, don't you? At least some of them?"

"Yes."

"Is there a single family that contributes several of the men?"

Anthony nodded. "The Matsons. There are three of them. Two brothers and one brother's son. They all live together in one house. But how are you going to make sure they're sick?"

"There are herbs that will do the trick. Aren't there, my dear?" Benedict looked toward Camilla.

She grimaced sourly. "I wouldn't know. *I* am not in the habit of trying to poison people."

"It won't seriously injure them," Benedict argued. "We'll slip it in their food at noon, and it will make

them sick at their stomachs for a while, long enough
for the smugglers to realize that they will be short-
handed. When you hear this—'' he nodded toward
Anthony ''—then you can tell them that there's a gar-
dener or groom or some such at the Park whom you
know would love to earn a little extra money, no questions asked.''

Anthony nodded. "I can do that."

"You are all mad," Camilla said flatly. "You will
wind up getting killed."

"Do you have some other suggestion?" Benedict
challenged her quietly. "Another way that we could
trap the man who is betraying this country to our enemy? Or perhaps you think we should allow him to
continue to do so?"

"No, of course not." Camilla gazed back at him, a
trifle sulkily. He had her neatly trapped. She could not,
of course, sanction letting the traitor work at will, but
neither could she think of another way to capture him.
"I am simply saying that it is dangerous."

"My dear girl…a little danger is the spice of life."

"Yes, and I have known from the beginning how
much you like spice," Camilla retorted bitterly.

Both Woollery and Anthony looked at her oddly.
Only Benedict could guess the reason for her bad humor, and he could say nothing to soothe her in front
of the others. He cursed his bad luck. This was not
the way he had meant for her to find out about his
true identity. He could see now how wrongheadedly
he had handled the whole thing. He should have realized that Camilla would not be mixed up in treason,
or even in the smuggling—not even to help out her
cousin. He should have revealed to her who he was

and what he was seeking. Then he would have had her help the whole time. She would have come to him and told him all about their mysterious patient. Everything would have been easier—and she wouldn't be in such a snit now, either.

"Well," Camilla went on coolly, "I have other things to do. I shall leave you gentlemen to make your plans for your expedition."

She turned and strode out of the room.

"Camilla! Wait!" Benedict started to follow her, but Anthony laid a restraining hand on his arm.

"I would let her be alone for a while if I were you," Anthony told him. "She'll just take your head off if you try to talk to her now. I know. I've tried it often enough." He gave a rueful smile. "She's angry because she can't go with us on the smuggling run. But she will come around, you'll see. She's always been a right 'un. And she won't tell anyone about it, either."

"No, I am sure she will not," Benedict agreed, looking after her in indecision. He suspected that Anthony was right, and if he did try to talk to her now, it would only lead to a furious argument. They both might very well say things they did not mean, and he would end up in a worse position than he was in now. He sighed. "You are right. I will talk to her later." *In their bedroom, where he could soften her with kisses and caresses.*

Camilla stormed off the island and across the path to the beach, ignoring the water that lapped only inches from her feet. Such angry emotions churned within her that she felt almost physically sick. *Lord*

Rawdon, indeed! She did not pause to examine her emotions. She only knew that she felt utterly betrayed and bereft. Her life was ruined, and it was Benedict who was the cause.

When she reached the house, she did not go into the breakfast room. She was feeling too ill. Instead, she went up to her bedroom and rang for her maid. It was there that Benedict found her, directing the activities of two footmen and the maid, when he came in an hour later.

He stopped and looked at the cot, set up in one corner of the room, on which the maid was busily tucking in sheets. The footmen, standing at either end of the cot, busily avoided his eyes. Benedict looked from the group over to Camilla, who folded her arms across her chest and gazed back at him coolly. He turned back to the servants.

"Out." His clipped voice and the peremptory jerk of his head were enough to send the three servants scurrying out of the room. The maid prudently closed the door behind her.

"What is this?" Benedict nodded toward the make-shift bed.

"That is a cot. Surely you have seen them before. I imagine in the army that you even slept on one."

"Stop playing the fool. You know what I mean. What is it doing here?"

"I should think that would be obvious. As for playing the fool, I am afraid I can be nothing else. After all, isn't that why you chose me for this charade?"

"If you will remember," Benedict said through clenched teeth, "it was *you* who chose *me,* not the other way around." He realized that over the past few days he had forgotten how utterly maddening the girl was.

"Of course. I suppose that makes this all my fault, then."

"It is no one's fault." He struggled for a reasonable tone, though he was not even sure any longer what they were talking about. "It just happened, and we need to make the best of it."

"That is what I am doing. We have been trying to think of a way this whole time to get you a bed to sleep in, and now I have. You will remember we even talked about our having a spat and your sleeping on a cot in the dressing room. Well, it's been long enough now. A fight would be quite believable—and not at all difficult for us to pretend, don't you think? So I had the men bring down a cot from the attic. I tried it in the dressing room, but it seemed terribly cramped and dark. I thought this was a better place."

Benedict moved closer, his eyes fierce. "Stop it! You know damn good and well I need no place to sleep. My place is in your bed."

Camilla met his eyes and replied flatly, "No. It is not."

"Damnation, Camilla, stop acting this way!"

"What way? Like someone whom you have deceived? Someone you have lied to and tricked? Like a woman whom you seduced and betrayed?"

"I didn't!" He flushed. "Well, I mean, yes, I suppose I did seduce you. I should have waited. I would have, if I had been stronger. But, dammit, Camilla, I'm only flesh and blood. There was only so much I could stand. Being so close to you all the time, seeing you, smelling you, sleeping ten feet away from you— it drove me insane.''

There was such raw need in his voice that it raised an answering heat in Camilla's abdomen. She turned away, flustered. "All right, I will admit it," she said in a muffled voice. "You did play the gentleman most of the time, and I was just as much to blame as you yesterday. But—" she whirled around, eyes flashing, her voice breaking on her words "—why did you lie to me?"

"I didn't lie to you."

"You never told me the truth!"

"My God, Camilla, what did you expect me to do? I was looking for a traitor. I came here, not knowing anyone, only knowing that this is where it happened. I couldn't tell anyone what I was really doing."

"I knew nothing about you," Camilla pointed out. "But I trusted you enough to take you into my home, to introduce you to my family as my fiancé. I even let you in here, in my bedroom, trusting that you would not take advantage of that."

"That is another matter entirely. I am not talking about personal trust. If *I* was wrong, it was my country that would suffer."

"You believed that I could be a traitor?" Camilla's voice was like ice.

"No, of course not. I never thought that *you* were the person I was looking for."

"Only because I am a woman, and you don't think a woman capable of carrying it off."

"No! That is not why. I was certain that you were not capable of betraying your country. But I couldn't risk your telling anyone the truth about me. I couldn't risk it getting back to him.''

''So it was just that you thought me incapable of keeping a secret. I see.''

''Are you trying to tell me that you would not have told Anthony? You certainly told him quickly enough that we were not really married.''

''For heaven's sake, he already knew that. He knew that the story I had told Grandpapa was a sham. And he isn't as gullible as Aunt Lydia. He would not believe that I had actually met and married a man at the same time that Aunt Lydia was telling everyone I had. Or perhaps you thought Anthony was the traitor?''

''He could have been. I did not *think* it was Anthony, but it was too important a thing to let my personal feelings interfere. Do you think I enjoyed deceiving you? Or lying to your grandfather? Or any of the other things I had to do?''

''You mean things like charming your way into my bed? Was that part of your scheme? Perhaps a way of ensuring my loyalty to you, in case I discovered who you really were? Well, let me tell you, *Lord Rawdon*, that it did not work.''

Benedict flinched as if she had struck him, and bright spots of color stained his cheeks. ''Dammit all to bloody hell! God knows I am not fool enough to think that you would be more loyal to me than to your cousin—or to a stranger you find feverish and bleeding among the ruins. You certainly held their secrets from me well enough! And I can promise you that there was no calculation in my making love to you. There was never the least thing in it except blind, unreasoning lust!''

Camilla paled. For a long moment, there was nothing but silence in the room. Then she said, her voice a trifle shaky, "Thank you for explaining your motives to me. I suppose I should be grateful that even though there was no higher feeling involved in your lovemaking, at least there was no thought or planning, either."

Benedict groaned. "I did not mean it *that* way. My God, do you think that I would marry you if lust was all that moved me?"

Camilla stared at him. "*Marry?* What are you talking about? No one said anything about marriage."

"*I* did. Did you not notice that I told young Woollery that you were Lady Rawdon?"

"Yes, but I—I could not understand why you had done it. You cannot marry me. I mean—the scandal!" It came to Camilla in a blinding flash exactly why she was so furious about Benedict's deception. She had fallen in love with him and, deep down, she had been nursing the dream that they would actually marry, despite the resulting scandal. With an ordinary man, it might have been possible, but not a nobleman. Certainly she would have been horrified if Anthony considered tying himself to a woman whose name was as besmirched as hers would be once their pretense of marriage was known. "Your family would never allow it."

"My family has nothing to say about it. I am the only one who decides whether I marry or not."

"But you cannot have a wife whose name is tainted, as mine will surely be when all this comes out."

"Your name will not be tainted. That is the whole

point of what I am saying. If you and I are married in truth, there is no scandal.''

"Oh." Camilla looked at him. "It won't work. My entire family thinks that your name is Lassiter and that I am already your wife. Now, suddenly, you say you are Lord Rawdon, and we will get married? They will still know that you and I slept in this room together without benefit of marriage for days, weeks, before we were married. If you think that Aunt Beryl won't talk about it, then you are sadly mistaken. And Cousin Bertram! No wonder he thought you were familiar-looking. No doubt he has seen you about London. It will be a wonderful bit of gossip for him, and there is nothing Bertram likes better. No, it's impossible.''

"It is not. I know a clergyman who will marry us and keep absolutely quiet about it. I saved his son's life in battle. He will never dispute it if I tell everyone we were married two or three weeks ago. I don't believe anyone will go so far as to check a country parish's records to see if the dates are right.''

"But what about your name? Everyone will suspect something havey-cavey when Aunt Beryl tells them that we said you were Mr. Lassiter!''

Benedict smiled smugly. "Not after we have explained to your family that I was pretending not to be myself because I was hunting a traitor. When this is all over, Jermyn and I shall explain to them how it was all for country and king. I married you secretly, and we came here with this story about who I was because we could not let the traitor suspect my real identity or he would know why I was here. I promise you, by the time Jermyn is through talking, your aunt Beryl will be convinced that she helped capture an enemy and that she knew all along who I really was but kept quiet in order to save England. So you see? Your family won't go spreading it around, or if they do, they will tell it as we told it to them, with our being married the whole time."

Camilla turned away. Benedict was offering her exactly what she wanted, yet she felt only cold. He wanted to marry her for the wrong reasons. There were no words of love on his lips, only reason and propriety. He did not love her, but he had felt an overwhelming lust for her, and because he had allowed his lust to overcome his good sense, now, as a gentleman, he was bound to marry her. As soon as the lieutenant, who knew him as Lord Rawdon, arrived on the scene, he had realized that he must marry her in order to avert a scandal. "I see."

She walked to the window and stared out sightlessly. She had never imagined that anything could hurt so much. Tears welled up in her eyes, and she swallowed hard.

"No."

Benedict stared. "I beg your pardon?"

"I said 'No.' I will not marry you."

"What?" Benedict's insides turned to ice. In all his planning, it had not occurred to him that Camilla might refuse to marry him. He had thought that her passionate response had told him all he needed to know about her feelings, just as his lovemaking had expressed his love for her. "Are you this angry about my deception?"

"It is not a question of anger." Camilla was proud of the way she managed to keep her voice level, despite her anguish. "I told you when we first met that I intended never to marry."

Benedict exploded. "The devil! This is no time for some silly bluestocking idea! For God's sake, Camilla, think of your family. Think of your own future! Don't you realize what this scandal will do to all of you? You are absolutely right about the gossip being all over London as soon as your cousin and aunt return. Even if your aunt has the brains to realize how her gossip will affect her own daughters' futures, I don't believe she will be able to keep from telling the choicest tidbits to her close friends. Once that is done, everyone in the ton will know. Your reputation will be ruined."

"Then I will live in seclusion the rest of my life. I shall retire to the Park. I can live without the social rounds, and country life will suit me well enough."

"I am glad to hear that you like the country life, because I prefer it, too, and as soon as I am no longer needed in London, I intend to spend most of my time on my estate. As my *wife*, you shall be there, too."

Camilla whirled around, her eyes flashing. Benedict was so infuriating that it made her forget her own pain and regret for the moment. "I will not! Are you deficient in understanding?"

"No. Apparently I have far better understanding than you do. But surely even you will be able to grasp this. You will marry me. It is the only course for you, and I don't care whether you wish it or not. You *will* marry me."

With those words, he swung around and threw open the door with a crash, then stormed out of the room. Camilla let out a shriek of frustration and ran after him to slam the door shut. Well, she thought, as she turned and ran across the room to fling herself onto her bed, at least no one in the house would have any trouble believing that the newlyweds had had a fight. Then she burst into tears.

17

If the shouts and slamming of doors left anyone in the house unaware of the "newlyweds'" spat, they soon realized it from Benedict's and Camilla's behavior over the next few days. They stayed apart from each other, speaking rarely and then only if they had to. It was well-known among the servants that they slept in separate beds, equally rumpled and disturbed, as if by fitful slumbers, and only a fool would have missed Camilla's icy, remote demeanor or Benedict's air of controlled fury.

Camilla spent most of her time talking in a spritely manner with her aunt Lydia or her cousin Bertram, or locked up in her bedroom, from which retreats she always emerged with reddened eyes. Benedict, on the other hand, spent most of his time in various gentlemanly pursuits, primarily riding horses or playing cards, with Anthony or the other young man, James Woollery, whom they had brought in and installed in one of the other nursery rooms.

Camilla had been rather surprised when Anthony and Benedict brought Woollery into the house, saying that he was a friend of Anthony's and explaining his need to stay in bed the first few days by saying that he had been thrown from his horse on the ride to Chevington Park. It seemed to her a foolhardy move.

"Aren't you afraid that his attacker will try again to kill him?" she asked Anthony, pulling him aside after supper that evening. "It seems to me that you are making him an obvious target."

"Mm. Probably."

"What? How can you be so casual about it?"

"It is part of a plan. Benedict thought it up." The young man's face glowed with enthusiasm, as it always did nowadays, whenever the subject of Benedict came up. Camilla's hand itched to slap him. "James is the bait with which to catch the killer. We are hoping he will try to sneak in some night and dispatch him, and we will be waiting to nab him."

"Is that where Benedict has been sneaking out to in the middle of the night?"

"Yes. He and I take turns standing watch for intruders."

"And I suppose poor Lieutenant Woollery was fool enough to agree to this plan."

"Of course. He thought it was a jolly good idea, and so do I. Really, Camilla, I don't understand why you are so hard on Benedict. Ever since we found out that there is nothing wrong with him, you have been acting exceedingly strangely."

"You would, too, if you had discovered that you had been taken advantage of by someone you trusted."

"That's doing it a bit brown, don't you think?" Anthony replied with brutal candor. "You never trusted him. You thought he was a thief until I convinced you that he was a customs officer. We always regarded him with suspicion."

"But I didn't suspect him of being a lord or a war hero."

"You aren't making any sense." Anthony regarded her with puzzlement. "Honestly, Milla, you are not acting like yourself at all."

Camilla knew that she wasn't. She realized that a great deal of what she said nowadays was bitter, and she spent most of her time either crying or acting far happier than she was. She missed talking to Benedict and being with him; most of all, she missed making love with him. She lay awake half of each night, it seemed, tossing and turning and thinking about Benedict's hands on her body. It seemed bizarre that the absence of the passion which they had shared so briefly should make such a huge hole in her life.

"I don't understand why you won't marry him," Anthony went on quietly.

Camilla narrowed her eyes at him. "Did he tell you that?"

"He told me he had asked you. Well, you wouldn't both be so miserable, would you, if you had accepted?"

"I am not miserable."

"I'm not a green 'un, you know," Anthony retorted. "If you are happy, I would hate to see someone sad. Even Grandpapa knows there's something wrong. He was asking me yesterday what it was. He likes Benedict, you know."

"I am well aware of that. My entire family *loves* him."

"Honestly, Milla, how much more could he do? It wasn't his fault, you know, that my mother told that silly story about your being married to him. Nor was he the one who wanted to pretend to be your fiancé. But when you are faced with a ruined reputation because of those things, he up and offered for you, which seems to me the gentlemanly thing to do."

"If that isn't typically male!"

"Well, I *am* a male," he pointed out reasonably. "But I ain't the only one here who would say he did the right thing. So would Mother and Aunt Beryl, if they knew about it."

"Oh, yes, he's done the *right* thing," Camilla responded in a goaded tone of voice. She looked at her beloved cousin with exasperation. How could she make him understand that she didn't want Benedict's *duty,* she wanted his *love?* She sighed. "Can't you understand? I don't want to hold a man because my mistakes have put us in a compromising position. It would be punishment, not marriage, and I refuse to do that. How would *you* like it if you had been put in Benedict's position, if you had offered to help a girl, even with ulterior motives of your own, and then you wound up having to marry her in order to save her reputation?"

Anthony looked taken aback at the thought. "I wouldn't like it by half."

"You see? How can I hold him to it? It was gentlemanly of him to offer, but I can't be cold and calculating enough to accept it. Especially after I've heard the lieutenant go on about what a catch Benedict was on the Marriage Mart and how he did not want to marry."

"I daresay it is hard on him," Anthony agreed undiplomatically. "But, Milla, you *have* to accept. Your reputation is ruined otherwise. Just think of what Aunt Beryl will say."

Camilla let out a low groan. "Please, don't remind me."

There was a pause. Finally Anthony said, "So you aren't going to change your mind?"

"No. I think not."

Anthony sighed. "And everyone says *I* am the one who doesn't think!"

Camilla retired early. She had grown to hate the nights, the lying awake and thinking about Benedict, wondering what he was thinking and whether he, too, missed the passion they had shared. There were times when she thought that she *was* a fool not to accept Benedict's proposal. Surely marrying a man who did not love her would be better than these long, aching nights alone.

She looked over at his cot against the far wall. It made it ten times harder, his sleeping in the same room. She ought to have insisted that he move up to the nursery with Anthony and Lieutenant Woollery. They could turn it into bachelors' quarters and leave her in peace.

Camilla sighed and began to take down her hair. Perhaps one could make a good marriage out of a mutual lust. Certainly couples married who did not have even that much. At least if they were married, she would not feel so restless and unsatisfied all the time. She grimaced, aware of the persistent, throbbing ache between her legs. She wondered if Benedict knew how his sleeping here affected her, and if that was why he continued to do it. *It would be just like him.* Last night she had lain in bed, pretending to be asleep, while she watched him undress through slitted eyes. There had been a moment, as he lingeringly pulled his shirt off his shoulders and arms when she was convinced he knew she was watching and was making sure she witnessed every little movement. It had been enough to make her close her eyes and turn away.

She rang for her maid, undressed and crawled into bed, determined that tonight she would get some sleep. However, the minutes passed slowly, and still she could not sleep. After some time, it occurred to her that Benedict was rather late coming to bed. He usually followed not too long after her.

She found herself waiting for the sound of his footsteps in the hall or the door to their bedroom opening. Sleep grew more and more distant. Eventually, she gave in to the need to look at the time. She got out of bed and walked over to the clock on the mantel. It was getting close to midnight. *Where could he be?* There was nothing to do; everyone in this house retired by this time, even night owls like Aunt Lydia and Cousin Bertram.

She supposed he could be upstairs, playing cards or drinking with James Woollery and Anthony. Or he could have just stayed there to guard Woollery instead of sneaking out of her bedroom later to do it. *Or he could be slipping through the dark outside, with Anthony and the almost-recovered lieutenant, on a smuggling mission.*

There was a tap on her bedroom door, and she opened it to find her grandfather's ancient valet standing there, her grandfather's spyglass tucked under his arm. It confirmed her worst fears. "Jenkins!"

He nodded lugubriously. "Miss Camilla. I have been keeping watch out His Lordship's window, just as you asked me to."

Something he did half the time anyway, Camilla knew; it was why she had asked him to keep watch for her. "Yes? Did you see—my husband?"

"Yes, miss. Him and the young master, going furtively across the garden not ten minutes ago. I barely saw them, dressed all in black as they were, but I caught a glimpse of the young master's face when he took off his hat for an instant."

"There were only two of them?"

"Yes, miss."

"They must not have taken Lieutenant Woollery. I wonder why." She chewed thoughtfully at her lip. "All right. Go down and get Purdle. He is the only other one we can trust. You will go with us to keep watch at the top of the cliff." The old man was not fast enough or strong enough to be of much help in a fight, but his eyes were still eagle-sharp, and, armed with the Earl's spyglass, he would make a good lookout for them. "I will get dressed and enlist Lieutenant Woollery. We shall meet you and Purdle downstairs in a few minutes."

"A stranger, miss?" Jenkins looked doubtful.

"He has great loyalty to Benedict, and therefore he will help me." Camilla was not entirely sure of his assistance, particularly if Benedict had ordered him not to help her. But, hopefully, Benedict had not had the foresight to suspect that she would follow them, and she was confident of her ability to bully the young man into helping her. After all, having been left behind, he would doubtless be champing at the bit for an opportunity to get in on the adventure.

She dressed quickly in some old, dark clothes of Anthony's that she had pulled out of one of the trunks in the attic a few days ago in preparation for this moment. Anthony had worn them when he was much younger, so she had to roll up the trousers only a little to make them fit. Piling her hair atop her head and cramming a cap over it, she thought she made an adequate lad, at least in the dark. She ran lightly upstairs to the nursery, where she knocked and went in before Woollery could get out a word. He was sitting at the table, looking sulky, a bottle and glass and a pistol lying on the table in front of him.

"Lady Rawdon!" He popped up, staring at her odd attire and trying to look as if he were not. "I am sorry, ma'am. I wasn't expecting company." He pulled his jacket from the back of his chair and started to pull it on.

"Don't bother, Lieutenant. I came unannounced. I can hardly expect to find you prepared for company." She did not address the subject of her clothes. "So, they have gone."

He stared. "How—how did you know?"

"Really, Lieutenant Woollery. This is my home, after all, and my servants. And I make it my business to know what is going on."

"Yes, ma'am. Of course."

"I see they did not take you with them."

"No, ma'am." He could not entirely conceal his disappointment. "Lord Rawdon said my shoulder wasn't healed enough. I feel no pain," he said, somewhat aggrievedly. "But he was afraid I wouldn't be up to lifting barrels. Besides, he wanted me here in the house in case someone used the smuggling foray as a diversion to dispatch me." He gestured toward the gun. "I'm healed enough to shoot."

"It's just as well. I need your help."

"You do?" He looked puzzled, but said gamely, "Whatever I can do…"

"Good. We are going after them."

"I beg your pardon?"

"I am taking some men and following them. I don't like this plan of Benedict's. There are too many pitfalls—he and Anthony alone with all those smugglers, trying to figure out which one of them is the traitor. I am afraid they will be far more obvious than he."

"But, my lady!" The young man looked shocked. "You can't go bursting in on a bunch of smugglers!"

"I don't plan to burst in on them. That would be foolish indeed. We will simply follow them, keeping safely out of sight. We will come to their aid only if they need it. If they get into trouble."

"But—what if someone sees us?"

"We shall simply make sure that no one does," Camilla assured him with a smile. "Come, come, Lieutenant, time's a-wasting. Are you coming with me or not?"

"I am sure Lord Rawdon would not like this."

"Perhaps not. But would he like your letting me go off on my own? That is really the only question."

Woollery looked rather taken aback. He could well imagine the verbal hiding he would get if he allowed Rawdon's wife to get into some mess by herself. "Yes, my lady. You are right."

She waited outside in the hallway for him to pull off his white shirt and substitute a dark sweater of Anthony's. Then they went downstairs to the kitchen, where Purdle and Jenkins were waiting for them. Both the servants had changed from their starched uniforms into dark, rough workmen's clothing. Camilla could sense Woollery's astonishment as he stood beside her, staring at the two servants.

"I— Are they going with us?"

"Yes. These are my men." Purdle, though his hair was thinning and his middle was growing, was still able-bodied. Jenkins, of course, was another matter, but she could not turn him down.

"Come, gentlemen, let us go." She started out the kitchen door, one hand on her jacket pocket, inside which lay one of her grandfather's pistols. Jenkins, she noted, had the other one of the pair stuck into his belt. Purdle, on the other hand, was armed with a stout wooden cudgel and a lantern.

They set out through the dark, keeping the lantern's shields down on all but one side. Jenkins led the way. He was slow, but surefooted, even in the dark.

They left the gardens and made their way toward the shore. They angled along the cliff, stopping now and then for Jenkins to search the beach with his spyglass. Finally, he let out a grunt.

"There they are," he said in a low voice, crouching down. The others all followed suit.

He handed the glass to Camilla and explained to her what points to pick out, and finally she was able to make out the dark, low boat out at sea, and the two smaller boats making their way between it and the shore. She was even able to see the two dark, almost invisible figures of the men who Jenkins said were the smugglers' lookouts.

"They will be coming up from the beach down there, miss," Jenkins told Camilla in a whisper, pointing a knobby finger toward a well-used path. "They need a good path for the pack animals."

Camilla nodded. "And from there, where will they go?"

"Your guess is as good as mine about that, miss. You had best find a good place to hide and follow them."

Camilla nodded. She, Purdle and Lieutenant Woollery worked their way back from the edge of the cliff, careful not to stand up and reveal their silhouettes against the lighter darkness of the sky. She knew that it was easier to spot them standing on the cliff than it had been to see the men working down on the beach and ocean. They found an outcropping of stone and took up their positions behind it and the low bush that grew at its base. Then they sat down and waited.

And waited.

Camilla's knees grew stiff, and her back began to ache. On one side of her, she saw that Purdle had drifted off to sleep and was softly snoring. On the other side, Lieutenant Woollery shifted restlessly. She suspected that he was thinking uneasy thoughts about Rawdon's reaction if his wife got into trouble while she was in his care.

It did not surprise her when, a few minutes later, Woollery began to tell her all the advantages of her going back to the house. She dealt with him in the way she had found best with lecturing males. She nodded now and then and made vague sounds, all the while without really listening. Seeing her, the lieutenant thought that he was making headway, though Anthony could have told him that she had not heard anything he said.

"Well, my lady?" he said at last, when Camilla made no response to his repeated suggestion that she return to Chevington Park. "Don't you agree?"

"Agree with what?" Camilla asked, turning to look at him with wide eyes.

"That it would be far safer for you at the house. I am sure it is what Lord Rawdon would wish."

"No, what Lord Rawdon would wish is to be out there, exactly where he is. But if you feel it's best, you are perfectly welcome to return to the house."

He stared at her, his eyes bulging. "I didn't mean me! I don't want to go back."

"Good. We are in agreement. Neither do I," she said, leaving him gaping like a fish in need of oxygen. "Ah, here comes Jenkins now."

The old man appeared in the darkness, shuffling toward them as quickly as he could. "They have finished unloading," he said as he squeezed into place beside the others, panting from the effort he had made. "Or near enough. They're starting the ponies up the trail. It may be a long walk, Miss Camilla."

Camilla stuck out one foot, showing the sturdy brogan that decorated it. "I wore my best walking shoes."

They fell into silence, mindful of the men who would soon be approaching. Before long, there was the muffled jingle of a harness. The four of them crouched behind the rock, hardly daring to breathe, as the quiet procession drew closer and then passed them by.

Cautiously Camilla peeked around the edge of the rock. She had thought that she would recognize Benedict and Anthony, even in disguise. She had thought that a gait, a movement, would give them away, that she knew them so well that she would know their height or body shape. But, in fact, even though the men walked by not fifteen feet from her, she recognized no one. There were only the dark, lumpy forms of men, shapeless in dark, full shirts, hats pulled low on their heads, and faces wrapped around with kerchiefs, mufflers and masks. The best she could do was eliminate three of the men as being far too short to be either Benedict or her cousin.

She thought about the fact that these were probably all men she knew, men she saw regularly around Edgecombe, and yet they were completely foreign to her. She felt Jenkins beside her and realized that he was peering at the passing parade through his spyglass. She wondered if he was having any better luck identifying Anthony or Benedict.

The pony train seemed to go on forever, but finally the last of the animals passed them. They waited for a few moments to make sure that no stragglers came along, then slipped out from their hiding place.

"I'll go back to the house. I would only be a hindrance to you now," Jenkins whispered regretfully, handing Camilla his spyglass. "Here, you might be able to use this." He handed the old dueling pistol to Woollery, who tucked it into his belt on the side opposite his own army pistol.

Jenkins headed back toward the house. The other

three started cautiously after the pony train. They could not use the lantern, even shuttered, because their light would give them away, so it was slow going. Camilla only hoped that she would not turn an ankle in the darkness. It was all they could do to keep the end of the train in sight as they struggled along over the dark countryside. More than once the ponies disappeared over a hillock and they were afraid that they had lost sight of them altogether, but each time they were able to get a glimpse of them a while later.

It seemed as if they would walk all night. Camilla wondered if they would make deliveries tonight. It seemed most unlikely, but she could not imagine why they kept hiking. The smugglers finally turned away from the cliffs and the shore and headed inland. They reached a wooded area that Camilla recognized as Varner Wood, and she nearly groaned. Surely they were not going to plunge into the woods, where it would be even darker and more difficult to see.

But then, ahead of her, she saw a faint flicker of light. She and the others moved even more slowly, creeping toward the light, until finally they saw a clearing, where the pack ponies stood. The smugglers had placed their lanterns around on the ground and lifted up one or more shields, so that the lanterns put out enough glow to allow them to see what they were doing.

Camilla and her companions crouched behind a rock and a couple of bushes, spreading out a little from each other. Camilla watched as the men, still dark and featureless in the dim glow, unloaded the ponies and carried the boxes and barrels—*down into the ground?* It took a moment for Camilla's mind to make sense of the scene. Then she realized the men must be going down steps built into the ground. There was some sort of cellar there, where they stored their smuggled goods until they could deliver them. Now Camilla could even make out the outline of a wooden door flung open against the ground. They probably even camouflaged it to keep it from being discovered.

It was a far cry from the caves, which she had always assumed must be the hiding places for the smuggling activity in the area. It felt odd to watch the men going about their tasks, almost as if she were witnessing some secret, sacred rite. She supposed in a way she was. No doubt it would be blasphemy to these men to give away this location.

They watched until the men had unloaded all the ponies and closed the door to the secret cellar, covering it up with a tangle of brush and branches. Moving quickly, but without particular haste, the men began to pick up their lanterns, to separate and leave, some of them leading ponies with them.

Camilla squeezed down tightly under her bush as a man strode in her direction. She was breathlessly certain that he would discover her and all would be lost. She hated to think of what they would do to someone who had seen the secret hiding place of the smugglers.

But the man walked away along a barely visible path. Camilla crawled back farther into the brush, away from the path. She looked across to where Purdle had hidden, but she could see nothing of him. She could sense Woollery's presence behind her, much closer.

She watched intently, trying to keep track of all the men who were leaving, to see if any of them reminded her of Benedict or Anthony. Suddenly, her attention was drawn to a man. He was tall, and she wondered if perhaps he was her cousin or Rawdon. Then she realized that there were two men with him, following him by just a few steps. She understood, too, what had drawn her eyes to him. It had been the very furtiveness of his movements. He stopped now and glanced around, making sure that no one was watching him. Then he walked away quickly, almost melting into the brush. His two companions followed.

It couldn't be Anthony and Benedict. There were, after all, three of these men. Of course, it could just be a family of smugglers, a group who were more cautious about being known than the others. Perhaps a respectable family.

But Camilla could not get it out of her head that the furtiveness of the men's movements was sinister. She wondered whether they should follow the men. Just at that moment, two more men slipped off in the same direction, looking around them, then following the route the first three had taken.

Benedict and Anthony? They had both been tall, one slightly shorter and more slender than the other. The description would fit Anthony and Benedict. Camilla glanced back toward Woollery and found him right behind her. He pointed in the direction of the two men, and she nodded. They slipped out of the hiding places, joined by Purdle, and made their way cautiously through the trees.

She thought that they had lost all five of the men amid the growth, but when they left the shelter of the woods, Woollery spotted the figures of two men in front of them, walking purposefully up a rise in the ground. Camilla and her two companions followed them.

This chase went on for several minutes, with Camilla and her men finding their quarry, then losing them, then spotting them once more when they crested a hill or were in some other way silhouetted against a paler sky or rock.

The men were almost to the top of a long slope, a few feet from a low stone wall that crested the ridge. Camilla, Purdle and Woollery waited at the bottom in the shadow of a tree, not wanting to be exposed on the long, treeless slope, letting their quarry crest the hill and start down the other side.

But as the two men reached the top, there was a sudden loud pop, and one of the two men flung up his arms and staggered backward. Camilla sucked in a sharp breath, paralyzed, as she watched three men leap over the low wall, attacking the two men.

A shriek of rage erupted from Camilla, and she tore up the hill toward the struggling group. She pulled out the pistol in her pocket as she ran, but she knew that she was too far away to take a shot. Lieutenant Woollery, a faster runner than she, pulled ahead of her, firing his pistol in the air in hopes of startling the combatants. It was obvious that there was no hope of actually using the pistols against any of the men, for all five of them were in a seething, struggling mass.

Woollery reached the group of men and launched himself into the pile, laying about him with the butt end of his pistol. Two men rolled away from the others, punching and wrestling. The one currently on top still wore a mask; the other one's face was bare. It was Benedict.

Camilla threw herself onto the back of the man on top. He smashed his fist into Benedict's face, but then reared back at Camilla's sudden weight on his back, trying to throw her off. Camilla held on for dear life and sank her teeth into his neck. He let out a roar like a wounded bull and lashed backward with his hand, hitting her so hard on the cheek that she fell back. He completed her fall by whirling around and knocking her across the stomach with his arm. Benedict scrambled to his feet, roaring, and the man took to his heels. His two companions, one of whom Purdle had cracked across the back with his cudgel, quickly followed.

Benedict gave chase. Camilla sat up rather dazedly and shook her head to clear it. She looked across the grass and saw her cousin lying there, and fear gripped her chest. She crawled across the ground to him.

"Anthony! Anthony! Are you all right? Are you shot?"

Anthony let out a groan and sat up, clutching his arm. "Winged me, dammit." He stopped and goggled at Camilla, suddenly realizing how strange it was that she was there. "Milla! What the devil are you doing here? And what are you wearing?"

Lieutenant Woollery knelt beside Anthony and examined his wound. "Good. Ball went right through it. You'll do fine." He took a knife and slit Anthony's shirt at the sleeve, ripping the sleeve from the rest of it. He pulled it off and began to wrap it tightly around the wound, binding it.

Camilla gingerly felt the side of her face, where the attacker had hit her. It felt quite tender. She had the sinking feeling that she was going to be sporting a bruise the following day.

"Did you see him, Anthony?" she asked. "Did you see who it was?"

"No! Even when we were fighting, he didn't lose his mask. I got a look at one of the men with him, but he was nobody I recognized. A stranger."

Benedict was returning to the group, his face set in grim lines. "Bloody hell! I lost him!" He strode straight to Camilla, pulling her to her feet. "Camilla! Are you all right?" He pulled her to him, then held her at arm's length to search her face. "Did he hurt you? God, I wish I'd gotten hold of him!" He scowled. "What the devil were you doing here, anyway? You said you would stay home."

Camilla, who had almost melted against him when he took her in his arms, now jerked away from him, stung by his angry words. "I said I would not join the smugglers. I said nothing about not following you."

"Damn! You could have been killed, you little fool! I told you to stay home, and that is where you should have been. Woollery, I'll have your hide for helping her with this escapade."

"Escapade!" Camilla shrieked, goaded. "We saved your lives! We followed you to give you help, which you obviously needed. You didn't almost capture him, you almost got yourselves killed!" Fury bubbled up in her, fueled by the fear of the past few minutes and the unbearable tension of their recent life together. "I wish I hadn't come! I wish I had stayed at the Park and let him *kill* you!"

With those words, she turned and ran for home.

18

Camilla awoke the next morning with muscles that ached with every movement and a face that felt swollen to twice its size. One look in the mirror showed her that her face was indeed swollen around her eye and sported a swath of purplish blue. She looked like a street brawler. It did not help any that her eyes were bloodshot, her hair was tangled and her face was dirty, with streaks of tears running through the dust.

She had run all the way home last night and locked herself in her bedroom, ignoring Benedict's loud knocking on the door and repeated calling of her name, until finally Aunt Beryl came out and told him in no uncertain terms to take himself elsewhere. Camilla, who had been crying throughout the whole experience, then cried herself to sleep.

She unlocked her door in the morning to her maid, who had been gently scratching on it for several minutes. The maid, after one horrified gasp, left the room and returned with a piece of raw meat, which she insisted on laying upon Camilla's bruised and swollen cheek, shaking her head and making sympathetic noises.

"What happened, ma'am?" Millie asked, her eyes wide with horror and avid interest. "Were you hurt with Master Anthony, then?"

"Uh…" Camilla realized that she had no story ready to explain her injuries. "Yes," she said cautiously. "How is Anthony this morning?"

"Oh, fine, ma'am. The doctor came last night, even late as it was, and he said the young master's fixed up all right and tight. Mr. Lassiter said it was a climbing accident."

Camilla glanced up and caught the knowing look in the girl's eyes. No doubt all the servants suspected that Anthony had been involved in the smuggling and that likely his wound had come from that. The servants always seemed to know everything. Now they would have something new to speculate about—Camilla's obvious black eye and apparent involvement in Anthony's escapade. Camilla sighed. *Belowstairs would be buzzing this morning.*

"Yes," she said coolly. "I'm afraid I fell against a rock trying to help him. Foolish of me."

Millie helped Camilla clean up and dress. It took some time to get all the tangles out of Camilla's hair. But at last she was dressed and looking almost normal—if one ignored the black eye, of course, Camilla thought wryly.

She did not feel like eating breakfast, and she was afraid that she might run into Benedict if she went downstairs. He was the last person Camilla wanted to see. She didn't know where to go. She wanted to talk about her problems, but Anthony, she knew, would be no comfort. Millie had told her that he was upstairs in his bed, a sling supporting his wounded arm, letting Nurse fuss to her heart's content over him. *Besides, the way things had been going, he would probably side with his beloved Benedict over her!*

Feeling ill-used and miserable, Camilla decided to visit her grandfather. It had always been he she turned to in times of trouble. Jenkins opened the Earl's door at her knock and let out a shocked gasp. His reaction was quickly seconded by the Earl.

Chevington sent his man away and held out his arms to Camilla. With a little gulping sob, she flew to him and let him take her in his arms, as he had when she was little. She had thought that she had no more tears, but they flowed all over again. Haltingly she poured out the story of what had happened the night before, and Benedict's furious reaction.

"All I did was try to help him!" she wailed. "He hates me."

"I am sure he does not. He would not have reacted so violently if he did not care for you."

"Humph! He has an odd way of showing it."

"No doubt he does. But when one is scared, one reacts stupidly sometimes. Don't you remember that time when Anthony got lost in the caves when he was little, and you screamed at him when Silsby brought him out?"

"I was certain he had died!" Camilla exclaimed, remembering. "I was *so* furious with him."

"Because you were scared. Believe me, I wanted to give him a caning myself. 'Tis the same thing with Rawdon. He was scared by your showing up there and getting into the midst of a brawl. I have to tell you,

Camilla, it is not something I can think about with equanimity, either.''

"I didn't get hurt. I mean, not all that badly. It looks awful, I know, but nothing is broken. I did it to help him. There were three of them against only him and Anthony, and Anthony had been shot.''

"I suspect it is not a pleasant feeling to be saved by one's wife, either,'' Chevington mused.

"Poppycock! Masculine pride!'' Camilla scoffed, but she could not help feeling somewhat better. "Besides, I am not really his—'' She stopped abruptly, casting an apprehensive glance toward her grandfather.

"Not really what?'' the old man asked pointedly, raising an eyebrow. "Not really his wife, were you going to say?''

Camilla stared. "How did you— What are you talking about?''

The old man raised an admonishing finger. "Don't play sly with me, young lady. I've known you since before you could walk. I am talking about this story you've been trying to hoodwink me with since the day you walked in here. Before that, really. Shame on you, for trying to deceive an old man.''

"Obviously I didn't succeed. How did you know? Does everyone?''

"I shouldn't think so. The reason I know is because he told me.''

"Who?''

"Rawdon. Your supposed husband. He came to me and made a clean breast of the whole thing.''

"But...why?''

The old man shrugged and cast a significant look at his granddaughter. "I suppose *his* conscience was bothering him about deceiving me. It was the day you two almost drowned. He must have had second thoughts about meeting his Maker with a lie on his soul.''

''That was before he discovered Lieutenant Woollery,'' Camilla murmured, more to herself than to her grandfather.

''Who? Oh, that lad. Benedict told me about him.''

''What did Benedict say?''

''About Woollery?''

''No. About me, about marriage, that day.''

''I'm not sure I remember exactly. He told me who he really was and apologized for deceiving me. Told me why he was here, playing that sort of game, and how that featherbrained Lydia had put the two of you in a worse position. I told him it was going to be a damned scandal, and he said no, he would make sure that it was not. Then he told me that he had a scheme, but he didn't tell me what it was.''

The old man let out a loud ''humph'' and went on, ''Doesn't matter, I guess, since now it looks as though his saying he would marry you must have been a lot of folderol, too. Don't see any signs of it. I have been mightily deceived in him.''

''You know as well as I that he *did* intend to marry me,'' Camilla told him crossly. ''I refused. I am sure he came and told you that, as well.''

''Actually, he didn't, although I have guessed as much from the foul mood he's been in the last few days. Why the devil did you turn him down?''

''I didn't turn him down, exactly, because he never asked me to marry him, exactly. He just decided that we would.''

The Earl let out a grunt. "Bungled it, didn't he? Just as I thought. Young people today have no suavity. No sophistication."

"That has nothing to do with it. I told him I wouldn't marry him because I knew that he didn't *really* want to marry me. He did it because he was too much of a gentleman to compromise me and then not marry me."

"I see. So it's because he is a gentleman that you don't want to marry him?"

Camilla rolled her eyes. "Of course not."

"Oh. I thought perhaps you preferred the sort of man who would not offer marriage to a woman whose good name he had sullied."

"He *didn't* sully it. It was my fault, not his, that we were even in this stupid situation, and I am not going to make him pay for the rest of his life for my mistake. I am glad he is the sort of man who would offer marriage in that situation. But I am not the sort of woman who would take him up on it."

"I see." Chevington was silent for a few moments, then went on, "You know, he didn't seem reluctant about it the night he told me what he intended to do."

"No doubt he would put a good face on it in front of you."

"Have you asked him why he wanted to marry you? Or did you just assume that he did it for the sake of honor?"

"That is all he talked about," Camilla told him miserably. "Scandal and my reputation and how his plan was the only thing that would save me from disgrace. He never, *ever* said a word about love. I didn't have to ask him. I knew."

"Odd..." Chevington drawled, watching his grand-daughter. "He spoke to me of honor, also. He thought that argument would convince you. Don't think the fellow knows much about women. But I asked him why he was doing it, and he said it was because he loved you."

Camilla's head snapped up and she stared at him in astonishment. "What?"

"I said, he loves you. Does that make a difference in your thinking?"

"Oh, Grandpapa! Truly?"

He nodded, and she jumped up and threw her arms around him. "That makes all the difference in the world!"

Benedict rode to town in grim silence. Lieutenant Woollery, riding beside him, was wise enough not to try to initiate any conversation. Benedict had been like this all morning, and the fact that Camilla had not come downstairs to breakfast had not helped his mood a whit. When, a few minutes earlier, he received a note from Jermyn Sedgewick, informing him that he was back in Edgecombe and needed to talk to him, Benedict had crumpled the note up with a growl.

For a moment Benedict had thought about not answering Sedgewick's summons. He could not remember a time in his life when he had felt so low. Annabeth's jilting him seemed laughable now, in comparison to this pain. He knew that he had managed to ruin everything with Camilla.

Once he had had time to reflect, he had realized that Camilla's following him with that ragtag group of protectors had been an indication that she did, indeed, care about him. Obviously she must have been worried about what would happen to him, and she had done her best to protect him. Indeed, she had probably saved his and Anthony's lives by following them. But instead of thanking her for risking her own neck to help him, instead of taking her in his arms and pouring out his gratitude and his relief that she was herself safe, he had barked at her. He had been so filled with icy fear when he saw that it was Camilla who had launched herself at the man he was fighting that he did not think at all. He only reacted. It had not been anger that drove him, but sheer terror at the thought of what could happen to her.

But now he saw that he might as well have slapped her in the face. She hated him for what he had said. Benedict did not think he would ever forget her scornful, bitter words last night, when she had lashed back at him, telling him that she wished she had let him be killed.

He had tried to make it right with her after he got home, but she had locked her door against him. This morning she would not even come near him. He had lost the only woman he had ever loved—and he had not even managed to succeed in discovering the identity of the traitor. They were just as much in the dark as ever, unless he could somehow search through the village and find the man whose bruises and battered knuckles would prove that he had been in a fistfight.

Benedict sighed, his hand going up to gingerly touch the darkening bruise on his own cheekbone. It might work, if only he could think of some way to get a glimpse of everyone's hands and face. But the villain would know the marks would identify him, and he would be certain to stay in today—just as Benedict wished to do. He did not want to expose himself to his friend Jermyn's quick mind and probing questions. It wouldn't be long before Jermyn had the whole story of what had happened between Benedict and Camilla, and he would not hesitate to tell Benedict how he had mishandled the whole affair.

He knew he would go. He had to, given Jermyn's urgent summons. His decision, however, had been sped up by the fact that Purdle came in and announced that Harold Elliot had come calling. Benedict rose to his feet immediately, but he was unable to escape the vicar completely. Cousin Harold strode in, smiling beatifically, before Benedict could get out the door and commented in shocked tones on the bruised condition of Benedict's face. Another ten minutes had followed of Cousin Harold's regrets that they would not be able to enjoy another little chat before Benedict was able to make his escape. By that time, Lieutenant Woollery had risen to his feet and been following Benedict, explaining that he was certain Benedict would need help with his errand.

The ride helped clear Benedict's head a little of its cobwebs, and while he did not feel cheerful when he strode into the inn a few minutes later, at least he was no longer in the sullens. He and Woollery were immediately ushered into the private room. Jermyn Sedgewick, seated on a bench beside the fire, jumped up at his entrance.

"Benedict! It's good— Good God, man, what happened to you?"

"Oh." Benedict raised his hand ruefully to his

bruise. "That. An encounter with the man we are seeking, I'm afraid."

Sedgewick's face lit up. "Then you saw him? Did you capture him?"

"No. We came out on the worse end of it. He winged Anthony and managed to pop me a good one. Nor did I see him. He wore a mask, and I was unable to get it off. We were following him and his two cohorts, and they ambushed us. It was a complete, bloody failure. I handled it like the veriest raw recruit."

"I doubt that."

"You would not if you had been there," Benedict told him bitterly. "We were saved by Lieutenant Woollery here, and Camilla and her butler."

"Lieutenant Woollery!" Jermyn looked more closely at the other man. His face lit up. "My God, man, it *is* you! I hardly recognized you out of uniform. And you've lost a good bit of weight."

"Yes, sir. It's good to see you, sir."

"But this must mean that you made it through, that nothing happened to you."

Woollery and Benedict quickly disabused him of that notion, describing the attack on the young man and the way that Anthony had helped him. They went on to explain their plan to capture the traitor the night before, and its failure.

"I see," Jermyn said, sitting back in his chair and steepling his fingers in front of his mouth. "Perhaps my report will be of some use to us, then."

"You mean you've got something?" Benedict perked up. "Why didn't you tell us?"

"I'm not sure if it is going to lead us to the traitor.

It seems unlikely, but..." He shrugged. "All right. Here is what I learned about the guests at Chevington Park. First of all, Mr. Thorne. Apparently he is exactly what he appears to be, a young man of modest fortune who fancies himself a poet and is at the moment stricken with love for the Countess Marbridge. He came up from the country last year to acquire some town polish and to 'explore his muse.' He has doting parents— Well, he would have to, wouldn't he, to still be alive? But he seems to live within his means, not caring much for the more practical things of life, and the only crime he seems to have committed is writing excruciatingly bad poetry."

Benedict grunted. "What about Oglesby?"

"Ah. Mr. Oglesby is somewhat more interesting. His real name is Jack Cooper, and his father is a book-keeper. He has no visible means of support—except for his face and form."

"What do you mean?" Woollery asked, puzzled.

"He sells himself?" Benedict put in.

"Nothing quite so crass as that. However, he seems to depend for his food, clothing and shelter on other certain gentlemen with whom he lives."

Benedict stared at him in amazement for a moment. "Then you mean that Cousin Bertram is a—"

"Apparently he belongs to a crowd of men who prefer the company of other men."

"My God." Benedict let out a crack of laughter. "I never guessed. So Bertram is given to 'Greek love.' I'd like to see what Harold and Aunt Beryl would say if they knew. No, on second thought, I'd rather not." He chuckled. "So that was why they came into the cave that day—nothing so nefarious as smuggling or spying. Bertram and his paramour were looking for a lovers' nest away from his damnable relatives."

"I presume so." Sedgewick smiled. "I was loath to give up on this, though. After all, Bertram could have been blackmailed by the French into doing it. Or he could simply want the money. He does seem to run up an appalling amount of debt. Camilla's cousin likes the finer things of life."

Benedict looked interested again. "Do you think he might have done it for the money, then?"

Sedgewick shook his head. "I had to give up the idea. The thing is, he never has paid off any of those debts. He seems to still be living from allowance to allowance from his father. And the rumor mill is quite certain that he came to Chevington Park to escape his creditors for a while. There is still the possibility of blackmail, of course, but there's another...."

"Another? What are you talking about?"

"I checked up on everyone whose name you had mentioned to me as being at the Park. I found that the Reverend Harold Elliot makes frequent trips out of town. He supposedly goes to meet with this or that scholar or to consult with his bishop or to visit some holy spot, like Canterbury. But, in truth, he never goes to those places. Instead, he visits to London. I had it from Giles Annerwick. You remember him, Benedict?"

"Of course. He was a year ahead of us at Eton. Something of a carouser, as I remember." Benedict continued to look at his friend blankly.

"Still is. Drinks like a fish, and spends half his income on opera dancers. Well, he has no family, so I suppose it really does no one harm but himself. He's quite a likable chap. I was talking to him about Bertram Elliot, trying to find out what he knew, you see, and he said that he didn't know Bertram well. He ran in different circles. He said the one he knew was *Harold* Elliot. He ran into him last year in London, met him at a gaming hall. Giles said he thought it was rather odd, because he had thought the man had become a parson, but he supposed he must have been wrong. Since then he has seen him here and there, all in rather unsavory places, several times.''

"Good God!''

"So I did some checking on the good reverend. It seems he keeps a small apartment in London. He goes to London frequently, and visits the gambling clubs and brothels. He drinks a great deal, gambles far too much, and commits a variety of sins with a number of light women. In short, the man lives a life quite at variance with his chosen profession—and, more importantly for our purposes, quite above any apparent means of living.''

"Good God!'' Benedict shot to his feet, shoving back his chair so hard that it toppled over onto the floor.

"Interesting, is it not?''

"Interesting! Disastrous. The man is at Chevington Park right now. With Camilla!''

Benedict turned on his heel and rushed out of the room.

Camilla hurried out of the Earl's bedroom and down the stairs in search of Benedict. Her heart soared. Benedict's anger of last night no longer mattered—nor did the fact that he had concealed his name and title from her. None of it mattered, not even the fact that one of her eyes was puffy and bruised, and she would normally have been too embarrassed to let anyone see her. No, the only thing she cared about now was that Benedict had told her grandfather that he loved her. She had to find him and talk to him. She had to find out if it was true.

She rounded the corner and walked into the sitting room, where she found Lydia, needlework in her lap, and a rather glazed expression on her face. "Lydia, have—"

"Camilla! There you are at last," came Cousin Harold's voice from behind her.

Camilla groaned beneath her breath and turned. Cousin Harold was just rising from the small secretary where he had been sitting. No wonder her aunt had such a dazed look on her face; she had been having to listen to one of Harold's long expositions.

"Hello, Harold. I didn't realize you were here."

"I sincerely hope not, since I have been waiting here for you for half an hour."

Camilla's eyebrows lifted. "Waiting for me?"

"Don't you remember? You and I were scheduled to work on the church bazaar together this morning. You told me last Wednesday that you would be glad to help, and I suggested that today would be a good time—well, actually, I suggested yesterday, but then I remembered that I had an appointment, and so we settled on today."

"Yes, yes, of course," Camilla agreed hurriedly. "I remember now. I am so sorry, Cousin Harold. I forgot. It's terrible that you came all this way for nothing."

"Oh, it's not for nothing," Harold told her cheerfully. "We can work on it now. I have ample time."

"Actually, right now I need to speak to Benedict."

"Then there is no problem. Benedict isn't here. We met as I came in. He said he had urgent business in Edgecombe to attend to."

"Ah. I see." No doubt the urgent business had been avoiding Cousin Harold's company. Camilla wished she had some of the same business.

"So you are perfectly free. Isn't it wonderful how things always work out for the best?"

"Mmm."

Harold held out the chair in front of the secretary for her, and Camilla sat down resignedly. It did not surprise her that Lydia almost immediately rose from her chair, remembering a task that awaited her. The work would not have been that bad, Camilla reflected, as she began to compile a list of donated items from the various scraps and pieces of lists that Harold had accumulated, if it were not for having to listen to Harold drone on about his church, his parishioners and various other topics that interested only him.

Camilla listened with half an ear as she recopied the list in her neat copperplate handwriting. When she had finished, she gathered up the scraps and tossed them in the wastebasket.

"No, wait!" Harold gasped, looking horrified. "I had notes for my sermon on the back of one of those." He bent down and began to paw through the pieces of paper in the basket. He was still wearing his gloves— a bit formal, even for Cousin Harold, Camilla thought—and they made him clumsy. He stripped off his right glove and sifted through the paper until he found the right piece.

"Aha!" He smiled triumphantly and sat down on the edge of the chair that Camilla had just vacated, smoothing out the crumpled piece of paper. "This is it. I have a quote I heard from Dr. Livermore the other day, and I did not want to lose it. A most learned man, Dr. Livermore."

Camilla said nothing. Her throat was suddenly too tight to speak or even swallow. She was looking at her cousin's hand as he smoothed out the piece of paper. His knuckles were red and raw, scraped like a man who had been in a fight.

Harold looked up and caught sight of Camilla's face, as white as the paper in his hand, and her wide eyes. "Damn!"

His reaction was all the confirmation Camilla needed, but she reached out anyway and jerked at the glistening white stock that was tied around his throat. Harold jumped to his feet, but not before she caught a glimpse of the semicircle of reddish marks that her teeth had made in his neck the night before.

He started toward the door, but Camilla jumped in front of him, spreading her arms wide. "Harold! No!"

"Get out of my way, you little fool!" He grabbed her arm and pulled her aside. "Don't make me hurt you."

"You already have!" Camilla cried indignantly. "You can't leave. I won't let you! You are Benedict's traitor." She clutched at his coat.

"Damn that man to hell," he cursed, and flung her aside.

He stepped out of the room, but Camilla ran after

him doggedly, crying out, "Benedict!" *Oh, curse the man! Why had he chosen this morning to go into town?* "Anthony! Purdle! Help! Help me, someone!"

Two footmen came running at her cry and stopped in the hall, goggling at the sight of Camilla wrestling with the vicar in the hallway.

"Help me, you fools! Don't just stand there!"

Harold pulled away from her grasp, but before he had taken three steps, the front door flew open and Benedict charged in. Before Camilla could even take in what he was doing, Harold wrapped his arm around her waist, jerking her back against him so tightly that the air whooshed out of her lungs. In the same swift movement, he pulled a pistol from inside his coat pocket and jammed it against Camilla's temple.

Benedict stopped so fast that Lieutenant Woollery, running in after him, bumped into him. Camilla stopped struggling. The hallway was suddenly, utterly silent.

Benedict's eyes went to Camilla's face, and his hands clenched into fists. "Leave her alone, Elliot. You are in enough trouble, don't you think, without shooting the Earl's granddaughter? Your one hope to get out of this mess is his influence and mine. I am Lord Rawdon, not—"

"I know who you are, you fool!" Harold snarled. "I knew as soon as you arrived. I have seen you, heard of you. Do you think I'm such a fool that I don't investigate my opponents? From the moment you came, I knew that it was a sham, that your name was not Lassiter, that you were not really married to my cousin. I played along with you, all the while laughing up my sleeve at your attempts to investigate the smug-

gling. I know what all of you think of me. Old Cousin
Harold, pedantic and boring. I have used it to my advantage all my life. No one ever assumes that it is I
who has done something wrong. I am too staid, too
proper, too *boring,* aren't I? I'm sure my foppish
brother could tell you how many times he or Graeme
got blamed for something they didn't do. But even
they, like the rest of you, were too blind to see what
I was really doing. I am a comic figure, not a villain.
Why, Camilla could hardly believe the evidence when
it was right in front of her eyes."

"Harold, be reasonable," Benedict said, struggling
to keep his voice calm. "We know that you are the
traitor. That you killed Nat Crowder and one or more
of my men, as well. You tried to kill Lieutenant Woollery. You must see that you can't get away unscathed.
Not only Woollery and Camilla and I, but also Jermyn
Sedgewick, know about you. You cannot escape for
long. Hurting Camilla will only make it harder on
you." His face darkened. "I can promise you that I
will make sure you die a slow, hard death if you hurt
one hair on her head."

"A difficult threat to fulfill when you are dead,
Rawdon."

"Then shoot me." Benedict took a step forward,
opening his arms wide. "Go ahead. Kill me now.
Right here." He thumped his hand against chest.

"Benedict! No!" Camilla screamed. She knew what
he was doing. He was hoping to so enrage Harold that
he *would* fire at him, thus using up the single bullet
in his gun and making it possible for Camilla to get
away unharmed.

At that moment, Aunt Beryl came sailing down the

stairs, scowling, her daughters trailing her like pale shadows. "What in the world is going on down here?" she complained, stopping at the bottom of the stairs in between Harold and Benedict.

Benedict let out a curse.

"Why is everyone shouting? I have a headache," she continued pettishly.

"You had better speak to your son." Benedict pointed toward Camilla and Harold, frozen in the hall-way.

Lady Beryl looked at Harold. "What is going on? Why are you holding that gun—and, Camilla, why are you in my son's arms? It's not at all the thing, you know."

"He is threatening to *kill* me!" Camilla lashed out. "For pity's sake, Aunt Beryl, can't you see that?"

"Ridiculous," Aunt Beryl replied stoutly. "Harold, put down that gun at once and come here. Is this some sort of bizarre jest? I have told you a hundred times that I won't have you boys playing pranks in my house."

Camilla groaned. No doubt in another moment Mr. Thorne would come wandering through, trying to find a rhyme, or Cousin Bertram would walk in and comment that his brother's pistol did not go with his suit.

"Aunt Beryl, he is threatening to kill me!"

"Nonsense. Harold, I said put it down. This is absurd."

"No! I'll tell you what is absurd—it is trying to maintain any sort of decent lifestyle on that pitiful stipend a vicar makes. It's impossible, of course. That's why I jumped at it when Billouart offered me all that money to infiltrate the smugglers. I was never inter-

ested in becoming the vicar of St. Anne's. Everyone
assumed I would because Grandfather would give me
the living. Bertram would get everything important because he is eldest, and Graeme was allowed to go into
the army, as he had always wanted. And because I am
the youngest, I was expected to go into the Church.
Well, it's not right. It's not fair!''

''Are we back on that old argument again?'' his
mother said with a sigh. ''Honestly, Harold, what possible good can it serve at this point? It is a good living
and exactly what should suit a scholarly sort like
you.''

''Dammit! It doesn't suit me at all!'' he raged, the
gun trembling so in his hand that Camilla's stomach
knotted with fear that it would go off by accident. ''I
want to enjoy myself! I want to have fun! I don't want
to be old stuffy Harold and spend my life with my
nose in a book while everyone else is out having a
good time!''

''Of course you don't, Harold,'' Camilla said soothingly. ''And you shouldn't have to. I never realized. I
apologize. None of us knew— I always thought you
preferred to—''

''Sit inside with a musty old book about the Sac-
raments instead of running and playing outside?''

''Still complaining about that, old fellow?''

Everyone's head swiveled toward the other side of
the hall, where Cousin Bertram had just strolled in
from the conservatory, the silent Mr. Oglesby behind
him. He set the tip of his elegant gold-topped cane on
the floor and struck a pose, surveying the others sardonically.

"My, my, what a gathering. Have I interrupted anything?"

"Bertram, go away." Harold ground out the words. "I have no desire to listen to your witticisms just now."

"But, dear brother..." Bertram strolled languidly forward. "I am not planning to be witty at all."

Camilla looked out the corner of her eye toward Benedict, who was edging silently around Aunt Beryl toward Harold. She could only hope that Cousin Bertram's inanities would keep his brother occupied a little longer.

"I wondered what all this commotion was about," Bertram continued. "Why are you holding a gun to Cousin Camilla? It cannot be her attire which has offended you. I have to admit that Camilla always dresses in the best of taste." He directed a look toward his mother and sisters and sighed. "Something that cannot be said of all my family."

"Bertram, you are a fool," Harold snapped. "Now would you kindly go away and let me get on with this?"

"I can hardly do that," Bertram protested mildly. "After all, how would it look if you went about killing off our relatives?"

Suddenly, moving faster than anyone would have believed possible, Bertram lunged forward, whipping up his cane in the same motion and cracking it hard against Harold's wrist. The gun went flying, firing up into the air and shattering several crystal drops of the chandelier. Aunt Beryl and her two girls went into hysterics. Camilla threw herself forward and down, rolling across the floor, and Benedict leaped across the last few feet between himself and Harold and crashed into him.

Within seconds it was over. Benedict knocked Harold unconscious with two well-placed hits, then left him to Lieutenant Woollery to bind. He crossed the hall and dropped down on his knees beside Camilla, pulling her into his arms and squeezing her so tightly she could scarcely breathe. Camilla did not mind, however. She clung just as tightly to him, while he rained kisses over her hair and face, interspersing them with low, breathless endearments.

"Are you all right?" He released her for a moment to lean back and peer at her, searching for injuries, then pulled her back into his arms.

"I'm fine."

"God, I was so scared. I thought he was going to kill you, right in front of me."

Camilla nodded. "I know. But you were crazy to try to make him shoot you instead!" She thumped her balled-up fist against his chest. "What made you do such a crazy thing?"

For an answer, he kissed her thoroughly, and that seemed to satisfy Camilla.

Finally he rose to his feet, lifting Camilla up with him, and turned toward Cousin Bertram, who was vainly trying to calm his hysterical mother and sisters. He turned with some relief when Benedict strode over to him.

"Thank you, Elliot," Benedict said, heartily shaking his hand. "That was damned clever of you. I can never repay you for saving Camilla's life."

"No need, dear fellow, no need," Bertram replied

lightly, though his usual air of sangfroid seemed a bit shaky. "Always rather fond of Cousin Camilla."

By this time, all the servants and family members, who had heard the shot and the shouting, had arrived on the scene and were talking and exclaiming. Even the Earl and Jenkins were peering over the banister of the stairs at the hall below.

Benedict took Camilla's hand and pulled her away down the hall and into the room farthest from the commotion.

"But, Benedict," Camilla protested, "shouldn't you stay and clear everything up?"

"Woollery can handle it for the moment. If I'm not mistaken, Jermyn will be here any moment, too. He can take charge. I have something more important to do."

"What?" Camilla looked up at him with wide eyes.

"This." He went down on his knees before her.

"Benedict! Whatever are you doing?"

"What your grandfather told me to—begging."

Camilla stared. "Have you gone mad? Begging for what?"

"Your hand in marriage. You can't refuse me, Camilla. I cannot live without you. All I think about is you—being with you, hearing you laugh, listening to you talk, making love to you." He reached out and took her hands. "Please, say yes."

Camilla hesitated. "There is one thing very important that you haven't told me," she said. "Why do you want to marry me?"

"Why?" He stared at her. "I just told you—I can't bear to be without you. The last few days have been sheer hell."

"But why, blast it?"

"Because I love you, of course! Why do you think?"

Camilla broke into a smile and threw herself into his arms. They tumbled backward onto the floor.

Finally he lifted his head and smiled down at her. "Is that a yes, Lady Rawdon?"

She smiled and nodded, smoothing her fingers through his coal black hair.

"I thought you did not believe in marriage."

Camilla raised her eyebrow. "This time I think I'll make an exception."

Benedict reached up and turned the lock of the door, then bent to kiss her again.

Epilogue

Camilla held up her left hand, admiring the gold and ruby ring on the third finger. She turned it this way and that, letting the light bring out the glow in the ruby's depths. "You know," she said, amusement tinging her voice, "it turned out nicely that this ring actually *was* your grandmother's."

Benedict, across the room from her, smiled as he shrugged out of his jacket and tossed it on a nearby chair. "Mm. I never said that it wasn't. 'Twas you who assumed I had stolen it."

Camilla flashed a grin at him. "You know you gave me every reason to think you a criminal."

"Not every reason," he protested mildly, smiling a little to himself as he turned toward the dresser and began to remove the studs from his cuffs.

Camilla watched him, warmth stirring in her abdomen. Tonight, for the first time, she thought, she was watching her legal husband undress.

They had been married that afternoon in a small ceremony at the home of the vicar who, as Benedict had predicted, had willingly married them in secret.

Benedict and Jermyn had escorted Harold to London the day after he had been discovered to be the enemy spy in their midst. Then, yesterday, almost a week later, Benedict had returned, this time in his personal carriage, and had whisked Camilla away to the vicarage in Sussex.

Only the vicar's wife and son had been there as witnesses. As soon as she saw the son, Camilla had understood the debt the vicar owed Benedict. The young man, walking with the aid of a crutch, was missing the lower half of one leg, and he had, just like Lieutenant Woollery, greeted Benedict as "Major," his eyes lighting up with warmth and admiration. He had been under Benedict's command in the Peninsular War, one of those young men whom Jermyn had told her about Benedict's bringing back to the safety of their own troops.

Pressed by the vicar and his family, they had stayed for tea after the ceremony, but as soon as they could politely leave, they had returned to their carriage and started on the journey north to Benedict's estate. When night overtook them, they had stopped at this pleasant, redbrick inn.

Camilla leaned back against the pillows, watching her husband, aware of the growing sense of excitement inside her, enjoying the anticipation of the night ahead.

"You know," she said conversationally, "I'm not at all sure that Aunt Beryl really believes that you and I are married." Camilla had had to endure several days of such speculations from her aunt while Benedict was away in London.

"Probably not," he replied unconcernedly. "It doesn't really matter. We *are* married, and we don't have to prove it to anyone. The vicar won't tell anyone that it was not legal until today.''

"But everyone in the house heard Harold say that we weren't married.''

"Yes, and afterwards, you and I both said he was lying and affirmed that we *were*. Your relatives would all be uncommonly foolish to take a professed traitor's word over ours. Besides, if your reputation suffers, so does theirs. The only one foolish enough to hurt herself in order to slander you is your Aunt Beryl, and I think I can guarantee that she will not tell anyone.''

Camilla's eyebrows went up. "How?''

"I spoke to her yesterday. She agreed with me that this would not be a good Season for her and her daughters to be in London.''

"I should think not. I imagine even Cousin Bertram will stay in the country, with Harold's scandal hanging over our heads.''

"There will doubtless be some rumors.''

"Rumors!'' Camilla stared. "It will be common knowledge. The man is a traitor.''

"Agreed. But it will not be well known.'' He came across the room and sat down on the bed beside her, gazing seriously into her face. "Harold is to be exiled. He can never live in England or an English possession again. But he will not be tried publically as a traitor.''

"But why?''

He looked at her quizzically. "As I am sure Cousin Bertram would agree, it is not exactly the thing to have a traitor for a cousin-in-law.''

"But, Benedict! He is guilty! He ruined your network. He killed your messengers. And Nat Crowder. He tried to kill Lieutenant Woollery. He tried to kill me—and you and Anthony, too. You cannot let him go free!"

Benedict smiled at her. "You constantly amaze me. You would rather your name suffer such a blot than to let him escape?"

"Yes, of course. He betrayed his country!"

"I agree. He deserves the worst that we could do. But we have to be practical, as well. We cannot prove that Harold killed the other messengers. We have no bodies, no weapon, nothing—and Harold is denying everything. We can't even prove that it was he who attacked Lieutenant Woollery or who fought with Anthony and me that night. None of us saw his face. All we can say with certainty is that he had injured knuckles the day after I was attacked. He will deny that he had anything to do with the smugglers or with spying. You know Harold. Can't you see how well he would play the virtuous clergyman in court, drawing all the dignity and piety of his profession about him like a cloak?"

Camilla frowned. She could indeed imagine Harold fooling jurors with his act of being a good clergyman. He had, after all, fooled the townspeople, and even his own family, for years. "I suppose so."

"Besides, if he were tried for treason, it would also mean exposing Gideon. We would have to tell the public all about our spy network if we accused him of working to destroy it, and that very thing would destroy it completely. Neither Jermyn nor I—nor anyone in the government—wants that. It is too valuable. We lost a few messages, but he did not break our network. It can continue to operate against Bonaparte. And that is far more important than bringing one man to trial."

''I see.''

''The only charge left to bring against him is his attempted murder of you. If the government went forward with that, you and your whole family would be dragged through the courts. And your grandfather and I would both bring every scrap of influence we have to bear to prevent you going through that ordeal. 'Tis better by far simply to get rid of the man.'' He smiled wryly. ''I think that your Cousin Harold will find life unpleasant enough, being exiled from England, stripped of his clerical orders and without the influence of his family name. I think that he is going to find out what it is like to truly be without money, after all these years of considering himself penniless.''

''Yes, poor Harold,'' Camilla reflected without a trace of pity.

''However, as part of our agreement not to try Harold for treason or murder, or even attempted murder, he has agreed to sign a confession. He told us all, and wrote it down and signed it. So we know exactly how much damage he did to the Gideon network and how we can repair it. Moreover, I told Aunt Beryl that I have such a confession in my possession. I also explained to her that if ever any rumor that you and I were not legally wed should surface anywhere, I would expose her son for the traitor he is. I think the woman knows that she could not show her face again in Society if that happened. She assured me that the thought had never entered her head and would never pass her lips.''

Camilla chuckled. ''Now I know what an extraordinary man you are. I thought it was quite wonderful that you were a military hero, that you brought your men back to their lines through all sorts of incredible dangers, and that you captured a traitor. But to have defeated Aunt Beryl—now *that* takes a man of real courage.''

Benedict let out a laugh, the skin around his eyes crinkling. ''Saucy wench. What am I to do with you?''

Camilla's lips softened into a seductive smile, and she languidly raised her arms above her head against the pile of pillows, subtly emphasizing the thrust of her breasts. ''Indeed, my Lord Rawdon, I would have thought you had a good idea of what to do with me.''

His eyes flared with light, and he leaned closer, saying in a low voice, ''Indeed, my Lady Rawdon, I do. I do.''

His lips met hers, and all thoughts of further banter left Camilla's head. She wrapped her arms around his neck, pulling him closer, and they sank into the pillows.

Daniel MacGregor is at it again...

New York Times bestselling author

NORA ROBERTS

introduces us to a new generation of MacGregors
as the lovable patriarch of the illustrious MacGregor
clan plays matchmaker again, this time to his three
gorgeous granddaughters in

THE MacGREGOR BRIDES

Don't miss this brand-new continuation of Nora Roberts's
enormously popular *MacGregors* miniseries.

Available in November 1997
at your favorite retail outlet.

Available in December from

DIANA PALMER

Was she about to marry the wrong man?

Journalist Wynn Ascot liked small-town news reporting, but she understood the drive that took McCabe Foxe all over the world, courting danger in the search for good stories. Sidelined by a sniper's bullet, McCabe comes home, where he's too close for Wynn's comfort. McCabe is as dangerous as he is exciting for Wynn—a woman who's about to marry another man. And now she has to dig deep to find the truth…in her own heart.

ROOMFUL OF ROSES

Available in December 1997
at your favorite retail outlet.

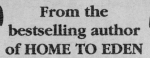

A showgirl, a minister—
and an unsolved murder.

EASY VIRTUE

Eight years ago Mary Margaret's father was
convicted of a violent murder she knew he
didn't commit—and she vowed to clear his
name. With her father serving a life sentence,
Mary Margaret is working as a showgirl in Reno
when Reverend Dane Barrett shows up with
information about her father's case. Working to
expose the real killer, the unlikely pair also
proceed to expose themselves to an unknown
enemy who is intent on keeping the past buried.

**From the bestselling author of
LAST NIGHT IN RIO**

Available in December 1997
at your favorite retail outlet.

The Brightest Stars in Women's Fiction.™

If you enjoyed this story of
passionate adventure and romantic
intrigue by award-winning author

**Don't miss the opportunity to receive her
other titles from MIRA® Books:**

#66035	SUDDENLY	$5.99 U.S. ☐
		$6.50 CAN. ☐
#66166	SCANDALOUS	$5.99 U.S. ☐
		$6.99 CAN. ☐
#66264	IMPULSE	$5.99 U.S. ☐
		$6.99 CAN. ☐

(limited quantities available)

TOTAL AMOUNT	$
POSTAGE & HANDLING	$
($1.00 for one book, 50¢ for each additional)	
APPLICABLE TAXES*	$ _____
TOTAL PAYABLE	$ _____
(check or money order—please do not send cash)	

To order, complete this form and send it, along with a check or money order
for the total above, payable to MIRA Books, to: **In the U.S.:** 3010 Walden
Avenue, P.O. Box 9077, Buffalo, NY 14269-9077; **In Canada:** P.O. Box 636,
Fort Erie, Ontario, L2A 5X3.

Name: _____

Address: _____ City: _____

State/Prov.: _____ Zip/Postal Code: _____

*New York residents remit applicable sales taxes.
Canadian residents remit applicable GST and provincial taxes.

**The Brightest Stars
in Women's Fiction.™**

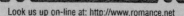

Look us up on-line at: http://www.romance.net   MCCBL3